The

D1534854

About the author

Mandasue Heller was born in Cheshire and moved to Manchester in 1982. There, she has found the inspiration for her novels: she spent ten years living in the infamous Hulme Crescents and has sung in cabaret and rock groups, seventies soul cover bands and blues jam bands. She still lives in the Manchester area with her musician partner.

MANDASUE HELLER

The Driver

HODDER

First published in Great Britain in 2010 by Hodder & Stoughton
An Hachette UK company

First published in paperback in 2011

3

Copyright © Mandasue Heller 2010

A CIP catalogue record for this title is available from the
British Library

B format paperback ISBN 978-0-340-95420-1
Ebook ISBN 978-1-444-71294-0

Typeset in Plantin Light by
Palimpsest Book Production Limited, Falkirk, Stirlingshire

Printed and bound by Clays Ltd, St Ives plc

Hodder & Stoughton policy is to use papers that are natural,
renewable and recyclable products and made from wood
grown in sustainable forests. The logging and manufacturing
processes are expected to conform to the environmental
regulations of the country of origin.

Hodder & Stoughton Ltd
338 Euston Road
London NW1 3BH

www.hodder.uk

To Carolyn Caughey and Betty Schwartz

Courageous, inspirational ladies – may you

both continue to be blessed by the angels

All of the usual love to my partner Wingrove; mum Jean; children Michael, Andrew, and Azzura (& Michael); grandchildren Marissa, Lariah & Antonio; sister Ava; Amber & Kyro, Martin, Jade, Reece; Auntie Doreen, Pete, Lorna, Cliff, Chris, Glen; Joseph, Mavis, Jascinth, Donna, Valerie, Natalie, Dan, Toni – and children.

And to the rest of our kinfolk – here and abroad, past and present.

Hello to the good friends who have been there from the start, and those we've re-connected with along the way. And never forgetting those we have loved and sadly lost.

Also, Liz, Norman, Ronnie, Wayne, Martina, and Jessie Keane.

Thanks to Cat Ledger, Nick Austin, and everyone at Hodder – Jamie, Lucy, Emma, Auriol, Aslan, Francine – to name but a few of the wonderful team.

And, lastly, as ever, immense gratitude to the readers, buyers, sellers, and lenders of my books – without whom none of this would be happening.

I

Shivering in the doorway, Katya gazed miserably out at the rain bouncing off the puddles. It had been lashing down all night, the wind driving it every which way so no matter where you tried to hide you still got soaked.

No wonder it's been so slow, she thought, pushing her chin deeper into her collar to let her breath heat her face. *Only an idiot would come out on a night like this.*

An idiot, or a *beast* – intent on having his way without paying, safe in the knowledge that nobody was around to stop him. Like that last punter. The ugly pig had lured her into his car by paying up front, then he'd driven her to a car park and forced her to do things that she would never have agreed to before taking the money back, head-butting her and kicking her out while the car was still moving. That had really hurt. Her cheekbone was grazed and swollen, and her shoulder was throbbing from the impact.

But at least he hadn't found her other money, or she'd really be in trouble.

A sliver of silvery-grey light began to slice through

the darkness. Stamping her feet to wake her frozen legs, Katya gritted her teeth when the burning pain rushed through her. Her friend Elena thought it might be herpes and had told her to get it sorted before it got really bad. But how could she go to the clinic when she wasn't allowed out in the daylight? And she couldn't risk going to one of the night drop-in centres because Eddie would go mad if he caught her taking time off from the street and losing him money.

His money – her body, *his* money.

What a sick joke that was. But there was nothing she could do about it because he'd already warned them what would happen if they tried to escape. And, even if they had the courage to try, where would they go? They knew nobody in this country. And they definitely couldn't ask the authorities for help because they all knew what would happen if *they* got hold of them.

A thin-sounding whistle floated up from the other end of the road: Elena's signal that it was time to go. Katya's stomach cramped. Horrendous as it was standing out here in the freezing cold, doing disgusting things to nasty men, it was almost preferable to going back to that prison.

Elena's mouth fell open when Katya joined her at the corner. 'What happened?' she demanded, turning her friend to face the dim street lamp so that she could see the damage more clearly. 'Who did this to you?'

'Red car,' Katya said, wincing when Elena touched her shoulder. 'Don't. It's really sore.'

'He didn't get your money, did he?'

'Only his own.'

'How much have you got left?'

'One-sixty. You?'

'Two-forty. But don't worry – Hanna's bound to have done worse than you.'

'Hope so.' Katya felt guilty for even thinking it but they all knew that the one who went home with the least was the one who would get the worst beating.

Elena saw the guilt and pursed her lips. 'Don't waste your pity on her. She's in the same boat as the rest of us but you don't hear us crying and going on about killing ourselves all the time. It's like she thinks she's—'

'*Sshhh!*' Katya hissed, nudging her friend when she spotted Hanna coming around the corner.

The girl looked awful. Her eyes were dark-ringed and dull and she was getting skinnier by the day. If Katya didn't know better she'd swear that Hanna was on drugs. But that was one luxury none of them could afford. Their money wasn't their own, and they all knew better than to risk trying to keep any back.

'I've only had one all night,' Hanna said when she reached them, her eyes already wide with the fear of what would happen when she got home. 'A few stopped, but Tasha kept jumping out and stealing them. She's such a bitch.'

'Maybe so,' Elena agreed unsympathetically. 'But it's your own fault for letting her do it.'

Hanna looked wounded. 'What am I supposed to do?'

'Stop being such a pushover and stand up for yourself,' Elena snapped, sickened by the pathetic whining.

'*How?*' Hanna's eyes were swimming with tears. 'I'm not like her; I don't want to fight.'

'None of us wants to,' said Katya, trying to calm the waters before the dam burst. 'But sometimes you *have* to. It's the only way.'

Before Hanna could reply to this Tasha yelled, '*Police!*' And, seconds later, stiletto heels clipping furiously on the pavement, she hurtled around the corner, screaming, '*Run*, you stupid bitches!'

'I *can't!*' Hanna wailed as Katya and Elena set off after Tasha. 'I'm scared!'

Turning back, the girls grabbed Hanna by the arms and hauled her along. Given a choice they would have left her there but they both knew that she would tell the police everything if she was picked up. And the consequences would be terrible for them all.

2

At just gone six a.m. the sky had brightened enough to show the Grange estate up for exactly what it was: a run-down dump consisting of four shabby high-rise blocks of flats, each one identical to the next apart from the faded painted panels beneath the windows: one block red, one blue, one yellow, one green.

They looked as if they had been flung up in the 1970s and left to get on with it, never to see the bristles of a paintbrush or the lick of a window cleaner's rag again. And there were bin bags littered around the pathways with rotten food spewing out of them, and empty beer cans dotted around the sparse grass like home-made daisies.

Driving slowly in through the gap where the gates should have been, Joe Weeks wondered if the high fence encircling the blocks and isolating them from the surrounding area had been designed to keep trespassers out or residents in.

Deciding that it was probably the latter, he pulled up to the front of the green block and gazed up at the grim façade.

Welcome to your new home, kiddo.

Shaking off the feeling of gloom that had begun to settle over him, Joe reversed up to the door and propped it open with one of the numerous bricks that were littered about. Unloading his stuff, he stacked the first boxes outside the lift at the end of the corridor. Hearing footsteps when he went back for the next lot he glanced around and saw four young girls hurrying towards him through the rain.

'Morning.' He flashed them a friendly smile.

Shielding their faces with their hoods they rushed past without acknowledging that they had heard him.

'Sorry about that lot,' he called after them. 'Give me a sec and I'll shift it so you can get in the lift.'

Bypassing the lift, one of the girls tugged open the door to the stairwell and they all disappeared through it.

Odd, Joe thought, wiping the sweat off his brow with the back of his hand. Most clubs stayed open until at least four in the morning these days so it wasn't that unusual to see a group of scantily dressed girls on the streets at this time. But, in his experience, girls who'd been out on the lash were usually at their flirtatious best if they came across a lone man on their way home and they hadn't so much as glanced at him.

But then, he was hardly looking his best right now, he supposed, and his old Vauxhall estate couldn't exactly be described as a babe magnet. In fact, compared to the Beemer and Audi parked up behind him it was a heap of old shit.

Those cars intrigued Joe because they just didn't fit in with the general air of neglect on the estate. He guessed that there had to be a couple of serious moneymakers living here – and with any luck it wouldn't take long for a friendly guy like him to meet them.

A few feet away, Cheryl Clark was checking Joe out through the nets of her living-room window while her two-year-old son Frankie sat cross-legged on the couch behind her, watching *Ben 10* and noisily gobbling his Sugar Puffs.

He was the reason that Cheryl was up so early today – the reason she was up so early *every* day while her friends had the luxury of sleeping in till noon and beyond. Much as she adored him, she wished the little bugger would stay in bed of a morning instead of always dashing into her room and bouncing up and down on her belly demanding breakfast. But she could have kissed him for waking her today because if he hadn't she'd have missed the arrival of the new tenant.

Cheryl watched him closely now as he took his things out of the car, and she guessed that he was in his mid to late twenties. Dark-haired and handsome, he was of average height and build but he had good strong thighs, which told her that he obviously took good care of himself. And he had an absolutely gorgeous smile – which he'd just wasted on the ignorant bitches from upstairs.

Impulsively snatching up her keys when he went to

park up, Cheryl ran into the kitchen and yanked the half-full bag out of the bin.

'What doin'?' Frankie asked, a look of alarm on his little face as she rushed past the couch heading for the door.

'Stay there,' she told him firmly. 'Mummy's just putting the rubbish out. Look . . .' She pointed at the TV to distract him. '*Dora the Explorer*'s coming on.'

Peeping through the spyhole, Cheryl waited until the man came into the corridor. Then, smoothing her hair into place, she casually stepped out – feigning shock when she bumped right into him.

'Oh my God! You scared the life out of me.'

'Sorry,' Joe apologised. 'Didn't think anyone would be up yet. Didn't wake you, did I?' he added, taking in the dressing gown and unbrushed hair.

Cursing herself for not thinking to get dressed before rushing out, Cheryl shook her head. 'No, you're all right – I've been up for ages. I was just taking this out.' Showing him the bag of rubbish, she caught a whiff of the week-old curry she'd only remembered to throw away last night and quickly switched it to her other hand. 'You moving in, then?'

'How did you guess?' Joe quipped, dropping his stuff and pushing it toward the lift with his foot.

'I suppose it was a bit obvious, wasn't it?' Cheryl rolled her eyes. 'What do you make of it so far? Bit grotty, isn't it?'

'It's not that bad,' Joe lied. 'Mind you, I haven't seen the flat yet so I might change my mind in a minute.'

'Didn't you come and see it before you signed for it?' Cheryl asked. 'They won't give you anything else now you've accepted it, you know.'

'It'll be fine,' Joe said more confidently than he felt. 'And if it's not, it's my own fault for winding my girl-friend up and getting kicked out. *Ex*-girlfriend,' he corrected himself quickly. 'Got to stop calling her that.'

Cheryl bit her lip, wondering if he'd said that to let her know that he was single. She kind of doubted it, considering what a sight she looked, but she could always dream.

Joe glanced at his watch. 'Well, it was nice meeting you but I'd best get this lot upstairs before the van gets here.'

'Sorry, didn't mean to hold you up.' Smiling, Cheryl walked backwards towards the door as he summoned the lift. 'Hope you like the flat, and you know where I am if you need any cleaning stuff. Oh, and I'm Cheryl, by the way.'

'Joe,' he said, waving as the lift opened behind him.

Cheryl wasn't the only woman on the block to have noticed the arrival of the handsome newcomer. Molly Partridge had been tracking his every move from the vantage point of her tiny balcony up on the fourth floor. Sheltered from the rain by the umbrella her son had tied to the washing line as a sun-shield on one of his rare visits that summer, she'd sipped at her tea and watched him through her compact binoculars.

He was a bonny one, all right, with his sparkly eyes and cheeky Jack-the-lad smile. And he had a fabulous backside – all nice and firm like her Archie's had been when they were courting. Forty-odd years they'd had together, and she hadn't half missed the sex when he'd gone and died on her. Not that she was supposed to remember stuff like that at her age but, hell's bells, she wasn't in her coffin yet. Although some of the young-sters around here seemed to think she *should* be and made no bones about telling her so.

When the young man finished what he was doing, Molly popped the binoculars back into the hanging basket and pushed the cat off her knee. Shuffling inside with the arthritic creature weaving stiffly around her ankles she brewed herself a fresh cuppa, then went to get washed.

It was brunch and bingo down at the centre today and she wasn't looking forward to it. The old biddies bored her and the young carers irritated the hell out of her with their patronising baby talk. But the nosy buggers would only come and bang the door down if she didn't show her face, sure they were going to find her lying face down in a pool of her own piss.

Or, rather, *hoping* that was how they'd find her, if it was that Ruth who came, because *she*'d have her pockets filled and the bank account emptied before she bothered calling the doctor, her.

Eeh, there was no dignity in death these days.

Carl Finch woke with a start when his girlfriend elbowed him in the ribs. 'Fuck was that for?' he demanded, giving her a dirty look.

'I heard a noise,' she hissed, pushing him towards the edge of the bed.

'What time is it?'

'They're at the *door*, Carl! What difference does it make what time it is?'

Knowing that she wouldn't quit bugging him until he'd checked it out, Carl shoved the quilt off and reached for his baseball bat. He couldn't blame her for panicking after those guys had booted the door in a few weeks back and ripped him off for two ounces of weed and near enough a grand in cash – *and* given him a good going-over while they were at it. But the bastards wouldn't be catching him out like that again.

Morning glory leading the way, he padded quietly out into the hall and pressed his eye up against the spyhole. The door of the flat directly opposite was standing open and he could see a stack of boxes lined up in the hallway. Jumping when a man suddenly came into view carrying a load of bin bags, he smacked his knee on the door frame. Gritting his teeth in pain, he threw the bat down angrily and hopped back to the bedroom.

'Who was it?' Mel was sitting bolt upright in the bed, chewing on her nails.

'No one,' he snapped, climbing in and rolling over to nurse his knee in peace.

'Can't be no one,' she argued, prodding him in the back. 'You sure they weren't hiding?'

Carl squirmed in disgust at the little wet spot her chewed fingertip left on his skin. 'It's just someone moving into Cynthia's old place.'

'Someone's moving into Cynthia's? Who? What do they look like? Have they got kids? *Carl* . . . ?'

'How am *I* supposed to know? It's just some random bloke – *okay?*'

'Anyone we know?' Mel persisted. 'Is he from round here?'

'For Christ's sake, go and ask him if you're that interested!' Carl yelled, losing patience as the pain throbbed. 'And quit eating yourself 'cos you're making me fuckin' heave!'

Joe had heard the noises behind the facing door and guessed that someone was checking him out. Conscious that he was disturbing people, he tiptoed the rest of his stuff in, glad that the lift was right beside his door so he didn't have too far to drag the bigger boxes.

The short hallway was crammed once it was all in and he couldn't close the door. Figuring that it would be easier to take the stuff out here and put it where he wanted it instead of clogging the other rooms up with packaging, he knelt down and started peeling the tape off the boxes.

Hearing a shuffling sound behind him a few minutes later, he snapped his head around. A middle-aged man wearing a tartan dressing gown and slippers and holding a steaming cup was staring in at him from the corridor outside.

'Tea,' the man said by way of explanation. 'Thought you could probably use one.'

Standing up, Joe dusted his hands on his jeans. 'Cheers, mate. That's really decent of you.'

'My pleasure.' The man turned the cup around and passed it to him. 'I take it you're the new tenant?'

'Yeah.' Joe extended his hand. 'Joe.'

'Phillip Kettler,' the man replied formally. 'I live next door. Thirty years now,' he added, as if for some reason he thought that Joe would be interested.

'That's a long time,' Joe said, taking a sip of the tea. It was weak and had no sugar in it – just the way he hated it.

'Boy to man,' Kettler affirmed proudly. 'Lived here with my dad until he passed on last year, but now it's just me. Not like it used to be, though.'

'No?' Joe peered at him questioningly over the rim of the cup.

'Used to be a lot of families,' Kettler told him, flicking a furtive glance along the landing before adding, 'but it's mainly singles now. Lot of *foreigners*.'

'I see,' Joe murmured non-committally. Then, deliberately changing the subject: 'Any good pubs round here?'

Pursing his lips thoughtfully, Kettler said, 'Well, I don't personally drink, but Dad used to quite like The Crown. I wouldn't recommend any of the others, though. Too many of *them*.'

Joe didn't even need to guess what he meant by that.

Un-fucking-believable, he thought in disgust. *Talk about laying your cards out from the off*!

He forced himself to finish the tea and handed the cup back, eager to get rid of the man before anyone saw them talking and assumed they were friends. Then, stepping forward so that Kettler had no choice but to back up, he said, 'Best get on. Removals van should be here in a minute.'

Still hovering, Kettler said, 'Oh, right. I see. Well, give me a knock if you need any help. That's me.' He waved his hand to indicate the door to the left. 'Just come round when you're ready.'

'Will do,' Joe lied, wishing that Kettler would just piss off and stop staring at him like that. It was starting to creep him out.

'Any time,' Kettler persisted. 'Any time at all. I'm always available.'

Joe's mobile began to ring. Mentally thanking whoever it was for rescuing him, he glanced at the name on the screen and smiled. 'Talk of the devil, that's them now,' he said, back-kicking an obstructing box up the hall and closing the door in Kettler's face.

Rushing back into his own flat, Kettler put the empty cup down and snatched up a glass. Pressing it carefully up against the dividing wall, he held his breath and listened.

'Not yet,' Joe was saying, his voice just about audible. 'But I've not long got here so you're going to have to give me a bit of time to suss out what's what.' Laughing at something the other person must have said, he said, 'Yeah, will do. Talk to you later.'

Frowning when his new neighbour stopped talking and started whistling, Kettler put the glass down and reached for his notepad. Flipping it open at a fresh page, he jotted down the date and time. Then:

New resident Number 312: Joe – no surname given. White. Approx 25–30. Occupation – not yet known, if any. To be watched.

Cheryl set off to take Frankie to the playgroup at nine. Tilting the pram back to pull it over the doorstep, she looked round to see who was coming out when the lift clanked to a noisy halt behind her. Seeing Molly struggling to get her walking frame over the lip where it hadn't stopped quite level with the floor she closed her door and went to help her.

'You are a good girl,' Molly puffed, clutching at the door to haul her overweight body out into the corridor.

'I don't know how many times I've reported this to the council but they never do nothing about it. Be the flaming death of me, it will.'

'They're terrible, aren't they,' Cheryl agreed, going back for the pram to walk outside with her. 'I've been telling them about the rats for ages but they've still not put traps down. It's them idiots from upstairs chucking their rubbish down that's doing it, but—'

'I'm off to the centre for my weekly bingo fix,' Molly cut her off. 'Hope in hell's chance of winning but they put a nice spread on, you've got to give them that. And it doesn't cost me anything, so I can't complain.'

Oh, sorry, was I boring you? Cheryl thought.

'That's nice,' she said, pushing the pram out into the rain and holding the door.

'Don't like the look of that,' Molly muttered as she stopped in the middle of the doorway and peered out. 'It'll proper mess me hair up, that.'

Wishing that she'd either hurry up and come out or go back in, Cheryl smiled when she caught a glimpse of Joe sheltering in the bin cupboard beside the door.

'Not lost your keys already, have you?' she called.

Leaning forward, Joe shook his head and blew on his icy hands. 'Nah. Still waiting for the van. Should have been here ages ago, but that's what you get for doing it on the cheap, eh?'

'Who's that?' Clanging her walker against the door, Molly craned her neck to have a nosy.

'New neighbour,' Cheryl told her, introducing them as Joe leaned further out of his hole. 'Joe, this is Molly. Molly, Joe.'

'Ooh, hello, handsome,' Molly cooed, holding out her hand. 'Come here and let me get a better look at you.'

Joe gave Cheryl a hooded look as he approached, unsure whether the old lady was expecting him to kiss her hand or shake it. He opted for the shake.

'I'm eighty-seven,' Molly informed him flirtatiously. 'But how old would you have *thought* I was if I hadn't told you, eh?'

A little alarmed by the drawn-on eyebrows and poppy-red lipstick, Joe shrugged. 'I'm, er, not sure. *Sixty?*'

'You fibber!' Cackling with delight, Molly gave him a playful slap on the shoulder.

Exchanging an amused look with Joe, Cheryl said, 'Well, that's her day made. You'll have a friend for life now.'

A car turned into the parking lot just then. Spotting who was at the wheel as it pulled into a space, Molly nudged Cheryl and nodded towards it. Glancing over, the smile slid from Cheryl's lips when she saw that it was Shay and his tart of a girlfriend.

'I'm off,' she muttered, stamping down on the pram brake to release it. 'See you later, Molly. Bye, Joe.'

She started to walk away but it was too late. Shay was already out of the car and striding towards her, the girl tottering along behind on clippety heels.

'What you playing at?' Shay demanded. 'It's pouring down and you've got my son outside without a cover. Are you off your head, or what?'

Cheryl gritted her teeth and her eyes flashed with anger when Shay's girlfriend squatted down to coo at Frankie. Jerking the pram away, she said, 'I was about to put it over, *actually*.' Then, yanking the plastic cover down, she stalked away with her nose in the air.

'See what happens if he gets a cold!' Shay yelled after her. Sucking his teeth when she ignored him, he shouldered past Joe and pushed his girl in through the door.

Joe gave Molly a questioning look. 'What was all that about?'

'He's Cheryl's ex,' she explained in a whisper. 'She caught him having it away with the other one a few months back and kicked him out, so he upped and moved in with her.'

'*Here?*' Joe grimaced. 'Bit cold, isn't it?'

'As ice,' Molly agreed. 'And now poor Cheryl's got to put up with them swanning about like love's young dream. Hardly ever visits his lad, neither,' she added disapprovingly. 'Unless you count the times he has a barney with *her*.' She jerked her head back to indicate that she was referring to the new one. 'Scuttles round fast enough then, all right. But I doubt he sees the lad while he's there – if you know what I mean.'

Joe shook his head. He didn't even know Cheryl but already he felt sorry for her.

'Ooh, here's my ride,' said Molly, waving when she spotted the minibus turning in off the road. 'Give us a hand, would you, luvvie?'

Joe helped her aboard and waved her off. But just as he was about to head back into the shelter of the bin cupboard the removals van turned up.

'What time do you call this?' he demanded, looking pointedly at his watch as he strode towards it.

'Sorry, cocker, I 'ad a flat,' the driver lied, wiping bacon-butty crumbs and ketchup off his chin. 'You'll have to guide us while I back it up to the door. Someone's nicked me mirror.'

'At the café?' Joe asked. Shaking his head when the man gave him a blank look, he said, 'Forget it. Just hurry up. I've got things to do.'

3

Up on the fourth floor Katya stepped wearily down off the chair she had been standing on. She'd been watching the man who had smiled at them earlier, wondering what he, the girl with the pram and the old lady had been talking about. It was impossible to hear any of their words from up here, but whatever it had been about she envied them their freedom to chat so easily. It had been a long time since *she* had been free to talk to a stranger without it involving money or swear words.

They had all gone now and the car park was deserted, leaving Katya with nothing more to watch. Not that she had seen all that much anyway, because it was difficult to see detail through the metal grilles that Eddie had fitted to the insides of the windows. She didn't know if he'd done this to keep anyone from seeing in or to stop the girls from flinging themselves out, but either way it really heightened the sensation of being in a prison. That, and the front door, which was so secure that it would be impossible for anyone to save them if there was a fire and Eddie wasn't on hand to let them out.

Katya jumped when she heard a bang out in the corridor and rushed to put the chair back under the table, scared that it might be Eddie on his way in. If he realised what she'd been doing he'd be bound to think she had been signalling to somebody and then he would cover the windows completely, leaving them in absolute darkness.

She was nervous now, and when she was nervous she got clumsy. Banging into the corner of the table, she bit her lip to keep the cry of pain inside and lifted her skirt to examine her already bruised thigh. Eddie had kicked her so hard this morning he'd left the imprint of his trainer behind and the pattern of its tread stood out in white welts against the purpling background. It looked bad and felt worse, but at least he'd only kicked her. Poor Hanna had been kicked *and* punched for daring to come back with just forty pounds.

The other girls were in their beds in the next room. They had fallen asleep as easily as they always did, exhausted by the events of the night they had just survived – and in need of regeneration for the new one they would be facing in a few short hours. Katya envied them their ability to switch off so completely but her own eyes had refused to stay shut when she'd closed them. And while she would usually have lain there until sleep came, her mind was too unsettled today.

Giving up after a while, she'd got up to wander around the flat, her head full of thoughts that she didn't want to think: fading memories of a better life in a better place that hurt almost as much as the reality she found herself in. Katya had tried to distract herself by watching people go about their business on the outside but that had made it worse, because they were free and she was not. She was a slave to the horrible man who had brought them here and put them to work on the streets, on the understanding that they could leave as soon as they had paid him back what they owed.

But how could they ever pay him back when half of whatever they earned went towards paying off the interest he'd heaped on, and the other half was classed as rent for this place?

Rent!

As if staying here was a voluntary arrangement; as if they were tenants, not prisoners, and Eddie was a landlord, not a vicious pimp.

This was not the life that she and the others had imagined they would be living when they came here, and she totally understood why Hanna was falling apart. And even, to a degree, why Tasha had allowed it to embitter her so. But Katya refused to allow her own spirit to be crushed. Her parents would be worried sick by now, wondering why she hadn't been in touch. And if the price of eventually being free to see them again was to do things that made her feel dirty and ashamed, then she would just have to be strong and get on with it.

4

The flat was smaller than Joe had initially thought so it felt cramped once all his stuff was in, even though he'd tried to keep things to a bare minimum. There was also a smell of damp that wouldn't shift no matter how much bleach and air-freshener he used; and the single-glazed windows let all the heat out and all the noise in, so he couldn't escape the thunder of traffic on the flyover.

Or the voices of anyone walking by down below . . . or the arguments that frequently kicked off in the surrounding flats . . . or the music that seemed to be blasting out from all sides day and night.

Joe didn't actually mind the noise because at least it broke up the feeling of solitude that came with being the new kid on the block. It was taking far longer to meet anybody here than in any of the other places he'd lived. He'd hear the other residents chatting in the corridors and knocking at each other's doors, but whenever he rushed out to introduce himself they had usually vanished. And those that he *did* manage to bump into were invariably rushing to or from somewhere, so he didn't get a chance to say anything more than hello as they whizzed past.

It seemed like Phillip Kettler was the only one who wanted to get to know him, and in the two weeks since Joe had moved in there hadn't been a single day that he hadn't come knocking with one excuse or another. But after the first couple of times Joe had stopped answering because the man made his skin crawl. And it wasn't just the fact that he was a racist, which was bad enough, but his habit of staring you in the eye long after you'd stopped talking, when any normal person would have felt awkward and said their goodbyes. That was just plain weird and Joe couldn't be doing with it.

Now that he'd explored all the local shops and checked out a couple of pubs, only to find that it was crap without someone to share a pint and a laugh with, the boredom was crashing in on Joe. So when Cheryl called round out of the blue one morning, panicking about a leak in her kitchen, he couldn't get out of his door fast enough.

'I'm sorry to bother you with this,' she apologised, rushing down the stairs ahead of him because the lift had broken down. 'But the council won't touch it if it isn't pipework, and there's no way I can afford a plumber. I'd usually ask Fred next door but he's at his daughter's this week. And my friend Mel's boyfriend got arrested last night, so he couldn't do it. You've seen her, haven't you?' Pausing, Cheryl slotted the key into the lock and looked back at him over her shoulder. 'Lives opposite you, long black hair? It was her who suggested I ask you, actually. Hope you don't mind?'

'Course not,' Joe said, wondering how women managed to talk so fast without fainting. He was exhausted just listening to her.

'You might not say that when you've seen it,' Cheryl warned, leading him through the flat.

Smiling at Frankie, who was sitting in a playpen in front of the TV, pushing toy cars in and out of a shoebox garage, Joe raised his eyebrows when she pushed the kitchen door open to reveal the soaked towels spread out all over the sudsy floor.

'Christ, you weren't kidding, were you?'

'It's that stupid old thing,' Cheryl grumbled, nodding towards the ancient washing machine that was sticking out at an angle from beneath a ledge. 'I tried to pull it out to get at the pipes but I think I made it worse. Do you think you can do anything with it?'

Joe scratched his head. He didn't have a clue about electrical things and had hoped that it would be something really simple, like a loose pipe that just needed tightening. But he couldn't bring himself to admit that to Cheryl while she was standing there looking so helpless. So, rolling up his sleeves, he said, 'Okay, let's see what we can do.'

Cheryl bit her lip as he knelt down with the washing-up bowl to catch the water that spewed out of the machine when he opened the door. She hoped he could get it going again, even if only for long enough to finish this load. Frankie was going to a party this afternoon, and she'd been washing the City tracksuit that Shay had bought him for his birthday. She could see the sky-blue pants through the glass door now, sitting perilously close to her red bra, and she just knew that the tracksuit was going to come out pink. Which would definitely cause a row, because Shay would swear she'd done it on purpose.

After a good fifteen minutes of poking about, during which time he got absolutely soaked, Joe yanked a sodden balled-up pair of baby socks out of the drainage pipe.

'I think that might have done the trick,' he said, feigning nonchalance even though he was actually quite proud of himself. 'Turn it back on; see what happens.'

There was an instant gurgling sound when Cheryl switched the machine back on and the water began to drain out properly. 'Oh, that's brilliant!' she beamed. 'Thank you so much! You're a lifesaver.'

'No problem,' Joe said, wiping his hands on his jeans.

'Here, use this.' Cheryl handed him a tea towel. 'And let me make you a brew for your trouble. Tea or coffee?'

'Coffee. But only if you're having one. I don't want to put you out.'

'Don't be daft, it's the least I can do. Sugar?'

'Two, please.' Putting the tea towel back on its hook, Joe looked around. 'Is it just me, or is this place bigger than mine?'

'Yours is a one-bed, this is a two,' Cheryl told him,

waving for him to sit at a tiny table tucked away in the corner beneath the window. 'That's why you're supposed to have a look at it before you sign up for it – in case you don't like it.'

'Ah, well, it's my own fault,' Joe said, pulling out a stool from under the table.

'For winding your girlfriend up and getting kicked out,' Cheryl finished for him. 'See, I do listen sometimes.'

'Glad to hear it.' Joe grinned. 'I know I'm boring but it usually takes more than one meeting for people to realise it.'

Sincerely doubting that anyone would ever find him boring – any *woman*, at least – Cheryl carried the coffees to the table. After popping her head around the living-room door to check on Frankie she sat down.

'So, what have you been up to?' she asked. 'Haven't seen much of you since you moved in. Have you been working?'

Joe shook his head. 'Nah. Seems there's not much call for crap painters and decorators round here.'

Cheryl tried to envision him in paint-splattered overalls and decided that she'd much rather see him in gym gear, all pumped up and sweaty.

'My last place went bust a couple of years back,' Joe went on. 'So I've been signing on ever since.'

'Nothing wrong with that,' Cheryl said kindly, sensing that he was a bit embarrassed about it. 'No one works round here. Well, apart from that lot in the yellow block, but they seem to think that makes them better than the rest of us – snobby tossers.'

'They sound like my ex,' Joe said with a hint of bitterness. 'It was all work work work, money money money with her. Makes me wonder how we lasted so long when I think about it, but you just get in the habit of someone being around, don't you?'

'I wouldn't know,' Cheryl replied, with a soft snort. 'Even when I lived with Frankie's dad he stayed out more than he stayed in. But at least I got to keep this place when we split, so it wasn't as bad as it could have been. I take it you were living at her place?'

'Yep. Her place, her mates – so she got to keep the lot.'

'God, don't you just hate all that taking-sides crap? That happened to me once, with this lad I was seeing a few years back. I got sick of him pushing me around and putting me down all the time, so I finished with him. Then he went and told all our mates *he'*d finished with *me* 'cos I'd been sleeping around behind his back, and they believed him and fell out with me.'

Guessing from her indignant expression that it still annoyed her, Joe said, 'I know what you mean. Angie told ours all kinds of crap about me, but I moved straight back here so they didn't get the chance to fall out with me.'

'Moved back?' Cheryl gave him a curious look. 'Were you living abroad, or something?'

'Nah, Angie's from Birmingham. And she already had the flat when we met, so it made sense for me to move in with her down there.'

Cheryl's expression told Joe exactly what she thought of *that*. 'So you left your friends and family for her, then she just kicks you out when she's had enough? Sounds like a right bitch.'

Amused that she'd already taken sides, despite professing to hate that, Joe smiled. 'It wasn't all her fault. Trust me, I'm no saint. But I suppose it helps having a couple of hundred miles between us 'cos I don't think I could be as civil as you if I had to put up with seeing her and her new fella around all the time.'

Cheryl narrowed her eyes, wondering how he knew about her and Shay, because she definitely hadn't told him anything about it. Then she remembered that Joe had seen Shay and Jayleen on the morning he was moving in – and the biggest gossip on the block had been right there to fill him in on all the gory details.

'Molly,' she said flatly.

Sensing that it might not have been something that she'd wanted him to know, Joe said, 'I didn't ask – honest. And she didn't tell me much 'cos she got picked up practically as soon as you went.'

'It's okay,' Cheryl assured him wearily. 'It's not exactly a big secret round here so you'd have heard about it sooner or later.' Standing up, she reached for a pack of cigarettes off the shelf above their heads. 'Truth is, I caught him cheating and kicked him out, so he moved in with her. But I'm dealing with it. Want one?'

Joe shook his head when she offered the pack to him. 'No, you're all right.'

'Oh, sorry, I just assumed you'd be a smoker,' Cheryl said, sounding surprised. 'I'll go outside if it bothers you.'

'It's your flat,' Joe reminded her. 'Anyway, it's not that I don't smoke,' he went on cagily. 'Just not like that.'

Cheryl was confused – but only for a second. 'Ah, I get you.' She gave him a knowing smile. 'Me, too – but only when Frankie's out of the way.'

'Christ, am I glad to hear that,' Joe exclaimed. 'The way Angie went on when she caught me you'd have thought I was a raving junkie. Makes you a bit wary of mentioning it.'

'This ex of yours sounds like a right stuck-up cow, if you ask me,' Cheryl said bluntly.

'Just a bit,' Joe chuckled, liking that she didn't censor herself before she spoke. 'Do you mind me asking where you get yours from?' he asked then. 'Only I haven't had any in ages. Most of my old mates moved on after I left and you can't just walk up to someone on the street and ask for the local dealer, can you?'

'Not unless you want your head caving in,' Cheryl agreed. 'They're a bit suspicious of strangers around here – in case you hadn't noticed.'

'Oh, I've noticed all right,' Joe told her. 'I've had some proper bad looks.'

'Ah, don't worry about it, they'll soon get used to you,' Cheryl assured him unconcernedly. 'But if you're after something, I'll get it for you. You should have just said.'

'Yeah, right. And risk having you grass me up?'

'No *way* are you saying I look like a grass?' Cheryl spluttered.

'If I knew what a grass looked like I'd be able to answer that,' Joe teased, reaching into his pocket for his wallet. 'But if you're serious I wouldn't mind a tenner bag.'

Promising to drop it round as soon as she'd got it, Cheryl took the money and slipped it into her jeans pocket. Leaning back to check on Frankie again and seeing that he was absorbed in *Fifi and The Flowertots* on the TV, she reached past Joe and opened the window an inch.

'Don't take this the wrong way,' she said. 'But can I ask how come you got a place so fast if you've only just moved back from Birmingham? Only you've usually got to be on the housing list for a good five years before they offer you anything.'

'I actually got back a few months ago,' Joe said, amused that, once again, Cheryl had come straight out with what was on her mind – although her face said that even *she* thought she was being nosy now. 'I stopped at my mum's for a bit, but we had a row about the fella she was seeing so she kicked me out and I had to go into the homeless. They sorted it.'

'Ah, that's why you ended up in this dump,' Cheryl

said, having heard from friends who'd been in homeless units that it was a case of *take-it-or-piss-off* when they offered you a place. 'Bet you wish you'd stayed in Birmingham.'

'No way,' Joe replied without hesitation. 'I knew me and Angie were on the skids, so I'd been wanting to come home for ages. Just didn't have the heart to walk out on her, so I had to wait till she'd had enough of me.'

Cheryl wondered if this ex of Joe's had any idea what she'd lost when she'd kicked him out, because it was nigh on impossible to find a man who was both gorgeous *and* nice. Round here it was either one or the other: gorgeous, but guaranteed to be a bastard; or nice, but you wouldn't want to be seen in public with them. Shay, for example: he was fit, but he didn't half know it, so you could never let your guard down because you were always having to keep an eye on him to make sure he wasn't slipping some other girl his number. Not that watching him had done her any good because he'd still screwed around behind her back. But at least he was now doing the same to Jayleen – *ha*!

Seeming to want to get it all off his chest now that he'd started, Joe said, 'Angie was ashamed of me not working, so she told her mates I was a freelance computer something or other. Bit stupid considering I don't know the first thing about computers and some of them know a *lot*,' he added with a sly chuckle. 'But it made for some interesting dinner parties – them quizzing me about RAMs and hard drives, and me talking shit 'cos I didn't know what the hell they were going on about.'

'*Dinner parties?*'

'Hey, if you think that's bad, you should have seen her wine and cheese parties.'

Cheryl pulled a face. 'That's so crap. You can't just drink wine and eat cheese and call it a party.'

'Oh, it's not any old wine and cheese,' Joe informed her with a straight face. 'It's got to be specially imported. And your guests have got to be really intellectual, so you can have amazing conversations about *really*, *really* interesting shit.'

Catching the glint of humour in his eyes, Cheryl narrowed her own. 'You're having me on, aren't you?'

'All right, so she didn't actually *import* the cheese,' Joe admitted. 'But the rest is true – honest.'

'Yeah, right.' Shaking her head, Cheryl lit her cigarette and sucked on it thoughtfully. 'You know, I can't remember the last time I went to a party. You get so knackered when you've had a baby you end up making up excuses when your mates want to go out, so in the end they stop asking and go without you.'

'Can't be easy,' Joe said sympathetically. 'But you must be doing okay – your lad seems happy enough.'

'Yeah, he's a good boy.' Cheryl smiled fondly. 'What about you? Have you got kids?'

'*Me?*' Joe drew his head back in horror. 'Christ, no.'

'Not met the right girl yet?' Cheryl ventured, wondering how he felt about girls who already had kids.

'Just don't want kids,' said Joe emphatically. 'Hard enough looking after myself, never mind a little 'un. *Way* too much responsibility for a selfish slob like me.'

Well, that's me told, Cheryl thought disappointedly. Then, forcing herself to smile, she said, 'You all say that but I bet you'll end up doing it one day. Anyway, never mind that. Let's talk about the party.'

'Party?' Joe wondered if he'd missed something.

'The one I've just decided to have,' Cheryl informed him excitedly. 'I can't believe I've never thought of it before, but it's a great idea. And it'll give you a chance to meet everyone – stop them giving you evils.'

'That would be pretty good,' Joe agreed. 'When are you thinking of?'

'Why? Need to check your diary to see if you're free?'

'Yeah, 'cos I've got *such* a busy life, me.'

They were both laughing when a hand snaked through the window and unlatched it all the way, letting a blast of cold air in. Glancing up in surprise, Cheryl felt a guilty blush spread across her face when Shay popped his head around the net curtain.

'*Shay!*' she squawked. 'What the bloody hell are you playing at? You nearly gave me a heart attack, you stupid idiot!'

'Aw, shut up moaning,' he grunted, cocking his leg

over the sill. 'Least I'm here, aren't I?' Dropping down into the kitchen now, he started dusting his jeans down but stopped abruptly when he spotted Joe. 'What's this?' he demanded, staring at Cheryl accusingly.

'I'm having coffee with a friend,' she told him, reminding herself that she'd done nothing wrong.

'A *friend*?' Shay looked Joe up and down with open suspicion. 'That what you're calling it these days, is it?'

Annoyed with him for having the cheek to have a go at her when *he* was the one who'd gone off with someone else, Cheryl said, 'Don't come round here trying to dictate who I can and can't have in my own house. It's got nothing to do with you any more. You moved out – *remember*?'

'Is that right?' Shay held her gaze, his expression giving little away.

Standing her ground, she folded her arms. 'Yeah, it is. And if you don't like it you know what you can do, don't you?'

'Yo, don't be mouthing off just 'cos you've got an audience,' Shay warned her.

'I don't need an audience,' Cheryl retorted defiantly. 'I'm just not having you telling me what I can and can't do.'

'*Hey fool!*' Mr T's distinctive voice suddenly boomed out. '*Pick up the goddamn message, fool – and don't make me have to tell you again!*'

'Sorry.' Joe grimaced, pulling his phone out of his

pocket. 'It's my text tone. Keep meaning to change it, but you know how it is.' Glancing quickly at the screen, he said, 'Oh, shit, gotta go.' Standing up now, he smiled at Cheryl. 'Got some mates coming round, didn't realise it was so late. Thanks for the coffee.'

Ashamed that he'd witnessed the argument and was obviously using his text as an excuse to escape the horrible atmosphere, Cheryl couldn't bring herself to look at him. 'You're welcome,' she said. 'And thanks again for fixing the machine.'

'Machine?' Shay repeated. 'What machine?'

'The *washing* machine,' she informed him tartly. 'It got blocked and Joe fixed it, so I made him a coffee to thank him.' She finished with a tight smile, hoping that *he* felt guilty now for jumping to conclusions.

'Could have asked me to do it,' Shay muttered, noticing the wet towels that were still spread across the floor and realising that she was telling the truth.

'Oh, yeah, 'cos I'm always welcome to come knocking on *her* door, aren't I?'

Shay sucked his teeth, irritated that Cheryl was using the situation as an excuse to have a dig about him cheating on her when *she* was the one who'd been caught red-handed with another dude. Not that this dude was any kind of serious threat, mind. He might have a pretty face, but the cruddy trainers and label-less clothes marked him out as just another no-hope estate rat, destined to live a hand-to-mouth existence until he died in bed with a dribble of Special Brew running out of his gob.

Catching the look that Shay was giving Joe, Cheryl's hackles rose. How dare he waltz in here and throw his scorn about like *he* was God's gift to women everywhere. He'd do well to get some of Joe's manners, in her opinion, never mind strutting around like the big I-am.

Thinking about manners, she realised that Shay had no intention of introducing himself so she thought she'd better do it.

'This is Shay, by the way,' she told Joe. 'And this,' she informed Shay frostily, 'is Joe. He's just moved in across from Carl and Mel.'

Joe held out his hand but Shay ignored it and hooked his thumbs through his belt loops. 'Met the nonce yet?'

'Your next-door neighbour,' Cheryl explained when she saw the confusion in Joe's eyes. 'Shay kind of caught him spying on a little boy last year.'

'*Perving* over him,' Shay corrected her, a glint of disgust flashing through his eyes. 'Cunt wants locking up, if you ask me. And see if he ever so much as *breathes* near Frankie, he won't just get a kicking, he'll be going head first off the balcony.'

'All right, you've made your point,' Cheryl admonished him quietly, wondering what Joe must be making of all this. He'd seen Shay twice now and both times her ex had been acting like a lout.

'Just letting the man know what we think of nonces round here,' Shay drawled, cracking his knuckles loudly and heading for the living room. 'My boy up yet?'

'What do *you* think?' Cheryl muttered, rolling her eyes. He knew damn well that Frankie got up at the crack of dawn every day. Not that it affected *him*, seeing as he wasn't the one who had to get up to see to him.

Turning to Joe when they were alone, she whispered, 'Sorry about that. He just gets a bit funny if he comes round when someone's here.'

'Don't worry, I'm thick-skinned,' Joe reassured her. 'But I've really got to go. Will you be okay?'

Cheryl nodded. She knew he was really asking if she would be safe on her own with Shay, but while she was grateful for his concern she was also deeply ashamed that he'd witnessed the argument in the first place. She was just glad that it hadn't turned into one of their *real* fights because they could both be vicious when they got going, so it always ended up looking and sounding much worse than it actually was.

Sighing when Joe went to show himself out, Cheryl reached for another cigarette. She usually couldn't wait for Shay to come round but she wished he hadn't bothered today. She'd been having such a nice time with Joe, and it had been great talking to a man who actually listened and who answered questions without jumping down your throat and accusing you of interrogating him. But, even if Joe hadn't already made it clear that he wasn't interested in having kids of his own, never mind someone else's, she knew that nothing could ever come of it because no man was ever going to come within a mile of her while Shay was still strutting around acting like he owned her.

Nodding when Joe said goodbye, Shay scooped Frankie out of the playpen and got down on the floor with him to play with the toy cars. Coming into the doorway when she heard him making brum-brum noises, Cheryl felt tears welling up in her eyes. Frankie idolised Shay but the poor little sod didn't understand that Daddy was only paying attention to him for Joe's benefit. And now that he'd pissed on his territory and warned the competition off, Shay would be gone again in a flash – leaving Cheryl to try and comfort their son.

Glancing up when he felt her watching, Shay said, 'I'll have tea, if you're brewing.' Winking, he added, 'And why don't you see if he's ready for a little nap, eh?'

Cheryl knew exactly what he meant by *that* and she felt like telling him to piss off back to his tart if that was all he'd come for. But she couldn't bring herself to say it. Much as she wanted to hate him for what he was doing to her and Frankie, she still loved him – and he knew it, which was precisely why he thought it was okay to keep flitting back and forth.

But Shay was wrong if he thought she was going to let him carry on doing it for ever, because the longer he stayed away the easier she was finding it to wake up without him. And one of these days he was going to get the shock of his life when he came knocking and found the door firmly closed.

But that day hadn't come quite yet. So, sighing resignedly, Cheryl turned back into the kitchen and reached for the kettle.

Joe thought about what had just happened as he made his way home. He wasn't stupid; he'd sensed that Cheryl liked him. But she was fooling herself if she thought that she was ready to start a new relationship, because she clearly wasn't over her ex. Despite acting coolly towards Shay when he'd arrived, her eyes had told a different story and Joe suspected that she'd been pleased by his show of possessiveness, because it proved that he still had feelings for her.

Just not enough to make him move back in, it seemed.

About to head up to the third floor, Joe hesitated when a man started coming down with a stocky white pitbull-type dog on a short chain. Seeing him, the dog immediately began to snarl and strain to get at him.

'Pack it in!' the man barked, yanking its chain so hard that it yelped.

'Cheers,' Joe said gratefully. 'Thought I was a gonner for a minute there.'

'You what?' Drawing level, the man stopped and gave him an aggressive stare.

'I said cheers,' Joe repeated calmly, wondering what

the hell the man had *thought* he'd said to make him react like this. 'Don't know what it is, but me and dogs just don't get along.'

A slight sneer replacing the scowl now, the man said, 'It's fear, mate. They *smell* it.'

Sensing that he'd just narrowly avoided a fight – which he'd have had no chance of winning – Joe shook his head and continued on up to his flat.

'Excuse me . . .' someone called out in a loud whisper just as he was about to open his door. 'You haven't got a spare fag, have you?'

Turning, he smiled when he saw the girl that he now knew was called Mel peeping out through a crack in her door. 'Sorry, I haven't.'

'Never mind.' She sighed. 'I'll get dressed and pop down to Cheryl's. Did you manage to fix that thing for her, by the way?'

'Yeah. It was just some socks blocking the pipe. Nothing major.'

'She came to ask Carl to do it,' Mel went on, opening the door a little wider and leaning against the frame. 'But he's not here just now so I told her to come to you. Didn't mind, did you?'

'No, it was no problem,' Joe replied, keeping his gaze firmly on her face because she was wearing one of the shortest dressing gowns he'd ever seen and he didn't want her to think he was leering.

'I keep telling her to get rid of the stupid thing, but

she says she can't afford a new one,' Mel told him, smiling slyly as she added, 'Don't be surprised if she comes knocking again now she knows you can fix things.'

'I'm sure her boyfriend will manage if it goes wrong again,' Joe said, slotting his key into the lock.

Tutting, Mel said, 'Great. I can't go down if *he*'s there. I'll have to wait for Carl to get out – I mean *home*,' she corrected herself quickly. 'Unless . . .' Biting her lip, she gave Joe a sheepish look. 'Don't suppose you could lend me a fiver?'

Joe had vowed not to get into any of that lending and borrowing stuff when he moved here but now that he'd been asked he couldn't bring himself to refuse. Saying, 'Give me a minute, I'll see if I've got it,' he left his door ajar and went inside.

He was just counting through the change he kept in a saucer on the dressing table when he heard the creak of floorboards behind him. Snapping his head around, he was surprised to see Mel looking in at him from the hallway.

'Thought I'd save you the trouble of bringing it over,' she said, her gaze flitting around the room. 'Wow, this is so different from how Cynthia used to have it. You've got it really nice.'

'I haven't really done anything,' Joe told her, passing the money over and stepping towards the door to indicate that he wanted out of there. Cheryl hadn't mentioned why Carl had been arrested but if it was something minor he could be home at any time, and Joe didn't think he'd be too pleased to find his girlfriend in here dressed like she'd just hopped out of bed.

'Must be your stuff making it look better,' Mel said, reaching down to stroke his quilt cover. 'I like this colour. *Very* sexy. Bet you're single?'

'Mmm,' Joe murmured, wondering where this sudden familiarity had come from. He'd seen her in the corridor a few times but this was the first time they'd ever actually spoken. He didn't know if this was her idea of being neighbourly or if she was trying it on because her boyfriend was out of the way, but either way he didn't like it.

'Do you mind if I have a look what you've done to the rest of it?' Mel asked, already strolling towards the living room.

Following, Joe stopped in the doorway, hoping that she'd take the hint and make this brief. But she sat down on the couch and reclined back against the cushions as if she was settling in for the day.

'Aren't you tidy?' she commented, casting an approving look around. 'I like that lamp. It's Ikea, isn't it? I think I saw it in the catalogue. *Well* expensive.'

'I got it from a charity shop, so I couldn't tell you,' Joe said, easing his sleeve back and glancing at his watch. 'Look, sorry, I'm not being rude, but I'm actually on my way out.'

'Aw, but I've only just got here,' Mel pouted, crossing

her legs and gazing up at him through her lashes. 'And I could really do with a brew but I've run out of milk.'

'Have mine,' Joe said, rushing into the kitchen and taking his almost full bottle out of the fridge. 'Here.' He thrust it towards her. 'I'll get some more while I'm out.'

'No point,' she purred. 'I've run out of tea bags as well.'

'No problem.' Going back into the kitchen, Joe grabbed a handful from the box. 'Don't need sugar as well, do you?'

Realising that her hints weren't working, Mel said, 'Wouldn't it just be easier to make me a brew?'

'Sorry, but I haven't got time,' Joe said firmly. 'And I've really got to go, or I'll be late.'

Sighing, Mel stood up at last. 'Thanks for the money,' she said, brushing against him as she passed him. 'I'll bring it round later.'

'No rush,' Joe said, grabbing his jacket and following her out. Saying goodbye, he set off down the stairs.

Coming out of the main door a couple of minutes later, he heard the unmistakable sound of a man's sexual grunting as he passed by Cheryl's bedroom window. Guessing that she'd settled her differences with her ex he shook his head and set off down the path. Going from what Molly had told him and what he'd seen for himself, Joe didn't think that Cheryl was doing herself any favours. But it was her business, not his. He just hoped that Shay didn't persuade her to change her mind about the party, because he was relying on that to make some new friends.

Cheryl had no intention of cancelling the party. Now that she'd decided to have it she was really excited, and was actually on the verge of telling Shay about it – sure in the post-sex glow that he would not only agree it was a great idea but might even suggest they use it as a celebration of getting back together.

But before she had a chance to mention it, Shay brought her back to reality with a gut-wrenching slam.

Relighting the spliff he'd left in the ashtray in his rush to get her out of her clothes, he said, 'Right, I'll have this, then I'd best get off. I told Jayleen I was only nipping into town to pay for the tickets. She'll go mental if I go home without them.'

'What tickets?' Cheryl asked, thinking that he'd better not be taking the bitch on holiday, because that really would be too much.

'Dubstep weekender in Leeds,' Shay told her. 'I was waiting to see if Bubba Ranks got his visa before I booked it 'cos it would have been a washout without him. But it came up on the website last night that he got it, so it's a deffo.'

'*Wow*,' Cheryl muttered sarcastically. 'You must be made up.'

'Can't wait,' Shay said. 'And Jayleen's well looking forward to it.'

Cheryl switched off as the familiar white-hot jealousy sparked to life in her heart. After sex, she always felt really close to Shay, as if he was still her man and none of this had ever happened. But it was becoming harder and harder to ignore the little telltale signs of Jayleen's presence in his life. Like his hair: he'd worn it in the same style the whole time they'd been together but it was shorter now and always had some fancy little logo shaved into the sides. And he was dressing differently, too, modelling himself on the American gangsta videos that he'd started watching since moving out.

Cheryl wondered how he could afford it all, considering he pleaded poverty whenever it came to handing money over for his son. And now he was splashing out on a weekender in Leeds, which wouldn't be cheap. But there was no point pulling him up about it because he'd probably only tell her that the whore was paying.

God, she was such a fool – and, *boy*, didn't Shay know it. But sack him. If he could make plans without giving a toss about her then she would do the same. And if the cat was playing away this weekend, then that was when the mouse would have her party – and just let him *dare* to try and have a go at her when he found out about it!

Frankie started shouting in his bedroom, letting it be known that he wasn't happy about waking up to find himself trapped in the cot with the sides up. Taking it as his cue to leave, Shay stubbed his spliff out and reached for his jeans. Cheryl had a sudden urge to rake her nails down his back but she resisted, knowing that the temporary pleasure she'd gain from imagining Jayleen's face when she saw the scratch marks wouldn't be worth the shit she'd get from Shay.

'Don't forget to say goodbye to your son,' she said when Shay slipped his jacket on.

'Nah, he'll only get mardy if he knows I'm going,' Shay said, patting his pocket to make sure he hadn't forgotten anything.

'Maybe if he saw more of you he wouldn't get so upset when you left,' Cheryl suggested narkily.

Sucking his teeth, because he couldn't stand it when she nagged him, Shay walked out, slamming the door behind him. Frankie immediately began to cry. Inhaling deeply to control the rage in her heart, Cheryl snatched her dressing gown off the floor and yanked it on.

'All right, all right . . . I'm coming.'

5

Joe had been out when Cheryl had called round later that day, so she'd dropped a note through his letter box telling him that the party was definitely on and that she hoped Saturday wasn't too short notice because she really wanted to introduce him to everyone.

He didn't see her for the rest of the week and couldn't ask what time she was planning on kicking things off, so he went down at nine on the night – hoping not to be the last, because there was nothing worse than walking into a room full of people who already knew each other but didn't know you.

Cheryl's face was flushed when she answered the door and Joe could tell that she'd made a real effort with her appearance. She looked much more feminine with her long blonde hair loose of its usual ponytail and she was wearing make-up which showed how pretty she actually was. And the dress and heels looked way better than the baggy jeans, oversized T-shirts and trainers that she usually sported.

He'd already guessed from the way she covered herself that she was self-conscious about her weight, and if it hadn't been so taboo to talk to women about that kind of stuff he'd have told her that most men didn't give a toss about a few extra pounds. But he'd made that mistake with an ex-girlfriend who had been a fair bit slimmer than Cheryl, so he decided not to mention it, sticking instead to a safe, 'Hey, look at you,' as he handed over the bottles of wine that he'd bought.

'Aw, thanks.' She beamed, giving him a quick kiss. 'Come in, come in.'

Grimacing when he followed her through and found that nobody else was there yet, Joe said, 'Aw, crap, I'm early. Do you want me to come back later?'

'Don't be daft,' she chided, heading into the kitchen and putting his wine with the beers and spirits already lined up on the ledge. 'What can I get you?'

'I'm easy,' he said. 'Whatever you're having.'

'BVR,' Cheryl told him, giving him a teasing smile. 'Sure you can handle it?'

Joe shrugged. 'Might help if I knew what it was.'

'You'll like it,' she assured him, twisting the cap off a bottle of brandy and pouring a large shot into a plastic beaker. 'Sorry about the kiddy cups,' she apologised, adding a healthy glug of vodka before topping it up with Red Bull. 'But I know what my mates are like when they get pissed, and I don't fancy spending all day tomorrow hoovering up broken glass.'

Saying, 'I don't blame you,' Joe took his drink and sniffed it cautiously. 'Christ, that's strong.'

'Don't be such a wimp,' she scoffed, topping up her own beaker.

A knock came at the door. Smoothing her dress down, Cheryl headed out to answer it. She came back a few seconds later with a couple.

'These are my friends, Mel and Carl,' she told Joe. 'The ones who live across from you.'

Joe hadn't seen Mel since he'd lent her that fiver – which she hadn't repaid – and he still felt uncomfortable about the way she'd followed him into his flat. But she'd obviously forgotten, or was deliberately making out like she had, because she gave him a polite smile and said, 'Nice to meet you,' as if it was the first time.

Deciding to let it go rather than remind her and embarrass her, Joe said, 'Yeah, you too.'

'All right, mate.' Carl extended his hand. 'Joe, isn't it?'

Nodding, Joe shook Carl's hand and swallowed a mouthful of his drink, shuddering when the bitter heat scorched his throat.

'Got you on the hard stuff, has she?' Carl chuckled, reaching for a bottle of beer. 'You wanna stick to the safe stuff, like me. It'll send you off your head, that shit.'

'You're such a *girl*,' Cheryl scoffed, pulling a beaker off the stack to pour a drink for his girlfriend. 'How do you put up with him, Mel?'

'I pretend he doesn't exist,' Mel replied, her flat delivery making Joe wonder if she was being serious.

If she was, Carl didn't seem to have realised it. Giving

her a playful slap on the backside, he took his beer over to the table and sat down. Reaching into his pocket, he hesitated and flicked a surreptitious glance at Joe before asking Cheryl if it was all right to smoke.

Guessing that he was checking if Joe was cool with it or not, she said, 'Don't worry, he's one of us.' As soon as she'd said it, she remembered the tenner Joe had given her. 'Oh, my God, I'm so sorry!' she apologised, clapping a hand over her mouth. 'I completely forgot about your weed.'

'Don't worry about it,' Joe said, shifting his weight onto his other leg because Mel was leaning against the ledge beside him and had started to press her hip into his.

'I've spent it,' Cheryl went on guiltily. 'But I can pay you back on Monday, if that's okay?'

'It's fine,' Joe insisted. 'I've gone without for months so a few more days won't kill me.'

Carl had pulled a pre-rolled spliff out of his pocket. Lighting it, he looked at Joe as if he couldn't believe what he'd just heard. 'You haven't had any for months? Jeezus, I'm climbing the walls if I don't have it every *day*, me.'

'That's 'cos you're a junkie,' Mel sniped under her breath.

Catching it, Carl's humour faded. 'What have I told you about calling me that? You know I never touch that shit.'

Unfazed, Mel held his gaze and downed her drink before coolly turning her back on him to pour herself another.

'Oh, don't start, you two,' Cheryl moaned. 'It's my first party in years – don't ruin it.' Giving them a warning look now when another knock came at the door, she said, 'Behave, or we're going to fall out.'

A heavy silence fell over the kitchen when she'd gone to answer the door and Joe felt awkward as the couple gave each other daggers across him.

Cheryl bounced back in a few moments later, dragging two women in with her; one a slim brunette, the other a small chubby redhead with enormous breasts.

'Look who's here.' She beamed at Carl and Mel before turning to Joe. 'This is Lisa, my old mate from school. And this is Vee – she used to live on the first floor. And this,' she told the girls now, 'is Joe – our new neighbour.'

'Ahh, so you're the one, are you?' Vee drawled, giving him a slow smile. 'You were right, Chez – he *is* fit.'

Hissing at her to shut her mouth, Cheryl turned to the drinks to hide her blushes. 'What you having?'

'Whatever's going,' said Vee, still eyeing Joe.

Looking around, Lisa flapped her hands. 'All right, where've you hidden my future husband?'

'He's at my mum's,' Cheryl told her, grateful for the change of subject. 'But you're not having him, so give it up. You'll be sixty by the time he's old enough.'

'Er, try thirty-two, you cheeky cow,' Lisa protested.

'Whatever!' Cheryl laughed, handing their drinks to them and heading for the door. 'Anyway, come and see what I got him from Primark the other day. They've got a sale on, and I got a gorgeous trackie.' Pausing, she jerked her head at Mel. 'You too. I'm sure Carl can manage without you for a minute.'

'Women,' Carl said wearily when they'd gone. 'Can't live with 'em, can't live with 'em.' Grinning at his own joke, he said, 'I take it you're one of the sensibles, Joe?'

'If you mean single, yeah.'

'Wish *I* was,' Carl muttered, offering the spliff to him. 'Here . . . you must need it by now. And if you don't, you soon will, 'cos that lot'll do your head in when they get going.'

Saying, 'Cheers,' Joe pulled out the other stool.

Carl leaned back against the wall and peered at him. 'Have we met before? Only I'm sure I've seen your face somewhere.'

'You have,' Joe told him, taking a deep drag on the smoke. 'Loads of times, in the corridor. Or, should I say, I've seen you, 'cos you didn't look like you'd seen me.'

'I bet you thought I was blanking you?' Carl asked. Rolling his eyes when Joe shrugged, he said, 'It isn't personal. I've just got so much crap in me head, I can't see what's right under me nose half the time. Me mates are always having a go at me for walking right past them.'

'Don't worry about it,' Joe said. 'I'm getting used to it. Anyhow, I'd rather be ignored than get some of the dirty looks I've been getting.'

'Ignorant load of fuckers round here, aren't we?' Carl grinned. 'But Cheryl's probably invited everyone on the estate, knowing her, so they'll be cool with you after this.'

'Hope so,' Joe said, handing the spliff back to him. 'Apart from Cheryl, and the old woman from upstairs, you're the first one who's actually talked to me. Oh, and my next-door neighbour, but I'd rather he didn't.'

'Give you the big welcoming speech, did he?' Carl asked knowingly. 'How long he's lived here, what a load of inbred scummy heathens we all are – that kind of shit?'

'Something like that, yeah.'

'Tosser,' Carl sneered. 'No one can stand him round here. And he's lucky he's still walking after Cheryl's ex gave him that going-over last year. She tell you about that?'

'Shay mentioned it,' Joe told him, lowering his voice to add, 'That is his name, isn't it – her ex?'

Nodding, Carl said, 'Sorry, didn't realise you'd met him. What did you make of him?'

'Seemed okay,' Joe replied neutrally, aware that Carl and Shay might be mates. 'He came round while I was fixing her washing machine; didn't really say too much.'

'Caught you and her alone in here?' Carl sucked a breath in sharply through his teeth and gave a soft chuckle. 'Bet he wasn't happy about that?'

'Didn't look too impressed,' Joe admitted, grinning now as the weed started to take hold. 'Can't be sure, but I think he might have made a dig about me being a nonce.'

'That'll be 'cos you live next to the freak. Probably thinks youse are setting up a paedo ring or something.'

'No way!'

'Only messing.' Carl grinned, his eyes as red now as Joe's were beginning to feel. 'Anyhow, take no notice of Shay. He talks big but there's worse than him around.'

'Yeah, I think I've met one of them. Big fella with a pitbull.'

'Eddie.' Carl smirked. 'Yeah, he's bad, all right. How did you meet him?'

'We passed on the stairs and his dog tried to go for me,' Joe told him. 'I thanked him for keeping it off, and I swear he nearly kicked my head in.'

'You'd be lucky if that was all he did,' Carl said ominously. Then, abruptly changing the subject: 'So, which side are you on?'

'Eh?' Joe gazed at him blankly.

'Footie,' Carl explained. 'City, or a dickhead?'

Grinning, Joe shrugged. 'Guess I'm a dickhead.'

'Bloody hell, it's not often you hear a man admit *that*,' Vee laughed, coming back into the kitchen just then. 'Hear that, girls? Joe's a dickhead.'

Pushing past her, Cheryl gave him an apologetic smile. 'I'm so sorry. She's not with me – honest.'

Joe and Carl exchanged an amused glance and burst out laughing.

'Looks like someone's had a bit too much wacky,' Lisa observed.

'Oh, that reminds me,' Vee said, reaching into her

bag for her purse. 'Can I get a twenty, Carl? And make sure it's bigger than the last one, 'cos that was well under.'

A tiny wave of paranoia washed over Carl as the self-preservatory part of his mind reminded him that he'd only just met Joe and didn't yet know if he could be trusted. But a quick glance at the man's wasted eyes and inane grin soon dispelled it. Like Cheryl had said, he was one of them – and he definitely didn't look the type to grass. Relaxing, he took some bags out of his pocket and handed one to Vee.

'Anyone else while the shop's open?'

'Can you do me a lay-on?' Lisa asked. 'I don't get paid till next Thursday.'

'No probs.' Carl handed a bag to her. 'What about you, Joe?'

'Er, yeah, why not? Can you do me a tenner?'

Passing a bag over, Carl shook his head when Joe put his hand in his pocket. 'Nah, keep it. Cheryl owes you, so she can give it to me instead.'

Sidling up behind him, Mel prodded him in the shoulder and hissed, 'You're not supposed to be doing lay-ons any more.'

'Leave it out,' Carl snapped, jerking his shoulder away from her. 'They're mates.'

'Well, don't blame me when you land yourself in the shit,' Mel huffed, flouncing away to get herself yet another drink.

Sticking two fingers up at her back, Carl downed his beer and waggled the empty bottle at Cheryl.

'God, you're such a lazy git!' she complained, tossing him a fresh one, as another knock came at the door.

More and more people began to arrive after that, and the small flat was soon heaving with bodies. Making sure that they were all introduced to Joe, Cheryl left him with Carl and the girls and went off to mingle. And Mel quickly followed when she spotted a group of lads congregating around the stereo in the living room, leaving Carl free to entertain without her miserable face to sour his mood.

Joe was more wasted than he'd ever been before, and he was having a great time. Carl's repertoire of dirty jokes was hilarious and everyone was cracking up as he reeled them out. Especially Vee, who had plonked herself on Joe's lap and kept jiggling up and down when she laughed so that her tits were bouncing in his face like lovely soft airbags. Yeah, he was having a great time.

At just gone twelve, a latecomer arrived and, picking up on a subtle shift in the atmosphere, Joe glanced around. Half expecting it to be Shay he was surprised to see that it was Eddie. And even more surprised to see how fawningly people were greeting him. Given his own less than friendly previous encounter with the man he'd have expected people to be giving him a wide berth, but they all seemed to love him.

Coming into the kitchen to find Cheryl, Eddie gave her a hug. 'All right, babe?'

'Yeah, great, thanks,' she said, looking a little flustered as she turned towards the drinks. 'There's not much left but there's still a few beers if you want one.'

'Nah, I'm not stopping,' Eddie told her. 'I'm on my way out; just thought I'd check everyone's behaving.'

'Everything's cool,' Cheryl assured him. 'But thanks, I appreciate it.'

Winking at her, Eddie glanced around to see who was here. Narrowing his eyes slightly when he saw Joe, he flicked his gaze onto Vee. 'Veronica.' He nodded.

'Edward.' She nodded back.

Casting a hooded glance in Carl's direction, Eddie turned back to Cheryl. 'Right, I'm getting off. Give us a shout if anyone steps out of line, yeah?'

'Thanks, but I should be okay,' Cheryl said, following him out to the door.

Waiting until she came back, Carl casually eased himself out from behind the table. 'I need a wazz,' he said to nobody in particular. 'Won't be a minute.'

Eddie was standing outside the main door lighting a cigarette when Carl came out. Jerking his head, he moved into the shadows of the bin cupboard.

Shivering as the icy air bit into him after the stifling heat of the crowded flat, Carl's hands were shaking as he pulled a wad of money out of his pocket and passed it over.

'There's two-sixty there, but I've done a few lay-ons tonight so there'll be more in a few days. And there's another ton or so upstairs, if you want me to go and get it?'

Shaking his head, Eddie said, 'I'll get it tomorrow. Just make sure you're keeping track of who owes what,' he added, peering at Carl's red eyes.

'I *never* forget when it comes to dosh,' Carl assured him. 'But while you're here, any chance of giving us a bit more? I'm running low.'

'Since when have I walked round with shit on me?' Eddie asked sharply, pocketing the money and taking another drag on his smoke. 'Who's the bloke, by the way?'

'Joe,' Carl told him, knowing exactly who he meant because that was the only new face at the party. 'He moved in across from me a few weeks back. Seems all right.'

A car pulled in off the road and stopped at the end of the path. Telling Carl to meet him at six tomorrow, Eddie strolled out and hopped into the passenger seat.

Back inside, Joe had caught the look that had passed between Carl and Eddie. Guessing that Carl hadn't really gone to the toilet when he came back now with his arms covered in goose bumps, he looked up at him over Vee's breasts and asked if everything was okay.

Nodding, Carl rubbed his hands together and looked around. 'Yo! Where's all the spliffs gone? I thought this was supposed to be a party!'

★

It was half-five before people started to drift home. Still sitting in the kitchen with Carl and the girls while Cheryl showed the rest out, Joe yawned loudly.

'Do you have to?' Vee complained, catching the bug and stretching her mouth so wide that Joe could see the fillings in her back teeth. 'God, I'm not looking forward to going home. It's going to be a right mission.'

'Oh, yeah, I forgot you'd moved,' Carl said, glancing up at her sleepily. 'Where was it you went?'

'Moved in with that Dave,' she reminded him, her expression clearly displaying what a mistake *that* had been. '*Oh, please come, babe*,' she mimicked. '*I really need you.* Yeah, till the next tart come along, then it was *see ya, wouldn't wanna be ya!*'

'You what? He dumped you?'

'Yeah, 'cos he's a two-faced lying piece of shit who can't keep his dick to himself,' Vee snarled. 'So now I'm stopping with my sister, waiting for the council to get its arse in gear and give me something. I should *never* have given my flat up,' she added bitterly. 'I loved it here.'

'Sorry it didn't work out, love,' Carl said sympathetically. 'But you'll get something soon.'

'That's life,' Vee said philosophically. 'But you can give us a lift if you're feeling sorry for me.'

'Sorry, no wheels,' he told her. 'Pigs confiscated it a few months back and I can't be arsed looking for another one.'

'What about you?' Vee twisted around on Joe's lap and looked hopefully down at him.

'Sorry.' He shook his head. 'I'm well too wasted to drive.'

'Any room in your bed for a little one, then?' She grinned.

'Oi! I like how you didn't ask *me*,' Carl blurted out, giving her a mock-offended look.

'Oh, yeah, 'cos I really want to snuggle up next to your skinny bitch of a girlfriend,' she snorted. Sighing now, she flapped her hands and gave Joe a regretful look. 'Sorry, babe, you took too long to answer, so I'm going to have to give it a miss.'

Smiling, because he knew she was joking, Joe said, 'Maybe next time, eh?'

'If I can be bothered,' Vee said, winking at him. 'Ah, well . . . suppose I'd best ring a cab.'

Lisa's head shot up. 'Wanna share?'

'Thought you were skint till Thursday?' Vee reminded her bluntly.

'Yeah, but I'll pay you back,' Lisa wheedled. 'Come on, don't be tight. It's on your way.'

Muttering 'Whatever,' Vee stood up, leaving Joe with a big cold spot across his thighs.

'Time I hit the sack,' Carl croaked, getting stiffly to his feet when the girls had gone and stretching his arms above his head. 'Hope Mel ain't locked me out. She was proper in one 'cos I didn't go home with her, but there was no way I was going to bed that early.'

'Early?' Joe grinned. 'It was gone four by the time she left, wasn't it?'

'Yeah, and there was still two hours of party left,' Carl reminded him. Touching fists with him now, he said, 'Laters,' and stumbled out.

Cheryl was singing softly to herself when she came into the kitchen a couple of minutes later. Jumping when she saw Joe still sitting there, she said, 'Bloody hell! I thought you'd gone.'

'Nope, still here,' he told her. 'Thought you might need a hand with the cleaning.'

'Don't be daft,' she protested. 'It's my mess, I'll do it. It won't take long.'

'Be faster with two,' he pointed out. 'Anyway, most of this is mine, not yours.' He indicated the table, which was covered in empty bottles, dimps and ash.

Cheryl gave him an amused look. 'God, your ex must have had you well trained.'

Joe shrugged, but he didn't deny it, she noticed. Thinking again what a fool his ex had been to let him go, she took a roll of bin bags out from under the sink and handed them to him. She had known most of the people who'd come to the party for a long time, a couple even since primary school, and yet not one had offered to stay behind and help clear up. But here was Joe, a man she'd known for a matter of weeks, not only offering but insisting.

Scooping all the mess off the table and the ledges into

the bag, Joe tied a knot in the top when it was full. Tearing another off the roll, he glanced up at Cheryl. 'It was a good night, wasn't it?'

'Yeah, it was great,' she agreed, switching the kettle on and taking a couple of cups out of the cupboard. 'I'm just amazed there were no fights. There's usually at least one, isn't there?'

'I think your friend might have had something to do with that,' Joe commented, carefully tipping an over-loaded ashtray into the second bag. 'The big guy – Eddie, is it?'

'I suppose he might have had a hand in it,' Cheryl conceded, spooning coffee into the cups.

'What's the score with him and Vee?' Joe asked. 'I got the feeling things were a bit strained between them.'

'They just don't like each other.' Cheryl shrugged. 'She used to be mates with his girlfriend, but they had a big fallout so they don't speak.'

'I see,' Joe said, going on casually, 'And what about you? You seem to know him pretty well.'

'Mmm,' Cheryl murmured. 'I kind of went out with him once.'

'Really?' Joe was surprised. 'He doesn't seem your type.'

'He's not,' Cheryl agreed, avoiding Joe's eye as she poured water into the cups. Sounding embarrassed now, she said, 'I was only fourteen, but he was twenty, so I lied and said I was older. We hadn't been seeing each other long enough to *do* anything, but we were getting there, so he went off his head when he found out. When I got this flat I found out he was already living up on the fourth. But there was nothing either of us could do about it by then, so . . .' Trailing off, she shrugged. 'We just sort of agreed to put it behind us.'

'So you get on all right now?' Joe asked, understanding why she'd seemed flustered when Eddie had arrived, because it was obviously a bit of a sore subject.

'I think he feels like he's got to look out for me,' Cheryl told him. 'But there's no way I'd ever go out with him again. I know he's good-looking but he's not the kind of man I'd want to get involved with.' Looking at Joe now, she gave him a sheepish smile. 'Now you know my dirty secret. Do you think I'm terrible?'

'For what?' Joe asked, knotting the second bag. 'Everyone's done stuff they wish they hadn't. Doesn't make you a bad person.'

'Suppose not,' Cheryl agreed. 'Doubt Shay would see it like that, though. He'd go crazy if he knew. I'm sure he thinks I was a virgin when we got together.'

'Some guys are weird like that,' Joe told her, picking up the bags. 'But women can be just as bad. I've had a few of those *let's be honest and tell each other everything* conversations, and believe me it's easier to lie, 'cos they just chuck it all back in your face when you have a row. Probably best to let Shay carry on thinking he was the first and last, eh?'

'In his dreams,' Cheryl snorted, having already decided that there was no way she was spending the rest of her life licking up the crumbs that Jayleen left on her plate when there were so many gorgeous men out there for the eating.

Leaving her to her thoughts, Joe carried the bags out and dumped them in the communal wheelie bin. Just as he was heading back inside, the four girls he'd seen on his first morning appeared. Holding the door for them, he wasn't surprised when the first three scuttled through without looking at him. But the last one glanced up at him as she passed and their eyes met for the briefest of moments, leaving him with a strange feeling in his stomach.

'What's up?' Cheryl asked when he came back into the flat with a thoughtful frown on his face.

Reaching for his brew, Joe said, 'Nothing, really. I just saw some girls and they got me thinking.'

'Four of them? Dressed like tarts?'

'Mmm. I saw them when I was moving in, and they just seem a bit – I don't know . . . *odd*.'

'They're not odd, they're ignorant,' Cheryl corrected him with a sneer. 'You can be standing right in front of them and they'll make out like they can't even see you. And you know they're prostitutes, don't you?'

'Really?'

'Well, obviously I don't know for *sure*, but that's what everyone round here thinks. Why else would they come in at this time every morning and only ever go out late at night? And normal girls don't dress like that, do they?'

'I guess not.'

'I think it's disgusting,' Cheryl went on, lighting a cigarette and pursing her lips prudishly. 'But Chrissie's obviously not bothered what they do for a living so long as they pay their rent.'

'Chrissie?' Joe repeated.

'Oh, sorry, I forgot you don't really know anyone yet.' Sitting down, Cheryl pulled the ashtray across the table. 'She's Eddie's girlfriend. She's got the flat next to his, but she lives with him.' Pausing, she gave Joe a guarded look. 'You'd best not repeat any of this 'cos I don't think anyone's supposed to know.'

'Course I won't. But you don't have to tell me if you're worried.'

Feeling guilty, because he obviously thought she didn't trust him, Cheryl said, 'It's Molly I'm thinking about, not me. She lives a few doors down, and she let slip that she'd seen him letting the girls in and out of Chrissie's place. Only she begged me not to say anything in case he found out and had a go at her.'

Joe couldn't help but smile. 'Very James Bond,' he teased. 'What's the big deal about someone renting a flat?'

'The DSS,' Cheryl told him, as if he really shouldn't have needed to ask. 'Molly reckons Chrissie's still signing on from there, and she'll get in trouble if anyone finds out she's really living at Eddie's.'

'But if those girls rent her place,' Joe said, trying to put it together in his head, 'surely they'd have their own keys?'

'We figure she's trying to make it look like they're just visiting,' Cheryl explained. 'Mind you, I don't know why they're being so careful, 'cos no one would dare grass her up. Eddie would *kill* them.'

'Well, I certainly won't be saying anything,' Joe assured her. 'I'm getting the impression that it's not too smart to get on the wrong side of Eddie.'

'It isn't,' Cheryl said flatly, taking a last drag on her cigarette and stubbing it out. Glancing out of the window now and seeing how light it was, she said, 'God, look at me keeping you up with all this gossip. I can finish the rest off. You go home and get some sleep.'

Joe couldn't deny that he was tired, and there didn't seem to be an awful lot left to do, so he said goodnight and straggled home to his bed.

6

As Joe fell asleep on the floor below, Chrissie Scott was being dragged out of her dreams by insistent knocking on the front door. Knowing that it would be Eddie's bitches, she threw her arm over to his side to tell him to go and deal with them. Furious when she found that he wasn't there, she shoved the quilt off and staggered into the kitchen to get the keys, calling him all the lying bastards under the sun for saying that he was only nipping out for half an hour last night.

Stepping into a pile of dog shit, she screeched, 'Oh my fucking *God*!' when it squelched up between her toes.

Eddie had used up the kitchen roll and put the empty tube back in the drawer, and Chrissie refused to go to the bathroom and risk getting crap on her lovely carpet so she was forced to rinse her foot in the sink. And all the while the stupid bitches were still knocking, as if they thought she was deaf or something.

Chrissie yanked the door open when she'd cleaned herself up, stalked past them and unlocked the adjoining flat. Following when they scuttled inside, she held out her hand, impatient to get this over with and get back to her bed.

Elena gathered the money from her friends and handed it over, glad that Chrissie had come instead of Eddie, because he always took it from them individually and would have seen that Hanna had yet again brought home the least and Tasha the most.

Standing beside Elena with her arms folded, Tasha stared at Chrissie with barely concealed contempt. Wrinkling her nose when Chrissie snatched the money and shoved it into her pocket, she sniffed the air exaggeratedly. 'What's that disgusting smell?'

'Probably your body telling you it's time to get a wash,' Chrissie sniped, pulling the door open and backing out into the corridor.

'Liar!' Tasha hissed when Chrissie closed the door. 'It's *her* who stinks. You could smell her as soon as she came out.'

'Oh, give it a rest,' Elena said, slipping her jacket off and heading for the bathroom.

'Make me!' Tasha yelled, yanking her own jacket off and hurling it into the corner. 'What are you staring at?' she demanded, catching Hanna looking at her.

'Nothing,' Hanna muttered, rushing into the bedroom to escape.

Katya was sitting on the couch taking her boots off. Tutting softly now, she said, 'Do you have to be so nasty?'

Spinning on her heel, Tasha gave her a dirty look. 'What?'

'I'm sick of you picking on Hanna,' Katya told her wearily. 'She hasn't done anything to you – why can't you just leave her alone?'

'She's an idiot,' Tasha snapped, taking a crumpled cigarette out of her pocket and looking around for a lighter. 'And what's got you talking all of a sudden? We usually can't get two words out of you.'

'I speak when I have something to say,' Katya said quietly. 'And this needs saying, because you're upsetting Hanna and that affects us all.'

'You're making my heart bleed,' Tasha sneered, inhaling deeply on her smoke and eyeing Katya with the same contempt she'd aimed at Chrissie. 'You really think you're something special, don't you? But you're no better than me. You're exactly the same.'

'I know,' Katya agreed. 'But I don't take my frustrations out on everybody else like you do. We're all trying to get through this as best we can but you're making it unbearable. Can't you see that?'

'Trying to get through this?' Tasha repeated nastily. 'You're as stupid as *she* is if you think you're ever going to see a happy ending. In case you haven't figured it out yet, this is *it*, sweetheart.'

Tasha was voicing what Katya was constantly struggling not to allow herself to think, and the words settled over her like a cold, dark cloak of hopelessness.

A glint of malice in her eyes, Tasha said, 'Oh, *please* . . . you're not going to *cry*, are you?'

Holding it together with difficulty, Katya said, 'We all cry, Tasha – even you. You might hide it better than we do but you're not so different on the inside.'

'You're so wrong,' Tasha informed her. 'You're all weak, but I'm a fighter, and I'll get out of here while you're still sitting here accepting your fate like little sheep.'

'What's she going on about now?' Elena asked as she walked back in just then with a towel wrapped around her hair.

Raising her chin, challenging her to deny it, Tasha said, 'I'm saying that you're all pathetic little sheep who do as you're told without question. But I'm a *wolf*, and I'll bite and claw my way out of here – and I don't care *who* I have to hurt in the process.'

'A *wolf*?' Elena gave a mocking laugh. 'Have you any idea how ridiculous you sound? You're a child, you silly girl. A spiteful, vindictive bully of a child.'

'And you're a whore,' Tasha spat. 'A dirty, disgusting whore.'

'Just like you,' Elena reminded her. 'And if you're so tough, how come you're still here?'

Tasha's lips tightened. They all knew why she was still here – why they were *all* still here: because Eddie Quinn had them so terrified of what would happen if they tried to run that they could barely put one foot in front of the other when they were outside. But she *would* get out of this situation one day, and then they would see who was the strong one.

Tired of Tasha's nonsense, Elena turned her back on her and smiled at Katya. 'Don't fancy making me a coffee while I dry my hair, do you?'

'Sure,' Katya said, glad of an excuse to get out of the room. She hadn't planned to tackle Tasha tonight, but she was so sick of these poisonous atmospheres. She had hoped that they could reach some sort of compromise and stop this constant bickering, but she'd known even before she started that it would be a waste of time.

Staring at the wall now as she waited for the kettle to boil, her thoughts floated off Tasha and onto the man in the hallway. She'd seen him from the window several times but had never been able to see his face clearly. That was why she had looked at him when she'd passed him today, so that she would know what he *really* looked like instead of what her imagination had built him into.

And, almost impossibly, he was even better-looking than she'd thought, with the kindest eyes she had seen in a long time. She never looked into those of the men who slobbered over her in their cars at night because she wanted to stay as far removed from them as possible. And she actively avoided looking into Eddie's for fear of seeing the devil staring back at her. But the man's had been such a lovely dark shade of blue, like a river in the moonlight.

Snapped out of her romantic reverie by the kettle clicking off, Katya made the coffees and carried them through to the living room. Handing Elena's and Tasha's to them, she took her own and Hanna's through to the bedroom. Hanna was in bed with the quilt pulled over her head. Leaving her cup on the bedside table, Katya undressed and headed into the bathroom for a shower.

Standing beneath the water, she reached for the soap and rubbed it listlessly over her body. It would barely skim the surface, because God alone could reach the parts of her that *really* needed cleansing. But since it was becoming increasingly obvious that *He* had abandoned her, it would have to do.

Next door, Chrissie had locked herself in the bedroom. The dog had leapt up at her when she'd walked back in and she'd kicked out at it to punish it for making a mess. It had immediately bared its teeth, forcing her to run for her life. So now she was pacing the floor, pressing redial on her mobile.

It was almost an hour before Eddie answered.

'Where the flaming hell are you?' Chrissie launched into him. 'You said you were only going to be half an hour, you lying swine! I've been up all night waiting for you.'

'Something came up,' Eddie said unconcernedly. 'What's up?'

'What's *up*?' she squawked. 'Your flaming dog, that's what! It's crapped all over the place, and I stood in it – with my *bare feet*!' Gasping with indignation when she heard him laugh and relate what she'd just told him to whoever he was with, she said, 'It's not funny, you dickhead. The vicious little bastard's got me trapped in the bedroom!'

'Give it a kick,' Eddie suggested, still chuckling.

'The only one who'll be getting a kick is *you* if you don't get home and sort it out,' Chrissie snarled, deciding not to mention that kicking it was what had got her into this mess in the first place. 'And you'd best be quick, 'cos I've already had to deal with your tarts. And I don't see why I should have to lose sleep over them when I didn't even want them here in the first place.'

'Thought you said you hadn't been to bed,' Eddie reminded her.

'Don't take the piss,' Chrissie retorted icily. 'I don't have to do your dirty work, you know.'

'Yeah, whatever,' Eddie said dismissively. Then, 'How much?'

It was a random-sounding question and most people wouldn't have had a clue what he meant by it. But Chrissie did, and it infuriated her that, after everything she'd said, *that* was all he was bothered about.

'Six-forty,' she lied, her voice thick with resentment.

'Take fifty,' he said, his tone giving nothing away so she didn't know if he thought it was an acceptable amount or not. 'And go get some girl stuff.'

Making a strangled screaming sound when he disconnected the call without another word, Chrissie threw the phone down onto the bed and herself down after it. No doubt whoever he was with would assume that he'd just told her to go out and treat herself, but he'd actually been telling her to go shopping for the whores – as if she didn't hate them enough already. But *he* certainly wouldn't waste his precious time shopping, and he refused to let *them* do it, because he reckoned they would take the piss and spend his money on crap. So it was left to Chrissie. And after the hiding he'd given her for threatening to grass them up to the immigration people that time she'd learned that it was easier to do as she was told where they were concerned.

She just wished they would hurry up and pay Eddie back. They were the ones who'd been desperate to come over here and they couldn't have thought he was paying their fares out of the goodness of his heart. It was a business arrangement and he'd upheld his side of it. But they weren't even *trying* to uphold theirs; always making excuses about why they hadn't made as much as they should have, and lying that there weren't enough punters when everyone knew that town was crawling with the bastards at night.

Still, like everything else he toyed with Eddie would tire of them eventually. And when that day came Chrissie would take great delight in turfing their skanky arses out. Until then, she would carry on taking her revenge where she could get it.

She only ever did little, sly things, because there was a very fine line with Eddie and if you crossed it you usually regretted it. The bitches were so terrified of him that they'd never dared complain about the times when she'd 'forgotten' to buy them sanitary towels or toilet roll, or when she'd given them nothing but beans and Spam for a whole week. But then, they had come from a country where she imagined they probably picked shit off the rubbish dump for dinner, so what did they care?

Today she'd held back eighty quid from their money. She didn't usually get a chance to get her hands on it, because this was the one area that Eddie maintained complete control over. But it was his own fault for staying out and giving her the opportunity. And if the bitches tried to say that they'd brought back more, it would be their word against hers – and Eddie would believe her every time.

Cheered by the thought of a nice new dress, or maybe a pair of shoes to compensate for her disturbed sleep, she got up off the bed now and, braving the dog, went to take a shower.

Eddie switched his phone off after the call. Watching him out of the corner of his eye, Clive said, 'Missus after money again?' Smirking when Eddie nodded, he said, 'Mine's the same. And it don't help that her sister's gone and shacked up with that loaded cunt. All I ever hear these days is *Chantelle's fella's got her this, Chantelle's fella's got her that.* Does my bleedin' box in.'

Amused by Clive's camp imitation of his wife. Eddie

glanced over the seat at the two lap dancers snuggled up together in the back. Chrissie had been spot on about him being cagey because he was in the company of someone who didn't know about his girls, although it hadn't even crossed her mind that it might possibly be a female – or two. But she could blame Clive's wife Letty, not him, because it wouldn't have happened if Letty hadn't abandoned Clive and pissed off to Lanzarote for a hen week. And Eddie was way too good of a mate to abandon him in his hour of need, so he'd had no choice but to go along when Clive had invited the tarts back to his for a party last night.

And what a party it had been. Eddie couldn't remember the last time he'd necked so much coke and downed so much cognac, and his poor dick had never worked so hard in its life. He was absolutely knackered now, with the mother of all hangovers, so there was no way he was tagging along while Clive dropped the tarts back in Bury. He was just getting a lift over to his boy Kenny's to pick up his money, and then he was going home to his bed for a well-deserved rest.

When Clive pulled up at the corner of a row of terraced houses in Moss Side, Eddie got out and strolled down the alley. Letting himself into one of the small backyards, he smiled when Kenny's mum answered the door.

'Morning, darlin'. He up yet?'

'He's still in his pit,' she told him, stepping back to let him in. 'Go straight up, love.'

Eddie took the stairs two at a time and crept down the landing. Pressing his ear against Kenny's door, he grinned when he heard a faint snoring sound. Then he hammered his fist on the wood, yelling, 'Get your hands where I can see them, you little prick – you're busted!'

Kenny was out of bed and halfway out of the window when Eddie pushed the door open a second later. 'Fucking hell, man,' he croaked when he realised who it was. 'What d'y do that for?'

'Just keeping you on your toes, matey,' Eddie said, laughing at the sight of Kenny's bare arse. 'Ain't warm out there – best watch nothing drops off.'

Kenny climbed back inside and snatched his crumpled jeans off the floor. Pulling them on, he reached under his mattress and took out a cloth money-bag.

Scowling now, Eddie snatched it out of his hand. 'See, that's what I'm talking about. You would have fucked off and left this, wouldn't you?'

'I was asleep,' Kenny muttered, as if that made any difference.

'Well, strap it round your fucking cock if you're going to do any naked flits in future,' Eddie warned him. ''Cos I'm telling you now, if you let the pigs waltz off with my money you're dead.' Looking into the bag now, he stared at Kenny accusingly. 'Where's the rest?'

'Aw, come on, man, don't be making out like you think I've been dipping into it,' Kenny moaned. 'I'm not like Tommy.'

'No, 'cos *you* can still feed yourself,' Eddie said, grinning again as he headed for the door.

He went back downstairs, taking a couple of twenties out of his pocket on the way. Popping his head around the parlour door, he tossed them onto the couch beside Kenny's mum.

'I'm off, sweetheart. Get yourself a little something with that, eh?'

'Oh, no, love, you can't keep giving me money,' she protested, scooping them up and flapping them at him. 'Here, take it back.'

Winking, Eddie closed the door and let himself out. She always tried to give it back but they both knew she didn't mean it. Anyway, it made him feel good to bung her a few quid because the poor cow reminded him of one of those women in those old black and white films who spent their lives scraping by – and trying to make out like they weren't complaining about it. She was so far back in the dark ages that she didn't even have a flat-screen TV.

But that was for her son to sort, not Eddie. He might be soft-hearted but he wasn't running a fucking soup kitchen.

The lap dancers had woken up by the time he got back into the car and they spent the next ten minutes desperately trying to flirt a repeat of last night's drugs fest out of him. Ignoring them, Eddie told Clive to drop him a couple of hundred yards back and on the opposite side from the flats when they reached Ardwick, in case they clocked where he was going and got any funny ideas about coming looking for him.

Eddie waited until the car was out of sight, then crossed over and slipped through a broken section of fence. Bypassing his own block, he headed down behind the other blocks to the red one at the far end.

The stench hit him as soon as he opened Patsy's front door. It was always rank in there, but after sitting in the car surrounded by the tarts' perfume it seemed way worse than usual, and for a moment he wondered if he was about to find her dead.

Patsy was sprawled across the couch when he pushed the living-room door open. Approaching her with caution, he was relieved to see the flickering movement behind her parchment-thin eyelids.

'Wha'?' she croaked, snapping her eyes open when he shook her.

Wiping his hand on his jeans, Eddie felt a shudder of revulsion ripple through him. Patsy was twenty-four but she could easily have passed for fifty with her body turning to skin and bone, and her cheeks sinking into the hollows where her teeth had started to disintegrate. And the smell was coming from her, he realised, trying not to inhale the rank odours of urine, BO and vomit.

'Jeezus,' he muttered, giving her a look that would have made any normal woman crawl away in shame. 'Have you seen the state of yourself?'

Grinning up at him as if he'd just complimented her, Patsy said, 'Hiya, Ed. I've been waiting for you.' Licking her lips now, she sat up and put her hands between her knees like an excited child.

Eddie knew exactly what she was waiting for but she wasn't getting klish until he was good and ready to give it to her. Leaving her, he went into the bedroom. The baby was lying in its cot on the far side. Roused by the harsh light spilling out of the bare bulb when Eddie flicked the switch, it made a pathetic mewling noise that lacked energy and conviction, as if it had already given up hope that anybody would respond.

Sickened by the sound, Eddie squatted down at the foot of the cot and shoved his hand under the heap of clothes and dirty nappies that were stuffed beneath it. Glancing through the bars as he peeled the damp carpet back and dislodged the loose floorboard, he frowned when he saw how clearly the veins were showing through the see-through skin of the baby's head.

'When did you last feed the kid?' he demanded when he'd pulled his case out and gone back to the living room.

The look of confusion that flickered across Patsy's face told him exactly what he'd suspected: that she'd forgotten she even *had* a baby, never mind remembered to feed it. He wondered if she'd even been into the bedroom in the three days since he'd last been here, or if she'd been sleeping, waking, pissing, sweating, and sleeping again right here with her beloved crack pipe.

'You'd better get a grip,' he warned her, sitting down and unlocking the case. 'It'll die if you're not careful.'

'I'll see to it in a minute,' she replied offhandedly, licking her lips again as she eyed the little white rocks inside the numerous clear plastic bags in the case.

'*Now*,' Eddie ordered her, lifting his gun out and pointing it at the wall. He wasn't going to use it – he just liked the feel of it in his hand.

The thought of her baby dying hadn't registered as important with her but the sight of the gun brought Patsy to her feet in an instant. Scared that he was going to shoot her, she stumbled through to the kitchen and scooped a bottle out from under the slime-coated dishes in the sink. Tipping out the clotted gunk inside, she gave it a quick rinse before spooning some powdered milk into it and topping it up with warm tap water.

'Done it,' she declared, rushing back to show Eddie.

'So give it to the fucking kid,' he told her exasperatedly.

Patsy darted out and came back with the baby clutched in her skinny arms. Watching as she stuck the teat into its mouth, Eddie wrinkled his nose at the smell of shit and sour milk. But at least it was getting fed, so it wouldn't die just yet. And that was his main concern, because he could really do without the hassle of trying to find a new stash-house as convenient as this one.

He pocketed the drugs now and replaced the gun before relocking the case. Then, tossing three of the bags onto the table, he said, 'Make it last, 'cos there's no more till Friday.'

Pausing in the hallway after putting the case back in its hiding place, he lit a cigarette to rid his mouth of the taste of decay before rushing outside into the fresh air.

Glad to find when he got home a few minutes later that Chrissie had done as she was told and gone shopping, he fed the dog and cleaned up its shit. Then he made himself a brew and settled down to count his money.

Eddie had recently branched out into the protection business and had added three pubs and a couple of clubs to his list so far, each yielding a few hundred a week. It was absolute peanuts compared to what the guys running the venues in the town centre were taking but he'd spent too long in prison ever to want to go back, so he was keeping it low-key so as not to draw unnecessary attention to himself while he was getting established. He planned eventually to run the whole of East Manchester – and maybe a bit of the north, the south and the west as well. But he wouldn't make the mistake of branching out too fast, as so many gang leaders did when they let self-importance override sense.

He was doing all right with the club money added to what he got off the girls and the dealers, but it was still nowhere near enough to think of himself as loaded. People might have thought he was rolling in clear profit but they didn't take the overheads into account: the lads' wages, for example; and having to pay up front for the drugs to supply them. Then there were the inevitable losses when one of them got jacked or arrested, and the expense of feeding the hookers, paying for the electricity they used and replacing the clothes that got ruined by rough punters. It all added up. And that was without his own day-to-day expenses – which weren't cheap. But he didn't see why he should do all the hard work and deny himself the benefits.

When he caught himself counting the same stack of notes twice Eddie decided it was time to get some shut-eye so he took the money and the drugs he'd picked up from Patsy's into the bathroom and stashed them behind the vent above the door – checking to make sure that Chrissie wouldn't notice it had been tampered with – before he went to bed. He'd lived with her for over a year, which was way longer than he'd entertained any other bird, but that didn't mean he'd trust her to keep her sticky fingers off his gear if she got a chance.

The dog jumped straight onto Chrissie's pillow when Eddie whistled for it. He knew she'd go ballistic if she came in and saw it but he didn't give a toss. All that mattered was that it had ears like a bat, so no one would be sneaking up on him and catching him unawares.

7

Joe had made a load of new mates at Cheryl's party, which was great because it was infinitely better to be on the inside than the out. But he'd never come across such a bunch of hardened weed-heads before and he was finding it hard to keep up as days blurred into nights in an endless stream of smoking and boozing.

His head was banging when he woke up today and for a moment he couldn't remember how he'd got home, never mind whose flat he'd been in last night. All he had was a vague recollection of being pleased not to have to tackle any stairs on his way home, so he thought it was a pretty good bet that he'd been at Carl's.

Yes, he definitely had been, because he remembered Carl loading up yet another bong – and taking the piss when Joe said he couldn't take any more. And then Mel had followed him out, offering to put him to bed, but Carl had told her to leave him alone, so he'd escaped unscathed.

Mystery solved, he got up and crept into the kitchen for a strong-coffee and painkiller breakfast – just about all he'd been able to face lately. Leaning down to get the milk out of the fridge, he was disgusted when he caught sight of his reflection in the microwave door and saw the dark hollows under his eyes and the roll of flab that was spilling out over the waistband of his boxers. He'd never been particularly fanatical about the gym, but he had always kept himself in reasonable shape so he was ashamed that he'd let himself go so badly – and in such a short space of time.

Renewing the vow that he'd made the previous morning – and the morning before that, and the one before *that* – to get a grip and stop letting himself get into such a state, he waited for the tablets to kick in. Then he took a shower and got dressed.

Carl called round twenty minutes later. Laughing when he saw the state of Joe, he said, 'Christ, you look half dead. Didn't you get any kip?'

'Less than you, by the looks of it,' Joe grumbled, taking his jacket off the hook and checking that he had his keys. 'And I don't see how, seeing as you were still at it when I left.'

'I haven't been to bed yet,' Carl told him, trotting jauntily down the stairs. 'I find it easier not to if I know I've got to get up early.'

'Hope you didn't do that on my account,' Joe said, following slowly behind. ''Cos trust me, I wouldn't have minded staying in bed for a few more hours.'

'And waste this?' Carl gushed, stepping outside and

raising his face to the sunshine. 'First day in ages it hasn't been chucking it down. Come on, mate, you can't say you're not glad you're up and out on a day like this.'

'Suppose not,' Joe conceded, heading across the car park.

His car had been playing up for a while but he had less of a clue about fixing it than he'd had about Cheryl's washing machine that time. But there was no way he was risking doing any of the wish-and-prayer poking about that he'd done then, so he'd been keeping his fingers crossed that it would hold out until he could afford to get it to a garage. Only trouble was, he was *never* going to be able to afford it at the rate he'd been going through money lately. He didn't know how his neighbours managed, because he found it hard enough just buying food and paying his electric bills. But add a tenner bag every couple of days – or every *day*, in some of his mates' cases – and you were left with less than nothing. Still, at least he had Carl and his lay-ons to fall back on, so it wasn't all bad.

And since Carl had decided to reveal out of the blue the other day that his dad had been a rally freak who had taught him all sorts of shit about engines, it looked like his car troubles might actually be resolvable without having to get down on bended knee to the bank manager.

Carl propped the bonnet open now while Joe brought his tools out of the back. Shaking his head when he saw the pathetic collection, he said, 'What am I supposed to do with that lot?'

'Sorry, it's all I've got,' Joe told him. 'How am I supposed to know what you need for this kind of thing? The most I've ever done is change a tyre – and it wasn't easy, I can tell you.'

'I wonder about you sometimes,' Carl muttered, rolling up his sleeves. 'If I didn't know better I'd swear you was gay. You're not, are you?' He gave Joe a probing look. 'Not that it'd bother me or owt, but the amount of times you've seen my cock I'm not sure I'd be too happy if I knew you'd been wanking over it when you got home.'

'Er, you've got no worries about that, mate,' Joe assured him. 'But if you didn't keep whipping it out for a slash in the middle of every road I wouldn't have seen it at all, would I?'

'Can't help having a weak bladder,' Carl protested. 'Anyhow, pass us one of them shit spanners if that's all you've got. And you can skin up while you've got nowt else to do.'

Joe wasn't thrilled by the thought of a spliff at this time of day but he could hardly refuse while Carl was helping him out, so he took his gear out of his pocket and climbed into the front seat. Leaving the door open because the sun had already made the car unbearably stuffy, he'd just finished rolling when a shadow passed over him. His heart sank when he looked up and saw Phillip Kettler staring in at him.

'I was on my way out,' Kettler said, looking stiff and ridiculous with his coat buttoned up to the throat. 'But it can wait if you need a hand.'

'Er, no, you're all right,' Joe said, jumping out. It was bad enough having to talk to Kettler at all without being at a height disadvantage as well. 'It's under control, thanks.'

'I've got plenty of time,' Kettler persisted. 'And you know what they say about two heads being better than one. Anyway, I haven't seen you for quite some time so it'll be nice to catch up. I've called round a few times but you've obviously been busy.'

'Er, yeah, I've had quite a lot on,' Joe lied.

'Oi, where's my smoke?' Carl called out from under the bonnet just then. 'A man can't concentrate with a straight head, you know.'

A strange look came over Kettler's face when he heard the voice. Having approached from the rear, he hadn't noticed that somebody was at the front. Glancing in that direction now and seeing Carl, he looked at Joe as if he'd just betrayed him in the worst possible way.

'I've, er, just remembered I've got to . . .' Trailing off on something unintelligible, he turned and rushed away.

'What did *he* want?' Carl asked, coming out from under the bonnet and sneering at Kettler's back.

'Offered to help me fix the car,' Joe told him, handing the spliff over. 'But I told him you were already on it.'

'Bet he loved that,' Carl snorted. 'Hates my guts, him.' Sucking his teeth dismissively now, he turned back to

Joe. 'Anyhow, you'll be pleased to know it's nothing major. Just a bit of shit in the carb.'

'You sure?' Joe asked, following him around to take a look.

'I'm sure,' Carl said confidently, pointing at something that could have been a tin of spaghetti hoops for all it meant to Joe. 'We'll take it for a run down the motorway,' he suggested, tossing the tools back into the bag and slamming the bonnet down. 'Give it a good blow-out.'

The flats' door slammed back against the wall just then and Eddie stalked out, yelling into his mobile, 'You're taking the fucking piss, mate. It's *Sunday*, not bleeding Christmas! Tell you what, forget it, but you'd best watch your tyres – that's all I'm saying.'

He cut the call and made a gesture as if he was about to smash the phone down on the concrete. Shoving it into his pocket instead when he spotted Carl, he shouted, 'Yo! Whose is the motor?'

'Joe's,' Carl told him, nodding towards his friend. 'Lives opposite me,' he added in case Eddie had forgotten.

'I know who he is,' Eddie said, walking over and nodding at Joe. 'Any chance of a lift?'

'Yeah, sure.' Joe shrugged. 'Where to?'

'Rochdale Road, then on to Moss Side,' Eddie told him, already heading for the passenger-side door. 'I was trying to get a cab but them jokers down at the rank reckon they can't get anything out for forty minutes – and I've got to be there in five.'

'They've been running funny on Sundays lately,' Carl said, climbing into the back. 'Took Mel over an hour to get to her mam's last week. She ended up getting the bus instead.'

Giving him a look that said he wouldn't be seen dead on a bus, Eddie took a twenty note out of his pocket and offered it to Joe when he got behind the wheel.

'No, you're all right,' Joe said. 'It's only a five-minute drive. I was about to take it for a run anyway. Carl says something needs blasting out.'

'Carb,' Carl reminded him.

Joe would never have said it out loud but he was glad to do Eddie a favour. Apart from Shay, who still gave him dirty looks whenever their paths crossed, Eddie was the only person on the block that he still hadn't spoken to. And given how much everyone seemed to look up to him, Joe was intrigued to see the side of him that he'd previously missed.

'You still not got your licence back?' Carl asked Eddie as they set off.

'Nah, I've got another two years yet,' Eddie told him, glancing at his watch.

'That would kill me,' Carl said sympathetically. 'I know I haven't got wheels now, but if I had a motor like yours gathering dust I'd be well tempted.'

'Yeah, well, I'm not that stupid,' Eddie said bluntly. 'The pigs would be all over me like a rash if I got spotted, and I'm not giving them any excuses.'

'I know what you mean,' Joe chipped in. 'I got pulled loads of times when I was living in Birmingham. And it was the same coppers every time, like they were specifically looking out for me. I threatened to do them for harassment in the end.'

'Did that stop them?'

'Did it hell. But I got smart and made sure it was legal so they couldn't do me for anything. Didn't half piss them off.'

'That's the only way to deal with that lot,' Eddie said scornfully. 'It's a game of them and us, and you've just got to learn how to play it better.'

'Yeah, that's what I've always thought,' Carl agreed. 'Pisses me off when I hear the other guys moaning about getting pulled. If you're smart, you can see them coming from miles off and make sure there's nothing they can do you for. They still keep you in if they can get away with it but at least it's only for the night.'

'Pity everyone's not as sussed as you, eh?' Eddie murmured.

Unsure if it had been a compliment or a dig, Carl stopped talking and they continued the rest of the journey in silence.

Partway down Rochdale Road, Eddie pointed out an entrance to a lane. 'You can stop here, mate. I'll only be ten minutes.'

Joe pulled over. Watching as Eddie got out and disappeared down the lane, he said, 'You know, that's the first time I've spoken to him since that business with the dog. But he's all right, isn't he?'

'Yeah, so long as he thinks you are,' Carl replied, winding his window down. 'But you still wouldn't want to get on the wrong side of him.'

'I kind of gathered that,' Joe laughed, rolling his own window down and lowering the sun visor to cut the glare. 'God, it's boiling in here.'

'Stop complaining,' Carl said, relishing the heat. 'It could easy go back to rain tomorrow and then you'd be moaning about that again.'

'I know,' Joe conceded, flipping the radio on and drumming his fingertips on the wheel in time to the music.

It was a good half-hour before Eddie reappeared. 'Sorry about that,' he apologised. 'Took a bit longer than I expected. Do you know Quinney Crescent?'

Joe nodded and started the engine. He'd been falling asleep in the stifling heat so it was good to be moving again and get a bit of breeze circulating.

They reached the Alexandra Park estate ten minutes later but as they turned onto Quinney Crescent they saw a couple of police vans blocking the far end and several uniformed officers milling around. A group of locals had gathered on the grass separating the Crescent from the Princess Parkway and a horde of hooded youths were circling on BMX bikes.

'Pull over,' Eddie ordered. 'And keep it cool so you don't draw attention to us.'

'Wonder what's going on,' Carl murmured, sitting forward in his seat to get a better look as Joe parked behind a row of cars. 'That's not Beanie's gaff, is it?'

'Don't know,' Eddie muttered unbuckling his seat belt.

'You're not getting out, are you?' Carl asked. 'Looks like a bust to me.'

'That's why I need to check it out,' Eddie told him, sliding a plastic bag out from under his jacket and tossing it into Carl's hand. 'Yours is in the blue bag inside. Drop the rest at Clive's.'

'Righto,' Carl said, shoving the bag up under his own jacket.

Turning to Joe now, Eddie said, 'Everyone seems to think you're okay. I hope you don't prove them wrong by opening your mouth about what you've just seen.'

'Didn't see a thing,' Joe replied sincerely. 'Just giving a mate a lift, that's all.'

Eddie held his gaze for several seconds, then nodded and climbed out.

Reversing back out the way they'd come as Eddie strolled down the road, Joe said, 'Where to?'

'Cheetham Hill,' Carl told him as he climbed over into Eddie's vacated seat. Glancing back and seeing the big man standing easy among the crowd, he turned his attention to keeping an eye out for coppers. There was a strong scent of weed coming from the bag and it would only get worse in the heat. But that was a minor concern compared to how much crack was probably in the bag

94

along with it. Chuffed as he was that Eddie had entrusted it to him, he definitely didn't want to get caught with all of that shit on him.

Relieved when he'd offloaded it to Clive a short time later, he came back to the car with his own bag causing an unsightly bulge in the front of his jeans. Shaking his head when Joe asked if there was anywhere else they needed to go, he said, 'Not unless you still fancy that motorway run. We're not that far from the sixty-two.'

Joe glanced at his petrol gauge and saw that it was already touching red. 'Best not. It's lower than I thought.'

'Should have taken that twenty off Eddie,' Carl told him, taking his skins and tobacco out of his pocket. 'It's not like he can't afford it.'

'No, it was way too much for a couple of short trips,' Joe said, setting off. 'Talking about Eddie, though, what was all that about people saying I'm okay?'

Shrugging as he licked his papers and stuck them together, Carl said, 'He just likes to know who's who on the estate, so he's been asking around about you.'

'Has he asked you?'

'Course. But don't worry, I told him you're sound.' Carl stuck a hand down his pants, pulled out a small clump of weed and sniffed it before ripping it apart and lacing his spliff.

'Jeezus, do you have to?' Joe pulled a face. 'Now I know where it's kept before it gets to me I'll be paranoid about hairy bits.'

'Hey, the pubes are a bonus,' Carl quipped. 'Think yourself lucky I don't charge extra.'

'Gee, thanks,' Joe muttered.

Arriving back at the estate, Carl shielded his eyes against the sun when he heard somebody shouting down to him from the fifth floor. He waved when he saw his friend Damien leaning out of his window and said, 'All right, mate. What's happening?'

'Just getting ready for Mischa's party,' Damien told him. 'Got that thing yet?'

'Just.' Carl patted his crotch. 'How much you after?'

'Half for now. I've got a load of mates coming over from Leeds. Youse are still coming, aren't you?'

'Too right,' Carl said, answering for both him and Joe. 'I'll drop it round in a bit.'

Giving him the thumbs-up, Damien retracted his head and closed the window.

Phillip Kettler was walking along the path at that moment. Annoyed when he saw the man watching them out of the corner of his eye, Carl yelled, 'What you gawping at, freak?'

Smirking when Kettler rushed inside without answering, he said, 'Bet he wears a Nazi uniform when he's at home. That's probably why he always looks like he's got something stuck up his arse, 'cos he's stopping himself from breaking into that stupid walk. Heil Hitler!'

Laughing as Carl goose-stepped up to the door, Joe

followed him inside. The light at the top of the lift said that it was up on the third floor but it didn't move when Carl pressed the button.

'See if I get up there and he's stuck something in it to stop it coming down, he's dead!' Carl hissed.

Cheryl's door opened just then and she backed out into the hall with the pram. 'What you moaning about now?' she asked amusedly.

'Aw, nothing. Just that idiot upstairs arsing about with the lift,' Carl told her. 'How's you?'

'Same as usual.' She rolled her eyes. 'Bored, skint, fed up, fat.'

'You're not fat,' Carl scoffed. 'You've got a great figure – hasn't she, Joe?'

Nodding, Joe winked at her and squatted down to pull faces at Frankie, who immediately started giggling.

'Going to Damien's party tonight?' Carl asked now.

'Doubt it.' Cheryl sighed. 'My mum's going out, and I can't find another babysitter.'

'Get Shay to watch him.'

'No way! He's not taking my baby anywhere near that slag.'

'Fair enough. Shame, though, 'cos it would do you good to get out for a change.'

'Ah, well, that's life,' Cheryl said resignedly. 'Anyway, I'd best go. We're going to Vee's for dinner and the bus'll be here in a minute.' Turning to Joe now, she said, 'Are you free for a brew sometime this week?'

'Any time,' he told her as he took a coin out of his pocket and put it into Frankie's pudgy hand.

Wondering why all men couldn't be as nice as him, Cheryl said, 'I'll try and pop round tomorrow after I've dropped him at nursery.' Pushing the pram down the hall now, she paused at the door. 'Oh, by the way, Carl, tell Mel my new catalogue came yesterday. I'll be home around six if she wants to pop down for a look.'

Carl pulled a face and said, 'I'll tell her, but only if you promise not to let her order anything. I know what you lot are like when you start drooling over shoes and handbags.'

'You're such a tightarse,' Cheryl flipped back, grinning as she manoeuvred the pram out.

'Great girl, her,' Carl said when she'd gone. 'Shay don't deserve her.'

Joe couldn't have agreed more but he kept his opinions to himself as they headed for the stairwell. He hadn't seen much of Cheryl since the party because they had formed a kind of unspoken agreement that she would visit him up at his place instead of him coming down to hers. She hadn't actually said anything but Carl had told him that Shay had had a go at her when he'd found out about the party, accusing her of having it behind his back so that she could screw every Tom, Dick and Harry. It wasn't true, but Joe wasn't about to interfere by trying to set the man straight. Anyway, Cheryl was still letting Shay go round there, so she could obviously see something in him that the rest of them couldn't.

The lift was on its way back down to the ground floor by the time they reached their landing. Carl banged on Kettler's door and yelled, 'Yeah, very funny, knobhead! But you'd best watch your back, 'cos you're gonna get what you're looking for one of these days.'

'Don't bother,' Joe said quietly, guessing that Kettler would be watching them through his spyhole. 'He'll be trying to get a rise out of us – don't give him the satisfaction.'

'I know, but he pisses me off,' Carl grumbled. 'Anyhow, what you doing? Fancy a brew?'

'Nah, my headache's coming back,' Joe told him as he took his keys out of his pocket. 'Think I'd best try and sleep it off.'

'You're a right old woman, you,' Carl laughed. 'I haven't even been to bed yet, and I'll be off to work in a bit.'

'Rather you than me,' Joe said, yawning at the mere thought of it.

'Lazy bastard,' Carl jeered, backing towards his own door. 'See you at the party – if you can stay up that late. I should be back around two.'

'I think I'm going to give it a miss,' Joe told him. 'You have a good one, though. I'll see you tomorrow.'

Tutting, Carl shook his head. 'Such a lightweight.'

Joe grinned, stuck two fingers up and closed his door.

*

Mel was in the bedroom when Carl let himself into his own flat, playing on the games console that he'd taken off one of his customers in lieu of payment. Carl went in to get his scales out of the drawer and said, 'Don't tell me you've been there since I went out?'

'Shut up – I'm trying to kill the monster,' Mel replied snappily. 'It's already eaten me about a thousand times.'

'At least *some*one's getting lucky,' Carl muttered, heading through to the kitchen.

The sink was full of dirty dishes, the ledges covered in empty pizza boxes and beer bottles. Swiping some of the mess aside, Carl laid the scales on the flat surface and retrieved the weed from his jeans. Mel had been really lazy since he'd set up that console; she hadn't cleaned up, or so much as *sniffed* at his dick in days. But if she didn't get it sorted he was going to lob the damn thing out of the window. A man had needs and if his woman wasn't fulfilling them she'd have no one but herself to blame when she found herself being replaced by someone who would.

Someone like Cheryl.

Now *there* was a face you'd be glad to see when you got home of a night. And how great it would be to snuggle up with a curvy lass instead of having to dodge jutting elbows and knees. He'd never understand why Shay had played away from home when he had a woman like her. Jayleen might be pretty, slim, and fashionable – and all the shit that seemed to matter to men who were as up their own arses as Shay was. But Carl had tried to talk to her at a party once and she'd had about as much personality as a watermelon.

But there was no point thinking about Cheryl while she was still hankering after the idiot so he pushed her out of his mind and got on with weighing out his deals. Stashing them in his inside pocket when he'd done, along with the bags of crack that Eddie had allotted him, he went back to the bedroom.

Mel was still trying to kill her virtual monsters. Watching from the doorway, Carl's mood softened as his dick began to harden. She wasn't that bad, he supposed, and she looked quite raunchy sitting there in her bra and knickers with her unbrushed hair trailing down her back.

'Fancy a quick break?' He fingered his fly hopefully.

'*Carl!*' she barked, her eyes never leaving the screen. 'This is difficult enough without you distracting me, you dickhead.'

Hard and soft parts swapping back to their original positions in a flash, Carl said, 'Forget it. Oh, and Cheryl said to tell you she's sacked the catalogue off, by the way.'

That got Mel's attention. Miraculously remembering where the pause button was, she twisted her head around and stared at him.

'You'd better be joking – I was relying on that for some new boots. And I need a coat as well.'

'Tough.' Carl shrugged into his jacket and zipped it up. 'Just have to save up like everyone else, won't you?'

Hurling a dirty look at his back when he walked out, Mel went back to her game.

After delivering Damien's half-ounce Carl made his way down to his spot under the canal bridge to see to his regular customers. He had a busy day ahead, starting with flogging as much shit as he could down here before meeting up with Kenny and the other guys to go collecting Eddie's money from the pubs and clubs. Then he'd finally be free to go to Damien's party – and, *man*, was he looking forward to that, because Damien's sister and her mates were bound to get wasted and start dirty dancing. And once they got going it was touchy-feely lesbo-hooker action all the way. Carl couldn't wait!

8

Carl's day had gone a lot slower than he'd anticipated. His customers had come along in dribs and drabs so he'd been forced to stay down by the canal for far longer than he'd wanted to. And, so far, the night hadn't been much better because the pub managers had seemed determined to hold up the handovers for as long as possible. But, finally, they were on their last pick-up and he couldn't wait to get it over and done with so he could get to Damien's.

He, Kenny, Matt and Daz had just arrived at Frost, a seedy little club situated in an old warehouse in a particularly rough area on the outskirts of Gorton. There were no houses nearby and the no-through road was way off the beaten track so there was no danger of casual passers-by or locals catching onto what they were doing and calling the police.

But the same remoteness that made Frost a sitting duck for Eddie's protection racket also made the crew vulnerable should a rival gang decide to muscle in and take it as their own. So they were alert as they got out of the motor now, watching out for silhouettes in the parked cars that were dotted around.

Carl went inside with Kenny and Matt when they reached the door, leaving Daz outside to keep an eye on the bouncers and watch out for police.

It was half-one by now, and this club closed at two on Sundays so the DJ had already started playing his wind-down music. Leaning against one of the pillars as Kenny and Matt made their way to the manager's office, Carl watched the desperate antics of the customers making their last-ditch attempts to find a bedmate for the night.

Outside, Daz had wandered around the corner into the shadows at the side of the club. He was supposed to watch the door but he figured it could take care of itself for a few minutes while he had a couple of lines of speed. Eddie didn't like them getting high on the job but Daz was safe as long as Kenny didn't find out and grass him up.

Just as he'd finished he heard the sound of footsteps. Thinking it might be Kenny checking up on him, he wiped his nose and rushed back out to the road. But it wasn't Kenny, it was a drunken girl.

'All right, love.' He nodded as she staggered towards him. 'Off home?'

'Yeah,' she slurred, grinning up at him. 'Wanna come with me, handsome?'

'Wish I could,' Daz drawled, looking her over. Her dress

was short and tight, and her hair was all mussed up from dancing.

The girl took a step towards him and giggled when her heel caught on the concrete. She fell against him. 'Oooh, you're a big boy, aren't you?' she purred when he caught her. 'Bet you work out.'

'A bit,' Daz admitted, catching the scent of her perfume mixed with the alcohol on her breath and feeling a stirring down below.

'I like a man who works out,' she said huskily, giving him the green light with her eyes as she stroked his arms. 'They reckon it makes you last longer 'cos of all those push-ups. Is that true?'

'Why don't you come and find out?' Daz suggested. He grabbed her hand and led her back into the shadows as the temptation became too strong to resist.

The doormen watched as Daz and his conquest disappeared. Then, exchanging a quick glance, they checked that the road was clear and went inside, locking the door behind them.

Carl turned his head when he felt a tap on his shoulder. 'Yeah?'

'Your mate's getting jumped outside,' one of the doormen told him. 'Just thought you'd want to know – 'cos there's three of them.'

Tutting, Carl pushed himself away from the pillar and headed out into the foyer. Under any other circumstances you'd expect a doorman to wade in if there was a fight.

But he could hardly blame this one for staying out of it, because it *was* a bit of a piss-take expecting the guy to help one of the men who were stealing money from the club. And that was effectively what they were doing, because they certainly weren't doing any of the security dirty work to justify it. That was all left to the doormen, who had to deal with the troublemakers *and* mop up the vomit and blood – all for a fraction of what Eddie was taking.

The foyer light had gone out. Trying the door and finding it locked, Carl presumed the doorman had done it to keep the fight from spilling over into the club. But as he turned to ask him to open it he heard a whooshing sound. Too late to duck – he felt like he'd been hit by a train when the baseball bat connected with his forehead.

At that same moment Kenny and Matt had just stepped out of the manager's office. When he found the previously lit corridor in darkness, the hairs rose on the back of Kenny's neck. And when the manager suddenly closed and locked his door behind them, he dropped instinctively to his haunches and eased his gun out of his inside pocket. He'd never used it and had hoped he'd never have to, but if something was going down there was no way he was being taken out without giving himself a fair chance.

Narrowing his eyes now, Kenny squinted into the void, watching for movement in the shadows as Matt edged his way along the wall in search of the light switch. When he heard the same distinctive whooshing sound that Carl had just heard out in the foyer Kenny yelled, 'Get down!' But it was too late, and he winced when he heard the dull *thwok* of wood connecting with bone, followed by the sound of Matt's body hitting the deck like a sack of potatoes.

'Don't be a prick,' Kenny said calmly, guessing that the doorman had whacked Matt with a bat. 'I've got a gun, so drop it or I start shooting!'

'Fuck you,' the doorman hissed, swinging out wildly and jarring his elbow when he hit the wall. 'Mistake you made was thinking that we were gonna sit back and let your boss carry on ripping us off,' he went on. '*We* run this place, not him.'

'Know him, do you?' Kenny asked, edging away from the door, aware that this was most likely where the man was heading for.

'Are you deaf, you little cunt?' the doorman snarled, getting closer. 'We don't give a flying *fuck* about Eddie Quinn – and you can tell him that from me. This is over, do you hear me? As of now, he ain't getting another penny.'

The light came on suddenly as Carl burst through the door and flicked the switch. Seeing the gun in Kenny's hand and realising that he'd been telling the truth, the doorman stopped in his tracks. It genuinely hadn't occurred to him that they would be armed, because they looked like a bunch of kids playing hard men to him. If anything, he'd thought they might have knives, but he always wore a stab vest when he was doing doors so that hadn't bothered him.

'All right, lads, no need to get stupid,' he said, raising his hands. 'Just leave before the pigs get here, yeah?'

Seeing Matt on the floor, Carl swiped at the blood running from the cut on his own head and aimed a vicious kick into the small of the doorman's back, sending him sprawling to his knees.

'Where's the other one?' Kenny asked, strolling towards the doorman and pointing the gun at his head.

'Spark out in the cloakroom,' Carl told him, wiping his face on his sleeve.

'And Daz?' Kenny asked, wondering why the hell Daz hadn't stopped the men from coming after them in the first place, or at least alerted them – unless they'd got to him first.

'No idea,' Carl said, squatting beside Matt and slapping his face to rouse him. 'All I know is, this one's mate told me he was getting jumped so I went to help him out. But they'd locked the doors, and he took a swing while my back was turned.'

Nodding, Kenny turned his attention back to the doorman. He lifted his foot and slammed it down on the top of the man's head.

'Try anything like this again and you're fucking dead, mate!' he warned him. 'Now get up and let us out. And lock the door behind us, 'cos if anyone tries to follow us they're gonna seriously regret it.'

Hauling the doorman to his feet now, Kenny shoved the barrel of the gun into his back and pushed him out through the clubroom as Carl helped Matt out.

Daz was strolling around the corner, adjusting his flies, when Kenny and the others came out. He frowned when he saw Carl holding Matt up, his face covered in blood, and said, 'Jeezus, what's happened?'

'Fetch the car,' Kenny ordered coldly, his eyes flashing fire as he took in the fact that Daz looked totally unscathed.

When Daz pulled up alongside them Kenny stashed the money he'd just taken into the bag with the rest and slid it under the passenger seat. Then, after helping Matt onto the back seat, he climbed into the front and told Daz to drive to the nearest hospital.

After dropping Carl and Matt off outside the A&E department Kenny kept his eyes peeled for a suitable spot in which to have it out with Daz when they set off again. He felt like whacking the idiot and didn't want his movements to be restricted by the confines of the car, so he told Daz to pull in behind a boarded-up warehouse just off the main road.

'Aw, I hope you're not planning on waiting for them,' Daz complained, doing as he was told. 'They'll be hours yet.'

Kenny didn't bother answering this. He climbed out

when they stopped and paced on the spot until Daz got out the other side.

'What the fuck were you doing back there?' he demanded, launching straight into him. 'All you had to do was watch the door and make sure them clowns stayed put, so how come you didn't see them following us in?'

Daz folded his arms, pursed his lips and gazed down at his trainers. He'd been having a knee-trembler with the pissed-up bird in the car park but he could hardly admit to that after what had happened. So he lied, and said, 'I thought I heard my alarm going off, so I went to check it out.'

'Bullshit!' Kenny spat. 'You were nowhere near the car. Anyway, you were zipping yourself up when we saw you. So what were you really doing? Having a wank? 'Cos I'll tell you what, that's the only muscle *you* ever use. The one in your *head* certainly never gets any fucking exercise.'

Incensed by the way Kenny was going off on him, Daz puffed out his chest aggressively. 'Who the fuck d'y think you're talking to? I could knock you out with one punch, mate.'

'Come on, then,' Kenny challenged him calmly. 'Let's see what you got.'

'You make me laugh,' Daz sneered, circling him. 'You gob off like some kind of hard man, but you're nowt but Eddie's lapdog.'

'You reckon?' Kenny's eyes glinted a warning. 'So what's stopping you from taking a pop, then? Come on – *do* it!'

Daz's burst of bravado fizzled out as quickly as it had come over him. He'd always relied on his size and his tongue to intimidate people into submission before they realised that he couldn't actually back up his words with actions. But Kenny wasn't intimidated and Daz's instincts told him that it would be a mistake to get into it with him. Kenny might be smaller but he was rock-hard on the inside – where it counted.

'Didn't think so,' Kenny jeered when Daz headed back to the car. 'You're a bottler, mate. I've been thinking it for ages and now you've proved it. And I'll tell you what: Eddie's gonna go fucking *ape* when he hears what you did tonight.'

Still fronting, because that was his last defence, Daz gave a slow smile as he climbed back in behind the wheel. 'You're full of shit,' he drawled. 'Only reason I'm not touching you is 'cos I don't wanna break you.'

Muttering, 'Whatever,' Kenny walked around to the passenger side. But just as he reached it, Daz activated the central locking and reversed away. Shocked, because he hadn't seen it coming, Kenny ran after him, yelling, 'Stop, you idiot! You've got the money!'

Kicking the kerb in frustration when Daz turned the corner with a screech of rubber, he yanked his mobile out of his pocket. But Daz's phone went straight to answerphone so he ran out onto the main road and looked around for a cab.

★

Joe woke with a start when his phone rang. Groping for it on the bedside table, he croaked, 'Yeah?'

'It's me,' said Carl. 'Didn't wake you, did I?'

'Yeah, but it's okay.' Joe rubbed his eyes. 'What time is it?'

'Nearly three,' Carl told him. 'Sorry for disturbing you but I need a favour. I'm at the hospital. Can you pick us up?'

'Hospital?' Joe sat up now. 'Why, what's happened?'

'Long story,' Carl said wearily. 'I'm okay but I left my dosh at home, so I really need a lift.'

'Course.' Joe was already pushing the quilt off. 'Which hospital?'

'Fuck, I don't even know,' Carl murmured. 'Hang on. Let me just ask.' His voice sounded muffled as he spoke to somebody else. Then, coming back to Joe, he said, 'Stepping Hill. Do you know it?'

'Yeah – Stockport. I'll come now. Do you want me to tell Mel?'

'Nah, I'll see her when I get back. No point worrying her. Just hurry up, yeah?'

Carl was sitting on a bollard when Joe pulled into the ambulance bay a short time later. He'd been having a smoke while he watched two policewomen try to convince a bloody-faced young girl that she needed to let the doctors have a look at her. He stood up now, flicked his cigarette butt away and shouted, 'Yo, I'd go with them if I was you, love. That nose is gonna look like you've gone ten rounds with Tyson come the morning.'

He grinned when the girl called him a wanker and yelled at him to go fuck himself, climbed into the car and touched fists with Joe. 'Cheers for coming, mate.'

'Don't worry about it,' Joe said, frowning as he checked out the glue holding his friend's forehead together. 'What the hell happened?'

'I had a run-in with a baseball bat,' Carl told him, shrugging as if it was no big deal. 'Don't hurt that much now.'

'Bet it did at the time,' Joe remarked, taking in the size of the lump surrounding the wound. 'Who did it?'

'Just some joker,' Carl said evasively. 'But he came off worse, so I reckon he'll think twice before he tries it on with anyone else.'

Shaking his head, Joe turned the car around and headed home.

Mel hadn't been back long from Damien's party and she was still pretty pissed. But she sobered up fast when she saw the state of Carl.

'Oh, my God!' she squawked, leading him to the couch. 'Sit down – let me have a look at you.'

'I'll leave you to it,' Joe said when she rushed into the kitchen for a bowl of warm water and some cotton wool to wash off the dried blood. 'I'll pop round in the morning, see how you're doing.'

'You don't have to go,' Carl insisted, looking as pleased

as a pig in shit as he lapped up Mel's attention. 'Get my gear out and roll a couple.' He nodded towards the sideboard.

Mel came back in just then. 'Aw, don't go,' she said. 'I've just put the kettle on. You can stop for a brew, can't you?'

'Okay, I'll stay for half an hour,' Joe agreed. 'But you should try and get some sleep, mate, 'cos you've already been up for two days.'

'Don't worry about me,' Carl scoffed. 'They don't call me the Duracell bunny for nothing, you know.'

'They don't call you it at *all*,' Mel pointed out, softening what would normally have sounded quite bitchy with a smile.

Joe was pleased to see the couple being nice to each other for a change. Carl had been complaining about her constant sarcasm and the lack of sex he'd been getting recently. But if seeing him hurt had given Mel a wake-up call, then there was hope for them yet.

Joe had just started to roll the spliff when somebody knocked on the door. Mel jumped, sloshing water out of the bowl onto Carl's leg.

'Who the hell's that at this time?'

'Want me to go?' Joe offered. He knew the reason for her nervousness because Carl had told him all about the gang raiding them before he'd moved in.

'If you don't mind,' she said gratefully, her hand rising automatically to her mouth for a good old chew. When she remembered that she'd been touching blood, she dropped it and scooted a little closer to Carl. 'Be careful, though. See who it is first.'

Joe told her not to worry, went to the door and peeped out. When he saw Eddie standing out in the corridor he opened up.

'Carl in?' Eddie asked, seeming a little surprised to see Joe here at this time.

'Yeah, he's in there.' Joe stood back. 'Go through.'

Mel hadn't had a chance to ask Carl exactly what had happened yet, but she figured it must have been serious for Eddie to be making a house call. Sensing that this was a men-only moment, she made them all a brew and then took herself off into the bedroom.

Eddie sat on the armchair opposite the couch and peered at Carl's wound. 'Looks painful.'

'It's not that bad,' Carl told him. 'Hurt like hell when it happened but they gave me some really strong painkillers so I can't feel a thing now.'

'And Matt?'

'Not sure. I had to leave him at . . .' Trailing off, Carl looked at Joe. 'Where were we again?'

'Stepping Hill,' Joe reminded him, passing the finished spliff over.

'Yeah, there,' Carl said. 'I didn't have any money on me so Joe came and picked me up.'

'Good of you.' Eddie cast an approving glance at Joe.

'It was no trouble,' Joe said, getting up. 'Anyway, I'll leave you to it. See you tomorrow, Carl.'

'Don't forget your brew,' Carl reminded him as he headed for the door. 'Might as well take it with you while it's still hot. And cheers again, mate.'

Nodding, Joe said goodbye to Eddie and let himself out.

'So what happened?' Eddie wanted to know when Joe had gone. 'Kenny's already told me his side but I want to get yours before I decide what I'm going to do.'

Shrugging, Carl said, 'Well, I can't tell you what was going on with the others 'cos I was on my own at the time. But the bouncer told me Daz was getting jumped by three blokes so I went to help him. And that's when I got whacked.' Grinning now, he added, 'Lucky I've got such a thick skull or I'd have been out for the count. And he must have thought I was staying down 'cos he didn't half look shocked when I jumped back up and kicked the fuck out of him.'

'What then?'

'I went back to help Kenny and Matt.'

'And where was Daz when all this was going on?'

'Outside,' Carl said. 'Can't blame him, though, 'cos they'd locked him out.' Narrowing his eyes thoughtfully, he added, 'Mind you, I don't know why he didn't ring one of us when he realised they'd locked it down. That's still puzzling me, that.'

'Maybe because he was in on it,' Eddie mused.

'You what?' Carl drew his head back. 'No way. He wouldn't switch sides on you like that. He wouldn't dare.'

'Yeah, well, I'll soon find out,' Eddie said quietly. 'Right now I'm more interested in finding my money.'

'Eh?' Carl frowned. 'What's going on, Ed?'

'Nothing for you to worry about,' Eddie told him. 'I just need to know where Daz might have gone.'

'Hasn't he gone back to his place?'

'No. Kenny's sitting outside waiting for him but there's still no sign. Can you think of anywhere else?'

Carl shook his head. 'We don't get on too good, to be honest. I tolerate him because we work together but that's it.' After thinking about it for a moment, he added, 'I suppose you could try his mum's. I know he goes round there when he needs money, 'cos I've heard him on the phone to her.'

'Do you know where she lives?' Eddie asked, downing his brew in one.

Thinking that Eddie must have a cast-iron stomach, because the coffee was still boiling hot, Carl shook his head again. 'Somewhere in Rusholme, I think. I know a few of his mates, so I could ring around and see if anyone's heard from him if you want.'

'Yeah, you do that.' Eddie stood up. 'And let me know as soon as you hear anything.' As he went towards the door he paused. 'Your mate, Joe . . . you trust him, yeah?'

'Absolutely,' Carl said emphatically. 'He's a good lad. I woke him up tonight but he got straight out of bed to come and pick me up. And there's not many who'd do that for you round here.'

Nodding, Eddie said, 'Ask him if he wants a job. You're going to need a driver now Daz is out, and it might as well be him if he's up for it.'

'He will be,' Carl said, sure that Joe would jump at the chance of earning a bit of extra money, considering he was always flat broke. 'You definitely think Daz has ripped you off, then?'

'If he has he'll regret it,' Eddie said darkly. 'If not, he'd better have a fucking good explanation for taking off with it and dumping Kenny. You just keep your ears open. And tell Joe I'll be needing him tomorrow. You, too. I'll give you a ring when I'm ready.'

Exhaling through his teeth when Eddie had gone, Carl lit his spliff and sucked deeply on it. Whatever had happened after he and Matt had been dropped at the hospital, he didn't envy Daz when Eddie got hold of him. Kenny was the only one authorised to hold the money and Daz would be lucky if he didn't get his hands cut off for taking it. That said, Carl still couldn't believe Daz would be that stupid. *Or* that brave.

Still, either way he was off the team. And that was great news for Carl because he couldn't stand the idiot. And it would be really good to work with Joe, so long as Joe agreed to do it. But there was only one way to find out.

Easing himself up off the couch, Carl headed for the door. When Mel heard the movement she came out of the bedroom and blocked his path.

'Where do you think you're going?'

'To see Joe.'

'I don't think so,' Mel scolded, watching as Carl staggered into the wall. 'You've just come out of hospital and your head's all over the place. You need to lie down.'

'I just need to ask him something,' Carl protested.

'It can wait,' Mel said firmly. 'Bed – *now!*'

'Yes, miss!' Carl chuckled, doing as he was told.

She was right. Joe would keep.

9

It was four in the morning, and Kenny was bored and freezing on the steps outside Daz's flat. But Daz wasn't coming home. Not now he'd found the money.

He hadn't known it was in the car when he'd driven off earlier and had assumed that Kenny was chasing him because he was mad about being dumped so far from home. But Daz hadn't seen why he should do Kenny any favours after the grass had said that he was going to tell Eddie about him disappearing off the job. They both knew that Eddie would sack him on the spot for that – *and* give him a kicking to make an example of him while he was at it. So fuck him.

Still heading for home at that point, Daz had taken a turning too fast and had dropped his cigarette in his panic to avoid smashing into a parked van. After slamming his brakes on when it rolled out of sight under the passenger seat he'd groped around for it. And that had been when he'd found the money.

Realising then why Kenny had really been chasing him, he'd thought about taking it back. But he knew it was already too late because they'd be bound to think he'd *intended* to steal it but had bottled out at the last minute. Either way he'd still be sacked – and would still get a kicking.

And it would take a bigger fool than Daz to hand himself over on a plate if he knew *that* was coming. So he'd sat and stared at the money for a long time, coming to the eventual conclusion that he might as well keep it. It was only two and a half grand – peanuts compared with what Eddie must be making off all his other shit – so *he* wouldn't miss it. But it would really help Daz out until he'd found another earner. And Kenny couldn't prove he'd left it in the car, so if Eddie caught up with him Daz would just deny he'd ever seen it.

But he couldn't face Eddie just yet because he was way too jumpy to pull off the innocent act. So obviously he couldn't go home because that was the first place they would go looking for him. He also couldn't go to any of his mates' places because none of them could be trusted to keep their mouths shut. Same with his mum – although she'd probably ring Eddie herself if she knew he was looking for Daz. There was only one person he'd be safe with and that was Billi: the junkie he'd been seeing but hadn't told any of his friends about because he hadn't wanted them to think he'd let his standards slip so low. And that made her flat the perfect hideout until he knew what Eddie was planning to do to him.

Parking up behind Longsight's Dickenson Road

market now, Daz pulled his hood up to shield his face in case people were already looking out for him and made the rest of his way on foot. Billi's flat was above a launderette and the only access was a door at the top of a steep flight of metal steps around the back. There was no lighting around there so it was always pitch black at night – and only marginally less so in the daytime, thanks to the huge factory that backed onto the alleyway behind and blocked out all the natural light.

Daz wasn't surprised when Billi didn't answer the door when he knocked, because she'd be well out of it by now. But it was easy enough to get in through the knackered kitchenette window and he was soon making his way to the bedroom – his dick already twitching in anticipation. He didn't know what it was, but there was something about the look on a bird's face when she woke up and found you sticking it to her that really did it for him.

The bedroom door squeaked when Daz pushed it open. Billi woke with a jolt, sat up and clutched the quilt to her naked breasts.

'What d'y want?' she squawked, squinting into the darkness. 'My fella and his mates will be here any minute, so you'd best get out while you've got a chance.'

Daz shushed her from the shadows and felt his way to the end of the bed.

Realising who it was when he slid his hand under the quilt, Billi's fear turned to anger. 'What the fuck do you think you're doing?' she hissed, kicking out at him. 'You can't go round breaking into people's gaffs whenever you feel like it!'

'I knocked,' Daz told her, as if that excused him. 'Not my fault you didn't hear me.' Stroking his way up her calf now, he stopped when he felt sharp stubble graze the back of his hand. He snapped his head around and frowned when he saw the shape of a covered body lying beside her. 'Who the fuck's that?'

'None of your business,' Billi said, jerking her leg out of reach. 'Anyway, get out. You've got no right coming round here in the middle of the night and questioning me.'

Daz inhaled deeply as a surge of rage coursed through him. He'd already had Kenny talking down to him like he was some kind of muppet and there was no way he was tolerating more of the same from a bird.

'Out here, *now*,' he growled, getting up and heading for the door.

Billi snatched up her dressing gown and tugged it on. She stomped after him and scowled when she found him sitting in her scabby armchair. 'Don't bother making yourself comfortable – you're not staying.'

'Oh, I think you'll find I am,' Daz informed her through gritted teeth. 'But *he*'s not.' He nodded towards the bedroom. 'So do him a favour and get him out before I *put* him out.'

'Are you for real?' Billi demanded indignantly. 'I invited him here. He's going nowhere.'

'Sorry – did I make that sound like I was asking?' Daz said quietly.

'No way.' Standing her ground, Billi raised her chin in defiance. 'This is *my* flat, and *I* decide who comes in, not you. Anyhow, what's the deal with all this jealousy shit? We've only had a few shags – we're not a couple or anything.'

It was true but Daz wasn't in the mood to be reasonable. 'Last warning.' He cracked his knuckles as if he was getting ready for a fight. 'Get rid of him, or I'll do it myself.'

A light clicked on in Billi's head and she gave Daz a knowing look. 'You're on the run, aren't you? So come on, what have you done? 'Cos I'm telling you now, I've got enough shit of my own to deal with without getting mixed up in any of yours.'

'You won't get mixed up in nothing,' Daz told her. 'So long as you do what you're told. And you've got about thirty seconds to get on with it 'cos I'm running out of patience.'

Billi had never seen him like this before. As she'd just reminded him, they'd only hooked up a few times, which hardly made them an item. But they'd always had a laugh and she'd thought he was all right, so it was unnerving to see him like this. Daz was like a completely different person and she realised that she didn't really know him at all. He'd already broken in and crept up on her in her bedroom, so God only knew what else he was capable of.

Deciding that it was probably safer to do as he asked for now and get rid of him when he'd calmed down, she went back to the bedroom and woke the lad, telling him that her boyfriend had come home unexpectedly, pissed and spoiling for a fight. She hustled him out when he'd dressed hurriedly and heard him curse as he missed his footing on the steps. Hoping that she wasn't going to find him lying at the bottom with a broken leg in the morning, she went back to Daz.

'Happy now?'

Daz eyed her as she sat down on the couch. 'Not really. I'm still thinking about that crack you made about me having no rights.'

'Look, I'm not being funny,' Billi said, reaching for her cigarettes. 'But come on, Daz . . . you know there's nothing serious going on with us. We've only known each other a few months.'

'So?' Daz had a nasty edge to his voice. 'If I'm fucking you I've got the right to expect you not to fuck anyone else, haven't I?'

Billi's mouth dropped open. 'This *is* a joke, right?' Shaking her head when he carried on looking at her, she said, 'Don't you think this is a bit twisted?'

Daz was off his chair and on her in a flash. 'You taking the piss, you fucking whore?' he growled, straddling her and pinning her down. 'Think I'm gonna let a skank like you talk to me like that?'

'Get off me, you nutter!' Billi yelled, squeezing her

eyes shut when he started slapping her across the face. Screaming when he sank his teeth into her cheek, she said, 'All right, all right, I'm sorry! Stop it – *please!*'

Daz peered down at her with a glint of satisfaction in his eyes. 'You ever mouth off at me like that again and you won't get off so lightly. D'y hear me?'

'Okay,' Billi croaked. 'Just get off me. You're on my ribs; I can't breathe.'

Daz stood up and snatched her cigarettes off the table. 'I need a drink. What've you got?'

'Nothing,' Billi muttered, rubbing at the circle of indentations marking her cheek. 'I do drugs, not booze – remember?'

Daz didn't like the tone of her voice but when he turned to give her a warning look he saw that her dressing gown had fallen open. His dick sprang back to life when he glimpsed the dark regrowth of her shaved pubic hair.

'Are you serious?' Billi gasped when he unzipped his fly and came towards her.

'What do *you* think?' Grinning, Daz slipped his dick out and waggled it in front of her face. 'Come on – you know how I like it.'

Billi was shocked that he was actually expecting her to have sex with him after he'd attacked her like that. But she wasn't about to set him off again by refusing, so she took a deep breath and leaned forward. Gagging when he put his hand on the back of her head and rammed himself deep into her throat, she prayed that he would finish as quickly as he usually did.

Daz didn't disappoint her. Climaxing after a couple of minutes, he waited until the shudders had subsided and then flopped down onto the couch beside her with a smile of satisfaction spread across his face.

'I've got a right thirst on me after that. Got any brewing gear?'

Billi pulled a face as the disgusting froth of his sperm slithered down her throat. 'I'll see what I've got. But I need to clean up first.'

'Don't be long,' Daz said, reaching for the remote for her portable TV as she headed for the bathroom. 'And make us a butty while you're at it.'

He was watching *Family Guy* when Billi came back after swilling her mouth out. Hoping that he would go when he'd had what he wanted, she made him a cup of tea and a cheese sandwich. But Daz had no intention of leaving just yet, and when he'd finished eating and the programme had ended he wiped his mouth and stood up.

'Think I'll hit the sack,' he said, yawning as he headed into her bedroom.

Billi stayed on the couch after he'd gone, infuriated that he was acting so normal after being such a beast. Spying his jacket draped over the back of the couch, she cast a furtive glance at the bedroom door before easing her hand into a pocket. She was looking for loose cash or drugs, but when she came across the money bag her eyes widened as she peeped inside and saw the thick bundle of notes.

'You coming or what?' Daz called just then.

Jumping as if she'd been electrocuted, Billi stuffed the bag back where she'd found it. 'Won't be a minute. Just making sure everything's switched off.'

She couldn't take the money there and then because Daz would beat the crap out of her if he caught her. And there was no way she could do a runner with it because he would only chase her and she had no chance of outrunning him. But if he was as set on staying as he seemed to be, it would give her time to figure out a way of getting her hands on it. And if she had to pleasure him to keep him sweet in the meantime, so be it. She'd done worse.

10

Cheryl knocked on Joe's door at nine-thirty the next morning and Joe immediately felt guilty when he opened it. He'd forgotten that she'd said she was coming round and he'd just made arrangements to go out with Carl to pick up Eddie.

'Sorry,' he said, grimacing. 'I'm going to have to give it a miss. Something's come up.'

'Good.' Cheryl looked relieved. 'I was only coming to tell you I couldn't come – if that makes any sense. I've got to go and see Molly. You know she's in hospital?'

'No, why?' Joe asked.

'She had a fall,' Cheryl told him. 'I'm surprised you didn't hear the ambulance, 'cos Fred next door said it happened yesterday just after I went out and you came in. They had the full sirens going and everything.'

'I had a headache so I went to bed to sleep it off,' Joe said. 'Is she okay?'

'Broken hip.' Cheryl sighed. 'I only heard after I got back from Vee's so I nipped over last night – to see if she needed a nightie or anything. She was proper upset, poor thing. They've told her she might have to stay in for a few weeks, and she was fretting about her cat. But I've said I'll feed it till she gets home.'

'That's nice of you.'

'Couldn't have left her like that, could I? Anyway, it's only twice a day so it's not going to kill me.'

'I've hardly seen her since I moved in,' Joe said guiltily. 'Do you think I should get her some flowers or something?'

'Are you kidding?' Cheryl smirked. 'She'll be telling all the nurses they're from her toyboy. Maybe you could go in instead, though, 'cos she needs to be told off about leaving her spare key in the plant pot, and she might listen to you. I told her last night. I said it might have been okay to do stuff like that in the olden days – but not nowadays, 'cos anyone could get their hands on it. But she said it makes her feel safer to know that someone can get in if she ever needs help. Stupid, isn't it?'

'Not too smart,' Joe agreed. 'But my nan was exactly the same, and there was no talking to her.'

'Mine too,' Cheryl admitted. 'Anyway, best go. She asked me to fetch her some juice and biscuits, and I've only got a couple of hours before I have to pick Frankie up.'

'Tell her hello from me and I hope she's better soon.'

'Hope who's better soon?' Carl asked, coming out of his door in time to catch this.

'Molly,' Cheryl said, turning to look at him. 'The foot of her walker got stuck on one of the broken slabs outside, and she fell over and broke her hip. Didn't you hear the ambulance either? It happened just after I went out and you two came in.'

'Nah, I went straight back out. Hope she's okay.'

'She will be now she's got all the nurses fussing over her,' Cheryl said. 'Subject of nurses, that's a hell of a cut you've got there. What happened?'

'Got into a bit of a fight,' Carl admitted, grinning sheepishly. 'But if you think this looks bad, you should have seen the other four.'

'*Four?*' Joe raised an eyebrow.

'All right, three,' Carl said. 'But you'd have thought there was four if you'd seen the size of them.'

Cheryl already didn't believe him. Tutting, she rolled her eyes at Joe. 'Can't help himself, can he?'

Joe shook his head and reached back inside for his jacket before pulling the door shut.

'So, where are you two off to?' Cheryl asked, linking her arms through theirs as they set off down the stairs. 'If it's anywhere near the hospital I wouldn't say no to a lift.'

'Sorry, babe, we're off to Levenshulme,' Carl told her – walking a bit taller than usual, Joe noticed. 'He's just got a job, haven't you, mate?'

'Really?' Cheryl gazed up at Joe. 'That's great.'

'I think so,' he agreed. 'And it couldn't have come at a better time, 'cos my electric bill's just come in and I didn't know how I was going to pay it.'

'Oh, that reminds me . . .' Carl pulled a twenty out of his pocket. 'Eddie said to give you this for petrol.'

'You're working for Eddie?' A shadow crossed Cheryl's eyes. 'Are you sure that's wise?'

'Don't be daft,' Carl scoffed. 'He's not going to come to any harm.'

'You reckon?' Cheryl murmured, pointedly eyeing his forehead.

'Aw, this was nothing to do with Eddie,' Carl said dismissively. 'Not in the way you're making out, anyway.'

Shaking her head, Cheryl let go of their arms when they reached the ground floor. 'I've just got to get something from my place,' she said, giving Joe a hooded look to let him know that she wanted a quick word.

Picking up on it, Joe said, 'Oh, that reminds me. I didn't leave my watch here the other day, did I? Could you just have a quick look?'

'I'll wait outside,' Carl said, heading for the door. 'See you later, babe.'

'Bye,' Cheryl said, waving. Turning to Joe when Carl had gone, her smile disappeared and she peered up with concern in her eyes. 'Please be careful. I know Eddie, and he's got a way of letting other people take the rap while he stays squeaky clean. I don't want to see you get into trouble because of him.'

'Nothing's going to happen,' Joe reassured her. 'I'm only going to be driving.'

'Yeah, well, I hope it works out like that,' Cheryl

murmured. Then, feeling a bit guilty about putting such a dampener on things because she knew he needed the money, she smiled. 'Go on, then. Get moving. You don't want to keep Eddie waiting on your first day.'

Winking at her, Joe went out and joined Carl who was waiting patiently by the car.

'Did you find your watch?' Carl asked.

'Er, no.' Joe shook his head. 'Must have left it somewhere else.'

'Take it it's not that one?' Carl nodded towards Joe's wrist. 'That's the kind of stupid thing I'd do,' he added with a grin. 'Turn everything upside down looking for it, only to find out I've been wearing it all along.'

'No, it's not this one,' Joe told him. 'But I know what you mean.'

Driving over to Levenshulme now – which turned out to be purely to give Eddie a lift to Clive's place in Cheetham Hill – Joe thought about what Cheryl had said. But while he was grateful for her concern he was sure that she was worrying about nothing. He was actually really pleased that he'd been given a way into Eddie's world, because the man intrigued him. Unlike the guys in the younger gangs, who seemed to flash their guns the instant there was even a *hint* of a dispute, Eddie seemed to keep control without having to resort to that kind of posturing. People spoke about him as if he was some kind of maniac, and yet they also seemed to adore him and would do anything for him. Like his dealers.

From what Carl had told him, no matter how many times they got arrested in possession of Eddie's drugs they *never* gave him up. But then, they knew that their fines would be paid if they were lucky enough not to get time. And if they weren't lucky, they knew that their jobs would still be there when they got out. It was pure old school but it obviously worked, and Joe was glad that he'd been invited to be a part of it.

'It's gonna be a buzz, this,' Carl said just then, interrupting Joe's thoughts. 'Daz was a right selfish git. He was the only one with wheels but he never picked none of us up, and only ever dropped us back at home if he couldn't get out of it. It'll be ace coming out of my gaff and hopping straight into the motor.'

'You'll get fat,' Joe warned him.

Lighting the spliff he'd just rolled, Carl twisted his head and pulled a face. 'Shut up, you woman!'

'Only saying,' Joe laughed, enjoying himself already. 'It's getting paid I'm looking forward to. Job seekers' is a joke. I've never had so many debts in my life.'

'That's what you get for letting that ex of yours keep you for so long,' Carl scoffed. 'None of us were lucky enough to find a rich bird. That's why we're all a load of dodgy bastards round here, 'cos if we had to survive on the dole the estate would be full of skellybobs. *Stoned* skellybobs, mind,' he added with a chuckle. ''Cos if it was a toss-up between food and weed, we'd choose weed every time. Suits me, though, 'cos I'd be out of work otherwise.'

'You never wanted to do a proper job?' Joe asked.

'Fancied being a mechanic when I first left school,' Carl admitted. 'But I was too thick to get on the course.'

'You're not thick.'

'Yeah, I know that *now*, but it's too late to do anything about it. Anyhow, I'm all right working for Eddie. And you will be, too. So long as you don't mind dropping whatever you're doing to pick him up or drop him off whenever he calls. 'Cos that's what'll happen now he's got a taxi on the doorstep – you do know that, don't you?'

'I don't mind,' Joe said truthfully. 'He's all right.'

'Yeah, so long as you stay on the right side of him,' Carl said ominously. ''Cos I've seen how he deals with people who cross him and, trust me, it ain't pretty.'

'Well, I've got no reason to cross him, so I'll be okay.'

'Course you will,' Carl said, passing the spliff to Joe. 'Next left,' he said then. 'And you'd best start remembering, 'cos he'll expect you to know where you're going without having to be told.'

Grinning, Joe said, 'Best get myself a satnav, eh?'

'You can buy one with your first wages,' Carl teased.

'God, that'll be a good day,' Joe said. 'Then I can pay you off and get you off my back.'

'It'll never happen,' Carl declared confidently. 'You might pay me off this week but you'll be after another lay-on next week, I guarantee it.'

'We'll see.' Joe smirked. 'We'll see.'

11

'Downstairs, five minutes. Wear black.'

Squinting at the phone when Eddie abruptly disconnected, Joe groaned when he saw that it was two in the morning. He'd only been in bed for an hour.

A quick wash later, he was dressed and heading down to the car park. Shivering as the freezing air bit into his cheeks when he stepped outside, he nodded when he saw Carl already standing by the car.

'What's going on?' he asked, jumping in and starting up the engine to get the heater going.

'No idea,' Carl told him as he clambered onto the back seat. 'Eddie just said to meet him down here in five. Didn't he say anything to you?'

Shaking his head, Joe glanced out of the window. When he saw Eddie coming out a couple of minutes later, he frowned and said, 'Oh, great, he's bringing the dog.'

'Fuck,' Carl muttered, scooting right up against the door. He eyed the dog warily when Eddie shoved it in beside him before hopping into the front. Eddie made out like it was some kind of baby, and it might have looked sweet if it had been any other dog lying there with its head on its paws, sighing as if it had been woken in a hurry. But its red eyes and battle-scarred head made it look positively demonic to Carl.

'Just had a call from Kenny,' Eddie told them. 'Daz is hiding out in Longsight.'

'Really?' Carl was surprised, because he'd started to wonder if Daz had skipped town.

'He's at some junkie bird's flat,' Eddie went on. 'She turned up at a smack dealer's house over in Rusholme earlier on and bought a load of gear. Long story short, there were a load of guys there and she offered to pay some of them to go to her place and sort out this dude who she reckoned had been holding her hostage for three days. She said she'd spiked him with Temazepam so she could get out, and now she wanted rid. But one of the guys had heard I was looking for Daz, so he put two and two together and got word to Kenny. He's there with her now, and he reckons she's got my money – apart from what she's already spent getting high, but I'll deal with that later.'

'At least you're getting most of it back,' Carl said.

'Better than not getting any,' Eddie agreed, glancing at his watch. 'But I still want to catch up with the cunt before he wakes up and legs it.' Turning to Joe now, he said, 'Head for Dickenson Road. I'll tell you where to go from there.'

Joe set off, a grim expression on his face. He didn't

mind driving but he hoped that Eddie wasn't expecting him to get into any rough stuff, because he hadn't signed up for that.

When they reached Longsight, Eddie told Joe to pull into a deserted car park at the rear of a block of Asian clothes shops.

'Stay here,' he said, getting the dog out of the back. 'And if you see any coppers hanging about, give us a ring.'

Nodding, Joe watched as Eddie, the dog and Carl set off down the road.

Daz was still sprawled on the couch where Billi had left him. Roused by the sound of scratching at the back door, he didn't immediately know where he was, or even if it was day or night.

Peering out through the gunk that was still partially gluing his eyes together, he felt an icy breeze waft over his face as the back door opened and closed. He peeled his lips apart and croaked, 'Billi?'

'Try again,' Eddie drawled, strolling in and looking down at him.

Scrambling to sit up as everything came back in a sickening rush, Daz's mouth flapped open and his eyes swivelled furtively.

'All right, Ed, I was, er, going to ring you in a bit.'

'That right?' Eddie said quietly, sitting down on the armchair and crossing his legs.

'Yeah, about the money,' Daz waffled. 'Kenny left it in the motor the other night, so I brought it back here for safe keeping. I've, er, been a bit sick, or I would've got word to you before.'

'And what made you think you had the right to make decisions about where my money would be safe?' Eddie asked.

Nervous of the dog, because it looked like it was just dying for the go-ahead to attack, Daz said, 'Kenny was wasted, man. I mean like really, *really* wasted.'

'Was he fuck,' Carl blurted out from the doorway. He couldn't believe that Daz was lying through his teeth when he knew that Carl had been there that night. And everyone knew that Kenny *never* touched shit when he was working.

'You didn't see him after we dropped you off,' Daz argued, twisting his head to look back at Carl. 'He had a couple of proper big sniffs and went totally off it, waving his gun about and talking shit. That's why I did one, 'cos I thought he was going to get us both banged up.'

'And you thought you'd take my money along for the ride, did you?' Eddie said calmly, not believing a word of it so far.

'Nah, man, it wasn't even like that,' Daz protested, sweating like a pig now. 'I didn't even know it was there to start with. But when I realised, I figured I'd be best holding on to it 'cos Kenny probably would have lost it.

And if you think about it, he *did*,' he added, giving strength to his argument. 'He left it in the car. And you're lucky I found it when I did, 'cos it's not exactly safe round here. Anyone could have caved the window in and nicked it.'

'So why didn't you let me know what was going on?' Eddie asked, wondering if Daz thought he was a complete numpty.

'I didn't want to disturb you,' Daz said lamely. 'But you're here now, so you can take it.' He stood up unsteadily, his head still woozy from the drugs he didn't even know he'd had. 'It's all here, safe and sound. I'll get it for you.'

He staggered past Carl and stumbled into the tiny bathroom. Dropping heavily to his knees, he rested his cheek on the toilet seat and reached around to the outlet pipe at the back. Shoving his fingers into the gap between it and the wall, he almost yanked the toilet off its moorings when he didn't feel the money bag, hoping that it had just slipped further down into the gap. But it wasn't there.

Going back into the living room, Daz looked around frantically, his groggy head telling him that he must have moved the cash and forgotten where he'd put it. He'd never been so relieved when he saw a corner of the bag sticking out from between the couch and the sideboard. But when he grabbed it, it was obvious that it was empty.

'No way,' he gasped, his face as white as a sheet

now. 'No fucking way! It was there, I swear it was. Billi must have took it!' Turning, Daz rushed towards the kitchenette, yelling, 'Billi . . . *BILLI*! Where are you, you fucking bitch?'

Carl blocked his path and gave him a forceful shove, sending him sprawling over the couch.

'She's took it,' Daz bleated, his eyes swimming with tears of injustice and fear. 'I can't believe she's done this to me. I'll kill her when I catch up with her, I swear to God!'

Still sitting quietly, Eddie stared at him. He could have put him out of his misery and told him that he already knew exactly where the money was, but he didn't see why Daz should get off the hook that easily.

'Kenny was right about you,' he said, reaching down to unclip the dog's lead. 'You are a fucking bottler. And a thief.'

'No, man, you've got it all wrong,' Daz cried, scrabbling back on the couch as the dog snarled and strained to get at him. 'Honest, you've got to believe me, there's no way I was going to keep it. I was going to ring you, I swear.'

'*And* a barefaced liar,' Eddie added softly, holding on to the dog's collar. 'And if there's one thing worse than a thief in my book, it's a liar. You've got thirty seconds to tell the truth.'

'Please, Ed, just hear me out,' Daz pleaded. 'This isn't my fault, I swear.'

'Twenty-eight . . .' Eddie drawled, skipping the first twenty-seven because he couldn't be arsed with all that counting. 'Twenty-nine . . . *Thirty.*'

Screaming when Eddie released the dog, Daz threw his arms up to protect his face. But the brute wasn't fussy: flesh was flesh, and it went for whatever was available.

As the blood started to spurt, Eddie sucked a loud breath in through his teeth and shook his head at Carl. 'Now that's what you *call* an animal!'

Watching in horror as the dog mauled Daz, Carl nodded. He felt sick to his stomach but he wasn't about to show it in case Eddie took it as a sign of weakness.

Glancing at the window after a torturous couple of minutes and seeing that it was an ancient single-glazed one, Carl warned, 'Don't you think you'd best make it stop now, Ed? Pigs could be on their way if someone's heard him.'

'Yeah, I know,' Eddie agreed with obvious disappointment. 'Should have taken him out into the sticks and finished the job in peace, eh?'

'Mmm,' Carl murmured, wishing that Eddie would hurry up and call the beast off – it sounded like it was having way too much fun.

At last Eddie yelled, '*Leave!*' Annoyed when the dog didn't obey immediately, he punched it in the back of its head and yanked it off by its collar. Resecuring its clip as it cowered at his feet, he passed the lead to Carl to hold.

Daz was curled up on the floor, sobbing like a baby as he tried to hold a loose flap of skin over a bloody gash on his arm. Squatting down beside him, Eddie said, 'I've already got my money back, you thieving cunt, and that's the *only* reason you're not dead right now. But if I ever see you again, you *will* be. You got that?'

Daz nodded his agreement.

'Don't test me,' Eddie warned him quietly, sticking one of his fingers into the wound and smearing the blood down Daz's cheek. Then, getting up, he took the dog back and followed Carl out.

'Everything all right?' Joe asked when they got back in the car.

'Sweet as,' Eddie said, grinning at Carl over the back of the seat. 'All went nice and smooth, didn't it?'

'Yeah, fine,' Carl said sickly, even more wary of the dog now that he'd seen what it was capable of.

'Where to?' Joe asked.

'Platt Lane,' Eddie told him. 'But don't worry, we won't be stopping. I've decided to give the bird a break for handing that muppet over. I'll just pick up my money, then you two can get back to your beds.'

'Great,' Carl mumbled, doubting whether he'd sleep for a week now that he had all those images to haunt him.

Arriving back at the flats a short time later, Eddie said, 'Cheers, guys. I'll see youse right tomorrow.'

Breathing a sigh of relief when he took the dog and left, Carl flopped his head back and ran his hands through his hair. 'Thank God that's over.'

'What happened?' Joe asked.

'Trust me, you don't wanna know,' Carl told him, opening the door and climbing out. 'But I'll tell you this for nowt: I am *never* getting a dog. They're fucking dangerous, man.'

'You don't have to tell me,' Joe agreed, getting out and locking the doors. 'I can't stand the things.'

'Anyway, let's not talk about it any more,' Carl said, rubbing his hands together. 'I need a drink and a smoke. You up for it?'

'Your place or mine?' Joe asked.

'Ooh, baby, I thought you'd never ask,' Carl quipped in a girly voice.

Glad that he seemed to be shaking off whatever had made him look so sick, Joe shoved him in through the door.

12

Eddie's night had started out pretty good. Earlier in the week Clive had bumped into the lap dancers they had partied with that time, and he'd arranged for him and Eddie to take them out again. So Eddie had splashed out on a meal at a fancy Italian restaurant for the four of them tonight, followed by a couple of hours at a night-club before they'd headed over to the casino in Chinatown that was fast becoming Eddie's favourite haunt.

Gambling was his latest passion. He loved the rush when his chips were in place and the wheel was spin-ning. And the buzz when the ball landed in his chosen slot was better than an orgasm. But like all addictions, this one had gripped him and was now happily strip-ping him of everything he owned.

They had been having a great time for the first hour or so, lapping up the complimentary champagne and flying on the coke that Eddie had been handing out like sherbet. But when Eddie's luck turned, it turned with a vengeance. And the more he lost, the darker his mood became, until even Clive had had enough. He'd tried to persuade Eddie to quit while he was still ahead, but the coke had made Eddie incapable of admitting defeat and he'd refused to leave the table, so Clive and the girls had eventually left him to it.

By four a.m. Eddie's pockets were so dry that he didn't even have enough for the bus fare home, never mind a cab. He still didn't want to leave, though, because he was convinced that he was about to hit another winning streak. But the casino management thought differently and he quickly found himself out on the street. Which would ordinarily have resulted in an almighty kick-off – if he hadn't been alone. And if the casino hadn't been run by Triads.

No amount of coke could make Eddie stupid enough to think he could take *them* on single-handed, so he set off in search of his whores, intending to take whatever they'd made so far so that he could try to recoup some of his losses at a different casino.

Hanna was nowhere to be seen when he reached her spot, and neither were Tasha or Elena when he went on to theirs. So he headed over to see if Katya was around, ringing Joe on the way and telling him to come and pick him up – just in case. Yes, it was late, and he'd probably be sleeping. But so what? He got paid plenty for the inconvenience.

Katya was in trouble. The car's headlights had been dipped when it had come slowly around the corner, and she'd stepped back into the shadows, only moving back out into the light when it pulled alongside and she saw that it wasn't a police car.

'How much?' the man asked, sliding his gaze down her body and back up again.

'For what?' Katya asked, knowing better than to state a price up front, because that was how the vice squad trapped you.

'Anal,' he said.

It wasn't the word that stirred the hairs on the back of her neck but the way he'd said it and the glint of something predatory that she glimpsed in his eyes.

'Sorry.' She shook her head. 'You'll have to find somebody else.'

'Nah, I want you,' he drawled. 'Get in.'

Katya's mouth dried up and her legs began to wobble. Her instincts were screaming at her to run, but the street was long and totally deserted, and her feet were sore from the hours she'd been standing in her heels, so he would easily catch her.

'Please, just go,' she said, managing to sound much calmer than she felt. 'I can't do what you want.'

'You'll do whatever the fuck I tell you,' the man growled, pushing his door open and leaping out.

'Get off me!' Katya cried, struggling when he grabbed her and tried to drag her towards the car. 'I'll scream!'

'I've got a knife,' the man warned her, pinning her up against the side of the car. 'So shut your mouth and do as you're told, or you're dead.'

Releasing a strangled scream when he shoved his hand up her skirt and tore at her knickers, Katya sank her nails into his cheek and raked the flesh as hard as she could.

Infuriated, the man headbutted her. Then, glancing around to make sure that no one was about, he threw her back into the shadows of the doorway and slammed her face into the wall. But just as he'd pulled her skirt up and her knickers down and was unzipping his fly, somebody grabbed him from behind and yanked him back out onto the pavement.

Squealing in terror when Eddie started punching the man and kicking him in the head, Katya squatted down and covered her face with her hands. The man had been about to rape her but she still couldn't bear to watch him being battered.

Joe drove around the corner just then. Still half asleep from having been dragged out of his bed, he squinted out at the fight that he could see going on up ahead. Assuming it to be a couple of pissed-up idiots, he wasn't going to interfere. But when he suddenly recognised the silhouette of the one who was stamping on the other's head, he drove quickly on up the street.

Eddie heard the car's engine and glanced wildly around. He'd expected it to be the police so he was relieved to see that it was only Joe.

'I told you to wait at the corner,' he barked, wanting to finish what he'd started.

'Get in,' Joe told him firmly, flicking a glance at the mess on the floor. 'Come on, man, before you end up in serious shit.'

Eddie inhaled deeply. If anybody else had told him what to do like that, they might have pressed all the wrong buttons and sparked him right back off again. But Joe rarely spoke out of turn so his words penetrated to the zone of reason in Eddie's mind and made him look at what he'd done. And he immediately saw that he'd come dangerously close to killing the man. One more kick and it might have been over.

Turning to Katya, he held out his hand. 'Give me what you've got and get moving.'

Katya didn't need telling twice. Picking herself up, she took the money out of her bra and edged out of the doorway. Passing the cash to Eddie, she sneaked a glance at the man in the car – and froze when she saw who it was. But shame quickly replaced the shock, followed by horror that this lovely-looking gentle-eyed man could possibly be a friend of Eddie's.

'What the fuck are you gawping at?' Eddie growled, kicking out at her and sending her sprawling on the pavement. 'I told you to get moving, you stupid bitch!'

Joe was sickened, and he gritted his teeth as he watched the girl pick herself up and stagger away.

'Let's go,' Eddie said as he hopped into the car.

Joe set off without a word but his mind was racing. He'd been working for Eddie for several weeks now, and everything had been fine. He got on well with the other guys on the crew, and they'd had no trouble at any of the clubs or pubs since Eddie had taken whatever revenge he'd taken on the manager of Frost for letting his bouncers get out of line that time. Which had made Joe's job a lot easier than he'd thought it would be – *and* it had given Eddie some kind of boost, because he'd been walking with an extra spring in his already cocky step ever since. But while Joe had known that Eddie was up to all sorts of illegal activities, it had never occurred to him that the man was involved with those girls in any way other than as a landlord.

Eddie had calmed down by the time they got back to the flats. 'Cheers for that back there,' he said when Joe pulled up at the door. 'I get a bit carried away some-times, so you did me a favour calling me off when you did.'

'No problem.' Joe forced a smile.

'Not coming in?' Eddie asked, unbuckling his seat belt.

Joe shook his head. 'I need some fags so I'm just going to nip back to the garage. Want me to get you anything while I'm there?'

'Nah, I'm cool.' Eddie yawned as he pushed his door open. Turning back to Joe before climbing out, he said, 'Keep shtum about the girl, yeah?'

'Nothing to do with me,' Joe said, shrugging.

He turned the car around when Eddie had gone in and drove back out of the estate. But instead of stopping at the garage he headed back into town and drove slowly around the streets, looking for the girl.

Katya jumped when Joe pulled up alongside her half an hour later, and he saw the blind panic in her eyes.

'Don't be scared,' he said, climbing out and holding up his hands to show her that he wasn't going to touch her. 'I just wanted to make sure you were okay.'

Katya's breath caught in her chest and she felt as if her legs were going to give way as she stared mutely back at him. He sounded sincere but it could easily be a trick. Eddie could have sent him.

Joe's thoughts were also on Eddie: wondering how the hell he was going to explain this away if the girl went back and told him that Joe had come looking for her. But he was here now, so there was no point leaving without at least trying to find out what was going on.

'Can we talk?' he asked.

'I – I can't,' Katya murmured, glancing past him to see if Eddie was hiding somewhere. 'I'm working,' she added, her cheeks flaring with shame at having had to admit it, even though he surely knew already.

Joe saw the blush and felt genuinely sorry for her, thinking that it was no wonder she'd looked so unhappy whenever he'd seen her, because she obviously didn't want to be doing this.

'Look, I don't want to cause any trouble,' he said as an idea came to him. 'But if you'll give me half an hour of your time I'll pay you whatever you usually make. And I swear I don't want anything from you.'

'Why would you pay me for doing nothing?' Katya asked, her instincts confusing her because they were giving her a dual reading. Yes, he could be here at Eddie's behest to check up on her. But he sounded so genuine, and his gaze was so sincere.

'I just want to talk,' Joe repeated. 'And if you'd feel more comfortable around other people, there's a café a few minutes away. You could clean your face up while we're there.'

Katya raised her hand when he said this and wiped at the blood still trickling slowly from her nose.

'Half an hour, and I'll bring you straight back,' Joe persisted. 'Eddie doesn't know I'm here,' he added, guessing that this might be concerning her when she glanced out along the street again.

Katya bit her lip. Then, nodding, she shoved her hands into her pockets and walked around to the passenger-side door.

The only other customers in the café when they got there were two old men. Sitting Katya in a corner well away from the window, Joe went to the counter and bought two coffees and a cheese sandwich. He took them back to the table and sat down across from her.

'I didn't know what you'd like, so I went for the safe option. Hope it's okay.'

Tears welled in Katya's eyes as she gazed down at

the sandwich. 'Thank you, you're very kind. But I can't eat it. I'm sorry.'

'God, no, it's no problem,' Joe assured her. 'Take it with you. Eat it when you're ready.'

'I'd better not,' Katya murmured, wishing that she didn't feel so sick right now because she probably did need to eat. But there was no way she could take the sandwich with her, because one of the other girls would be bound to wonder why she'd thought it was okay to slope off and buy food when they had been stuck working.

Katya and Joe sat in silence for the next few minutes, sipping at their coffees and listening to a tap dripping behind the counter – and to the constant snorting and sniffing of the old men who were both ignoring the 'No Smoking' sign and sucking on foul-smelling roll-ups.

Clearing his throat after a while, Joe said, 'My name's Joe.'

Glancing up briefly, Katya nodded. But she didn't offer her own name in return.

'I know you're probably wondering why I came back,' Joe went on. 'And, to be honest, I'm not really sure myself. But something just didn't feel right about what happened earlier. Why was Eddie fighting with that man?'

Katya felt the heat rise to her cheeks and she couldn't bring herself to look at him as she admitted, 'He was hurting me, and Eddie . . .' Pausing, she shook her head as if she still hadn't made sense of it herself yet. 'I don't know why he came; he doesn't usually. But he stopped the man from – from doing what he was doing.'

Joe knew exactly what she meant without her having to spell it out, and it sickened him to hear the guilt in her voice. Men who did those kinds of things to women were scum, but most people would probably say she'd asked for it. And never mind if she actually had any choice about what she was doing.

'Is Eddie good to you?' he asked now. 'I mean, I take it you do work for him?'

Katya's fears came rushing back as she wondered why he would ask such a question. All she could think was that Eddie must be testing her: setting her up to see if she was stupid enough to reveal his business to a total stranger.

'This was a mistake,' she murmured, pushing her chair back. 'I should go.'

'Wait.' Joe reached for her hand across the table. Releasing it when she flinched, he said, 'I'm sorry, I didn't mean to do that. I just don't want you to go running away while you're upset. I promise I'm not going to hurt you, and I won't repeat anything you say to me.'

'You're Eddie's friend,' Katya reminded him. 'It's too dangerous for me to talk to you.'

'No, I *work* for Eddie,' Joe corrected her. 'And if it makes it any easier for you, I think it would probably be just as dangerous for *me* if he knew I was talking to *you*.'

Holding his gaze for the longest period so far, Katya's pretty face suddenly crumpled and she buried it in her hands.

'Please talk to me,' Joe said softly. 'Let me help you.'

'There's nothing you can do,' she sobbed, struggling to contain the emotions that she had vowed not to succumb to. 'There's nothing anybody can do.'

'There are plenty of people who can help you if you need it,' Joe insisted, reaching out and tentatively touching her shoulder.

Again, she flinched, but nowhere near as violently as the previous time. Then, shaking her head, she reached for a paper napkin and gingerly wiped her nose. 'You shouldn't get involved. It isn't your problem.'

'You don't have to live like this,' Joe persisted, sure now that she wasn't doing this voluntarily. 'If you want to get out, there are people who can help, places you could go where you'd be safe.'

'No!' Katya blurted out, her eyes fearful again. 'Thank you for your kindness – I won't forget it. But, really, I don't need help.'

Standing when she did, Joe took a couple of notes out of his pocket. 'I know it's not much but it's all I've got on me.'

'No, I don't want it.' Katya shook her head.

'Take it,' Joe insisted. 'Please.'

Katya bit her lip. She really didn't want to take his money. But she couldn't afford to be proud, so she took it and slipped it into her pocket, murmuring, 'Thank you,' as she rushed out.

Joe sighed as he watched her go. Then, turning to pick up his keys off the table, he shrugged when he saw the old men watching him. 'Women, eh? One minute they want you, the next minute they can't stand the sight of you.'

'Still took your money, though, eh, son?' one of the old-timers pointed out, cracking a toothless grin. 'Nowt much changes there, does it?'

'Not when it comes to pros, it don't,' the hag behind the counter chipped in snidely, as if she'd thought that Joe hadn't known. 'The sob stories you hear when they come in here of a night. But they cheer up fast enough when they get what they're after. You can bet your life *that* one's already sticking a needle in her fanny. Filthy mare.'

Disgusted, Joe gave the woman a dirty look and snatched up the sandwich. He didn't even want the damn thing, but there was no way he was leaving it behind for her to make a profit on.

His mind was full of unanswered questions as he made his way home. Now that he'd actually spoken to the girl he knew that she wasn't just scared of Eddie, she was absolutely terrified of him. But had she chosen this line of work and then got herself in with Eddie and found herself unable to get out of it? Or had Eddie forced her into it from the start? Her accent was foreign, and her reaction when he'd suggested that she could get help from the authorities had been one of absolute dread.

There was more to this than met the eye, Joe was sure. And whatever the truth, now that he'd started he knew that he wouldn't rest until he found out.

13

It was gone twelve when Eddie woke up the next day, and he had the hangover from hell. Reaching across to wake Chrissie and send her to get something for his head, he was disgusted when the dog licked his hand. Knocking the beast flying, he wiped the slime on the quilt and sat up gingerly.

'Chrissie . . .' he called when he heard the TV in the next room. 'Get us some tablets. Me head's banging.'

Forced to get up when she didn't answer, Eddie walked through to the living room in his boxers, the dog trotting along beside him. Annoyed to see that Chrissie had gone out and left the TV on, he switched it off and snatched up the note she'd left on the table. Sucking his teeth when he read that she'd gone to see her mum and wouldn't be back for a few hours, he counted the small pile of money she'd left beside the note. Furious to find that there was only four hundred and forty quid, he dropped it in disgust. What the fuck was he supposed to do with that? And what the fuck were those girls doing if this was all they could bring home between them?

They must think they were on holiday or something. But that was what he got for leaving Chrissie to see to them for the last couple of weeks – they obviously thought she was some kind of soft touch.

But they were in for a shock if they thought he was going to let things carry on slipping, because he was about to take over the reins again. And Chrissie was another one who'd best buck her ideas up, because it was her fault he'd blown all the money he'd gone out with last night. If she could've been trusted he'd have left it at home instead of taking it out. But since she'd taken to ordering shite off of Bid-Up TV – and rooting through his pockets for the money to pay for it – he'd been forced to carry everything around on him. And now look . . . from the eight grand he'd had last night, he was down to the poxy five hundred or so that he'd got off those useless bitches.

Kicking the dog out of the way now when it followed him into the kitchen and whined for its breakfast, Eddie took a couple of painkillers and lay on the couch to wait for them to take effect. He felt like shit, and it was all down to Charlie. Good old everyone's best mate, Charlie, building you up to think you were some kind of king with a right royal pot of money to spend, then robbing you of your senses so that you woke up a pauper. Much as he loved the buzz, he really couldn't stomach the comedown and he knew it was time to think about knocking it on the head for a bit. That, and the wallet-watching tarts he'd been screwing around with lately.

Like those slags Clive had gone off with last night. They'd said they were going to a house party when they'd left him at the casino, so they shouldn't have needed any money. But Eddie would bet they'd found a way to scrape the last penny out of Clive's pocket and the gold fillings out of his mouth before they'd let him go.

As the banging in his head began to ease at last, Eddie got up and fed the dog before hopping into the shower. Dressed and ready to leave a short time later, he finished off the last of his coke to get the day kick-started. No point suffering the shitty comedown if you didn't have to, and all that.

Patsy rushed out into the hall when Eddie let himself into her flat. Immediately suspicious because she was twitching even more than usual and her eyes were wide and wild, he said, 'What you up to?'

'Nothing,' she mumbled, pressing her back against the wall to keep a distance between herself and the dog. 'I just heard a noise and came to see who it was.'

'Who else *could* it have been?' Eddie demanded, looping the dog's lead over the doorknob. 'You'd best not have been letting people in.'

'I haven't,' Patsy insisted, hurrying into the bedroom behind him because the dog looked like it wanted to eat her. 'I never let anyone in. Not even the social worker. She's always knocking, but I pretend I'm not here.'

'So why are you acting so jumpy?'

'I'm not,' Patsy lied, wrapping her arms around her skinny body. 'I just need a bit of stuff.'

'I don't know about that,' Eddie muttered, kneeling at the foot of the cot. 'You're starting to need it too much, if you ask me.'

'No, I'm not,' Patsy blurted out, chewing on her knuckles now. 'I just need a little bit to get myself straight, and then I'll cut down. Honest.'

'Yeah, right,' Eddie drawled, not believing a word of it. Glancing into the cot as he reached through the rubbish below it, he said, 'Where's the kid?'

Patsy's eyes swivelled wildly. 'My, er, my sister took it.'

'Thought you said no one had been in?' Eddie reminded her.

'They haven't,' Patsy said, scratching at her arms. 'She knocked and asked if she could take him, so I passed him out to her.'

Eddie wasn't sure he believed her but, wherever the kid was, he thought it was probably better that it was out of here because Patsy was definitely getting worse. Every time he'd called round lately she'd been wearing the same clothes she was wearing now. And whatever maternal instinct she might once have possessed had been well and truly swamped by her addiction, to the point that she looked confused whenever he mentioned her child.

Getting back to the task at hand now, Eddie reached

down to move the floorboards. But as soon as he touched them he knew they'd been moved since he'd been here last. Yanking the cot out of the way, he shoved the mess aside and hauled his case out. Furious when he saw the scratch marks around the lock, he glared up at Patsy.

'You been messing with this?'

'No!' she protested. 'I haven't touched it, I swear.'

'So what are all these marks?' he demanded, standing up and thrusting the case out to show her.

Wincing, because she was sure that Eddie was going to hit her, Patsy said, 'Mice. There's loads of them. They crawl all over everything. And they bite. Look . . .' She held out her scabby arms. 'Teeth . . . sharp little teeth.'

Grimacing when she mimicked a mouse nibbling, Eddie pushed her out of the way and laid the case down on the bed to examine it. It looked like she'd stuck some-thing into the lock, because the metal was distorted on the inside of the cut-out. But, fortunately for Patsy, she hadn't managed to get into it, and he found everything as he'd left it when he opened it.

'Touch this again,' Eddie warned her, taking out the money and the thirty or so bags of crack that were still in there, 'and I'll chop your fucking hands off. You got that?' He looked up at her now, his stare cold and hard.

'I haven't,' Patsy repeated lamely, her gaze riveted to the crack that was already disappearing into his pocket.

'This is your last chance,' Eddie said, relocking the

case and putting it back into the hole. 'Any more nonsense and I'll move the whole lot out.'

Patsy's body twitched in anticipation when he put everything back in place and came towards the door. But when he shouldered past her and headed into the hall without giving her anything, she said, 'What about me?'

'What about you?' Eddie looked coldly back at her as he unhooked the dog.

'You can't just leave me like this,' she whined, bravely going after him and clutching at his arm. 'Come on, Eddie. I *need* it.'

'Get your fucking hand off me,' he warned her quietly. 'Unless you want me to show you what I do to people who try to rip me off?'

'I'll give you a blow job,' Patsy blurted out, falling to her knees and scrabbling to get at his flies. 'You know you like it when I do it special.' She gurned up at him now, her gunk-coated tongue flicking in and out of her mouth.

Disgusted, Eddie had to draw on every last ounce of willpower not to lay into her. But he knew he would probably kill her if he hit her properly, so he just swatted her out of the way instead, sending her sprawling across the filthy floor.

Sobbing, Patsy screamed, 'I'll do anything! *Anything!*'

'You're a wreck,' Eddie sneered. 'What do you think I could possibly want from you?'

'You said you were going to look after me,' Patsy

reminded him, licking at the snot that was running from her nose.

'I will,' Eddie said calmly. 'But not while you're like this, 'cos you're putting me at risk.'

'I'm not,' Patsy said sincerely. 'I'd never do anything to hurt you, Eddie. I love you.'

'So show me you're making an effort to sort yourself out and I'll think about giving you something in a day or so,' Eddie told her firmly. She was suffering but he was glad, because it would make her think twice about disobeying him again.

When he walked out, Patsy scuttled back into the bedroom and started licking the sheet in case he'd dropped any traces of crack there.

Joe was woken by the sound of the letter box's flap. He reached for his watch and groaned when he saw that it was almost one in the afternoon. He hadn't meant to sleep in so late but he'd sat by the window after getting home that morning, keeping himself awake with strong coffee while he waited for the girl whose name he didn't even know to come home. It was half-six before she'd finally appeared, and she'd looked as if she was carrying the weight of the world on her frail shoulders. But one of the other girls had been linking arms with her, so Joe had figured that she would be okay.

He pulled on his dressing gown now and staggered

out into the hallway. Seeing the neatly folded note on the doormat – the third in as many weeks – he snatched it up and yanked the door open, hoping to catch the anonymous sender in the act. There was nobody out in the corridor but, just as he was about to go back inside, Eddie came around the top of the stairs.

'Not up yet, you lazy cunt?' Eddie called when he spotted what Joe was wearing.

'Didn't get much sleep,' Joe told him, trying not to look as paranoid as he suddenly felt about his secret trip back into town to see the girl after dropping Eddie off last night.

'Likely story,' Eddie scoffed. 'You've got a bird in, haven't you?'

'I should be so lucky,' Joe muttered. 'Been out walking the dog?'

'Yeah, I've been neglecting it a bit lately,' Eddie admitted, reaching down to stroke its head. 'Need to remind it who I am before it forgets what it's here for. Anyhow, you get back to your bed,' he said now, tossing Joe a conspiratorial wink. 'And don't go doing anything daft like moving her in. Take it from someone who knows, that's the beginning of the end, that.'

Smiling, Joe was about to say goodbye when the sound of an argument suddenly erupted on one of the lower floors.

'See?' Eddie said, as a female voice started screaming at someone to fuck off. '*That*'s what happens when you let a woman think she's got the better of you.'

Joe frowned and stepped closer to the stairwell. 'It sounds like Cheryl,' he murmured.

Eddie cocked his head. 'Yeah, I think you're right,' he said. 'Come on, boy.'

As Eddie and the dog turned and dashed back down the stairs, Joe nipped back into the flat and grabbed his keys before following them.

Cheryl was furious and heartbroken all at the same time, and the combination of emotions had given her a strength she'd never known she possessed. But Shay was still stronger, so even though she'd managed to push him as far as the doorway she couldn't quite get him out into the corridor.

'Just *go*!' she screamed, beating his chest with her fists as the tears streamed down her cheeks. 'You're a bastard and I wish you were *dead*!'

'You'd best quit hitting me before I hit you back,' Shay warned her, gripping her firmly by the wrists. 'I mean it, Cheryl . . . pack it in, or you're gonna be sorry.'

'Get your filthy hands *off* me!' she bawled, hurting herself even more than she was hurting Shay as she struggled to yank herself free. 'Just go back to your bitch and leave me alone! I hate you!'

'Carry on cussing me out like I'm a piece of shit and you're gonna know about it,' Shay hissed. 'You've got it all wrong, as usual, you stupid cow.'

'You're the one who's got it wrong if you think I'm

listening to any more of your lies,' Cheryl screamed. 'And don't think you're seeing Frankie again, 'cos you're not!'

'Oh, so you're going to try and pull that one on me now, are you?' Shay snapped, clenching his fist. 'No one tells me when I can and can't see my own son.'

'Put that fist anywhere near her and I'll put your fucking head through the wall!' Eddie barked, coming out of the stairwell door just then and marching towards them.

Inhaling deeply, Shay released Cheryl and took a step back. 'Everything's cool,' he said smoothly, his gaze flicking from Eddie to the dog as it bared its teeth. 'It's just personal stuff, man. Nothing for anyone to get worked up about.'

'What are *you* saying?' Eddie asked Cheryl. 'You want him here?'

'No,' she sobbed, shaking her head and swatting at the tears.

Turning back to Shay, Eddie jerked his chin. 'You heard her. Do one.'

'Fine by me,' Shay drawled. 'I was going anyhow.' Flashing a quick hooded glance at Cheryl now, he turned and strolled nonchalantly away.

'Take her inside and make sure she's okay,' Eddie said to Joe. 'I'm going to have a quick word.'

'Leave him,' Cheryl begged, immediately regretting having involved Eddie because now it was bound to end in blood. 'It was just a stupid row. He didn't hurt me.'

'Don't worry – I won't touch him if you don't want me to,' Eddie reassured her. 'I just want to make sure he's not planning on coming back and kicking off after I've gone. Okay?'

'There's no need,' Cheryl insisted. But Eddie just winked at her and went after Shay. Turning to Joe when he'd gone, she said, 'Oh, God, I hope he doesn't hurt him. You don't think he'll set the dog on him or anything, do you?'

'Course not,' Joe said gently, taking her by the arm. 'Come on, I'll make you a brew.'

'I'm okay,' she insisted, still worriedly eyeing the door.

'*You* might be, but I need a coffee,' Joe told her. 'And I could really do with getting off the corridor before someone sees us and thinks I've been knocking you about.'

'Do I look that bad?' Cheryl asked, allowing him to lead her inside at last.

'You've looked better,' Joe admitted, closing the door behind them. 'But don't worry, the red nose kind of suits you.'

'Gee, thanks,' she murmured, giving him a tiny smile.

While Joe made the coffees, Cheryl peered out through the nets at the kitchen window and chewed nervously on her nails as she watched Eddie catch up with Shay at his car. Relieved when they started talking, with no sign of flying fists or biting dogs, she slumped down onto a stool and reached for her cigarettes.

'So what's he done this time?' Joe asked over his shoulder.

Cheryl lit up and inhaled deeply to calm herself. 'He's got engaged,' she said after a moment, her chin wobbling again.

'You're joking?' Joe glanced back at her. 'To what's-her-face?'

'Yeah, I couldn't believe it either,' she muttered, her heel beating the floor as she agitatedly bounced her leg. 'Two years we were together, and we've got a baby, but he never bought *me* a ring. But you know what he said when I collared him? That he's only done it to shut her up, 'cos she's been nagging him about it. Don't you think that's pathetic?'

'Ridiculous,' Joe agreed. 'So what are you going to do?'

'I've already done it,' Cheryl said, pulling a tissue out of her pocket and dabbing at her nose. 'That's why we were fighting when you and Eddie came down, 'cos I'd just told him I never want to see him again.'

'And do you mean it?' Joe asked cannily, knowing that if she went by form she'd punish Shay for a while before letting things slide right back to where they had been.

'Yeah, I do.' Cheryl raised her chin proudly. 'I know it'll hurt for a bit, but I'll get over it. *You* did,' she added. 'You'd only just split with Angie when I met you, and it was obvious you still had feelings for her because you were always talking about her. But look at you now. You haven't mentioned her in ages.'

'I didn't realise I'd talked about her that much in the first place,' Joe said, bringing the coffees to the table and passing Cheryl's to her before he sat down.

Cheryl thanked him and said, 'Yeah, well, you did. But you're loads happier now. And I will be, too – so long as *he* stays out of my life.'

'Probably for the best,' Joe agreed, doubting that she'd stick to what she was saying.

'Best for *him*, maybe. But he obviously doesn't care what it's going to do to his son. The poor thing's confused enough already without all this. But if Jayleen thinks she's going to be his new mummy, she can fuck off. And you know I don't usually swear, so that's how much I mean it.'

'Frankie will be fine as long as he's got you,' Joe assured her, wondering if the boy would even notice if his father stopped coming round. 'Shay's not exactly dad of the year, from what I've seen so far.'

'No, 'cos that bitch has got him all tied up,' Cheryl spat. 'But he'll regret it when he realises what a waste of space she is. I wouldn't mind, but she can't be all that special or he wouldn't have been coming round to see me the whole time he's been with her, would he?'

'No. But I still think you can do better for yourself. And so does Carl.'

'Carl can't talk,' Cheryl snorted. 'Mel's an absolute

bitch to him but he's still with her. I bet *you* wouldn't put up with someone treating you like that, would you?'

'Not a chance!' Joe laughed. 'But that's love for you. He probably doesn't see her like we do.'

'No, 'cos he can't see past her great figure and gorgeous face.' Cheryl sniffed. 'Typical man.'

Joe was amazed that Cheryl thought Mel was better-looking than her just because Mel was slimmer. And she obviously had no idea that, given the choice, Carl would swap Mel for her in a heartbeat. Not that Carl had ever actually said that as such but Joe had seen the way he looked at her, so he knew.

Finishing her smoke in silence, Cheryl stubbed it out and exhaled wearily. 'Thanks for letting me spout off. I got myself into a right state after I saw her and that flaming ring.'

'You've seen it?' Joe raised an eyebrow. 'How come?'

'She was standing outside when I took Frankie to play-group this morning,' Cheryl told him. 'Holding her phone to her ear with *that* hand so I couldn't miss it.' Sneering now, she shook her head. 'I bet there wasn't even anyone on the other end. She just did it to spite me, the slag. But if she thought I was going to let her see I was bothered, she was wrong. I just made out like I hadn't even noticed and walked right past her.'

'Good for you,' Joe said approvingly.

'Yeah, I thought so. Should have seen her – she was gutted. But she'll be even more gutted if she tries to get in my face again, 'cos I'll get Shay to come round and then I'll take a picture of us in bed together and Bluetooth it to her. See how she likes that.'

'And would that make you feel better?'

'I'll let you know when I've done it,' Cheryl said, grinning slyly. 'Anyway, enough of me and my problems. I haven't even asked how you are.'

'Same as usual.' Joe shrugged. 'You know me, nothing much changes.'

'Glad to hear it.' Cheryl gave him a meaningful look. 'I was a bit concerned that Eddie's ways might rub off on you when you hooked up with him.'

Assuring her that he was basically just a glorified taxi driver and therefore in no danger of becoming a gangster, Joe said, 'I'm doing it for the cash more than anything. And I'm definitely getting fitter now I've not got as much free time to spend boozing, so I'm pleased about that.'

Cheryl smiled and took a sip of her coffee. Joe hadn't needed to tell her that he was getting back into shape because she'd already noticed for herself. He'd begun to look drawn before getting this job, but the old sparkle was coming back into his eyes lately. And that was nice to see.

The post arrived just then. Reminded of the note he'd stuffed into his pocket, Joe pulled it out to read it when Cheryl went to get hers.

FAO Tenant of No. 312: Your neighbours have the right to expect peace and quiet whilst at home, so it would be appreciated if you could reduce the volume of your television set and/or hi-fi equipment as it has been noted that you are causing a regular disturbance. Thanking you in anticipation of your cooperation.

Shaking his head when Cheryl came back, he said, 'Have a look at this.'

Reading it, Cheryl's eyebrows knitted together. 'Who the hell sent that?'

'Who do you think?' Joe rolled his eyes. 'It's not signed so I can't prove it, but it's got to be Kettler, hasn't it? No one else round here is that anal.'

'I wouldn't mind, but you don't even make that much noise,' Cheryl said indignantly. 'There's plenty of times I've been at yours and I couldn't hear the TV properly, and I was in the same room.'

'Well, I didn't think I was noisy,' Joe agreed. 'But he's obviously got a problem with it. Either that or he's got superhuman hearing.'

'Nah, he's just being a wanker,' Cheryl said bluntly, passing the note back. 'I hope you've told him to get lost.'

'He'd only deny it, so I can't be bothered,' Joe said, shrugging it off. 'Anyway, I reckon he's only doing it to get a reaction, so it must be killing him that I haven't said anything.'

'What, you mean this isn't the first?' Cheryl asked.

'Third,' Joe told her. 'First was a complaint about me dropping rubbish on the stairs. Which is crap, 'cos I always double-check my bags before I take them out. But according to the note, someone could fall and break their neck because of it. Second one was about me slamming my door when I come in or go out late at night. Apparently, I do it so hard I make things fall off shelves.'

Cheryl laughed now and shook her head. 'Wow, he's really got it in for you. You want to watch he doesn't report you to the council, or you'll have them spying on you.'

'Couldn't be any worse than *him* doing it,' Joe said, slapping the note down on the table. 'But I'm just going to carry on ignoring him. Wait till he finds someone else to obsess over.'

'Good luck with that.' Cheryl's tone implied that she thought he'd be waiting a while. As she opened her own post her brow creased into a frown. 'Oh, great, that's all I need,' she muttered. 'The Social are threatening to cut my benefits if I don't tell them who Frankie's dad is.'

'So tell them,' Joe said, wondering why she hadn't already.

'I can't,' Cheryl moaned. 'He went mad when I said the CSA had been asking for his details, said he'd deny he was the dad if I dropped him in it.'

'Send them the birth certificate,' Joe suggested. 'That's all the proof they need.'

'His name's not on it,' Cheryl admitted. 'He wouldn't come with me when I registered the birth, and you're not allowed to put the dad's name on the certificate unless he's there.' Tutting now, she slapped the letter down on top of Joe's note. 'See what a bastard he is? It's all right for him living up there with no responsibilities, but he obviously doesn't give a toss that me and Frankie could end up with no money.'

'There must be something you can do,' Joe said, wondering why so many men felt no guilt about denying their own children. 'How about a DNA test?'

'And who's going to pay for that?' Cheryl gave him a weary look. 'Even if he agreed to do it in the first place – which he wouldn't. I've got a good mind not to give him this.' She tossed down the other letter she'd been holding and stared at it resentfully. 'He thinks he's smart keeping this as his address. Thinks if people don't know where he's living they can't catch up with him if he gets into debt.'

'You're the one who's letting him do it,' Joe pointed out.

'Yeah, 'cos I'm soft in the head,' Cheryl said bitterly. 'But enough's enough,' she added, a new resolve coming into her voice. 'I'm going to see who it's from, then ring them and tell them he doesn't live here any more and to stop sending shit here for him.'

She snatched up the letter and tore the envelope open. But when she saw the credit-card bill inside and scanned down the list of recent purchases that Shay had made, her mouth dropped open and fresh tears sprang into her eyes.

'He spent nearly two grand at a jeweller's a couple of weeks ago,' she croaked. 'How could he do that? He said he was broke when I asked him for twenty quid to get Frankie some new trainers but he can spend that much on a ring for that brain-dead whore. And he told me it only cost him fifty quid from a pawn shop when I asked him this morning.'

Joe got up when she started sobbing, put his arms around her and rocked her gently. 'I know you're hurt, but at least you know the truth now. And you're way too good to let him treat you like this – you know that, don't you?'

'I just can't believe he's done this to me,' Cheryl cried, burying her face in Joe's shoulder. 'He tells me he loves me when he comes round; says it was a mistake going with her, and he wishes he'd stayed with me. Even today, he said he was going to leave her as soon as he's paid her brother back the money he owes him.'

'And you believed him?' Joe asked.

'Not now,' Cheryl conceded, the pain in her heart eased by his closeness. This was the first time they had ever actually hugged, and it felt totally different to be held by him than it did to be in Shay's arms. With Shay it was all about sex: every touch designed purely to get her out of her knickers. But Joe's arms felt warm and safe, like those of a true friend.

Fearing that she might become too comfortable and stay there for ever, Cheryl eased herself away from him after a while and reached for the kitchen roll to wipe her eyes. 'Sorry, I didn't mean to fall apart like that. Hope I haven't ruined your dressing gown.'

'It'll dry,' Joe said, going back to his seat. Waving his hand over Cheryl's letters he said, 'Know what I'd do with them? I'd ring them *both* and give them his name and her address. Sooner he realises you've stopped making things easy for him, the sooner he'll have to sort himself out.'

'Yeah, you're right,' Cheryl agreed, blowing her nose noisily. 'No more Mrs Nice Girl. From now on I'm going to be the bitch queen of Ardwick.'

'You couldn't be a bitch if you tried,' Joe laughed.

'Trust me, I can,' Cheryl told him. Glancing at the clock now, she sighed. 'Time to go and pick the little monster up from the nursery. I'll only be twenty minutes if you want to stay and make yourself another brew. But no peeking in my knicker drawer,' she added with a cheeky grin.

'What do you take me for?' Joe gasped, giving her a mock-offended look, although he was glad that she'd recovered her humour so quickly.

'A gay,' she teased, going to the sink and splashing cold water over her eyes.

'Don't you start,' Joe groaned. 'I get enough of that shit off Carl, if you don't mind.'

'Shouldn't be so nice, then, should you?' Cheryl said as she used the tea towel to dry her face. 'Subject of nice, Molly said to thank you for the card you sent in the other week. She was really chuffed.'

'I forgot about that.' Joe smiled. 'How's she doing?'

'Okay,' Cheryl told him, heading out into the hall. 'But not as well as she should be, according to the nurse I had a word with the other day.' Shrugging as she slipped her coat on, she said, 'All I can think is that she's either loving the attention too much to want to come home or she's giving up. 'Cos they say old people do that, don't they?'

'Nah, she's got way too much character for that,' Joe said, opening the door and going out into the corridor.

'Well, she'd best hurry up or she won't have a cat by the time she gets out,' Cheryl replied darkly, following him out and pulling the door shut. 'I'm getting seriously tempted to throttle the little shit. Look at this.' She thrust her arm out and pulled back her sleeve to show him a mess of scratches on her wrist.

'Painful.' Joe grimaced. Then, chuckling, he said, 'Ever thought that might be why she's staying put – 'cos she knows the moggie'll be waiting for her when she gets home? She's probably loving the break.'

'Well, I'm not,' Cheryl huffed. 'Anyway, I'll see you later. And thanks again for letting me drip all over your shoulder.'

'My pleasure,' Joe said, walking backwards to the

stairwell. 'And you just concentrate on yourself and Frankie from now on. Never mind Shay. Okay?'

'Okay,' Cheryl agreed.

Joe winked at her and went home.

He'd stayed with Cheryl a lot longer than he'd intended to, so he dropped his dressing gown and took a quick shower when he got in. He'd arranged to meet up with some old friends for a drink that evening and he had a few things to sort out beforehand, so he'd have to get a move on.

14

Chrissie had been feeling queasy for a couple of weeks. It came and went so she'd thought nothing of it, reckoning that it was probably just a mild stomach bug. But her mum had thought differently, and despite Chrissie telling her that she couldn't possibly be pregnant she'd gone ahead and bought the test anyway. And, purely to prove her wrong, because Linda Scott was the infuriating kind of woman who always thought she was right, Chrissie had used it.

So now she was sitting here in her mum's bathroom, gazing in disbelief at the little blue line glaring out at her from the window of the pissy little stick.

'Well?' Linda called, rattling the door handle impatiently. 'Who was right? Me or you?'

The shock on Chrissie's face when she opened the door was answer enough. But Linda resisted the urge to say, 'Ha! *Told* you!' even though that was what she was thinking.

'So, are we pleased?' she asked instead, testing the water. 'Or should I be nipping down to the hardware shop for a coat hanger and a bottle of paraffin?'

'*Mum!*' Chrissie squawked, reflexively encircling her stomach with her arms. 'Don't be so horrible.'

'So we *are* pleased, then?' Linda gave her a questioning look. Flapping her hands when Chrissie just scowled back at her, she turned and went back down the stairs, muttering, 'I give up. Let me know when I'm allowed to smile – or not. I'm only the grandma. Nothing important. No big deal.'

Chrissie closed her eyes and waited for her irritation to lessen before going after her mother. She found her in the kitchen looking for things to clean, which was what she always did when she was upset. Chrissie pulled out a chair and sat at the table.

'Sorry, mum. Didn't mean to snap at you. It's me, not you.'

'Tell me something I don't know,' Linda huffed, squeezing a dollop of Fairy Liquid into the washing-up bowl and turning on the hot tap. 'I only wanted to know if I was supposed to congratulate you or not. I mean, it's not like you're fifteen and I'm supposed to be giving you a beating, or anything. You're a grown woman.'

'Yes, I know,' Chrissie groaned, putting her elbows on the table and running her hands through her hair. 'I just don't know how I feel about it yet. It's a shock.'

'Mmm, well, I suppose it must be if you've been taking your pill like you reckon,' Linda said, softening her tone. Of her four children Chrissie was the only girl, and their relationship had never been easy. Her own mum had always said that you couldn't have two queens ruling one castle, and Linda had found out just how true that was when Chrissie had hit her teens. If Linda said the sky was blue, Chrissie would say it was red just to start an argument. But Linda still loved the silly bones of her and wanted the best for her.

'What am I going to do?' Chrissie asked now, sounding like the helpless child she'd never been.

Sighing, Linda reached for the tea towel. 'What do you *want* to do?' she asked as she wiped her hands and joined her daughter at the table.

'Smoke myself stupid,' Chrissie said, fingering the pack of Superkings her mum had left on the table. 'But I'm not supposed to, am I?'

'For God's sake, you've only known for two minutes so what difference will it make?' Linda said, reaching for the pack and taking a couple out. 'Here, have one if you need it. Worry about the baby when you've decided if you're keeping it or not. I'm presuming that's what's bothering you?'

Chrissie nodded and leaned forward to get a light.

'So, what will Eddie say when you tell him?' Linda asked, squinting through the smoke as she lit her own. 'Will he want it?'

'I've got absolutely no idea what Eddie wants,' Chrissie admitted glumly. 'I've hardly seen him lately. He's always out. *Working*,' she added quickly, realising that she'd come perilously close to giving her mum an excuse to launch into one of her *I told you not to move in with him until he'd put a ring on your finger* lectures. Like she was any kind of advertisement for marriage when she had not one but *four* failed ones behind her.

'You're going to have to tell him if you're thinking of keeping it,' Linda told her, pointing out the obvious. 'But it's probably best to say nothing until you know for sure. And if you decide you *don't* want it, I'll come to the clinic so you won't be on your own. Okay?'

'Okay.' Forcing a smile, Chrissie nodded. 'Thanks, mum.'

'No need to thank me,' Linda sniffed. 'It's all part of the job. How old are you now?' she asked after a moment.

'*Mum!*' Chrissie spluttered, shocked all over again. 'How can you not know how old your own child is? Don't you feel ashamed having to ask?'

'Not my fault I've got early-onset dementia.'

'You have *not* got dementia. And I wish you'd stop saying it, 'cos one of these days someone's going to believe it and have you put away.'

'Maybe I have, maybe I haven't.' Linda shrugged. 'But what I *have* got is a mental mother, two bitchy sisters, four kids, and three grandkids – and another on the way, depending what you end up doing. So you tell me how I'm supposed to remember every single birthday?'

'We're only talking about mine,' Chrissie informed her. 'Your only daughter – who happens to be twenty-six, for the record. Twenty-seven next month, and you'd best not use that lame excuse to try and get out of buying me a present. You got that?'

'Loud and clear,' Linda chuckled, seeing from Chrissie's face that she wasn't being serious. 'Anyhow, I was only asking out of concern for my new grandson.' She nodded towards Chrissie's stomach. 'You know there's more risk of disabilities with babies of older mums, don't you?'

'That's mums of *your* age, not mine,' Chrissie corrected her. 'And please don't give it a sex when we don't even know what it is. That'll just make it harder if I decide to . . . you know.'

'Fair enough.' Linda held up her hands. 'Consider the subject closed until you choose to reopen it. And now we've got *that* out of the way, why don't you tell me about this work that's keeping your Eddie from spending any time with you? Good pay, is it?'

'Great,' Chrissie said evasively, wanting to talk about Eddie even less than she wanted to talk about the baby. Changing the subject, she said, 'So what's our Steven's new girlfriend like? Have you met her yet?'

'Pftt,' Linda snorted. 'Don't talk to me about that little madam. He brought her round the other day and she sat there like Lady Muck. Didn't want a cup of tea, didn't want to look through me catalogue . . . didn't even want to stay for dinner, but he made her, 'cos you know how much he loves my steak and kidney. The *face* on her while she was eating, though. Well, I say eating, but it was more like watching a bird pecking.'

Trailing off, she shook her head. 'Nah, she won't last two minutes, her.'

'I hope you didn't say that to him?' Chrissie asked, knowing how well that would have gone down with their Steven.

'No point,' Linda said, flicking her ash. 'You know how stubborn he is. But he'll find out for himself soon enough. Just like our Neil did. Remember that Gaynor he brought round that time? She was another one who looked down her nose at me the whole time she was here. But she got her marching orders fast enough, didn't she?'

'*She* finished with *him*,' Chrissie pointed out.

'Same difference.' Linda shrugged. 'At least your Eddie treats me with respect,' she said now. 'When I see him – which isn't that often.'

'Join the club,' Chrissie muttered, stubbing her cigarette out and standing up.

'You're not going already, are you?' Linda asked, a look of dismay coming into her eyes. 'You've only been here an hour.'

'I've got some things to do,' Chrissie lied, pulling her coat on. She leaned down to kiss her mum and said, 'I'll see myself out.'

'When are you coming round next?' Linda asked, annoyed with herself for sounding so desperate. But she couldn't help it. Much as they butted heads, she loved spending time with her daughter. And since

Chrissie had moved in with Eddie last year she hadn't seen anywhere near as much of her as she'd used to.

'Not sure.' Chrissie backed towards the door. 'I'll give you a ring.'

'Don't leave it too long,' Linda said, looking pointedly at her daughter's stomach. 'You could be further on than you think, so you'll need to move fast if you want rid.'

Chrissie left without answering and walked quickly to the taxi rank, pushing her hands into her coat pockets as she went and cupping the tiny swelling that she imagined she could feel there. It was unreal and too real all at the same time, and she didn't know how she was supposed to make such a massive decision on her own about whether or not to keep it. It was Eddie's responsibility as much as it was hers, but she knew exactly how he'd react when – *if* – she told him. He'd say it was *her* fault; that she was the one who was supposed to be taking the pill, so she should have made sure that she didn't slip up. And he'd be right – if she *had* slipped up. Trouble was, she was positive that she hadn't. Only she must have, or she wouldn't be in this position.

Eddie was out when she got home twenty minutes later, but he'd left the dog behind and it slunk out of the kitchen when it heard her coming in and gave her a baleful look. Usually she'd have told it to piss off, or at least given it a dirty look to let it know to stay away from her. But today she squatted down and called it to her.

'It's not your fault, is it?' she said, stroking its scarred ears as it pressed itself up against her like an unwanted child craving affection. 'You're just lonely, aren't you, fella? 'Cos your master's not paying you enough attention. Not nice, is it?'

The dog looked up at her as she spoke, pitiful adoration in its pink-rimmed eyes. Feeling a little tug in her heart when it licked her hand, Chrissie got up and went into the kitchen. Sighing when she saw the pile of shit in the corner, she said, 'Come on, let's get you some dinner.'

She cleaned the mess up while it ate and then made herself a cup of tea and carried it through to the bedroom. She stripped down to her bra and knickers, stood in front of the dressing-table mirror and scrutinised her stomach from every angle. She'd been wanting to do this ever since she'd left her mum's, desperate to see if there were any visible changes to her body.

The dog trotted in a few minutes later and sat down to watch her. 'Can *you* see it?' Chrissie asked. Smiling when it waggled its tail stump, she said, 'I take it that's a no? Well, good. If you can't see it, neither will he.'

15

Joe was exhausted by the time he got home that night. It had been great to see his old friends again, but they'd had so much to tell him about what had been happening in his absence that he felt as if his ears had been chewed off, so the last thing he wanted or needed now was company. But not five minutes after he'd made himself a cup of tea and flopped down in his chair to watch a bit of mindless TV – with the volume low so as not to spark Kettler off again – Carl came round with a couple of four-packs of beer and a bag of weed, reminding Joe that they were supposed to be watching the City v Chelsea match together – and scolding him for being late and making him miss the kick-off.

Just about resigned to having to endure that, Joe's mood dipped when Damien called round soon after. He'd gone to Carl's looking for a score and had been redirected here by Mel. When he too made himself comfortable after getting what he wanted, Joe was on the verge of feigning a migraine and asking them to go and watch the match some-where else when three more of Carl's customers turned up.

Football chants and obscenities were soon bouncing off the walls as they all got sucked into the match, and the air was so thick with smoke as the spliffs flew round that Joe was surprised they could see the screen. But the noise didn't end when the match did, because they were all buzzing by then and in no rush to move the party on.

By half-eleven Joe's head was banging for real, so he escaped into the kitchen. Sure that none of the guys had even noticed that he'd gone, he made himself a coffee and took a couple of paracetamol before wandering out onto the tiny balcony.

This was his favourite view from the flat, especially at night when lights were twinkling all across the city, punctuated by the silhouettes of skyscrapers and ghostly-looking industrial cranes. As the cool air cleared the stuffiness from Joe's head and eased the tension in his shoulders, he was seriously contemplating getting his quilt and settling down out here for the night when he heard the sound of the door clanging shut below. Glancing over the balcony in time to see the four girls from the floor above hurrying down the path in their peculiar little huddle, he tried to pick out the girl he'd spoken to last night. But they all looked the same from behind. Same short skirts, boots, and hoodies; same skinny legs and barely-there hips. And same general air of misery causing their thin shoulders to hunch around their hooded ears.

As Joe watched them leave the estate, he once again

found himself wondering how one man could exert so much control over them that they would continue to do what they blatantly didn't want to be doing. From everything he'd heard about enforced prostitution, most of the women were unable to get away because they were either imprisoned in a physical sense or by their addictions to whatever drugs their pimps had forced them onto. But the girl he'd spoken to hadn't shown any signs of being on drugs. And they were free right now, in as much as they were walking around on the outside without Eddie watching over them. So why didn't they just keep on going while they had the chance? It didn't make sense.

'*There* you are,' Carl said just then, yanking the door open and peering out at Joe. 'I've been looking everywhere for you. What you doing out here?'

'Headache,' Joe said, rubbing at his forehead. 'Just needed a bit of fresh air.'

'You mean you'd had enough of the noise?'

'Well, yeah, kind of.'

'So why didn't you just tell them to piss off?' Carl said, rolling his eyes. 'What are you like?'

'Didn't want to break up the party.' Joe shrugged. 'Don't worry about me. You go back to your mates.'

'Nah, not without you,' Carl said loyally. 'Come back in. I'll tell them to keep the noise down.'

'Actually, I was just thinking about nipping out,' Joe said, glancing at his watch. 'I was supposed to see someone earlier on but I forgot. He should still be up, though, so I might call in on him for half an hour.'

'*Him?*' Carl repeated disbelievingly. 'Come on, mate, do you think I fell out of the stupid tree? Blokes don't go out in the middle of the night to see a *him*. You've got a bird waiting for you, haven't you?'

'Maybe,' Joe said evasively.

'Dirty dog.' Carl grinned, slapping him on the back as he came inside. 'I knew you had it in you. Just don't go doing anything Mel won't let me do.'

'I won't,' Joe assured him, rinsing out his cup at the sink. 'You can let everyone out, can't you?'

'Sack that,' Carl scoffed. 'I'm off to see if Mel's still awake. I'm not having you getting laid if I can't.'

'Good luck,' Joe chuckled as he headed into the living room.

Carl clapped his hands loudly as he followed him in. 'Party's over, guys! My man's got a hot date and we're cramping his style, so come on . . . move it!'

Joe smiled as the guys gathered their things together without argument and started traipsing out, all of them either shaking his hand or slapping him on the back as they went and telling him to have one for them.

He was still smiling as he headed down to the car a few minutes later, amused that they had all been so surprised to hear that he was going to see a woman. Although it made him wonder what the hell they thought of him if it was such an unexpected event that they felt the need to congratulate him. Carl joked about him being gay, but could they really have been suspecting that he was this whole time? If so, it was great that they were being so chilled about it, because people who lived in places like this usually had a reputation for being outspokenly anti-everything. But he supposed it just went to show that nothing was ever quite what it seemed from the outside.

Including the situation of the girl he was hoping to see again now. Although what he would say when he found her, he didn't know.

Katya had felt rough all day and she was no better by the time she and the other girls reached town. She'd thought that the infection from which she'd been suffering on and off for the past few months had cleared up, but it had kicked in again that morning and her bladder was aching now because the burning pain made her terrified to go to the toilet. And, thanks to that man headbutting her last night, both of her eyes were black and swollen. But at least her nose didn't appear to be broken, so that was something to be thankful for.

When the girls had separated at the entrance to Piccadilly Station and gone off to their individual spots, Katya had put her head down and rushed past Dale Street, afraid to look as she passed in case the man was still lying there, even though she knew that it was extremely unlikely.

The new spot she'd found for herself that morning was more exposed because it was closer to the town centre, which put her at more risk of being spotted by the police. But she figured she'd be safer there if that man came looking for revenge because he'd have to think twice about attacking her if he thought that somebody might see.

Keeping an eye out for him now as she settled into the doorway, Katya felt the ice of fear in her heart when, within minutes, a car pulled up at the kerb ahead. Relieved to see an unfamiliar young man smiling hopefully out at her, she almost returned the smile as she climbed in beside him.

Almost – but not quite. Because no matter how young and innocent he looked, she knew that he would still cause her pain. And she was right. Although, unlike most of the men she had to deal with, this one had come prepared, and the lubricated condom eased his passage into her considerably. But the friction had still exacerbated her pain and she knew it would only get worse as the night progressed.

Katya soon realised that she'd picked out a busy spot for herself when a second car came along almost as soon as the first one had dropped her back in the doorway, quickly followed by a third and a fourth. At just over an hour in, she'd have been lucky to have had one punter down on Dale Street so she was already well up on her usual. But just as she was beginning to think that she could weather the pain for the increase in earnings, the two girls who had been watching her from the shadows on the opposite side of the road decided that it was time for her to move on.

'What d'y think you're doing, standing round here?' one of them demanded when they marched over to confront her. 'This is our street, so fuck off and find your own.'

More scared of being forced to go back to Dale Street than she was of them, Katya stood her ground. 'You've got that side, I've got this,' she pointed out reasonably. 'I'm not doing any harm.'

'You ain't listening, darlin',' the second girl informed her aggressively. 'We said fuck off. And we ain't messing about, so do one before I slice your fucking face open.'

Catching a flash of light out of the corner of her eye, Katya glanced down and swallowed nervously when she saw the razor blade in the girl's hand. 'Okay, I'm going,' she murmured, taking a step back.

'Not so fast,' the first girl said, gripping her by the arm. 'What you got for us first?'

'Nothing,' Katya lied. 'I've only just got here.'

'Don't try and mug us off, you foreign bitch,' the girl hissed. You've already nicked four of our jobs, so we'll have that money for starters. And where's your phone?' she demanded.

'And your drugs,' the other one said, glancing furtively

around. 'Come on, hand everything over. And hurry up, we ain't got all night.'

'I haven't got a phone, and I don't do drugs,' Katya protested, struggling to fend them off as they tried to search her pockets.

'Is that right?' the first girl said, closing in with a nasty sneer on her lips. 'Or is it that you just don't like sharing where you come from? What are you, anyhow? A Pole? We hate Poles round here. Nicking our punters with your cheap nasty arses.'

'She ain't legal, whatever she is,' the second girl said knowingly. 'Want us to ring the pigs, do you, darlin'?'

Desperate to get away now, Katya tried to push past them. But they weren't letting her go that easily, and she cried out when they shoved her deeper into the doorway and her back slammed up against the large brass door-knob.

Hissing, 'Shut your fucking mouth!' the girl with the blade slashed at her leg. 'And get your money out. We know you've got it. Don't make us have to strip you for it.'

Shocked by the feel of blood trickling down her leg, Katya instinctively kicked out, catching one of the girls on the shin.

'You're fucking dead!' the other one snarled, laying into Katya with her fists and battering her about the head and shoulders as her friend hopped around in pain.

Katya tried to fight back, but when the other girl

recovered and joined in she knew she stood no chance, so she threw her arms over her head and sank to the floor.

Just as she thought they were never going to stop, a car screeched to a stop, and a man yelled, 'Oi! Pack it in, you two!'

Hesitating, one of the girls glanced around to make sure that it wasn't the police while the other one kept a firm grip on Katya. Seeing that it was just an ordinary bloke, she said, 'Fuck off. This has got nowt to do with you.'

'You reckon?' Joe said, getting calmly out of the car and walking towards them.

Facing up to him, the girl looked him up and down. 'So what are you? Her man, or something?'

'Do I look like a pimp?' Joe asked, knowing that that was what she'd meant.

Something in his icy stare unnerved the girl and after a couple of seconds she jerked her head at her friend. 'Come on, leave it.'

Joe watched until they had gone and then turned to see if Katya was all right. Having seen the state of her last night, he'd known that she would have at least one black eye but he was shocked to see how bad she looked now. *Both* of her eyes were badly bruised, and her lip was freshly split. And there were clumps of her long hair all over her jacket and the floor, and a streak of blood running down her bare leg.

'Christ, what did they do to you?' he asked, reaching out to her.

'I'm fine,' Katya muttered, jerking away from him. Pulling her sleeve down over her hand now, she dabbed at her lip before gingerly examining her leg. Relieved to see that the cut was superficial, she raised her chin proudly. 'You didn't need to get involved. I can look after myself.'

Joe raised an eyebrow, as if to say *Are you sure about that?*

'Really, I can,' she insisted, smoothing her hair down. 'You can go now.'

'I think you should get that cut looked at,' Joe told her. 'Why don't you let me take you to hospital? It's only five minutes away.'

'*No!*' Katya blurted out. 'It's just a scratch. I'll put a plaster on it when I get home.'

'Okay, if that's what you want,' Joe said, aware that he couldn't force her. Feeling awkward now, because she clearly wasn't pleased to see him, he said, 'Can we talk?'

'Why?' Katya looked at him with suspicion.

'Because I'm worried about you.'

Unable to hold his gaze, Katya dipped hers. He sounded sincere, and the kindness in his eyes was making her heart flutter painfully. But her head wouldn't allow her to believe that he was here of his own accord. It was too much of a coincidence that he should just happen to be passing at the exact time when she was being attacked – just like Eddie had turned up out of the blue last night.

'I've got to go,' she said.

'Will you at least tell me your name?' Joe called after her as she hurried past him. 'Please. I'd really like to know.'

Katya hesitated, wondering why Eddie wouldn't have already told him if he'd sent him to spy on her. But then, Eddie so rarely spoke to the girls that it wouldn't surprise her if he'd forgotten.

Taking heart from the fact that she'd stopped walking, Joe stepped around her so that he was facing her again and held out his hand. 'I'm Joe.'

'You already told me,' she murmured, folding her arms.

'I know, but I didn't know if you'd heard me,' Joe said. Sighing now, unsure what else he could say to convince her that he meant her no harm, he spread his hands. 'So what do we do now?'

'You should go,' Katya replied wearily. 'I've got to work, and I'm sure you must have something better to do.'

'Not really,' Joe told her. 'I came to find you because . . . well, because I want to talk to you – to find out more about you. But if you're too busy right now, why don't you call round to my place when you've got the time? I live on the third floor, number three-twelve.'

'That's not possible,' Katya murmured.

'Well, how about meeting up and going out for a coffee?' Joe suggested.

Confused by his persistence, Katya gazed up at him.

'Why are you doing this? You must know I can't do what you're asking of me.'

'Why not?' Joe frowned. 'It's only a coffee. And I didn't mean when you're working. I meant some time when you're free and feel like having a chat.'

Katya felt the terrible pain of longing pulse through her body. She so wanted to believe that she could trust him. But it would be a huge mistake to even think about getting involved with anybody from the outside world, because one wrong word would bring everything crashing down not just on her head but Elena's and the other girls' too. And, worse, their families would suffer terrible things.

'I'm sorry, I can't do this,' she mumbled, blinking quickly to hold the tears at bay. 'Please just leave me alone and forget about me.'

'If it was that easy, don't you think I'd have done it by now?' Joe asked.

'Not if Eddie has told you to watch me,' she replied flatly. 'That is why you're here, isn't it?'

'No.' Joe shook his head. 'He's got absolutely no idea that I've spoken to you. I'm here because I've been thinking about you all night, wishing there was something I could do to help you. I know I can't force you to talk to me,' he said now. 'But will you at least take my number in case you change your mind?'

'I don't have a phone,' Katya told him.

'There's plenty of public phone boxes around,' Joe

said as he went back to the car. He scribbled his mobile number on a scrap of paper and handed it to her, along with a pound coin. 'Call me,' he said. 'Any time.'

Katya held the items tightly in her hand. She knew that she would never use them but it felt strangely comforting to have them nonetheless.

Watching now as Joe walked back to his car, she bit her lip. Then, taking a leap of faith, she blurted out, 'It's Katya . . . my name.'

Pausing, Joe smiled. 'Thank you.'

Katya stayed where she was after Joe had driven away, gazing down at the number in her hand. She screwed up the paper after a while and was about to throw it away when something stopped her, and she found herself slipping it into her boot instead. Then, pulling her hood up, she walked quickly away in search of a less dangerous place to work, because she had no doubt that those girls would come back to finish what they'd started now that Joe had gone. She just didn't have the strength to fight them.

16

Patsy was going crazy cooped up in the flat. She knew that Eddie was punishing her for messing with his case, but he'd promised to come back and he hadn't. And she didn't know how long ago it was since he'd been here but she was sure it had been a few days, if not a week.

Her skin was raw from scratching at the invisible insects that had been crawling all over her, and the inside of her head felt like a shattered mirror from the baby's constant crying. Desperate for something to calm the bubbling craziness, she'd taken Eddie's case out of its hole numerous times. And it didn't matter that she'd seen him take all the little baggies out, just knowing that they had been in there in the first place had turned it into a giant magnet, pulling her back time and again. But the tiny part of Patsy's brain that was still functioning normally reminded her that he had threatened to chop her hands off if she tampered with it again, so each time she took it out she put it straight back again.

When she could stand it no longer, Patsy wandered out into the hall and tested the water by opening the door and peeping out. Becoming braver when nothing terrible happened, she opened it a little wider and stepped tentatively up to the threshold before eventually setting foot in the actual corridor – for a fraction of a second – before darting back in again. She couldn't remember the last time she'd been out, and it felt big, bad and dangerous beyond her front door, like a world she no longer belonged in. She knew she shouldn't go out, because she'd promised to stay home and look after Eddie's stuff in return for him looking after her. But something must have happened to stop him from coming round, because there was no way he would have left her for this long. He loved her; he would never deliberately torture her like this.

Patsy went back into the living room; slapping at her ears as the baby's cries reverberated through her head and twanged at every nerve in her body.

'Shut up,' she muttered, pacing up and down past the bouncing chair tucked away between the armchair and the couch. 'Shut up, shut up, shut *up*!'

But it didn't stop. It went on and on and on, until she was forced out into the hall again. And this time she knew that she had to find Eddie before she completely lost her mind.

The corridor outside her door was cold, and it had eyes: buried in every wall, spying from behind every door. Head swimming, she clutched at the door frame for support.

'Are you okay?' somebody asked.

Patsy swung her head in the direction of the voice. A white-haired old lady wearing fluffy slippers and a patterned dress was standing a few doors down. She had a miniature watering can in her hand.

'Who are you?' Patsy's tongue clicked as it unpeeled itself from the roof of her mouth.

'Mrs Thomas,' the old lady reminded her, a frown of concern creasing her kindly old face. 'Is everything all right, dear?'

'Sorry,' Patsy mumbled, pulling her door to behind her to block out the sound of the baby's wailing. 'He's just . . . he's . . . he's waiting for his bottle. But I've not been very well. Haven't been able to get my money.'

'You haven't got any milk?' Mrs Thomas clucked. 'Oh dear, that's not good. Why don't I get you some of mine?'

'No!' Patsy blurted out. 'It's got to be proper baby powder. From the shop.'

'Ah, I see,' Mrs Thomas murmured, bending to put the watering can down. 'Just a moment, I'll see what I can do.'

Patsy scratched at her arms while she waited, creating a little line of blood droplets from her wrist to her elbow. She was licking at them when the old lady came back out and her eyes widened when she saw the ten-pound note in her hand.

'Thanks,' Patsy mumbled, snatching it and rushing back inside. Watching through the spyhole until Mrs

Thomas had finished watering her potted flowers and had gone, she let herself back out and edged along the wall until she reached the lift.

Carl was in the parking lot, drooling over the Golf GTi that Damien's friend had brought over from Leeds to sell. He wanted it – badly – but there was no way he could afford it on the money that Eddie was paying him. Still, it did no harm to look – and touch, and smell, and fantasise about driving it.

'State of that,' Damien said suddenly, nudging him and nodding towards the red block.

Turning in time to see the skinny girl creeping out, Carl said, 'Jeezus, talk about rough.'

'You can say that again,' Damien chuckled, shaking his head as he took in the girl's filthy clothes and the hair standing out in tufty clumps around her head. 'Man, you just wouldn't, would you?'

Carl laughed. But he stopped abruptly when the girl spotted him and called out to him in a loud whisper, 'Carl! Over here . . . I need to talk to you.'

'Sorry, mate, didn't realise you knew her,' Damien said, giving him a strange smile. 'You'd best go see what she wants. See you later.'

Stranded when Damien and his friend hopped into the car and took off, Carl shoved his hands into his pockets and walked over to see what Patsy wanted. She'd been a bit of a babe back in the day and he'd enjoyed a couple of drunken snogs with her. But it had never gone any further than that because she'd had too many other men sniffing around her at that point in time and he'd never been a fan of sloppy seconds. It had been almost a year since he'd last seen her, and as he got closer and was able to see her more clearly he was truly shocked by the change in her. He struggled to keep the look of horror off his face – and he fought to conceal the revulsion he felt when he got a whiff of her, because she absolutely reeked.

'I need something,' Patsy blurted out when he reached her, speaking as if they still knew each other as well as they once had. 'I've got money. Look.' She thrust out the ten-pound note.

'Er, very nice,' Carl said cautiously, wondering why she'd targeted him – he hadn't even been dealing gear when they'd last seen each other. 'Is that all you wanted?' he asked now, already backing away. 'Not being rude, but I'm a bit busy just now.'

'I need something,' Patsy repeated, clutching at his arm. 'I know you've got some. I can smell it.'

Repulsed by the skeletal feel of her fingers digging into his flesh through his jacket, and seriously creeped out by her claim to be able to smell what he had in his pocket, Carl tried to shake her off. But she held on tight.

'Just one bag,' she whined. '*Please*.'

Paranoid about how bad this would look if anyone were to come along, Carl hissed, 'Leave off, Pat. I'm not into that shit.'

'I'll give you a blow job,' she wheedled, her tongue snaking in and out of her crumbling teeth.

'Nah, man, leave it out.' Grimacing, Carl shook her off at last and rushed back to his own block.

Mel was in the living room when he let himself in. She was sitting cross-legged on the couch with a mirror in one hand, a pair of tweezers in the other.

'I've just seen Patsy Mills,' Carl told her, going through to the kitchen to wash his hands to get the imagined grime off himself. 'You should see the state of her. She's proper lost it.'

'Great,' Mel murmured, her focus firmly on the dark hairs she was plucking from around her top lip.

'Christ, doesn't that hurt?' Carl asked, pulling a face as he watched her from the doorway. 'Can't you just shave it?'

'Can't you just fuck off and mind your own business?' Mel snapped, flashing him a dirty look. 'I thought you were supposed to be going out.'

'Yeah, I was, but—'

'So go, then,' Mel cut him off, glaring at him.

Muttering under his breath, Carl dropped the tea towel and snatched up his rolling gear off the table. Slamming the front door behind him, he went across to Joe's to have a moan. But Joe wasn't in so he wandered down to Cheryl's instead – just in time to bump into Shay on his way out.

Cheryl was in the hallway behind him, her loose hair

mussed up as if she'd just climbed out of bed. She blushed when she saw Carl but fronted it out with a smile.

'Were you coming here?'

'No, I'm on my way out,' Carl said, flicking a look of hatred at Shay's back as he swaggered down the corridor like the cat who'd got the cream. Noticing now that Cheryl's T-shirt was on inside out and the wrong way around, he said, 'I take it you two have sorted things out?'

'Kind of,' Cheryl admitted, feeling guilty, because she knew that Carl, like Joe, wouldn't understand why she'd let Shay back in after what had happened. But it was all right for them. Carl had Mel – for all her faults; and Joe liked being on his own. But neither of them knew how hard it was to try and bring up a child alone.

'Oh, well, it's your choice.' Carl shrugged. 'I just hope you know what you're doing.'

'I can't just cut him off, can I?' Cheryl said, sensing his disapproval and feeling strangely sad. 'He's still Frankie's dad.'

'And Jayleen's fiancé,' Carl reminded her. Groaning when her face immediately dropped and tears sprang into her eyes, he said, 'Oh, God, I'm sorry, Chez. I didn't mean it.'

Shaking her head, her eyes flashing with pain, she said, 'No, you're right. But he won't be for much longer. He promised he's going to leave her this time.'

'Babe, wait . . .' Carl said, stepping forward. But she closed the door in his face.

Feeling like the biggest git on earth, he walked to the main door and slammed it open, angry with himself for upsetting Cheryl. Whatever he thought of her situation, she had the right to make her own decisions and shouldn't have to base them on worrying about how her friends were going to react.

Chrissie was immediately behind him, but Carl hadn't noticed her, so he jumped when she said, 'You're going to break that, and we've all got to use it, you know.'

'Sorry,' he muttered. 'Got a lot on my mind, wasn't thinking. You okay?' he asked now, seeing her reddened eyes as he held the door for her.

Composing herself, because she didn't like people to see when she was upset, Chrissie said, 'Yeah, I'm fine, thanks. Sorry for snapping. I've not been feeling very well. Stomach bug.'

Carl gave her a small smile. She was clearly upset about something, and he'd have loved to offer her an ear for her troubles. But there was no way he was sticking his nose into her and Eddie's business.

A cab came into the parking lot just then. Chrissie said goodbye and walked down the path.

Staying where he was, Carl lit a cigarette and sneakily checked out her legs. Mel's were long and slim but they had no shape, and she insisted on wearing ugly flat shoes that did nothing for her – or for him. But Chrissie always wore heels, which made her look sexy – *and* made Carl wonder why the hell Eddie screwed around with so many munters when he had a fit bird like her keeping his bed warm.

Up ahead, Chrissie was holding her short skirt down as she climbed into the back of the taxi. She knew that Carl was watching her and might ordinarily have been flattered enough to put a little extra sway into her walk. He was a good-looking lad and he had something about him that reminded her of Eddie's nicer side – kind of like the bad boy without the bad bit: street enough to be cool, but not underground dangerous.

So, yes, ordinarily Chrissie might have been tempted to give him a thrill to show her appreciation for his interest. But she was too tired.

Just as she'd been too tired to be bothered trying to reason with Eddie after he'd woken in a foul argumentative mood – again.

She closed the cab door, told the driver where she wanted to go and waved at Carl as they set off.

Waving back, he sucked on his smoke and went off in search of someone to hang out with.

Seconds after Carl and Chrissie had gone, Patsy came out from behind the block and sidled up to the door. It should have locked automatically behind Carl, but his rough treatment had caused it to stay open so she was able to walk straight in.

The corridor smelled different from that of her own block, and that unnerved her, so she put her head down and rushed for the stairs. She wasn't even sure where Eddie actually lived but she had a vague recollection that it was on the fourth floor, so that was where she headed.

Eddie was stomping around the flat like a bear with a sore head. He'd woken on another comedown, and felt like his skull was literally caving in. But there was no way he was admitting that coke was the cause – not while Chrissie was determined to make him face up to his so-called addiction by nagging him to death about it.

He didn't know what had been up with her these past few days but she'd been narking at him like a proper bitch. Which had inevitably ended in them having a massive row this morning, during which she'd threatened to leave if he didn't lay off the coke and start paying her more attention. And he'd told her to go for it, sniping that he didn't need or even particularly want her here anyway. And then, just to hammer home the message that she had absolutely no control over him and never would have, he'd phoned Clive and ordered him to pick up two grams and bring it round asap. To which she'd responded by flouncing out.

Too edgy to stay inside now, Eddie decided to take the dog down and let it have a runaround on the grass while he waited for Clive to deliver his medicine. But just as he was about to put the animal on its lead it started growling deep in its throat. Aware that he might be about to be raided or hit when he heard a shuffling sound outside the door, Eddie reached down behind the hall table and slid out the machete he kept there. Then, pressing his eye up against the spyhole, he scanned the corridor.

A lone figure was mooching about in the shadows to the right of his flat's door, but there didn't appear to be any others hiding as far as Eddie could tell. Narrowing his eyes when the figure suddenly approached Chrissie's door and bent down to look through the letter box, he wondered if it might be somebody from the council or DSS checking up on her. Either way, he had to get rid of them before those stupid girls started making noise and raised their suspicions. So he put the machete back and straightened himself up, all set to tell whoever it was that he'd just seen his 'neighbour' going out.

Furious when he opened the door and saw that it was Patsy, he glanced around to make sure that nobody was watching, then darted out and grabbed her.

'Get in here!' he hissed, dragging her towards his own flat.

'I was looking for you,' Patsy yelped, her elbow cracking loudly under the pressure of his grip. 'You didn't come back. You said you would, but you didn't.'

Warning her to shut her mouth, Eddie threw her inside and slammed the door shut. He didn't want this stinking headcase souring his fresh, clean air, but rather that than have her squealing his business out for all his neighbours to hear.

Sure that he was going to beat her, Patsy made a dash for the living room. But Eddie chased her and pinned her up against the wall with his arm across her throat.

'What are you playing at, coming round here in broad daylight?' he demanded, slapping her harshly around the face with his free hand. 'And since when did I say you could go out?'

'I'm *hurting*,' Patsy cried, desperation tipping her over the edge and giving her the guts to answer back. 'You said you'd bring me something.'

'You tried to rip me off,' Eddie reminded her, fury causing spittle to spray out from between his gritted teeth and soak her face. 'So you'd better just fuck off home before I really do kill you, you skanky slag!'

'You said you'd look after me!' she screeched into his face. 'Me *and* the baby! You're his dad, you *owe* him!'

Slapping her again to shut her up because she was getting hysterical, Eddie dragged her back out into the hall. Pausing there, because he realised that he didn't actually know what to do with her, he mulled over his options. He couldn't chuck her out in this state because she would draw far too much attention to herself – and, therefore, to him. But she couldn't still be here when Chrissie got back, because it really would be the last straw if she found another tart in her castle – especially one who was screaming about

Eddie being the father of her bastard child. The only thing he could do was calm Patsy down and send her back to her own place before she did any real damage. So, much as he didn't want to, because it was the last thing she deserved after pulling a stunt like this, he reluctantly told her that he would give her what she needed – on the proviso that she went straight home, and stayed there.

Nodding her agreement, Patsy gasped for breath when he released her at last.

'Sorry for shouting,' she whimpered, following him back into the living room with a pathetic smile of gratitude on her face. 'I just thought you'd forgotten about me. But you hadn't really, had you? You were just punishing me for being bad. But I'm being good now, aren't I? I haven't stolen your drugs or touched your gun. I've been looking after business for you like I said I would, haven't I?'

'You still shouldn't have come,' Eddie muttered, rooting through his jacket pockets. A bag had slipped out of the batch he'd given to Carl the other day and he was sure it should be there somewhere.

'I won't do it again,' Patsy promised, willing to do or say whatever he wanted as long as she got her fix.

Finding the bag at last, Eddie handed it to her. 'Not here,' he said when she scrambled to open it. 'Go home. I'll sort you out properly later.'

'You won't forget, will you?' Patsy asked, gazing up

at him with distrust in her eyes. 'I didn't want to come out but I had to. You know that, don't you?'

'I won't forget,' Eddie assured her, checking that nobody was around before he ushered her out.

She'd just turned from a nuisance into a liability, but Eddie knew that he was partly to blame because he'd been meaning to sort out a new stash house for ages but had been too lazy to get on with it. It just wasn't going to be easy to find somewhere as close, or some*one* he trusted with his shit as much as he'd once trusted Patsy. And it galled him that he would have to keep her sweet until he did find an alternative, but he had no choice. If she felt the need to roam like this again, all it would take would be for her to say the wrong thing to the wrong person and he'd be fucked.

Next door, Tasha had squinted out through the spyhole when she'd heard Eddie showing his visitor out. She couldn't properly see the woman who she'd just heard arguing with him because she moved off too quickly towards the stairs. But she did catch a glimpse of dark bushy hair, which ruled sleek blonde Chrissie out.

Tasha rushed into the living room now, pulled a chair out from under the table and carried it over to the window. Standing on it, she pressed her nose up against the grille and peered down. A couple of minutes later a scrawny-looking girl scurried out of the main door below, followed shortly afterwards by Eddie who, even from this distance, looked shifty as he skulked off in the opposite direction.

Tasha pursed her lips. *Interesting*, she thought. *Very interesting.*

'What are you looking at?' Elena asked, coming in from the bedroom just then.

'Nothing,' Tasha said evasively, stepping down off the chair. 'Just the view.'

'*Really?*' Elena drawled sarcastically, clearly not believing her. 'Because it's so spectacular from here, isn't it?'

Tasha didn't care what Elena thought. This was her secret and she had no intention of sharing it – at least, not with her so-called friends. She didn't know yet quite what she would do with the information she'd just gleaned, but she would use it to her advantage if she got a chance. Maybe as leverage to get Eddie to dump that leech who called herself his girlfriend, because any fool could see that the bitch wasn't right for him. He needed somebody with the same fire inside her as that which burned in him.

A woman like Tasha.

Unlike the others, who were still childishly yearning to go home, Tasha had quickly realised that this situation might actually be more of a blessing than a curse. English men were so stupid – and rich beyond the dreams of any of the menfolk back home. And Eddie could give her everything she'd ever wanted: money, clothes, jewellery, protection – all the luxuries that bitch Chrissie took for granted but hadn't earned.

Tasha had earned it. And she wanted it. She just needed a way to get Eddie to see that she could handle his business better than his so-called girlfriend.

17

Joe left it a week before he went looking for Katya again. He didn't know if she would want to talk to him, considering that she already suspected he was following her around on Eddie's orders, but she had told him her name – after a little persuasion – so he was hoping that she would.

She'd been on Newton Street last time he'd seen her, but there was no sign of her there tonight. And nor was she back on Dale Street, so he was forced to trawl around looking for her. Eventually finding her a few streets away from where he'd started, Joe suddenly felt nervous as he approached her. Gazing out at her face through the wind-screen, he was dismayed to see the instant fear in her eyes. But then, amazingly, she almost smiled.

'Fancy a coffee?' he ventured, rolling his window down.

Katya bit her lip and glanced around before answering. She *had* been scared when she'd recognised the car but the fear had melted away as soon as their eyes met. Her heart was pounding now, and there was a fluttering of excitement in her stomach. She'd thought about him almost constantly over the last week, recalling his lovely soft voice and his beautiful eyes. But she hadn't dared to hope that he might come looking for her again. And now here he was.

'Yes, thank you,' she said shyly.

'Right,' Joe said, sounding as shocked as she herself was that she'd agreed. 'Great. Well, let's go then.' Leaning over, he pushed open the passenger-side door.

He took her to a different café this time, further out of town than the previous one. Again, he settled her at a table in the corner before going to the counter to buy their coffees. And, again, he spoke to her as if she was a lady, which made her feel strange because it had been so long since anybody had treated her so nicely.

'Thanks for coming,' Joe said when he'd settled into the seat opposite hers. 'I didn't think you would.'

'Neither did I,' she admitted. 'But, like you said last time, it's only a coffee.'

'Absolutely,' Joe agreed, unable to stop himself from smiling. 'So how have you been?'

Katya gave a tiny shrug. 'Nothing is ever very different. I work, I sleep, I work again. There's really nothing more I can tell you.'

Amazed that she was being so forthcoming after her previous reticence, Joe said, 'I'm sure there's a lot more to you than that.'

Blushing, Katya shook her head. 'This is all I do and all I am.'

'All you *think* you are,' Joe corrected her. 'But I'm guessing that you haven't always lived like this. Am I wrong?'

'No, but it doesn't make any difference,' Katya said, gazing down into her cup.

'I haven't told anybody,' Joe said. 'About us talking, I mean.'

'Thank you,' Katya murmured.

'I just wanted you to know, because I know you had your doubts – about Eddie, and that,' Joe went on. 'But I meant what I said about him and me not being mates. I just work for him, that's all. And I saw what he was like with you that time, so I would never do or say anything to put you in danger—'

'It's okay,' Katya interrupted. 'I believe you.'

'Good, because it's important that you know you can trust me,' Joe said. Then, holding up his hands when she gave him a mock-weary look, he said, 'Okay, I'll shut up about it.' After drinking some of his coffee he said, 'Do you mind if I ask where you come from? Only I've been trying to place your accent, and I can't.'

The caution returned to Katya's eyes. 'I can't tell you,' she murmured. 'Please don't ask me to.'

'Hey, it's fine,' Joe assured her. 'No pressure. You speak excellent English, by the way.'

'Thank you.' She gave him a small smile. Then, turning the spotlight onto him, she said, 'You were born here, yes?'

'No, Liverpool,' he said. 'Not that anyone can tell, 'cos I lost the accent years back. It was getting a bit rough back home, so my folks moved the family here when I was six. Thought we'd stand a better chance of staying out of trouble.'

'And were they right?'

Smiling at the memory of his parents' naivety, Joe shrugged. 'A city's a city. If you're the kind of person who seeks out trouble, you'll find it anywhere.'

'I think you're right,' Katya said thoughtfully. 'But sometimes you can't avoid it even when you try your very hardest to.'

Joe guessed that she was referring to her own situation. 'Life can be unfair,' he said, 'but we just have to find a way of coping with whatever it throws at us. It helps if we've got good friends to lean on,' he added pointedly. 'A problem shared is a problem halved, and all that.'

Katya repeated the phrase, saying the words slowly as if to digest them fully. 'That is very wise,' she concluded. 'Did you – how you say – *invent* it?'

'No, it's just an old saying,' Joe told her. 'We've got loads of them over here; things people have said that get passed down to the next generation, and the next.'

'Tell me more,' Katya urged.

Catching a glint of something he could only describe as hunger for knowledge in her eyes, Joe reeled off a few more sayings and their meanings, some of which she understood immediately, others that took a little extra translation and working-out before she could get to grips with them. But even Joe was stumped when it came to explaining why a bird in the hand was worth two in the bush.

Katya mulled it over for a few minutes, then said, 'I think maybe it means that it's better to have *some*thing, however small, than to chase that which is out of reach and have nothing.'

'Wow.' Joe gazed at her with admiration. 'So simple, yet so deep.'

Katya dipped her gaze as a blush flared across her cheeks. 'I could be wrong.'

Joe shook his head. 'No, I think you're spot on. And it makes perfect sense put like that. Very *wise*.'

Aware that he was teasing her by using her own word, Katya smiled.

It was the first proper smile she'd given him, and Joe thought she'd never looked more beautiful. She had the most stunning eyes he'd ever seen, large and dark, with long silky black lashes. Her hair was equally black, and, free of the hood, fell in a curtain all the way down her back. He thought she would look amazing if she were able to pamper herself like women were supposed to, but she was like a butterfly whose wings had been coated with dust, and that saddened him.

Conscious of his scrutiny, Katya began to fidget. She found him very attractive and had almost convinced herself that he liked her, too. But the pity she saw in his eyes right now reminded her that he was only being nice because he felt sorry for her.

'Thank you for the coffee,' she said. 'But I think I should probably go back now. Would you take me, please?'

'Of course,' Joe said, his mood dipping at the thought of her returning to work. The more he saw of her, and the more he spoke to her, the more he knew that she shouldn't be selling herself like this. She was too good, too beautiful, too intelligent for any random man to think that he was entitled to abuse her just because he had the cash in his wallet. And that she seemed so resigned to it was tragic. But he couldn't help her if she refused to let him.

Just outside town they passed an all-night pharmacy. Glancing back, Katya bit her lip. She'd been too frightened to stray away from her spot before, terrified of what would happen if Eddie caught her. But she'd been for a coffee with Joe twice now and the sky hadn't fallen in.

'Could you please stop?' she blurted out.

'Yeah, sure,' Joe said, doing as she'd asked. 'Is something wrong?'

Katya shook her head and unbuckled her seat belt. 'No, I just need something from that shop.'

Guessing that she meant the chemist's, because that was the only one that was open on the block, Joe reversed back.

Katya was relieved to find a female pharmacist on duty because she knew that she would never have been able to discuss such an intimate problem with a man. But she was still poised to run if the woman asked for her name or proof of identity.

Fortunately, she was asked for neither, and she came back out a short time later with the medicine and the cream that the woman had prescribed after Katya had confided her symptoms to her. She'd had to dip into her earnings to pay for them, which had worried her because she was sure that Eddie would realise she'd spent some of his money and would beat her. But it would almost be worth it just to have this awful pain taken away.

'Sorted?' Joe asked when she went back to the car.

Nodding, she held the small bag in her lap as he set off, already wondering where she could stash it. She definitely couldn't take it back to the flat, so it would have to be somewhere near her doorway. That way she could take some when she arrived each night, and more before she left in the morning.

Joe turned to her when they stopped and offered her thirty pounds.

'Please,' he urged when she shook her head. 'I don't want you to get into trouble with Eddie.'

'He is never satisfied no matter how much we make,' Katya told him, giving him the clearest glimpse yet into what life was like for her under Eddie's control. 'It will probably be his girlfriend who comes to take it, and my friend Elena always puts the money together when she comes so they don't know who has given what. So, really, I don't want it. You've already done enough.'

'Can we do it again, then?' Joe blurted out. 'The coffee, I mean.'

Katya inhaled deeply. Her head was telling her that she should stop this now before one or both of them got hurt. But her heart was screaming yes, yes, yes.

Her heart won.

Smiling, she said, 'Yes, please.'

18

Carl was freezing when he arrived home at just gone twelve in the afternoon. He'd planned to stay at his mum's the night before but had ended up going to a party at an old mate's place a few doors down and he'd got so wasted that he'd ended up flaking out on the guy's kitchen floor. So by the time he'd woken up this morning his mum had already gone out, locking his jacket in her place – along with his keys and money.

Cursing her for stranding him like that, and Mel for the row which had sent him there in the first place, he'd walked all the way back from Longsight only to get no answer when he knocked on his flat's door.

He shoved the letter-box flap open after several attempts, and yelled, '*MEL!* I know you're in there, you ignorant bitch, so quit arsing about and open the fucking door or I'll kick the fucking thing in!'

Kettler came out of his own door just then, buttoning up his coat. He cleared his throat as Carl stepped back to carry out his threat.

Twisting around, Carl gave him a thunderous look. 'What you gawping at?'

'I was just going to tell you that she went out about half an hour ago,' Kettler informed him. 'And I'm sure the council won't be too pleased if you damage their property,' he added disapprovingly.

'Fuck off,' Carl snarled. 'I pay the rent, I can do what the fuck I want with it.'

Kettler's eyebrows rose. He wanted to point out that Carl most certainly did *not* pay the rent: that it was paid for by the DSS, from the proceeds of the taxes they had taken from honest workers like his own father. But he sensed that the lout was in too volatile a mood for honesty, so he went on his way without another word.

Sucking his teeth as he watched him go, Carl booted the door before marching over to Joe's. Although, now that he knew Mel was out, it was more an act of defiance to piss Kettler off than a serious attempt to get in.

Joe didn't hear the first few knocks because he was sleeping, but he woke up when Carl started yelling through the letter box. And then he pulled the pillow over his head and tried to ignore the noise because he was too knackered to face any of Carl's usual morning exuberance.

Since his breakthrough with Katya last week, he'd been nipping into town almost every night to see her. And their conversations had deepened as her trust for him grew, so now he knew that she was twenty-four, and that she'd wanted to be a teacher but that she'd been too poor to waste time gaining the necessary qualifications because she'd been forced to take whatever jobs were available in order for her family to survive.

Joe also knew now that she and her friends were from tiny poverty-stricken Ukrainian villages with unpronounceable names and that they had all been fooled into coming to England with the promise of well-paid work and a safe place to live.

It was a classic scam and Joe had imagined that everyone the world over must be aware of it by now, considering how many documentaries had been made on the subject. But he hadn't taken into account the fact that people from Katya's background often didn't have access to TV, so they'd had absolutely no idea of what awaited them when they'd set off. And by the time they had arrived it had been too late.

Now that he knew, Joe was more determined than ever to help her. But, brave as she'd been in opening up to him, Katya was still too scared even to contemplate trying to escape from Eddie. When Joe had pressed her to explain how anything could possibly be worse than the way she was being forced to live now she'd clammed up and refused to discuss it any further, so he'd been forced to let it drop.

It had been four a.m. by the time he'd got home this morning, and it had taken him hours to get to sleep, so he didn't appreciate being woken now. Carl was being so insistent that he had no choice but to get up.

'Jeezus, mate, you took your time,' Carl complained, blowing on his hands and rushing in when Joe opened the door. 'It's fucking freezing out there.'

'I was asleep,' Joe told him, yawning his way to the kitchen. 'And it might help if you were wearing a coat instead of a T-shirt.'

'I was, but I left it at my mum's last night,' Carl told him. 'My keys are in the pocket and Mel's out, so I need a lift to Longsight to get it.'

'Wouldn't it be easier to ring Mel and tell her to come back and let you in?' Joe suggested, putting the kettle on.

'I tried, but her mobile was switched off,' Carl told him.

'Everything all right with you two?' Joe asked, guessing that it probably wasn't if Carl had spent the night at his mum's and Mel had gone awol.

'It's her not me,' Carl muttered. 'You know I told you I thought she was seeing someone else behind my back? Well, I came right out and asked her the other day, and she had the cheek to tell me that the bongs have fucked my head up and made me para. Can you believe that?'

'Well, they do say it's a side effect,' Joe said amusedly.

'Mate, the only side effect going on here is the one *she*'s picked up watching them twat-show hosts lecture-tossers about shit they know nowt about,' Carl retorted. 'I mean, when was the last time any of *them* had a good bong? But give 'em a microphone and they're experts all of a sudden. Paranoid, me backside.' He sucked his teeth. 'She won't be such a smart arse when I tell her I've got her lined up to go on *Kyle* to do a lie detector.'

'You haven't?' Joe laughed.

'Have I fuck,' Carl snorted. 'But *she* won't know that. And she'll crap herself when I tell her, 'cos she'll know it'll make her look guilty if she refuses.'

'She'll never go for it,' Joe said, handing Carl's coffee to him.

Sighing, Carl said, 'Yeah, I know. Guess I'll just have to keep following her till I catch her.'

'What do you mean, *keep* following her?' Joe asked. 'I didn't know you had been.'

'Yeah, man,' Carl said, as if it was a perfectly normal thing to do. 'Like last night, she went stomping off saying she was going to her sister's. But I know she can't stand her so I waited five minutes and went after her.'

'And did she go there?'

'Yeah, but only 'cos she probably clocked me. She'll have left as soon as she thought I'd gone.'

'How long did you wait?'

'About half an hour.' Carl shrugged. 'Got too cold so I walked to my mum's. And then my old mate invited me round to his for a party and I got wasted. That's why I need to get my keys asap, 'cos I did a bit of a dribble in my jeans and need to get changed.'

Sighing, Joe said, 'All right. But you'll have to wait till I'm properly awake.'

'Late night?' Carl asked, opening the window and shivering in the cold air as he lit a cigarette. 'Seeing that bird again?'

'No, I just couldn't sleep,' Joe told him.

'Not easy getting used to a strange bed, is it?' Carl gave him a knowing smile. 'Come on, mate, no point lying about it,' he went on. 'I already know you stopped out, 'cos Eddie called round for you, then rang me wanting to know where you were.'

'I forgot to take my phone,' Joe said, wondering if Eddie had somehow found out about him and Katya. 'What did he want?'

'A lift to some tart's place, knowing him,' Carl said. 'Anyhow, what's with you and your bird?' he asked now. 'Don't think I haven't noticed you sneaking out in the middle of the night. So what's with the secrecy? Is she a minger, or something? Or is *she* a *he*?' He raised his eyebrows.

'Don't be daft,' Joe scoffed. 'I just haven't known her long enough to start introducing her to my mates yet. Don't know if it's going anywhere – you know how it is.'

'Fetch her round. I'll soon tell you if she's a goer or not.'

'Cheers, but I think I'll just carry on taking it slow for now.'

Joe headed into the living room when he heard his mobile vibrating on the coffee table and his heart leapt when he saw that it was a withheld number. Hoping that it might be Katya, he was smiling as he answered it. But the smile soon slipped when the caller tartly informed him that this was the third time they had tried to reach him this morning.

'Sorry,' he apologised. 'I had a late night, didn't hear it.' Frowning now when he heard the reason for the call, he said, 'Yeah, sure. I'll be there.'

'Was that her?' Carl asked when he'd hung up.

'No, it was the dole,' Joe told him, checking the phone and seeing that he'd had nine missed calls in all: two from Eddie, three from Carl, the rest from a withheld number. Glancing at his watch now and realising that he didn't have much time, he said, 'Sorry, I'm going to have to give that lift a miss. They've called me in for a meeting.'

'Aw, come on, I was here first,' Carl protested. 'Ring them back and tell them you can't make it.'

'I can't,' Joe insisted. 'You know what they're like. They'll cut me off if I mess them about.'

'Wankers,' Carl sneered. 'You wanna do what I do and tell them you've got mental issues. Amazing how fast they want you out of there when you're rolling round on the floor foaming at the mouth.'

Joe grimaced at the thought of people looking at him the way they must surely look at Carl if he really did that kind of thing.

'No, you're all right, I'll stick to doing it my way,' he said. Then, 'Look, why don't you stop here till Mel gets back? I don't know how long I'll be, but you know where everything is. And you can take a shower if you want.'

'Nah, I need to get my gear and get out there before I lose my customers,' Carl told him. 'But you can lend us a couple of quid for the bus if you're feeling generous. And a jacket,' he added, rubbing at his arms.

'Take the one off the hook behind the door,' Joe said as he headed into the bedroom to get the money.

Carl was already in the hall, tugging the jacket on when he came back out. Handing the money over, Joe said, 'Don't forget my cups when you fetch it back. You've got four of mine now. I'm running out.'

'You and them bleedin' cups,' Carl snorted, pulling the door open and stepping out into the corridor. 'Anyone would think they were made of gold or something.'

'Just bring them,' Joe repeated firmly.

'Yes, *sir*!' Carl said, giving him a salute before marching away down the corridor.

'Tosser!' Joe called after him.

'Takes one to know one,' Carl called back, flipping him the finger before disappearing into the stairwell.

Joe closed the door and traipsed to the bathroom before reluctantly getting dressed for the meeting he'd been summoned to. He was dreading it because he had no answers for the questions he would undoubtedly be asked. Yes, he'd lived here for almost six months now, and no doubt most people would think that was ample time to have made some sort of headway. But he just hoped they would understand that it wasn't that easy.

19

As Joe drove through town a short time later he just missed seeing Chrissie and her mum making their way into the family-planning clinic. It had taken Chrissie a long time to make her mind up, and now that she had she wanted to get it over with as quickly as possible. But she was about to have her whole world dragged out from under her feet.

More than two hours after arriving, during which time she'd been questioned, examined, and then questioned again, she emerged from the nurse's room with her face ashen. Linda had been sitting in the waiting room the whole time. Dropping the magazine she'd been reading, she leapt up from her seat.

'What's happening? Have we got to wait, or come back, or what?'

'Keep your voice down,' Chrissie muttered, pushing her towards the door. 'People are listening.'

'I don't give a toss about them,' Linda retorted loudly. 'I want to know what's happening with *you*.'

'Nothing.' Chrissie trotted down the stairs and yanked

the door open. 'I need a fag,' she said, lurching out onto the pavement.

'Here.' Linda lit two and passed one to her. 'Now tell me what she said. When are they going to do it?'

'They can't,' Chrissie told her, swiping at a tear that was trickling down her cheek. 'I'm too far gone.'

Linda was confused. 'How come? I thought you said you were only twelve weeks.'

'Yeah, well, I was obviously wrong,' Chrissie muttered, pulling a tissue out of her pocket and dabbing at her eyes. 'What am I going to do?' she moaned, looking as forlorn as Linda had ever seen her.

They'd never been particularly huggy-kissy, and Chrissie especially didn't like being touched when she was upset, so Linda settled for patting her on the arm.

'Only one thing you can do, love. You'll have to have it.'

'How can I?' Chrissie wailed. 'Me and Eddie are arguing all the time. How can I bring a baby into that?'

Linda gave her one of her looks. 'You already know what I think. If it's that bad, move out.'

'And bring it up by myself?' Chrissie gasped, horrified by the thought.

'I brought you and your brothers up on my own,' Linda reminded her. 'And it's way easier these days, with all the benefits they chuck at you.'

Sniffling into the tissue, Chrissie shook her head. 'I don't want to bring up my baby like that. I want it to know its dad.'

'Oh, so I wasn't good enough for you, wasn't I?'

'I'm not saying that,' Chrissie mumbled, moving away from the door. The sign was discreet, but they might as well have been done with it and written 'Abortion Clinic' in foot-high letters because everyone knew that was what it was.

'You're going to have to tell Eddie,' Linda said firmly, figuring that there was no point pussyfooting around Chrissie at a time like this. She'd taken this long to decide she wanted rid, and now she knew she'd left it too late she still seemed to think that she had options. But she only had two, as far as Linda was concerned: tell Eddie and hope that he'd be man enough to step up to the mark; or cut her losses and get on with it by herself – like Linda and millions of other women had done before her.

Chrissie tutted and flashed her mum a dirty look. She knew she was right but she wasn't about to tell *her* that. Anyway, it was all very well for her to tell Chrissie to talk to Eddie, but she had no idea how difficult it was to pin him down for *any* kind of conversation, never mind one as important as this. He'd been up and down like a yo-yo recently, moody as hell one minute, jumping about like an excited firecracker the next. He was still doing way too much coke for her liking, smoking too much weed and drinking himself stupid. But he insisted that it wasn't a problem and the more she nagged, the more he did it to spite her.

Linda looked at her daughter's miserable face and decided that it was probably best to back off for now and give her time to get used to the idea that she was going to be a mother. Finishing her cigarette in silence, she turned to stub it out on the wall.

'Let's go home and get a cuppa,' she suggested when she turned back. But Chrissie was already halfway down the street. 'Oi!' she called, rushing after her. 'Where you going? Wait for me.'

'I need to be alone for a bit,' Chrissie said when Linda caught her up.

'So you just thought you'd take off?' Linda said indignantly. 'Stuff me, 'cos it's not like I put my own life on hold to come with you or anything. And not everyone's mum would do that for them, you know. None of them girls back there had *theirs* with them.'

'You know I appreciate you coming,' Chrissie told her. 'But I can't deal with this right now. I need to do some thinking.'

Linda sighed. 'Look, I know this is hard for you, love, but it's just as hard for me. I can't bear to think of you going back to the flat and getting no support. So why don't you come home and let me look after you? It'll be easy, the two of us together. We can get that cot off our Neil and—'

'Mum, stop.' Chrissie cut her off. 'This is my baby – mine and Eddie's. And we'll bring it up together, like we're supposed to.'

Linda struggled with her own emotions as she saw the determination flare in her daughter's eyes. She wanted to be a real, valuable part of her grandchild's life but she knew that Eddie would block her. Just like he'd blocked her and Chrissie from being as close as they had used to be. But Chrissie was a grown woman with a mind of her own, and if this was what she wanted then Linda was just going to have to swallow it.

'Good luck,' she said, conceding defeat. 'You know where I am if you need me.' With that, she turned on her heel and walked back down the road to the bus station.

Chrissie exhaled wearily and set off in the direction of home. But she didn't go straight there: she needed to think about what she wanted to say first, make sure she got it right first time. So she went to a café and wasted a couple of hours there, drinking coffees that she didn't want and could barely stomach. And then, when she knew that she'd overstayed her welcome, she wandered into the park and sat on a bench for a couple of hours more, staring unseeingly at the ducks on the dingy crap-littered lake.

It was almost seven by the time she finally plucked up the courage to go home and she was still no clearer about what she would say.

Eddie was in the bedroom, getting ready to go out. Instantly suspicious when she got a heavy blast of aftershave and saw the dressy clothes, Chrissie asked where he was going.

'Clive's,' Eddie told her, stuffing his shirt into his jeans and admiring himself in the mirror.

'Is that new?' Chrissie asked, trying to make it sound casual.

'Nah, I've had it for ages,' Eddie lied, hoping that he hadn't left the tag hanging out the back. 'Where've you been?'

'To my mum's, like I told you,' Chrissie replied. 'What are you going to Clive's for?'

'A bit of business I need to sort out,' Eddie told her, rubbing some gel between his hands and smoothing it through his hair.

'Is that all?'

Eddie glanced at her in the mirror and caught the suspicion in her eyes. 'What's that supposed to mean?' he demanded.

'Nothing,' she muttered. 'Just wondering why you're getting all dressed up if you're only going to Clive's.'

'It's called being respectful,' Eddie snapped. 'Do you expect me to turn up looking like a tramp when his missus is good enough to make dinner for me?'

'Dinner?' Chrissie said, giving him a tight smile. 'Oh, good, I haven't eaten yet. I'll come with you.'

'You can't,' Eddie informed her, going back to his grooming. 'I just told you me and Clive will be talking business.'

'Don't worry, I won't get in your way,' Chrissie came back smoothly. 'I'm sure me and what's-her-name will be able to amuse ourselves while you're talking. Women can always find things to chat about. Hair, nails, handbags, shoes, men . . . *other women.*'

She'd said that last bit so meaningfully, as if she actually knew something. And she'd stared at Eddie as she said it, hoping that he would betray himself in some small way. But there wasn't so much as a flicker of guilt.

'You wouldn't get on,' he said as he sat down on the bed to pull on his trainers.

'Oh, and why's that?' Chrissie demanded.

'Because you're white,' Eddie told her bluntly.

'So are *you*,' she gasped.

'That's different.'

'*How?*'

'It just is. Anyway, some of the other guys will be there and we're going for a drink after we've finished – no birds allowed.'

'Not even Clive's wife?' Chrissie asked jealously. 'After she's gone to all that trouble to make your dinner?'

'Put a sock in it,' Eddie said irritably. 'You ain't coming – end of.'

'So it's all right for *you* to go and eat some racist woman's food but I'm not good enough?'

'First off, Letty's no racist,' Eddie informed her. 'She just ain't fond of trashy white birds, 'cos she's got class.'

'You're calling me trashy?' Chrissie hissed.

'No, course not,' Eddie said wearily. 'But that's how *she*'d see you, 'cos you wear short skirts and low tops and that. You know what women are like about each other. I shouldn't have to tell you.'

Flaming with indignation, Chrissie marched into the living room and sat on the couch with her arms tightly crossed and her foot jiggling wildly. There was no way he was getting dressed up just because Clive's wife was cooking for him. There was more to it than that. But there was no point calling Eddie a liar, because he'd only lie again to cover himself. And then he'd get angry and use it as an excuse to stay out all night – again.

He was getting good at that lately: starting arguments, and then twisting it around so it looked like *she* was to blame. Clive's couch must have a permanent Eddie-shaped hollow in it by now, the number of times he'd claimed to have slept on it.

Eddie walked in a few minutes later and pulled his jacket on. Forcing herself not to sound as if she was nagging, because she needed to keep the lines of communication open, Chrissie asked what time he thought he would be back.

'Don't know,' he answered offhandedly, standing in front of the living-room mirror and running his hands through his hair again to make sure it was in place.

'Can you try and give me some kind of idea?' Chrissie persisted, her nostrils twitching as the tears began to sting the backs of her eyes. He looked so handsome, and it killed her to think that he was doing it for some other woman.

'What do you keep hassling me for?' Eddie snapped, snatching his cigarettes and lighter off the table.

'I'm not,' she protested. 'I just need to talk to you.'

Sighing, as if the thought of talking to her was a massive ball-ache, Eddie said, 'What now?'

'It'll keep till you get back,' Chrissie said quietly.

Closing her eyes when he'd gone, she dug her nails into her thigh and pinched it hard to prevent the tears from falling. She wouldn't fall apart; she was stronger than that. She would just wait until he came home, then sit him down and tell him that he was going to be a daddy. That – maybe, if she was really lucky – he was going to have a son. A little boy who would look just like him. He'd have to be over the moon about that, because men always wanted boys. And once he knew he'd be sure to stop messing around and make an effort to get things back on track for the sake of his new family.

The dog wandered in from the kitchen and licked Chrissie's ankle. Opening her eyes, she sighed and patted the couch beside her. Then, reaching for the remote as the animal snuggled up next to her, she switched on the TV and settled down to watch *EastEnders*.

Twenty minutes later, just as an interesting fight was kicking off, Chrissie heard raised voices coming through the wall from the flat next door. Leaning her head back, she yelled at them to shut up but they were making too much noise to hear her. Annoyed, she pushed the dog aside and got up, intending to bang on the wall.

But as she passed the window a blue light flickered across her face, and when she glanced out she saw a police van driving through the car park below.

Forgetting the girls and their argument for the moment, she pressed her face up against the glass. The van went all the way down to the block at the far end and, seconds later, a squad car followed with its sirens blaring. When six uniformed officers got out of the vehicles a man rushed towards them and started pointing animatedly back to where the land dipped into a boggy field beyond the perimeter fence.

Chrissie craned her neck to watch as two of the officers climbed through a gap in the fence and disappeared from view. When one of them reappeared seconds later and started waving his arms and shouting to his colleagues she pushed the window open in the hope of hearing what he was saying. She was too far away to catch any actual words, but it was clear from the urgency of his tone that something serious was going on.

More of her neighbours had begun to lean out of their windows by now, and yet more were gathering in little groups outside the main doors of their blocks, their cigarettes glowing like fireflies in the darkness. As a couple of officers began to tape off a wide area around the gap, one of the women in the group that was closest wandered over to talk to one of them. Rushing back to her friends a few minutes later, she excitedly relayed what she'd heard, and word soon began to spread as people ran around passing the news on and shouting up to those above.

Chrissie leaned further out of the window and attracted the attention of a man leaning out a few windows down. 'What's happening?' she asked.

'They've found a body in the brook,' he told her.

'No way!' she gasped. 'Who is it?'

'No one knows yet,' he said. 'They're calling forensics in, so no doubt they'll be doing house-to-house inquiries in a bit. They'd best hurry up if they want to talk to me, though, 'cos I'm off out.'

A loud thud sounded on the wall from the girls' side. Jumping, Chrissie pulled her head back in and closed the window. This wasn't good. The girls were making way too much noise, and if the police *did* start calling round they'd be bound to hear them. And then they'd be bound to wonder why they weren't answering the door. No, it wasn't good at all. She had to call Eddie.

Chrissie ran over to the table and snatched up her phone, but Eddie's went straight to answerphone. Cursing him under her breath, she ran into the kitchen as another thud shook the wall. She snatched the keys off the hook. Telling the dog to stay when it tried to follow her, she took a cautious peek into the corridor before going next door.

20

As usual, it was Tasha and Elena who had been making all the noise. And, as usual, Hanna had fled to her bed at the first sign of conflict, leaving Katya to try and keep the peace.

And she *had* tried. But to no avail, because the tension which had been simmering between the two for months had finally erupted into a full-blown fight. And it was over an egg, of all things; one stupid little egg that Elena had decided to eat, to the annoyance of Tasha who had argued that Elena should have asked if anybody else wanted it first.

'You're just pissed off because *you* wanted it and I got to it first,' Elena had sneered. 'And you're so greedy and selfish that you actually think you had more right to it than me.'

'You had one yesterday,' Tasha had shot back.

'So did *you*,' Elena had reminded her.

'Yes, but I did more punters than you last night,' Tasha had pointed out. 'So I *earned* it.'

Elena had laughed in Tasha's face at this, so Tasha

had slapped her and Elena had responded by slapping her back. And then they had both leapt on each other, so now their faces were covered in scratches and red marks from where each other's punches had landed, and the faded rug on the floor had a layer of hair coating it.

Katya was standing over them when Chrissie burst through the living-room door, shouting at them to stop as they rolled around on the floor biting each other's arms.

'*OI!*' Chrissie yelled. 'What the hell do you think you're playing at?'

Shocked, Elena scrambled to her feet and gazed past Chrissie in dread of seeing Eddie behind her.

But Tasha was still in a fighting mood, so she leapt up and glared at Chrissie with naked contempt in her eyes.

'Have you got any idea how much trouble you'd be in if it'd been Eddie who'd heard you and not me?' Chrissie hissed.

'We're sorry,' Katya apologised. 'It won't happen again.'

Chrissie flicked a cool glance at her but didn't say anything. This one wasn't like the others, with their aggressive body language and venom-filled eyes. She was much more polite, and a lot prettier with her long glossy black hair and massive brown eyes. But that just made Chrissie resent her all the more, because she suspected that *she* would be the one Eddie would go for if he had to choose.

Not that he ever would, because he'd always said that he would rather die than go with a prostitute.

'He's on his way back,' Chrissie lied now. 'So you'd best keep it zipped or there'll be hell to pay. And you'd better quit looking at me like that, you cheeky bitch,' she added, glaring back at Tasha.

'Or you'll do what?' Tasha challenged her, the adrenalin that was still coursing through her body making it impossible to keep her mouth shut.

'Ex*cuse* me?' Chrissie snapped, unable to believe that the girl was daring to talk to her like this.

'You heard,' Tasha snapped right back. 'You think you're such a fancy lady, don't you? Coming in here and talking down to us as if we're the dog shit you've trodden in.'

'Tasha, stop,' Katya hissed, clutching at her arm.

But Tasha shoved her roughly away. This had been a long time coming and she had no intention of stopping until she'd had her say.

'What makes you think you're so much better than us?' she demanded, her eyes flashing with spite as she approached Chrissie. 'Coming in here and throwing the rubbish you call food at us, and expecting us to be *grateful*. Snatching our money from our hands as if we owe it to you, when we owe you *nothing*.'

'No, you owe it to my *boyfriend*,' Chrissie reminded her sharply. 'Which makes it just as much mine as his.'

'*Boyfriend?*' Tasha repeated scathingly. 'He doesn't care about you.'

'I'd be careful what I was saying if I was you,' Chrissie warned her. 'He's on his way back, don't forget.'

'Liar!' Tasha said defiantly. 'Do you think we can't hear you through the wall, you stupid bitch? Just as you can hear us, we hear every word you say to each other. So we know that he's gone out, and that he wouldn't tell you when he was coming back. *That*'s how much he thinks of you!'

Chrissie's face was scarlet, she felt sick, and her heart was pounding in her chest. 'You'd best shut your mouth,' she warned.

'Or what?' Tasha repeated. 'Come on, then. Don't just threaten me. If you want to do it, *do* it!'

Elena had been watching all of this in a state of absolute disbelief. Much as they had all dreamed of speaking their minds to their captors, none of them would ever have dared to actually do it.

'Enough, Tasha,' she said firmly.

'Shut up, you coward,' Tasha sneered, her gaze still riveted to Chrissie's face. 'Why don't you ask your so-called boyfriend about the woman he was screwing in your bed while you were out last week?' she said.

'*Tasha!*' Elena barked. 'I said *enough!*' Then, reverting to their own language, she scolded her for going too far, reminding her that they weren't the only ones who would suffer for it.

'I don't care,' Tasha retorted coldly. 'She makes me sick, and she needs to know that she is not so special.'

'Stop talking like that just because you know I can't understand you,' Chrissie ordered.

'Why?' Tasha rounded on her again. 'Are we being rude? Does it make you feel uncomfortable to know that we can say whatever we like about you? That we can call you names, and tell each other how much we hate you?'

'I don't give a toss what you think of me,' Chrissie told her angrily. 'I just want to hear about this woman you supposedly saw with my Eddie. Which would be a hell of an achievement, considering you're locked in here and can't see *any*thing, don't you think?'

'You are so stupid,' Tasha snorted. 'I've just told you we can *hear* everything.'

'And precisely what *did* you hear?' Chrissie demanded, her instincts telling her that the bitch might actually be telling the truth.

'Tasha, *please*,' Katya implored. They had all heard Eddie arguing with a woman last week but none of them had paid any attention because they were so used to hearing him and Chrissie bickering. But Tasha had listened through the wall, and now they knew what she had heard – and what the fallout from telling Chrissie was likely to be.

Ignoring Katya, Tasha gave Chrissie a strange smile. 'You'd really like to know? Okay, I'll tell you. She was angry with him for not taking care of her and their baby, like he'd promised he would.'

'Now I *know* you're lying,' Chrissie said triumphantly. 'He hasn't got any kids.'

'Is that what he told you?' Tasha smirked. 'And, like a fool, you believed him? It seems that *we* know more about your man than you do.'

'You know nothing,' Chrissie snarled, touching her stomach reflexively.

Tasha saw the gesture and narrowed her eyes. 'Ah, you thought that *you* were the first,' she ventured. 'You thought that *your* baby would be his first child. And I bet you even thought it would make him love you!'

She was hitting the nails so firmly on the head that Chrissie's legs began to wobble and she thought she might actually faint.

'You're even more stupid than I thought you were,' Tasha went on. 'His other woman has his child, and she looks after his money, his drugs, and his gun. But you still think he's *your* boyfriend?'

'You're a liar,' Chrissie hissed. But she knew even as she said it that the only liar was Eddie, because the girl couldn't possibly know that he stashed all those things elsewhere unless she had really heard what she'd claimed to have heard.

'And you're an idiot,' Tasha retorted gleefully. 'Is it any wonder he'd rather have a junkie looking after his business than a useless tramp like you? Or should that be *trashy* tramp?' she added pointedly, letting Chrissie know that she'd even heard that. 'I wouldn't worry too much, though,' she went on. 'It didn't sound as if he thinks any more highly of her than he does of you, so it shouldn't be too long before he turns his back on her. And when he does, *I* will be there to step into the shoes of *both* of you.'

Elena and Katya exchanged stupefied glances. 'She's gone crazy,' Elena murmured. 'It's the only explanation.'

'Why am I crazy?' Tasha demanded. 'We all know I'm his favourite. He could have any of you any time he wants, but he always chooses me.'

'What are you talking about?' Chrissie asked, her voice as weak now as her legs already felt.

'What do you *think* I'm talking about?' Tasha sneered. '*Sex*, of course.'

'You're lying,' Chrissie mumbled. But one glance at the other girls' faces told her that she wasn't. Her mouth dried up. Licking her lips, she looked at Katya. 'How . . . how long?'

'From the start,' Katya admitted guiltily, feeling sorry for her because she obviously hadn't known any of this.

'All of you?' Chrissie asked. She didn't want to hear the answer, but she had to know the truth.

Blushing, Katya nodded and lowered her head in shame.

'Get out,' Chrissie said, finding it hard to breathe now. 'All of you,' she insisted, gritting her teeth and looking around at them. 'Get out of my flat – *NOW!*'

'Suits me,' Tasha said, tossing her hair back and heading for the door.

'Oh no you don't!' Elena yelled, rushing after her and dragging her back. 'None of us is going anywhere!'

'Get your fucking hands off me!' Tasha bellowed, struggling to get free. 'I'm going to find Eddie!'

Katya couldn't take any more. 'No, you're not!' she screamed. 'You might have stopped caring about *your* family, but we won't let you get ours killed. We're all staying until our debts are repaid and we can go home.'

'That will never happen,' Tasha reminded her forcefully. 'And I don't want to go home, for your information. I'm staying here to make my fortune.'

Katya turned to Chrissie and threw herself on her mercy. 'Please just leave and lock us in so she can't get out,' she pleaded, clutching at the other woman's hands in desperation. '*Please* – my baby will be murdered if Eddie tells the man that we have disobeyed him. I'm *begging* you.'

'What are you talking about?' Chrissie asked, snatching her hands away. '*What* man?'

'The policeman,' Katya sobbed. 'In my village. He advertised for girls to clean his house, but too many of us applied so he told us that his cousin owned a restaurant in England and that he would pay for us to go and work there. He promised that we would earn good money so that we could repay him and send something home to take care of our families.'

Chrissie gave her a disbelieving look. 'Why would anyone, never mind a *policeman*, pay for four of you to go and work in another country?'

'He said he wanted to help us,' Katya told her. 'And we believed him.'

'No, you're making it up,' Chrissie said. '*Eddie* paid for you to come over. That's why you're working for him – to pay *him* back. You wanted to come because you knew you'd have an easier life. You asked for this.'

'Katya is telling the truth,' Hanna said quietly, shocking them all because none of them had seen her slink into the room. 'Eddie is the third man who has owned us since we came here, and they have all warned us that they would tell the policeman if we disobeyed and then he would have our families killed to punish us.'

'And if they all know the same man they must be telling the truth,' Elena added.

Chrissie couldn't take this in. Their story was completely different from that which Eddie had told her and she didn't know which one to believe. All she did know was that Eddie had spent his entire life in this area, never straying any further than he absolutely had to, because he'd made a career out of being the self-appointed king of Ardwick. So if he had the kind of international contacts that these girls seemed to think he had, he'd have made damn sure everyone knew about it because that was what he was like – the big I Am.

'I've had enough of this,' Tasha declared. 'I need to talk to Eddie.'

'Shut your mouth!' Chrissie hissed, giving her daggers. 'You're not going anywhere near him.'

'Bitch, don't tell me to shut up!' Tasha yelled, shoving her roughly.

Chrissie's arms flailed as she struggled to stay on her feet but her heel caught in a frayed bit of rug and she went flying, smashing her back against the edge of the table.

'Look what you've done *now*,' Katya cried, giving Tasha an accusing look when Chrissie slithered to the floor with a look of agony on her face.

'I don't care,' Tasha snarled, scooping up the keys which had fallen out of Chrissie's pocket. 'You can all stay if you want to, but I'm going to find Eddie. And when I do, things are going to change around here. *I'll* be the one living like a queen.'

'Stop her!' Katya cried as Tasha marched towards the door.

'No, let her go,' Chrissie gasped. 'Let her find out the hard way that Eddie's not the big shot she thinks he is. He's got nowhere near as much money as he makes out, because he gambles most of it away and sticks the rest up his nose.'

'You're lying,' Tasha said, hesitating in the doorway. 'Of course he has money.'

'Not enough to keep a greedy cow like *you* happy,' Chrissie informed her, gritting her teeth as a painful cramp gripped her stomach. 'But if you really think he'd finish with me for you, then you go for it. Just don't forget that I'm the one who's carrying his baby. And when he hears about it he won't look twice at you.'

'He looked at *you* when he already had a child,' Tasha reminded her snidely.

'Just get out,' Chrissie groaned. 'All of you,' she added, rocking herself to ease the pain. 'I mean it. Go now while you've got a chance. Don't worry about Eddie. Whatever he told you, I guarantee it was a lie to scare you into doing as you were told. He doesn't know anyone outside *Manchester*, never mind in another country. He's full of shit.'

'But how could all of the men have said the same thing if it wasn't true?' Hanna reminded her.

'Oh, come on, you can't be that stupid,' Chrissie snapped. 'If they were selling you to each other, they would have told each other exactly what to say to keep you in line. It's obvious.'

'You're right,' Tasha said thoughtfully. 'It is obvious. But *they* probably don't believe it, because they *are* that stupid,' she added, flashing the other girls a scathing look. 'You've got your wish,' she told Chrissie now. 'I'm going, and I've changed my mind about taking your man so you can keep him. There are plenty more fools out there with the money to give me what I deserve.'

'Oh, you'll get what you deserve, all right,' Chrissie muttered as Tasha unlocked the door and stalked out. Turning back to Katya now, she said, 'The rest of you should go with her.'

'I can't risk it,' Katya said, kneeling beside her and

rubbing at her back. 'Please understand that I am not being disrespectful when I say this, but you obviously don't know everything that Eddie is involved in and I can't put my child or my family in danger. I just pray that you will be kind enough to tell him that we didn't have anything to do with this when he gets back.'

'I know more than you think about Eddie,' Chrissie snapped, shrugging off Katya's hand. 'And I'm telling you, he does *not* know this policeman of yours. And, in case you don't know, this is *my* flat, not Eddie's, and I want you out. *Now*, or I'll call the police and get them to take you. And they'd be here in two minutes, because there's loads of them outside right now.'

Elena rushed to the window and squinted out through the grille. Seeing the activity going on down below, spookily highlighted by the faint blue light that was still revolving on the top of the van at the far end of the car park, she said, 'She's right.'

'What are we going to do?' Hanna squeaked, biting nervously on her knuckles.

'Go,' Chrissie said again. 'Before Eddie gets back and stops you. He's the only one who can hurt you, not some man thousands of miles away.'

'We can't just go and leave you like this,' Katya said concernedly. 'You're hurt. The baby . . .'

'None of your business,' Chrissie said assertively, pushing Katya aside and using the edge of the table to haul herself up. 'See . . . I'm absolutely fine, so you can stop worrying about me. And don't test me, because I *will* call the police if you don't go right now.'

'Come on.' Elena jerked her head at the others. 'We've got to do as she says. We have no choice.'

'*Where?*' Hanna wailed. 'We don't have anywhere to go.'

'We'll figure something out,' Elena said, pushing her out of the door. 'Katya, come.'

Reluctantly, Katya turned and followed her friends out.

They had walked out of that flat and down those stairs thousands of times, but it was different now and they were terrified of drawing attention to themselves. Fortunately, everybody was far too interested in the police to be bothered with them, and they were able to get out of the block and off the estate without anybody so much as glancing at them. But just as they had made it out onto the main road, Katya suddenly stopped walking.

'What are you doing?' Elena demanded. 'We've got to keep moving.'

'I have to go back,' Katya murmured. 'She didn't look right. I think she was in real pain.'

'Good, she deserves it,' Elena said bluntly. 'That's the one thing I agree with Tasha about. She's never been nice to us, so why should we be nice to her?'

'But that was before she knew the truth,' Katya reminded her. 'She's only known the lies that Eddie had told her. And he lied to us, too, don't forget – telling us that he would set us free when we had repaid him. But Tasha was right about that as well, because it was never going to happen.'

'Maybe not,' Elena conceded. 'But we still shouldn't be standing here like this. What if Eddie comes along and sees us? Or the police?'

'You go and find somewhere safe to hide,' Katya said decisively. 'I'll find you when I've checked that she's all right.'

'How will you find us if we're hiding?' Elena pointed out exasperatedly. 'Come on, Katya, this is ridiculous. You don't owe her anything, and you're putting us all at risk if you go back.'

'I have to,' Katya insisted, already walking backwards. 'And I will find you. I promise.'

Elena flapped her hands in despair when Katya turned and fled back the way they had come. But there was nothing she could do to stop her, and she certainly wasn't going to follow her. So, pushing Hanna ahead of her, she put her head down and continued on up the road.

Chrissie had lied when she'd said that she was fine. The cramping pains were getting steadily worse and she'd already thrown up twice. All she wanted to do was go home and lie down, but Tasha had taken the keys so she couldn't get into the flat. She just thanked God that Tasha hadn't locked her and the other girls in here, because that would have been truly awful.

Feeling dizzy now, she clutched at the door frame and pulled her phone out of her pocket. Eddie's was still on answerphone, so she was forced to leave him a message.

'Eddie, you've got to come back,' she gasped. 'As soon as you get this. It's urgent. They – they've gone, and I don't feel too good.'

She slid the phone shut when she'd finished. Then, glancing around hopefully when she heard somebody coming out of the stairwell, she groaned when she saw that it was Katya.

'I knew something was wrong,' Katya said, rushing to her. 'Come back inside and sit down. I'll get you some water.'

'I don't want any flaming water,' Chrissie protested. 'I just want you to get the hell out of my life.'

'Oh, no,' Katya murmured, horrified to see blood spots appearing on the floor around Chrissie's feet. 'I think you're bleeding.'

'*No!*' Chrissie gasped, gazing down in disbelief. 'I can't be.'

'You need to go to hospital,' Katya told her. 'Let me call an ambulance. Please.'

Chrissie wanted to refuse but this was too important. She'd gone to that clinic this morning to have this baby removed, but now that it was under threat she suddenly knew that she didn't want to lose it.

'Okay,' she said, allowing Katya to lead her back in

and sit her down. 'Here.' She passed the mobile to her. 'Call them, then go. Promise me.'

'I promise,' Katya agreed.

She made the call and told the operator what was happening but said, 'I'm sorry, I don't know,' when she was asked for the patient's name. 'I was just passing and saw her.'

'Go now,' Chrissie urged when the call was done. Then, clutching at her hand, she said, 'And thank you.'

Touched, Katya said, 'I hope everything works out okay for you and the baby.'

She turned to leave then, aware that she had to be gone before the ambulance arrived or the paramedics would undoubtedly ask awkward questions. But before she'd taken a step out of the door she heard a crash, and ran back to find Chrissie unconscious on the floor.

She was still breathing, so Katya covered her with a coat to keep her warm. Then, retrieving Joe's number from the hole she'd made in her mattress, she took Chrissie's phone and slipped out of the flat.

A police officer was standing right outside the main door when Katya reached the ground floor. Stopping in her tracks, she thought about going back up the stairs but knew that she couldn't when she heard the sound of footsteps coming down. Glancing around, she saw that the door to the maintenance room at the far side of the stairwell was slightly ajar. Dashing in there, she pressed herself up against the wall.

The ambulance arrived a few minutes later and Katya heard the policeman talking to the paramedics as they entered the block and headed towards the stairs.

'Any idea whose baby it is?' she heard one of the paramedics ask.

'Not yet, but it shouldn't take too long to find out,' the policeman replied. 'So, what did you say you were attending? A miscarriage?'

'Sounds like it,' the paramedic said, adding grimly, 'Be a bit of a coincidence if she does lose it. Two babies in one night in the same place.'

'Ours didn't die tonight,' the policeman told her. 'It's been there for at least a week, from what we can gather so far. But the autopsy will . . .'

Unable to hear the rest of the sentence as the policeman and paramedics went up the stairs, Katya allowed herself to breathe again. She knew that she should get out of there but her legs were shaking too much.

The phone suddenly started playing music in her hand. Almost dropping it in fright, Katya glanced at the screen and saw that it was a message from 'Mum'. She felt guilty for having taken it now, not that Chrissie would have been able to reply to the message. Her mother should know what was happening so that she could go to her, but Katya certainly couldn't tell her.

She slipped the phone into her pocket and eased the maintenance-room door open. She peeped out, relieved to see that the corridor was empty. But, just as

she was about to make her move, three more police officers suddenly walked in so she was forced to retreat.

The officers started knocking on doors and Katya heard
them speaking to the tenants about the body they had
discovered. What seemed like an eternity later, they finished
with the ground-floor tenants and made their way up to
the next floor. But almost as soon as the police had gone
the ambulance crew came back down and Katya heard
one of them speaking into her radio, saying that they were
on their way in with their patient and to have a crash team
ready.

'What's happened?' a man's voice asked just then.

'Are you a relative?' one of the paramedics asked.

'No, a mate,' the man said. 'Is she okay? Where's
Eddie?'

'Is that the dad?'

'No, he's her fella, not her dad. Wasn't he in? Do you
think I should call him?'

'If you could,' the paramedic said gratefully. 'We're
taking her to St Mary's, and it'd be good if he could get
there sooner rather than later.'

They left then, and Katya heard the door clang
shut behind them. But the man hadn't gone, and she
heard him muttering, 'Come on, man, answer your
phone, for fuck's sake.' Then, tutting, he said, 'Eddie,
it's Carl. I've just seen your missus being carted off in
an ambulance. They're taking her to St Mary's, and you
need to get over there asap. Don't know what's wrong,

but she was proper out of it, man. Let me know if you need me.'

Katya closed her eyes in despair when she heard a door opening and a woman asking the man if he knew who had been in the ambulance.

'Eddie's missus,' he told her. 'He's not at home, so I've just left him a message letting him know.'

'What's wrong with her?'

'No idea, 'cos they won't tell you if you're not related. But it didn't look good. If you ask me, I reckon she could have taken an overdose.'

'No way!' the woman gasped. 'Why?'

'Well, they haven't been right for a while, have they?' the man said knowingly. 'Anyhow, what's with all the bizzies out there?'

'They've found a dead baby in the brook,' the woman told him. 'The police have just been round asking if I know anyone round here with a baby that I haven't seen for a while.'

'What, so they think it's a local?'

'Seems like it,' the woman said. 'Unless this is just what they do to start with: assume it's close, then widen the search as they need to.' Lowering her voice now, she said, 'Have you got anything?'

'Enough for a spliff,' the man said. 'Don't suppose you've seen anything of Mel?'

'No, why? Has she gone missing?'

'Yeah, and I can't get in 'cos I left my keys at my

mum's last night. She went out this morning and I've been over there all day waiting for her to come home. Had to give up in the end and walk back.'

'Poor you,' the woman chuckled. 'Fancy a brew?'

'God, yeah,' the man groaned. 'You're an angel.'

'Come on, then. You roll, I'll brew.'

'Tell you what, you put the kettle on,' the man said. 'I'll just go and check they shut Eddie's door properly. Can't risk leaving it if the coppers are about to go up there. Won't be a minute.'

Katya heard the stairwell door open and shut as the man ran up to the fourth floor, and the woman's footsteps as she went back into her flat. But she still couldn't leave the maintenance room because the policemen were still around, both in the block and out there.

Biting her lip, Katya ran her fingertips over the screen of the phone in her pocket. Then, deciding that it was her only hope, she tapped in Joe's number.

21

Joe was in a pub when the call came, having a laugh with a couple of his old mates and catching up on all the gossip about who'd been doing what since he'd last seen them.

His meeting earlier that afternoon hadn't been half as daunting as he'd thought it would be. As he'd expected, he *had* been asked some awkward questions but his answers had obviously been satisfactory. So, with the heat off for the time being, he'd decided to capitalise on the fact that he'd been called back to his old stomping ground by spending the rest of the afternoon mooching around the old haunts before meeting up with the lads.

When the phone rang Joe didn't hear it immediately because he was listening to a story about another old mate who had sold everything he owned and emigrated to the States, only to get stopped by Customs and sent straight back. Hearing the phone at last, he was laughing as he answered it. But he stopped abruptly when he realised who it was. Concerned when he heard the panic in her voice, he excused himself and went outside to find out what was going on.

'Where are you?' he asked when she'd gabbled out a condensed version of the story. 'Can you get out of there?'

'No, the police are everywhere,' Katya told him, crying now because she was just so relieved to hear his calm voice. 'And people keep coming in and out.'

Mulling it over, Joe knew that it was going to take at least an hour for him to get back. But it wasn't safe for Katya to stay where she was right now, because the police would no doubt do a search of all the public areas in and around the flats before too long. She obviously couldn't get into his flat, and there was nobody else that she could go to for refuge until he got there because nobody knew her. But there was one place . . .

'Look, you're going to have to get yourself together and do exactly what I tell you,' he said now. 'Go back up to the fourth floor—'

'No!' Katya gasped. 'I can't.'

'You *have* to,' Joe insisted. 'You'll be safe, I promise you. Do you trust me?'

'Yes,' Katya murmured.

'Then do as I say,' Joe told her gently. 'Go back up, but don't go to your flat. Go to the one across the landing, the one with the big plant-pot outside. Have you seen it?'

'I think so.'

'Right, well, there should be a key in the soil,' Joe told her, praying that Cheryl hadn't moved it. 'Let yourself in and stay there till I get back. I'll knock three times to let you know it's me. In fact, no, I'll ring you back on this number and tell you when I'm outside. Okay?'

'But won't somebody be in there?' Katya asked worriedly.

'No, the old woman who lives there is in hospital,' Joe assured her. 'A friend of mine feeds her cat, but she won't be going in until tomorrow so there's no danger of anyone finding you. Just stay quiet and sit tight till I get there. I'll be as fast as I can. But go now, before someone sees you.'

'Okay,' Katya agreed, trusting that he had to know what he was doing.

Going back to his mates, Joe made his excuses and left, promising that he would hook up with them again soon.

But he didn't realise that while he'd been busy saying his goodbyes, a lad in another group had been watching him. And was still trying to remember where he'd seen his face before.

Eddie had only noticed the missed calls and voicemail on his phone when he had gone to make a call. It was nine o'clock by then and he and Clive had just picked up a couple of birds. They were on their way to a club now, and from there they would go to the casino before eventually heading back to Clive's place. Letty had gone to Jamaica for a couple of weeks to look after her sick mum, so they were planning on having one of their while-the-cat's-away parties.

That was why Eddie had been about to make a call, to arrange for his coke man to drop off another couple of grams when they got back to Clive's. But he made the mistake of listening to his messages first, and what he heard blew their plans apart.

Carl's message alone wouldn't have done it but Chrissie's did. Not because he was concerned about her but because of what she'd said about *them* being gone. The only *them* that he could think she would be referring to were his girls. And he doubted she'd meant gone as in gone to work because it was way too early. But if Chrissie had been carted off to hospital, looking as bad as Carl had reckoned, he could only assume that something must have happened and they had escaped.

'Stop the car,' he ordered.

'Why, what's up?' Clive asked, frowning.

'Don't ask questions, just do as you're told,' Eddie barked.

'Yo, don't be dissing me like that,' Clive hissed, flicking his gaze towards the girls on the back seat.

'Fuck them,' Eddie said. 'This is important.'

Picking up on his tone, Clive slammed the brakes on.

'Out,' Eddie ordered, jerking his thumb at the girls.

'What, here?' one of them protested. 'We're not even in proper town yet.'

'And I haven't brought any money out,' the other one chipped in. 'So how am I supposed to get home?'

Eddie snapped his head around. 'Do I look like I give a flying fuck?' he roared. 'Get the fuck out!'

'Fuck you,' one of the girls hissed, sliding towards the door with a look of disgust on her painted face. 'I knew you were a tosser as soon as I saw you.'

Squealing with fright when Eddie tore his seat belt off and made to open his own door, the girls were out and running in a flash.

Eddie sucked his teeth and told Clive to get moving.

'Gonna tell me what's going on?' Clive asked, wishing Eddie had been gentler with the girls. He'd quite fancied his and had been looking forward to spending the night with her.

'Chrissie's in hospital,' Eddie told him.

'Aw, sorry, man,' Clive murmured, guessing from his agitation that Eddie must be really worried about her. 'Which hospital? Do you want me to take you straight there?'

'Do I fuck,' Eddie said sharply. 'I'm more concerned about the tarts right now. Not sure what's going on, but it sounds like they might have done one, so I need to get back to find them.'

'Shit,' Clive muttered, putting his foot down a little harder. 'That's not good, man.'

'No, it isn't,' Eddie agreed, staring out at the street in case any of the whores were walking around.

'So what time did you get the call?' Clive asked.

'How the fuck do I know?' Eddie snapped. 'What difference does it make?'

'Because then you'd know how long they might have been gone,' Clive told him reasonably. 'And then you'd have more of an idea how far they could have got.'

Eddie exhaled loudly and pulled his phone back out of his pocket. 'I see your point,' he conceded, checking the times of both Chrissie's and Carl's messages. They were twenty minutes apart, the first at eight-fifteen. And it was nine-twenty now. 'It's been an hour.'

'That's not too bad,' Clive said, turning along the approach to the Grange. Slamming his brakes on when he noticed all the people milling about, he said, 'What the fuck's going on here?'

'Reverse out,' Eddie ordered when he spotted the police. '*Now*, man!'

Clive did as he was told without argument. Pulling over around the corner, he waited while Eddie rang Carl to find out what was happening.

'Panic over,' Eddie said when he'd finished. 'Pigs are doing house-to-house because someone's found a dead baby. But they've already done my block so we're safe.'

'That's good,' Clive mused. 'An hour's plenty of time. So if the pigs aren't there for you, chances are the girls haven't even thought of grassing you up.'

'Yeah, but the longer they're gone, the more risk there

is that they'll get picked up,' Eddie said, checking his watch again.

'So what do you want to do? Check the flat, then go looking for them?'

'Nah, Carl checked, and it's secure,' Eddie told him. 'I need to talk to Chrissie and find out exactly what happened, so drop me at the hospital, then you go looking for them. They hardly know you, so they'll presume you're a punter. Then you can grab them and get them in the car.'

'What if I don't see them?'

'You will if you look hard enough. They don't know anywhere but town, so I doubt they'll stray too far. I'll get Joe to pick me up after I've seen Chrissie, make sure there's no trace of me in their flat – just in case.'

'Want me to bring them back there when I find them?' Clive asked.

'No, you'll have to keep them at yours till we can sort out somewhere else,' Eddie said. Shrugging when Clive gave him a horrified look, he said, 'What else can we do, man? I can't risk having them back there till we've got all four of them. One can still bring the pigs down on me like a ton of bricks.'

'I'm not happy about this,' Clive grumbled, setting off reluctantly.

Chrissie was lying with her back to the door when Eddie walked into her little room at the end of the ward. She'd regained consciousness in the ambulance en route to hospital so the paramedics had been able to prepare her for what was to come by explaining gently that she had lost the baby. After that, nothing that anybody said to her registered as important.

The doctor had told her that he wanted to keep her in for a couple of nights to keep an eye on her. She'd lost a fair bit of blood, he'd said, and he was concerned about the bruise that was developing across her back. He hadn't come right out and asked if her man was responsible, but Chrissie had known that was what he was thinking. Him and the nurses, with their sympathetic smiles, soft talk and hand patting. Little did they know that, albeit indirectly, it *was* Eddie's fault, because if it hadn't been for him bringing those girls into her life this would never have happened. Which was why, when the nurse had asked if there was anybody she wanted them to contact, she'd given them her mum's number, not his. She didn't want to see him yet; she had too much to think about before she could listen to any of his lies. And that was exactly what she would get, she knew, because he was incapable of telling the truth.

She stiffened now when Eddie approached the bed and put his hand on her shoulder.

'Babe?' he whispered. 'You awake?'

Chrissie squeezed her eyes shut, glad that he thought she was asleep.

'Babe?' A little louder now. 'Wake up, we need to talk.'

The door opened behind him, and Linda walked in with two cups of drinking chocolate in her hands. 'Oh, you made it, did you?' she said when she saw Eddie. 'I'm amazed anyone knew where you were. My Chrissie certainly didn't. But then, it seems she hardly ever does 'cos you're always taking off and leaving her from what I've heard.'

Eddie sighed. He hadn't so much as said hello to Linda yet but she was already launching into him as if she was some kind of authority on his and Chrissie's relationship.

'So what have you got to say for yourself?' she demanded.

'To tell you the truth, I haven't got a fucking clue what's going on 'cos I've just this minute got here,' Eddie told her. 'And she's asleep, so I haven't even spoken to her yet.'

'She's not asleep,' Linda sneered. 'She obviously just doesn't want to talk to you. What does that tell you?'

'It tells me that she's had *you* pecking her head for the past hour,' Eddie retorted angrily. 'So why don't you just back off and keep your nose out, 'cos it's got nothing to do with you.'

'Is that right?' Linda gave him a smug smile. 'So how come she asked them to ring me and not you?'

''Cos you've got her under your fucking thumb,' Eddie snapped. 'You've got no respect for boundaries, man.'

'Don't make me laugh,' Linda said dismissively. 'You're

nowt but a big bully, but you don't scare me. And what you looking at me like that for? This is your fault, this.'

'What's my fault?' Eddie asked. 'I haven't got a clue what's going on.'

'She's lost your baby, that's what,' Linda informed him. 'Because you couldn't keep your flaming hands off her.'

'What you talking about?' Eddie frowned. 'I haven't seen her all day.'

'No, but when you did you went to flaming town on her, didn't you?' Linda said accusingly. 'That bruise on her back didn't come out of thin air. And I know for a fact it wasn't there before she got home 'cos she was with me all day.'

'You're off your head,' Eddie shot back. 'I haven't laid a finger on her.'

'Yeah, right,' Linda said disbelievingly. 'But I'll tell you this much, you won't be touching her again. Not so long as I've got a breath left in my body.'

'You reckon you could stop me?' Eddie sneered, looking her up and down.

'Too right,' Linda said fiercely. 'You might think you're some kind of big man, but you're nothing to me, mate. I've seen hundreds of your sort in my time and you're all talk, the whole lot of you.'

Eddie had heard enough of her rubbish. 'Why don't you do yourself a favour and fuck off before I show you if I'm all talk or not,' he warned her. 'I've got better things to do than listen to you prattling on about your loser boyfriends.'

'Don't threaten my mum,' Chrissie said, turning over just then and struggling to sit up.

'Stay put, love,' Linda said concernedly, rushing to the bedside. 'Don't stress yourself – I can handle him.'

'Nobody's handling anyone,' Chrissie said firmly. 'This is between me and him.' Glaring at Eddie when he gave her mum a smug look, she said, 'Don't bother gloating, 'cos she's right about everything else. This *is* your fault.'

'What is?' Eddie demanded, pissed off with her now for trying to talk down to him in front of her bitch mother. 'I wish someone would just fucking tell me what's going on, 'cos youse are proper doing my head in.'

'I've lost the baby,' Chrissie told him, gritting her teeth determinedly to keep the tears at bay.

'What baby?' Eddie asked, having heard nothing about it before now.

'*Your* baby.' Chrissie stared at him, trying to gauge his reaction to the news. But there didn't seem to be any, which confirmed what she'd been afraid of: that he wouldn't have wanted it anyway.

Eddie pursed his lips and looked at Linda who was hovering protectively beside her daughter. 'Do you think you could just give us a minute?' he asked, struggling to be polite. 'There's some things we need to discuss, and I haven't got much time.'

'Really?' Linda said sarcastically. 'Got to go, have you?

Got better things to do than look after the mother of your dead baby?'

'Mum, pack it in,' Chrissie scolded her. 'I'll be fine. Just go and have a fag, or something.'

'Okay,' Linda agreed. 'But don't you go upsetting her, I'm warning you,' she said to Eddie.

'Fuck's her problem?' Eddie asked when Linda had gone. 'And why does she think I've been hitting you? What's this shit about a bruise on your back I'm supposed to have given you?'

'I never told her that,' Chrissie said wearily. 'She's just assuming it was you.'

'And you didn't bother setting her straight?'

'I haven't had a chance to set anyone straight yet,' Chrissie told him, giving him a cool, meaningful look.

'Yeah, well, you'd best just tell me what's going on, 'cos I need to get moving,' Eddie said, glancing at his watch.

'The girls have gone,' Chrissie informed him tartly.

'And you didn't try to stop them?' Eddie demanded, keeping his voice low in case anyone could hear them. 'What the fuck are you playing at, you stupid cow? You know what this means, don't you? It won't just be me who's fucked if they grass us up.'

'I don't care,' Chrissie replied icily. 'I never wanted them there in the first place and I'm glad they've gone. But I wouldn't worry – it didn't sound like they were in any rush to tell the police anything. They were all too scared of what you'd tell that policeman in their country.'

'What policeman?' Eddie asked.

A tiny humourless smile lifted Chrissie's lips and she shook her head. 'I knew it was a lie. Shame they didn't believe me, though, 'cos they could have been well on their way to a refuge by now. But they'll probably just carry on selling themselves 'cos that's the only thing they've got going for them, thanks to you.'

'So you're saying they're still around?' Eddie said, seizing on what she'd said and not how she'd said it. He didn't give a toss what she thought. All that mattered was finding those girls and getting them back under control.

'You don't care about me at all, do you?' Chrissie hissed, her eyes flashing with pain and hatred.

'Don't be stupid,' Eddie said, reminding himself that he would still need her flat if – *when* – he rounded up the girls.

'I might have been stupid,' Chrissie told him, her eyes watering up against her will. 'But no more. This is the end. I'm giving the flat up and moving back in with my mum.'

'You're just overreacting,' Eddie said, turning on the charm. 'You and me, we've got something special,' he went on, sitting on the edge of the bed and reaching for her hand. 'You're my woman. You belong with me.'

Chrissie's chin started to wobble but she snatched

her hand away, determined to stay strong despite her quickening heartbeat. She could never resist Eddie when he gave her those puppy-dog eyes. But, boy, didn't he know it.

'Come on, Chrissie, you know how I feel about you,' Eddie crooned, gently stroking her hair back off her face. 'I'm really sorry about the baby, but can we talk about it later? Clive's driving round looking for the girls on his own right now and there's more shit going on back at the flats, so I need to go back and make sure everything's all right. I don't want you coming home and having to deal with any crap, do I?'

He sounded so sincere, and Chrissie longed to be able to believe that he was truly doing this for her sake. Allowing him to hold her hand, she sighed, and said, 'All right, go. But you'd best come back tomorrow.'

'Course I will,' Eddie assured her, raising her hand to his lips. 'Just tell your mum to back off, eh?'

'Don't worry about her,' Chrissie murmured. 'She's only trying to protect me.'

'Yeah, well, that's *my* job,' Eddie said possessively. 'So just tell her to butt out.'

Chrissie nodded. Winking at her, Eddie got up and left.

'What happened?' Linda asked, rushing in before the door had closed behind him. 'Did you tell him you're coming home with me? How did he take it? He's not going to try and cause trouble, is he, 'cos I've already warned him I'll—'

'Mum, it's okay,' Chrissie interrupted. 'Just leave it, eh?'

'What do you mean, "leave it"?' Linda frowned. 'Don't tell me you've let him talk you round? Oh, Chrissie, I knew you were stupid, but not *that* stupid.'

It was the second time in a matter of minutes that she'd been called stupid and it incensed Chrissie that the people who were supposed to think the most of her obviously thought so little of her.

'I'm tired,' she said, feeling a sudden need to be alone with her thoughts. 'Why don't you go home? There's nothing you can do here.'

'I don't want to leave you,' Linda protested.

'*Please*,' Chrissie implored. 'I'm absolutely fine, honest. And you can come back first thing tomorrow.'

'Is *he* going to be here?' Linda asked.

'He said he would be, yeah,' Chrissie admitted.

'Oh, well, that's me told, then, isn't it?' Linda huffed, snatching her jacket off the chair.

'Don't be like that,' Chrissie said wearily. 'I know what I'm doing.'

'We'll see,' Linda said tetchily. 'You know where I am,' she added, heading for the door.

Chrissie flopped her head back on the pillow and squeezed her eyes shut when her mum had gone. But, hard as she tried, she couldn't hold back the tears any longer. It was all such a mess and she just couldn't see a way back to where they had been before. And she still hadn't had a chance to confront Eddie about the baby he'd supposedly fathered – with the woman he supposedly trusted enough to have stashed all his stuff round at her place.

But would he tell Chrissie the truth when she did confront him? She doubted it, somehow.

22

Katya was sitting on an armchair by the window, with the cat curled up on her knee purring contentedly and the curtains open just enough to let in a sliver of moonlight. She'd felt like a burglar when she'd let herself in, but she'd had to trust that Joe knew what he was doing because he was the only one who could help her now. She just prayed that he was the genuine man that she had come to believe he was, because if this all turned out to be a game and he brought Eddie here to catch her then she was as good as dead.

That thought was still on Katya's mind when Joe rang to let her know that he was parking the car and would be on his way up in a couple of minutes. Her legs were shaking wildly when the tap came at the door and she gazed out through the spyhole to make sure that Joe was alone before she let him in. Even then, she backed away from him, her fearful gaze fixed over his shoulder.

'It's okay,' Joe reassured her. 'I'm alone. I haven't spoken to anybody on my way here, and nobody saw me coming in.'

Relaxing a little when he locked the door and slid the chain across, Katya headed back into the living room. Following her, Joe smiled when she sat down on the chair and the cat climbed back onto her knee.

'It must like you,' he said, perching on the edge of the couch. 'My friend Cheryl reckons he's a bit vicious. She showed me her arms the other day, and they were covered in scratches.'

'He's just old and lonely,' Katya murmured, gently stroking the cat's ears. 'He must be missing his owner very much. This is probably her chair, because he came to me as soon as I sat down.'

'I still reckon he likes you,' Joe said. 'Especially if that *is* Molly's chair. Going off what Cheryl said about him, I think he would have had a right go at you for sitting there if he didn't.'

'Maybe,' Katya said quietly.

'So, you got in okay?' Joe asked, glancing around the unfamiliar room as his eyes began to adjust to the dark.

'Nobody saw me,' Katya told him. 'But I didn't enjoy doing it. It doesn't feel right to go into somebody's home without their permission.'

'I don't think Molly would mind if she knew why you needed to be here,' Joe said confidently. 'Have you had a drink, or anything to eat?' he asked.

'No, of course not,' Katya said, as if the thought hadn't even occurred to her. 'I would never touch anything that didn't belong to me. I'm not a thief.'

'And I'm not calling you one,' Joe assured her. 'But I'm sure Molly wouldn't mind if you helped yourself to a coffee. Although I doubt there'll be anything in that's fit for eating, because she's been gone for a while now. But if you can wait I'll fetch something up from mine when I get a chance.'

A look of alarm came into Katya's eyes. 'Why? How long do you think I'll be here?'

'Only until I can work out where else to take you,' Joe said. 'You'll have to sit tight till then, because the last thing we want is anybody seeing you and mentioning you to Eddie. That's why you can't come down to mine, because I've got people coming in and out all the time.'

'I should just go,' Katya murmured guiltily. 'I'm bringing trouble into your life.'

'Don't be daft,' Joe protested. 'I told you I'd help you, and I will. You've already done the hard part, so now it's down to me to find somewhere safe for you. I've got a few ideas but I need to make some calls. And we'll have to wait until there's no chance of anybody seeing us leave. Okay?'

'Okay,' Katya agreed, praying again that her instincts about him were correct because she had so much to lose if they weren't.

Joe's phone began to ring just then. He took it out of his pocket and tutted when he saw the name on the screen. 'It's Eddie.'

'Oh, no,' Katya cried. 'Please don't tell him I'm here.'

'Hey, stop panicking,' Joe said. 'I'm not even going to answer it. I'll just let it stop ringing, then I'll switch it off.'

'But won't that just make him suspicious?'

'Do I look like I care?' Joe said calmly. Doing as he'd said he would when the phone stopped ringing at last, he stood up.

'Where are you going?' Katya asked.

'You need a drink, so I'm going to see what I can find,' Joe told her. 'Please stop worrying. Nothing bad is going to happen.'

Joe went into the kitchen, filled the kettle and felt around in the cupboards until he found the cups. There was no coffee, he discovered, only tea. But there were some biscuits in a tin behind the kettle and they seemed quite fresh when he snapped one. Although the same couldn't be said for the milk that Cheryl had left in the fridge for the cat, so he decided not to risk that.

'Hope you don't mind it black?' he asked when he carried everything through.

'No, I don't mind. Thank you,' Katya said, grateful for anything wet and warm because her mouth was so dry with fear.

'Do you feel up to telling me what happened?' Joe asked, settling back on the couch as she sipped at the tea. 'You don't have to if you don't want to, but it might help.'

Katya shook her head. It was all too raw and confusing.

And Eddie calling just now had made her even more nervous because it reminded her of how close he was. How vulnerable *she* still was. At least Elena and Hanna were safe. But where were they – and how long would they be able to hide before Eddie found them?

'Hey, what's wrong?' Joe asked, coming over to her when he realised that she was crying. He squatted beside the chair and held her hand. 'You can trust me,' he told her. 'I swear on my mother's life.'

'Don't,' Katya sobbed. 'Don't ever say that.'

'Okay, I'm sorry, that was wrong,' Joe admitted, mentally kicking himself. 'I just want you to know that I would never do anything to hurt you. I want to help you, and I thought it might be easier if I knew what I was dealing with, that's all. But you don't have to tell me anything.'

'It's not you,' Katya sniffled. 'I'm just so scared of what will happen if Eddie finds us. Tasha was the one who hurt Chrissie but he'll blame all of us, I know he will.'

'Chrissie got hurt?' Joe prompted gently.

'I – I think she might have lost her baby,' Katya told him tearfully. 'Tasha pushed her and she hit the table quite hard. I knew she was hurt, so I came back after the others had gone. She was bleeding, so I made her let me call an ambulance.'

'When did all this happen?' Joe asked, wondering if Eddie knew about it.

'Not long before I called you,' Katya told him. 'Elena and Tasha had been fighting, and Chrissie came to warn them to stop because Eddie was on his way home. But we'd heard him going out and knew that he wasn't coming back, so Tasha called her a liar. And then she told her about the other woman who already had Eddie's baby and Chrissie got mad about it.'

'Eddie's got a baby?' Joe interrupted, thinking that it was the first he'd heard about it.

'That's what Tasha said,' Katya told him. 'She said the woman had been angry with him, because she'd been looking after his drugs and his gun but he hadn't looked after her and their baby as he'd promised he would.'

'Any idea who she was?'

'We didn't hear that conversation,' Katya said, sliding her hand free to dab at her nose. 'And if Tasha heard her name she didn't tell us.'

'Did Chrissie look like she knew who it was?'

'I don't think so. She called Tasha a liar and said that Eddie didn't have any children, but I think she might have believed her. Then Tasha said that she was going to take her place with Eddie, so Chrissie told her that he had no money because he had gambled it all away and spent so much on drugs.'

'That's true,' Joe affirmed.

'Well, Tasha changed her mind after that,' Katya went on. 'And that was when Chrissie told us all to get out. She said that Eddie had lied to us and that he couldn't get us into trouble with the man because he doesn't know anybody outside of this country. Tasha left then but we didn't want to risk it. But Chrissie told us that it was her flat, not Eddie's, and that she would call the police if we didn't go. And there were already so many policemen outside – Elena said that we had no choice.'

Joe went back to the couch and mulled all this over for several minutes.

'This man you say you thought Eddie could get you into trouble with,' he said. 'Who is he?'

Katya was wary of telling him but she had already placed her faith in him to an irreversible degree, so she figured that she might as well just get it over with.

'Wow,' Joe murmured when she'd finished. 'I guessed that you weren't doing this work out of choice, but I had no idea of the kind of hold that Eddie had over you. You must have been terrified.'

'We *are*,' Katya affirmed, using the present tense to emphasise that the fear was still every bit as paralysing as it had ever been. They might have escaped but that didn't mean that this was over. For all they knew, Chrissie could have been the one who was lying – and their families could be being murdered in their beds right now.

'If it helps,' Joe said quietly, 'I agree with Chrissie. Eddie hasn't got that kind of power. And he stays in his own territory – because this is where he feels safest – so there's no way he's been linking up with anyone in your country.'

'But how did he find us if he doesn't know the man?' Katya asked.

'Someone probably approached him in the pub,' Joe said scathingly. 'Trust me, that's how these sleazeballs usually find each other. Pub, internet, mate of a mate – the usual anonymous ways to conduct shady business.'

Katya was looking at him with a strange expression on her face.

'What are you thinking?' he asked.

'Just that you seem too nice to know such things and such people,' she told him. 'You are a million miles away from him in atmosphere. Do you understand what I mean by that?'

'Yeah, I think so,' Joe said, smiling because he guessed that it was a compliment. 'But you don't have to be involved in that kind of business to know how it works,' he added. 'Anyway, I suppose I'd best go and make those calls,' he said now. 'You'll be okay while I'm gone, won't you? You won't do anything daft like try to go it alone?'

'No, I'll wait for you,' Katya assured him. 'Do you think I might be able to take a bath?' she asked then. 'I wouldn't make any sound, and I'll keep the lights off.'

'I'm sure that would be fine,' Joe told her, getting up. 'I'll be as quick as I can, but you've got my number if you need me before I get back.'

'Thank you,' Katya said, gently moving the cat and getting up herself to show him out.

Joe walked down the hall, unaware of how close behind

him Katya was. Turning before he opened the door, he was surprised to find himself almost nose to nose with her. She too hadn't realised how close she was and she dipped her gaze shyly now.

'Sorry,' Joe apologised. 'I, er . . .' He jerked his thumb at the door. 'I'd probably best put the key back in the pot – just in case.'

'Oh, yes, of course,' Katya murmured, handing it over.

'Best go, then,' Joe said. 'I'll give you a ring when I'm on my way back.'

Nodding, Katya closed the door after him and leaned her back against it. They had been so close just now that she'd been able to smell the individual scents of him. And it hadn't been unpleasant. In fact it had been the absolute reverse.

But she had no right to be thinking such things at a time like this. Or feeling such things for him when she had brought nothing but trouble into his life. He'd said that he didn't mind, insisted that he wanted to help her, but he couldn't have expected things to become this complicated. And she felt guilty now, because he had his own life to live, his own job to worry about. She just prayed that Eddie never found out that Joe had been helping her, because that would be bad. Very, very bad.

But it was too late to stop him now.

23

Carl was knocking on his own front door when Joe came out of the stairwell. He frowned when he saw him and said, 'Where have you been? I saw you parking up ages ago.'

'Bumped into that girl on the sixth floor and she invited me up for a brew,' Joe lied, thinking on his feet as he headed towards his own door. 'You still locked out?'

'No, I'm just testing the knocker to make sure it works,' Carl replied facetiously.

'I take it Mel's not back yet?'

'If she is she ain't letting on,' Carl grumbled, following him into the flat. 'I don't even care where she is now or what she's been up to, I just want to get at my shit. I've been stuck down at Cheryl's for the past few hours. And I'm not complaining, 'cos you know I think the world of her. But we've only had a spliff between us in all that time and I'm gagging. Don't suppose . . . ?'

'Bedside table,' Joe said. Glancing at his watch when Carl rushed off to get the weed, he bit his lip, praying that Mel would get back soon, because he had to get on with finding somewhere to take Katya.

'Eddie was looking for you earlier,' Carl said, coming back with the gear and flopping down on the couch. 'He rang me when I was at Cheryl's, made me come and knock on for you.'

'I switched my phone off when I went for that meeting,' Joe told him. 'What did he want?'

'A lift back from the hospital, I think.'

'How come he's at the hospital?' Joe asked. 'He's not had an accident, has he?'

'Oh, yeah, I forgot you'd missed all the action,' Carl said, licking the Rizlas. 'And I saw how fast you came in after parking up so I'm betting you didn't even notice all the pigs down at the brook, did you?'

'Eh?' Joe frowned.

'Thought not.' Carl chuckled. 'Man, that bird up on the sixth must have some shit-hot coffee if you didn't see all the crap going on out there. They've found a body, innit.'

'Really? Who is it?'

'Some baby.' Carl shrugged. 'No one's got a clue where it's come from, though.'

'That's terrible.' Joe tutted, taking another peek at his watch.

Carl finished rolling his spliff. 'God, I needed this,' he sighed, lighting up and stretching his legs out. 'Don't mind if I take a bit down for Cheryl after we've had this, though, do you?'

'Help yourself,' Joe said, wishing that Carl would just go now.

'Cheers, mate. I'll sort you out after I get mine,' Carl promised.

It was another fifteen minutes before Carl eventually left and every second had stretched out like an eternity for Joe. As soon as he'd closed the door behind him he ran into his bedroom to find his address book.

Eddie rushed into the corridor seconds after Carl had gone back into Cheryl's. He'd called Clive from the cab on the way back, only to hear that he was having no luck finding the girls. Which made it even more imperative for Eddie to clean out Chrissie's flat. *And* his own, because he really didn't need traces of anything incriminating lying around if the pigs came calling.

The dog bounded out of the kitchen when it heard him coming in. Then, sensing his agitation, it slunk straight back in and cowered on its pillow, its gaze flicking from the door to the pile of shit it had left in the corner.

Tasha had taken the keys to Chrissie's place so Eddie was forced to look for the spare. Pissed off when he finally found it in the dressing-table drawer after half an hour of tearing the place apart, he stomped next door.

He rarely bothered going in there apart from when he went to take the girls' money or give them a slap, and he didn't want to be in here now, with its disgusting gloss-painted walls and crappy old furniture. But it just confirmed what he already knew: that Chrissie would never move back in here out of choice. And neither would she move back to her mum's if it meant giving up all the luxuries that she had round at Eddie's place. The sixty-inch TV he'd fitted to the wall, for example. There was no way she'd ever be able to afford one of them. Or the black granite fire surround he'd had imported for six grand; the state-of-the-art hi-fi, and the plush carpet. Shit, even the mirror had cost more than she got off the social in a year. Nah, she could say what she liked – she was going nowhere.

Which was just as well, because all this shit that had been going on tonight had given Eddie a kick up the backside and made him realise that he'd been pissing away some major opportunities. His girls, for example. If he'd done things right from the start he'd have been rolling in it by now. But he'd treated them like a hobby so far, when he could have been well on his way to setting up a shit-hot little harem of high-class hookers. But he wouldn't make the same mistake again. When he found them – and he *would* – there would be no more faffing about; it would be business all the way.

Satisfied, after a quick look around, that there was really nothing to show that he had ever been into Chrissie's flat, Eddie went home to scour every nook and cranny of his own place for traces of drugs or any incriminating amounts of money that he might have forgotten about. He knew what the cops were like. They'd been after him for ever and if they thought there was a hint of a chance of catching him with so much as a spliff's worth they'd be all over him with a pack of sniffer dogs.

It was gone twelve when he'd finished and he was sweating like a pig. So he lit up, opened the window and leaned his elbows on the sill to take a look at what was happening outside. The police had packed up and gone, leaving just the blue and white tape behind to mark the spot where they had made their grim discovery. And the locals had already trampled most of that down when they'd done a mass dash through the gap as soon as the last police van had left – they'd wanted to see the spot for themselves.

Eddie was still gazing out when someone knocked on the door a short time later. He tensed. It hadn't sounded like a copper's knock but it didn't sound like Clive's either. And all his lads knew better than to come up here without invitation – so who could it be?

It was Patsy.

'What the fuck are you doing here *again*?' he demanded, yanking the door open and dragging her inside. 'I told you to stay put at your place.'

'You left me again,' Patsy moaned. 'You said you'd come round this morning but you didn't.'

'Don't you think I've got better things to do than run around after you?' Eddie barked, lashing her across the face with the back of his hand and throttling her with the other. 'Get the fuck back to your place – and stay there this time or I'll fucking kill you!'

'I *can't*!' Patsy wailed, her voice rising to a screech as he raised his hand again. 'The police have been asking questions. I – I think they're coming to get me.'

'They fucking will if they see you walking round looking like *this*, you dirty little skank!' Eddie spat, hurling her against the door. 'And what the fuck d'y think's gonna happen if they see you coming round here?'

'They're going to kill me,' Patsy screamed.

'They won't, but *I* might if you don't shut it,' Eddie warned her, seizing her by the throat again and glaring down into her crazed eyes. 'Now, do as you're told and fuck off, or I really will lose it.'

'Can't,' Patsy croaked, her words coming out in strangled gasps. 'Baby . . . *baby* . . .'

'What about the fucking baby?' Eddie demanded. Then, a light flaring to life in his head, he hissed, 'No way! No fucking way was that your baby they found!'

'It wasn't me,' Patsy yelped. 'It was . . . it was sick. It fell out of the window.'

'And crawled to the fucking brook all by itself?' Eddie roared.

As the enormity of what she'd just told him hit home, Eddie felt the red mist of rage descend over his head like a blanket.

'What the fuck have you *done*?' he yelled, drawing his fist back and slamming it into her mouth.

Patsy's lips exploded as her last few secure teeth burst out through the skin. Oblivious to the blood that had sprayed over his hand and the pulp that had embedded itself in his gold-eagle ring, Eddie punched her again and again, yelling, 'They'll know it was mine if they test it . . . *YOU . . . STUPID . . . FUCKING . . . BITCH!*'

He switched to kicking her when her body slithered down the wall and landed in a heap on the floor. His chest was heaving when the mist began to evaporate at last and he blinked rapidly when he saw the mess he'd made of her. He ran his hands through his hair.

'Oh, for fuck's sake!' he muttered, prodding her with his foot. 'Oi! Get up. I'm not messing about – get the fuck up.'

Patsy's body flopped around like a lump of jelly under his foot. And then he noticed the blood. It was everywhere; the door, the wall, the floor beneath her.

Eddie kicked his trainers off when he realised that he was standing in it. Then he ran into the kitchen and filled the mop bucket with bleach and hot water.

'Wait!' he told himself firmly, holding up his hands and walking around in circles. 'Right, you've got to do this in order. Get her wrapped up, *then* clean up.'

And then what?

He ran back into the living room and tugged his mobile out of his jacket pocket.

'I need you to get back here right now,' he said when Clive answered.

'No can do,' Clive told him quietly. 'I've just been pulled over. The pig's just getting out of his car.'

'What the fuck are you talking about?' Eddie yelled, unable to believe this was happening to him. 'I need you here – *now!*'

'Listen, man, they're probably gonna try and do me for kerb-crawling 'cos I've been trawling the fucking streets for hours,' Clive hissed angrily. 'And we both know what'll happen if Letty finds out, so do me a fucking favour and sort out your own shit for a change, will you? I'll get back to you as soon as I can.'

Eddie wasn't used to having the phone put down on him and the rage bubbled up afresh in his chest now. He needed Clive but the man was just sitting there like a prick waiting to get booked when he should have just put his foot down and done one as soon as the pig gave him the blue lights.

But cursing Clive wasn't going to get him here any faster, Eddie realised. And he needed help right now.

'Where are you?' he demanded, calling Carl instead.

'At Cheryl's, having a smoke,' Carl told him, chuckling softly at something Cheryl had just said. 'Why, what's up? Not still looking for Joe, are you, 'cos—'

'Just shut up, and get your arse round to mine,' Eddie ordered. 'And don't be telling her who this is or where you're going – you got that? And fetch some rubber gloves while you're at it.'

'I can't, I'm locked out,' Carl told him, all humour gone from his voice as he picked up on the urgency in Eddie's. Excusing himself, he walked out into Cheryl's hall. 'Do you want me to go to the all-night garage and see if they've got any?'

'Get some off Cheryl,' Eddie snapped. 'She's a clean freak, she's bound to have some.'

'What should I tell her they're for?' Carl asked, whispering now.

'Carry on asking stupid questions and see what happens,' Eddie warned him.

Carl sighed when Eddie hung up abruptly. He wandered back into the living room.

'Don't suppose you've got any rubber gloves I can borrow, have you, Chez?'

'Rubber gloves?' she repeated, glancing up at him over the back of the couch with a questioning smile on her face. 'What the hell do you need them for at this time of night?'

'That was, um, a lass up on my floor. Her sink's blocked so I've said I'll take a look at it for her,' Carl lied.

'Proper little Sir Galahad, you, aren't you?' Cheryl laughed. Then, waving her hand towards the kitchen, she said, 'They're under the sink. Sorry, I've only got girly pink ones,' she added teasingly. 'And you'd best hope Mel doesn't find out you're rushing off to another girl's flat in the middle of the night or she'll string you up.'

'Like I care what *she* thinks,' Carl snorted, heading into the kitchen. 'I'll get you a new pair in the morning.'

'Don't be daft. I've got about a hundred pairs.'

'Cheers, babe,' Carl said, winking at her. 'See you tomorrow.'

Patsy's body was slumped right behind the front door. Eddie didn't have any intention of touching it if he could help it, so he moved her by pulling the door open when Carl tapped on it.

About to enter, Carl hesitated when he glanced down and saw the blood. 'What's happened?' he gasped. 'Are you okay?'

'Just get in,' Eddie hissed.

Hesitating again when he took a step in and saw that there was a body attached to the mess, Carl swallowed loudly and averted his eyes.

'Oh, shit, man. Is it . . . *you* know?'

'What's it fucking look like?' Eddie muttered, pulling him the rest of the way in and closing the door.

'Aw, man, it's not Chrissie, is it?' Carl gulped.

'Don't talk shit!' Eddie snapped. 'She's in hospital.'

'Yeah, yeah, course,' Carl muttered, stepping further away from the corpse and pressing his back up against the wall. 'Here.' He held out the gloves.

'I've already got some,' Eddie informed him. 'They're for you.'

'*What?*' Carl was horrified. 'Why, man? What d'y want *me* to do?'

'Help me get it out of here,' Eddie told him, pulling his own gloves on with a snap.

'And put it where?'

'Next door,' Eddie said, shoving his feet back into his trainers. He sat down by the living-room door, pulled a plastic bag over each foot and tied them around his ankles. 'Here.' He tossed a couple of bags to Carl.

'Why you putting it next door?' Carl asked, already sick to his stomach at the thought of touching the stiff.

''Cos I don't want it in here,' Eddie said simply. 'And there's a rug in there, so we're gonna wrap it up in that and wait for Clive to fetch the car round.'

'Is he on his way?' Carl asked, relieved to hear that Clive was coming because Eddie would probably want to deal with this just with him. That was the usual way they worked.

'He will be as soon as he's shook the pigs off,' Eddie muttered, cracking his knuckles now in preparation for the next step.

'The pigs?' Carl repeated.

'Just shut up and let's get this over with,' Eddie said irritably. 'Take a look outside and make sure no one's about. Then go and open up next door.' He tossed the spare key over.

Carl caught the key and determinedly avoided looking at the dead body as he edged his way out around it. There was nobody around out in the corridor but the paranoia had already settled over him like a cloak of thorns, pricking at his skin like little electric shocks and sparking mad images in his head of eyes watching from behind every door.

'I'll get the legs,' Eddie declared when he came back a few seconds later. 'You get the top end.'

'Aw, man, I can't do this,' Carl complained sickly.

'Yes, you fucking can,' Eddie snarled through gritted teeth. 'Now pick it up. And if I have to tell you again I'll slit your fucking throat and bury the pair of you together! Got that?'

Nodding, Carl squatted down reluctantly and slid his hands under the corpse's shoulders. Holding his breath for fear of accidentally inhaling any of its death spores, he hoisted his end up. Almost dropping it when Eddie *did* drop the legs in his quest not to touch anything more substantial than the toes of Patsy's shoes, Carl squeezed his eyes shut when the head rolled against his crotch.

'Open the door,' Eddie ordered.

Yeah, 'cos I'm fucking Superman, me! Carl thought bitterly. But he kept his mouth shut and did as he was told, using his elbow because his hands were already occupied.

Once they were safely in Chrissie's flat Eddie dropped his end of the body on the rug. Then, giving Carl a funny look when he didn't immediately drop his end, he said, 'What you doing, man? This ain't no time for fucking dancing with her.'

Even more sickened now that it had been confirmed that the corpse was that of a woman, Carl laid his end down with a little more care than Eddie had displayed.

Eddie took hold of the frayed tassels at the end of the rug. He told Carl to get the other end and they rolled the body up into a tight cylinder.

'Give us your belt,' Eddie said, holding the roll in place with his foot and snapping his fingers at Carl.

'I don't wear belts,' Carl told him.

'So go get something out of the bedroom. And hurry up – I need to get out of here and clean all that blood up.'

Carl felt awkward when he rushed into the bedroom and saw all the feminine stuff lying around and remembered that the four prostitutes lived here. He found a long scarf looped over the wardrobe door and took it back to Eddie.

'Do you think it's safe leaving it here?' he asked, nodding towards the bundle. 'What if them girls come back before you've moved it?'

'Don't worry about them,' Eddie said as he bent down to slide the scarf under the roll.

When it was tied he pushed Carl out into the corridor and slammed the door shut.

'I'd best go and see if Mel's back so I can get changed,' Carl said, backing towards the stairwell.

'You can help me clean this shit up first,' Eddie told him, jerking his head towards his own door.

Groaning, Carl reluctantly followed him back into the flat.

Across the landing, Joe had watched everything through Molly's spyhole. He'd nipped back up a short time ago to give Katya the sandwich he'd made for her and to tell her that he hadn't yet found anywhere to take her but that he was going to carry on trying. It would have been a damn sight easier if she had let him contact somebody in authority because he could have smuggled her out easily by now if she had. But she'd adamantly refused even to consider it and had threatened to run away if he kept on pushing it, so he'd been forced to promise that he wouldn't involve the police or any of the care services.

He'd been about to leave then but he'd peeked out through the spyhole first – just in time to see Eddie and Carl coming out of Eddie's flat and going into Chrissie's, carrying something that looked suspiciously like a body. Although he couldn't be sure about that, because the lighting in the corridor outside was so dim and the spyhole lens was dirty enough to distort his view.

Still watching as they went back into Eddie's flat, Joe jumped when Katya wandered into the hall behind him and asked what he was doing.

'Nothing,' he told her. 'Just saw someone going home down the landing, so I thought I'd best wait till they'd gone.'

It was a lie but Katya was already terrified and he didn't want to alarm her by telling her what he'd just seen – or *thought* he'd seen. Because if it *had* been a body then the chances were it would be that of one of her friends. And God only knew how she'd react if she thought that Eddie had found one of them already.

'I'd best get going,' he said now, thinking that he needed to make his move while Eddie's door was closed. 'Just stay quiet. And try to get some sleep if you can because this might take a while. And it's probably safer if I don't come back up until I've found somewhere to take you,' he added. 'But you've got my number, so give me a ring if you get worried. Okay?'

Nodding, Katya stayed in the living-room doorway and wrung her hands together as she watched Joe leave. He was trying to conceal his nervousness but she could feel it coming off him in waves and that did nothing to quell her own fears. She was already beginning to think that she would never get out of here alive.

Jumping when the cat coiled itself around her leg, she exhaled shakily. Then she reached down, lifted it gently and held it close to her heart – for her own comfort as much as for its.

24

Kenny's mum was a nervous woman by nature but she was always worse at night because, statistically, that was when most burglaries occurred, as well as most random drive-bys and police raids. Disturbed by the slightest little sound, she could usually be found huddled under a duvet on the couch in the small hours, watching whatever she could find on TV to keep the ghouls at bay.

She almost jumped out of her skin now when she heard a knock at the door. She crept out into the hall and pressed her eye up against the spyhole. Recognising the man who was standing outside, she pushed the letter-box flap open and whispered, 'Sorry, love, you'll have to come back tomorrow. He's in bed.'

'This is really important,' the man whispered back, speaking slowly because he recalled that she was a bit simple. 'So go and get him for me, there's a love.'

'I don't know,' she said uncertainly. 'He doesn't like being disturbed when he's sleeping.'

'He won't mind once he hears why I'm here,' the man

assured her, squatting down and flashing her a reassuring smile. 'Go on, be a love. Go get him.'

Sighing, she said, 'All right, just a minute.'

She went upstairs, tapped on Kenny's door, and then counted to twenty. She'd only walked in on him once without warning but she would never do it again because she'd seen things that a mother should *never* see.

She pushed his door open now and tiptoed up to the bed. 'Kenny?' she whispered, gently shaking his shoulder.

He woke as soon as she touched him and was out of the bed and waving a samurai sword under her nose in a flash.

'Jeezus!' he roared when his eyes cleared and he realised it was her. 'Don't fucking *do* that! I could have cut your fucking throat, you stupid cow!'

'I'm sorry,' she bleated, clutching her cardigan to her throat. 'But there's a pal of yours at the door. I told him you wouldn't be happy but he insisted. He said it was really important.'

'Who is it?' Kenny asked, already pulling his jeans on.

'I'm not sure,' his mum admitted apologetically. 'He's been here a few times with you, though. Big lad, very short hair. *Baz*! That's it.'

'I don't know anyone called Baz,' Kenny muttered, pulling a T-shirt over his head.

'Oh.' She frowned. Then, snapping her fingers, she said, 'Oh, no, it's not Baz . . . it's *Daz*.'

'You joking?' Kenny narrowed his eyes.

'No.' She shook her head. 'I remember, because I called him Spaz once when you brought him round and you told me off.'

'Move,' Kenny said, stalking towards the door. 'And don't come down.'

'You're not taking that, are you?' His mum eyed the sword with horror.

'Too right I am,' Kenny snarled as he trotted down the stairs.

'Whoa!' Daz yelped, holding up his hands and backing down the path when Kenny yanked the door open and lurched out. 'Wait, man, just hear me out. I've got something to tell you that Eddie really needs to hear. One minute – that's all it'll take.'

'One minute is all you'll have left of your life if you don't turn around and get the fuck back to whatever ditch you've just crawled out of,' Kenny warned him, glancing around to make sure that nobody was watching.

'Ken, please,' Daz implored, closing the gate to separate them. 'Just let me tell you, then I'll go. I swear to God that Eddie will want to hear this. And it affects you, too, so you need to listen, an' all. You don't think I'd have risked coming back if I wasn't serious, do you?'

Kenny caught a movement at a window across the road. Aware that he was being watched, he lowered the sword and jerked his head at Daz. 'Inside.'

Daz was shaking now as he followed Kenny into the house. Sitting at the kitchen table when Kenny told him to, he swallowed nervously, his mouth suddenly as dry as his pockets had been for the last few months.

'Well?' Kenny said. 'Say what you've come to say. And make it quick.'

Licking his lips, Daz said, 'It's about that guy who took over from me as the driver for the crew. Joe, is it?'

'What about him?' Kenny demanded.

'I saw him earlier on,' Daz said. 'Over in Wigan.'

'And?'

'And I didn't recognise him to start with but then it suddenly clicked.' Pausing, Daz cleared his throat. 'Sorry, man, any chance of a drink? I've been walking for hours and I'm all dried out.'

Kenny snatched a cup off the draining board and filled it with water from the tap.

'Cheers,' Daz said, taking a long drink. Then, after wiping his mouth on the back of his hand, he said, 'Before I tell you, will you put in a good word with Eddie for me? 'Cos I had to hitch to get here and walk the rest of the way, and I only did it to prove I've still got loyalty.'

'Expecting a medal?' Kenny snapped, struggling to contain himself. Daz was already pissing him off and he felt like slapping him upside his stupid head.

'No, I just wanna come home,' Daz said plaintively. 'I know I fucked up and it'll take time to get his trust back, but I'd do anything.'

'Just tell me what you've come to say,' Kenny said impatiently.

Daz took another swig of the water. Then, looking Kenny square in the eye, he said, 'I've been stopping with this lass I used to see in Wigan and some of her mates took me out for a pint earlier tonight.'

'*And?*' Kenny snapped, wishing he'd just get to the point.

'And there were some blokes there when we got there, and I recognised a couple of them,' Daz said. 'Well, one of them to start with, 'cos I couldn't place the other one straight off. But then it suddenly clicked.'

'Is there a point to this?' Kenny demanded, fast losing patience.

'Yeah, there's a point,' Daz said, reaching into his pocket for his phone. Squealing with fear when Kenny lunged forward and shoved the blade of the sword under his chin, he said, 'I was just gonna show you the pictures, man!'

'Of what?'

'That Joe with his dibble mates!'

'You what?' Removing the sword, Kenny peered down at him with narrowed eyes. 'What you talking about?'

'Honest, man,' Daz said shakily. 'Remember when Eddie sent us over to Leigh that time to look for Tommy after he ripped him off, and that big ginger-cunt traffic cop pulled me for having no brake light? Well, it was *him*, man. I recognised him from his hair. And that Joe was with him tonight – having a right laugh by the looks of it.'

'You don't even know Joe,' Kenny reminded him. 'You were long gone by the time he started working for Eddie.'

'Yeah, but I'd seen him a couple of times when I dropped Carl off,' Daz said. 'That's why it didn't click straight off. I recognised his face, but not where from, so at first I thought he must have nicked me at some point. But then it clicked, and I thought, *fuck* no! That's why I took the pictures, 'cos I couldn't believe it.'

'Show me,' Kenny ordered.

The pictures had been taken from the other side of the pub and the quality was poor because the phone was a cheap one. But Kenny immediately recognised the ginger copper that Daz had mentioned. And he could also see at a glance that the man sitting beside him definitely was Joe – either that, or someone who looked exactly like him. He was wearing the exact same jacket that Kenny had seen Joe wearing: the weird green one with the red stripe on the collar that Kenny had ribbed him about because it was so naff.

'That don't mean nothing,' Kenny said now, handing the phone back. 'Anyone can be at the same place at the same time. He'd probably been nicked by the cunt himself and was just having a bit of banter with him.'

'Come off it,' Daz snorted. 'He's one of them. It's *obvious*. Look again, and tell me you can't see it.' He thrust the phone out.

Kenny gazed at the pictures again. When you'd had as much contact with the police as he'd had over the years you came to recognise that unmistakable something they had about them: that air of arrogance that they could never quite shake off even after they had slipped out of uniform and into civvies. And it was right there in Joe – he could see it now.

'Don't move,' he said as he marched out of the door and bounded up the stairs.

Swigging at the water, Daz raised his eyes when he heard Kenny's mum ask her son if everything was okay.

'Keep your nose out,' Kenny retorted tetchily. 'And get to fucking bed. It ain't natural moping about at all hours like a fucking ghost.'

He came back down a few seconds later with his mobile in his hand. 'If you're lying and you've faked these pictures, you'd best tell me now.'

'On my life, I'm not lying,' Daz said calmly, already envisioning himself being welcomed back into the fold.

25

It had taken Clive ages to persuade the coppers who'd pulled him that he hadn't been kerb-crawling but had been searching for his teenage daughter who, he'd claimed, had gone missing after arguing with her mother earlier that afternoon. Fortunately, they had believed him. But that had created a whole new set of problems, because then they had insisted on circulating his fictitious daughter's description. And they had also wanted Clive's name, address, landline and mobile numbers so that they could contact him if they found her.

Already pissed off about that, his mood had plummeted when he'd arrived at Eddie's only to find that his friend expected him to drive back through town with a dead body in the boot.

'Are you fucking crazy?' he protested. 'What if them coppers see me and pull me to ask if I've found my daughter yet?'

'You've already talked them round once tonight – I'm sure you'll be able to do it again,' Eddie said unconcernedly. 'But the longer you hold us up, the more chance there is that they will see you. So quit moaning and go pull the car up as close to the door as you can get it. And, here . . . take him down with you.'

Sucking his teeth in disgust when Eddie thrust the lead into his hand, he yanked the dog out and dragged it down the stairs.

It took Eddie and Carl a good ten minutes to smuggle the body out of Chrissie's place and manhandle it down to the car. Carl was petrified that someone would spot them but they managed to get it into the boot without a hitch, so it was a job well done as far as Eddie was concerned.

He closed the boot firmly, pulled a key out of his pocket and handed it to Carl. 'You know Patsy's flat?'

'No.' Carl shook his head.

'Red block, six twenty,' Eddie told him, his voice so low that Carl could hardly hear him. 'There's a cot in the bedroom. My case is under the floorboards. Get it.'

A sickening realisation hit Carl. He frowned and his gaze flitted towards the boot. 'Is that . . . ?' Trailing off, he swallowed loudly.

'Wow, you're sharp, you, ain't you?' Eddie sniped. 'Just quit gawping and get my case,' he said, hopping into the passenger side of the car.

'What d'y want me to do with it?' Carl croaked, dreading the thought of letting himself into Patsy's place now that he knew it was her body he'd just carried down.

'Sit on it till I get back,' Eddie told him irritably. 'And get fucking moving, you muppet.'

Gripping the key, Carl pulled up the hood of Joe's jacket and ducked into the shadows.

Eddie took out his phone when Clive set off.

'It's me,' he said when his call was answered. 'Meet us at your place, quick as. We're on the way and we've got heavy shit we need rid of.'

Cutting the call, Eddie exhaled wearily. His head was mashed. And not because of what he'd done to Patsy – because that was just a nuisance sorted, as far as he was concerned – but because of that baby of hers. He'd never been completely convinced that it was his, but if it *was* – and the police traced it back to him – there would be awkward questions to answer. And he could really do without the hassle as long as he still didn't know where those bitches were or what they were saying about him.

His phone rang. It was Kenny.

'I'm busy,' Eddie told him. 'What do you want?'

'Where are you?' Kenny asked. 'Are you on your own?'

'Out with C,' Eddie told him. 'Why?'

'Don't kick off,' Kenny said. 'But I've got Daz round at mine.'

'You fucking *what*?' Eddie roared.

'Just hear me out, man,' Kenny said, urgency in his voice. 'He's just told me something that you really need to hear. It's about Joe – and you're not gonna like it, man.'

Switching to speakerphone so that Clive could hear

as Kenny relayed what Daz had told him, Eddie sucked his teeth when he'd finished and said, 'Bollocks!'

'That's what I thought,' Kenny said. 'But he showed me the pictures and it was definitely him. Either that or he's got an indentical twin,' he went on. 'He's even wearing that godawful jacket. You know the one. Red bit on the collar.'

'And you reckon the others are definitely coppers?' Eddie asked.

'*Definitely*,' Kenny affirmed. 'One of them pulled us when we were looking for Tommy that time.'

'Shit,' Eddie hissed.

'Hang about,' Kenny said just then. 'Daz wants a word.'

'All right, Ed?' Daz sounded nervous when he came on the line. 'I, er, just wanted to say sorry for all that shit that went down last time I saw you. I was well out of order, and I totally respect what you did 'cos I well deserved it. But I was thinking . . . now that I've worded you up about Joe, do you think there's any chance we can put the past behind us, 'cos I really want to come home? And I'd do anything to make it up to you.'

'Finished?' Eddie asked when he stopped speaking.

'Yeah, sorry, didn't mean to rant,' Daz said, hope dripping from his voice.

'Right, well, listen up, 'cos I'm only going to say this once,' Eddie said quietly. 'If you haven't disappeared by the time I get to Kenny's, I'm going to fuck you over. And this time I'll *finish* you. You got that?'

'But I've just done you a favour,' Daz gasped.

'Yeah, and now I'm doing *you* one,' Eddie told him coldly. 'I'm giving you the chance to walk away while you can still walk. Take it – or die. Your choice.'

Glancing around when Eddie snapped his phone shut, Clive said, 'What d'y reckon?'

'Fuck knows,' Eddie admitted. 'What do *you* think?'

'Kenny seemed convinced,' Clive said. 'And I can't see Daz having the bottle to turn up in person if he was bullshitting, can you?'

'No, I can't,' Eddie agreed. 'You've never trusted him, have you?' he said then.

'Who, Joe?' Clive frowned. 'No. But I told you that from the off. He's too . . .' Unable to find the right words to describe what he felt about the man, he shrugged. 'Just a bit too good to be true, I suppose. Always there when you need him, day or night. Never asks questions, never complains.'

'Yeah, I know what you mean,' Eddie murmured thoughtfully.

'And what do you really know about him apart from what *he*'s told you?' Clive went on.

'All right, you've made your point,' Eddie snapped. 'Shut up now – I need to think.'

'Well, you'd best hurry up and decide what you're going to do,' Clive said ominously. ''Cos if he *is* a pig, he knows everything.'

26

Carl hadn't been able to get straight into Patsy's flat because one of her neighbours had been messing about with a bike in the corridor when he'd first got there. He'd had to pretend that he was on the wrong floor and wait on the stairs until he'd heard the bloke go back into his flat.

Already paranoid, his legs had felt like butter dripping down a hot knife when he'd sneaked back out of the stairwell, and he'd dropped the key the first time he'd tried to slot it into the lock. But he'd made it at the second attempt – only to be knocked off his feet by the smell when he opened the door.

Carl had never smelled anything as bad in his entire life. It was like a mixture of everything rotten and putrid that anyone could think of: shit, piss, sweat, vomit . . . *death*.

Shuddering when he remembered that death was the reason he was here, he pulled the collar of Joe's jacket right up over his mouth and nose and ran into the bedroom. But just as he moved the cot away from the wall and dislodged the floorboards, his phone rang.

'Where are you?' Eddie asked when he answered it.

'Just getting that thing,' Carl told him cagily.

'Right, well, when you've got it fetch it down the arches,' Eddie told him. 'And bring Joe.'

'He's probably in bed.'

'So get him up,' Eddie said sharply. 'Tell him to park up by the station and fetch him the rest of the way on foot. And don't tell him nothing. You got that?'

'Is something wrong?' Carl asked – doubting, even as the words came out, that anything could be more wrong than what was already happening.

'It fucking *will* be if you don't quit asking stupid questions and do as you're told!' Eddie barked.

When Eddie cut the call, Carl groaned and yanked the case out. All he wanted to do was get a shower and go to bed – even if he had to kick his door off its hinges to do so. With any luck, by the time he woke up tomorrow the world would be back on its axis and none of this would have happened.

Joe had been back in his own flat when Clive had arrived. Already suspicious that something shady was going on after what he'd seen through Molly's spyhole, his suspicions had deepened when he'd watched Clive enter the flats only to reappear a couple of minutes later with Eddie's dog and reverse the car right up to the door below.

It had been impossible to see what Eddie and Carl

had put into the boot after that but Joe had thought it a fair bet that it was probably the *thing* he'd seen them carrying into Chrissie's flat earlier.

Eddie and Clive had driven away then and Carl had disappeared into the shadows, heading towards the far end of the estate. But he was on his way back now, clutching a large silver briefcase.

Two minutes later he was tapping at the door.

'Get your keys,' Carl hissed, almost knocking Joe over in his rush to get inside. 'We've got to take this to Eddie asap.' He held up the case.

'Why, what is it?' Joe asked.

'Fuck knows,' Carl said, stalking agitatedly into the living room and lighting a cigarette as he stared down out of the window. 'Come on, man. We've got to get moving.'

'What's going on?' Joe asked, frowning at him from the doorway.

'Aw, man, I'm not supposed to tell you,' Carl muttered, flopping down on the couch now and sucking on his smoke as if his life depended on it. 'But it's bad shit.'

'What kind of bad shit?'

'The worst kind,' Carl moaned. Then, thinking that he owed it to his mate to warn him so he didn't turn up and get the same kind of shock that Carl himself had already had, he said, 'If I tell you, you've got to promise not to say a word to Eddie.'

'Course,' Joe assured him.

'Remember that bird I told you about?' Carl said. 'The one I hadn't seen for ages, then she grabbed me the other week asking for gear?'

'Patsy?' Joe said.

'Yeah, her,' Carl muttered. Shaking his head now as he recalled what he'd seen tonight, he said, 'She's dead, man. Eddie called me round to his place earlier, and she was lying there in a pool of fucking blood.'

'You're joking?'

'Wish I was, man. I don't know what the fuck he did to her but I didn't even recognise her. Then he made me help him fucking move her. And it was gross, man.'

'So where is she now?' Joe asked.

'He's fucking getting rid of her,' Carl told him. 'Sent me up to her place to get his shit out of it.'

'The case?' Joe guessed.

'Yeah. And now he wants us to go over there – and I've got a horrible feeling she's still going to be there.'

'Where?'

'The arches,' Carl told him. 'You don't know it. Hardly anyone does. But that's the place where people *disappear* – if you get me.'

'Mmm,' Joe murmured. Then: 'Look, just chill out. There's nothing you can do about it now and he's obviously got it under control. So let's just go and do whatever he wants, then we can get back home and forget all about it, yeah?'

'Yeah,' Carl agreed, sighing wearily. 'Cheers, mate. Feels loads better getting it off my chest.'

'No worries,' Joe said. 'Just give me a minute to get my stuff and we'll get off.'

Joe went into the bedroom, eased the door shut and pressed his ear up against the wood to make sure that Carl hadn't followed him. Then he reached for his phone. After leaving a hushed message he put on his trainers and jacket and picked up his keys before going back to Carl.

27

The arches were a row of derelict workshops beneath a disused Victorian freight-railway line on the dark undeveloped outskirts of the city. The only access to the units was via a rough cobbled path that was just about wide enough for a carefully driven vehicle, and it dipped so steeply after it left the road above that it would have been invisible to anyone who didn't know it was there.

There was a canal to the immediate left, its dark waters made all the more murky by the shadows that were cast by the wall of the long-abandoned warehouse that loomed high on the opposite bank. And the path ended so abruptly beyond the last unit that someone could easily find themselves drowning in the centuries-old sludge below if they lost their footing. They'd be held fast by the discarded tyres, shopping trolleys and bicycles that had been lobbed off the bridge above over the years.

Fred Abbott had been running a motorbike-repair shop out of the end unit for some fifteen years, but business had declined to such a degree over recent years that he'd have been forced out if it hadn't been for shady fucks like Eddie Quinn bunging him backhanders for his waste-disposal facilities. And, as Fred had found out to his cost pretty early on, if you did it for them once, you were stuck doing it for life. So now he asked no questions. If they called, he came – simple as.

Fred parked his motor up some distance away from the unit now, and walked the rest of the way. Nodding a sombre greeting to Eddie and Clive who were already waiting outside he edged past the growling dog and squeezed past the car that they had reversed down the path. He took a bunch of keys out of his overall pocket and unlocked the numerous padlocks and mortise locks before shoving the door open and flicking on a dim overhead light.

Desperate to get the corpse out of his car before it tainted his carpet, Clive flipped the boot open. 'Yo!' he hissed when Eddie made to follow Fred into the unit. 'No fucking way am I doing this by myself, man. Get hold – or it's going straight in the canal. And I ain't messing.'

Eddie sucked his teeth but did as Clive had said without argument.

After dumping their burden on the oil-stained unit floor they both stepped away from it. Then they wiped their hands while they waited for Fred to move the huge stack of tyres away from the corner and open up the door behind it that connected this unit with the empty one next door. The unit where Fred kept the waste-disposal kit: a huge industrial barrel filled with lime.

'I'll need some rope,' Eddie said when Fred had

finished clearing a path for them. Plus a couple of chairs and the machete.'

Nodding, Fred shuffled off to set things up.

Shivering in the icy air, Clive poked the rolled-up rug with his toe. 'You sure it's proper out?'

'Over and,' Eddie affirmed.

'Hope so,' Clive murmured, lighting a cigarette and offering the pack to Eddie. 'It *stinks*, man,' he complained, wrinkling his nose.

'Soon be over,' Eddie said, squinting as he took a light.

'Not quite,' Clive reminded him. 'We've still got the bitches to find.'

'First things first,' Eddie replied, thinking that they were the least of his troubles right now. Glancing at his watch, he said, 'Right, I'm going to have a couple of lines before they get here. Make sure I'm nice and sharp. Having some?'

'Yeah, I think I better had,' Clive said. 'I've got a feeling this is going to be a long night.'

Carl was shivering as he and Joe traipsed down the path fifteen minutes later. 'God, I hate it round here,' he muttered, jumping at every shadow. 'Always feel like there's a shitload of ghosts watching me.'

Glancing out over the tarry waters, Joe gazed at the broken warehouse windows and gaping holes where cargo had once been hauled in straight off the barges. 'It is a bit spooky,' he agreed.

Fred was standing in the doorway of the last unit but they didn't see him until they were almost on top of him because his face and hair were as grey with ingrained oil as his hands and his overall.

'They're waiting,' he muttered, jerking his head at them to go in.

'About fucking time,' Eddie said when Carl stepped over the lip at the bottom of the metal door. 'You got my case?'

'Yeah, here.' Carl passed it over.

Taking it, Eddie waited until Joe was inside too. Then, nodding at Fred to lock up, he laid the case on top of a pile of tyres and took out his gun.

'You and you,' he said, pointing it from Joe to Carl. 'Move that through there.'

Joe glanced down at the rolled-up carpet. Even if he hadn't already known that it contained a body the smell would have given it away. 'You're not serious?' he said, frowning.

'Deadly,' Eddie said, coming nose to nose with him and peering down at him with malice flashing from his eyes. 'So be a good boy and pick it up, or you'll be joining it. You too, Carl. Chop chop.'

Carl recognised the tone and knew that Eddie wasn't messing about. And he wasn't about to argue, not while Eddie had the gun in his hand, that crazed look in his eyes, and the dog sitting close by. It might be tied up but it would take less than a second for Eddie to release it – and Carl had already seen the damage it could do.

'Just do it,' he urged Joe, his legs already shaking as he bent down to take one end of the bundle.

Joe had picked up the bad vibes off Eddie as soon as he'd stepped through the door, and he could sense that Clive was shooting him the evil eye even though he was standing in the shadows and Joe couldn't actually see him. There was something going on and Joe's instincts told him that he should get out of there. But the other man had not only locked the door, he'd padlocked it, so there would be no escaping that way. And there was no way Joe would be able to fight his way past all three of them – four, if push came to shove, because Carl would be a fool not to back Eddie up if something kicked off.

'Okay, where do you want it?' Joe asked, speaking calmly to make it sound as if he was still on side and hadn't realised that anything was wrong.

'Follow me,' Eddie said, snatching the dog's lead off the hook he'd tethered it to and heading for the door into the adjoining unit.

Carl felt as if his legs were really going to buckle. He struggled not to throw up when he lifted his end of the bundle and the smell gripped his nostrils.

'Man, this is gross,' he mumbled, wondering how Joe was managing to stay so calm.

'Stop thinking about what's inside and breathe through your mouth,' Joe advised him quietly.

'Quit arsing about, you pussy fucks,' Eddie barked, poking his head back out to see what was keeping them. 'We ain't got all night.'

Gritting his teeth, Carl carried his end of the carpet roll through. Then, dropping it like a hot brick, he stepped as far away from it as he could get and rubbed his hands on his jeans in disgust.

A thick plastic sheet was spread out on the floor and two chairs were resting against the far wall. Fred moved a stack of steel sheeting away from one of the walls, revealing an alcove in which a large metal vat was concealed behind yet more tyres. He pulled on a pair of welding gloves and removed the lid carefully.

Eddie lit a cigarette and jerked his chin at Joe. 'Unroll it.'

'Aw, fuck, man, don't make me have to see it again,' Carl groaned. 'I haven't got the stomach for this kind of shit. Can't I just wait outside?'

Ignoring him, his gaze still fixed on Joe, Eddie said, 'Didn't you hear me, *nark*?'

'Eh?' Joe tilted his head and gave him a questioning smile. 'What's that supposed to mean?'

'You saying you're *not* a nark?' Eddie asked.

'Don't be stupid!' Joe snorted. 'Fucking hell, man, I knew I was picking up weird vibes but I never would have figured you were thinking crap like that about me.'

'What's going on?' Carl asked, looking from one of them to the other.

'Interesting,' Eddie murmured, still gazing at Joe but with a slight smirk on his lips now. 'You're cool, I'll give you that.'

''Cos I haven't *done* anything,' Joe replied sincerely. 'Come on, man, think about it. If I was a nark, don't you think you'd have been nicked by now? I've seen all sorts while I've been working for you, but I've never opened my mouth, have I?'

Clive sucked his teeth with irritation. 'The chat can wait, man. Let's just get this finished and take it somewhere else.'

'Chill,' Eddie said, sauntering over to the chairs and sitting down. 'Our friend here is about to prove he's one of us. Ain't that right, Joe?'

'If that's what it takes.' Joe shrugged. 'What do you want me to do?'

'Unroll it, and put the stiff in there,' Eddie told him, nodding towards the barrel.

Carl grimaced when Joe coolly untied the scarf that secured the bundle and peeled back the top flap of the rug. Apart from his grandad, who he'd been forced to visit in the funeral parlour as a kid in order to pay his last respects, the only other dead body that Carl had seen before today had been a junkie who'd OD'd in the bin cupboards a couple of years back. And that corpse had started to rot by the time somebody had decided to investigate why the wheelie bin wouldn't go all the way into the shed, so it hadn't even looked like a real person.

But this one was by far the worst of the three dead bodies he'd seen because he actually knew Patsy. Or, rather, he had *known* her – he knew that he would never be seeing her again after this.

Carl didn't want to, but he couldn't stop himself from looking when Joe peeled the rug back. Patsy's eyes were open, the dark lashes matted into spikes around the dust-coated iris of one, while the other was almost completely out of its socket and facing the opposite direction. Her battered head seemed to have doubled in size, and the blue tip of her tongue was poking out grotesquely through the gash that her teeth had made when they had burst through her lip.

'Oh, fuckin' hell,' he croaked, as if he hadn't believed his eyes the first time around.

'Shut your mouth,' Eddie snapped. 'And help him get her in there.'

Carl wiped his sweaty hands on his jeans. 'She won't fit,' he said, mentally sizing her up against the vat.

'She will,' Eddie informed him, his gaze still on Joe. 'Give him the chopper, Fred.'

The grey man did as he was told without a word.

Joe looked from the machete to Eddie. 'What am I supposed to do with this?'

'Use your imagination,' Eddie drawled.

Carl gagged.

Snapping his gaze onto him, Eddie said, 'Puke, and you'll be licking every last drop of it up, you fucker. I'm not having you leaving your fucking DNA around to lead no one back to me.' Turning back to Joe when he was satisfied that Carl had got himself under control, he said, 'What you waiting for?'

'I'm not doing it,' Joe said firmly. 'Everything else, yeah. But there's no way I'm cutting up a body.'

'You disobeying me, cunt?' Eddie snarled, strolling over to him and ramming the nozzle of the gun under his nose.

'I'm *not doing it*,' Joe repeated slowly, gazing steadily back at him.

'So you're telling me you'd rather die?' Eddie asked, smirking nastily.

'No, but if you're going to do it you're going to do it,' Joe replied.

'Youse are doing my head in,' Clive snapped, losing patience with Eddie because he was messing about too much and costing them time. 'It's half fucking five, in case no one's realised. Give me that!' He stalked across the room, snatched the machete out of Joe's hand and shoved him out of the way. Then, dragging the body into the centre of the plastic sheet by its feet, he drew his arm back and hacked into one of its thighs.

It was the most horrendous thing Carl and Joe had ever seen or heard, and they both knew that the images would stay in their heads for ever. But Eddie was fascinated – a bit *too* fascinated, Clive realised when he glanced up after a few minutes and caught Eddie filming him on his mobile.

'What the fuck are you playing at?' he bellowed.

'Aw, quit moaning,' Eddie scoffed. 'You're not even in it – look.' He turned the mobile around and showed it to him.

'You can see my hand,' Clive protested. 'And my trainer.'

'Some fingers and the *toe* of a trainer,' Eddie corrected him. 'No one's gonna know it's you from that, you knob.'

'Yeah, well, you still shouldn't be doing it,' Clive admonished him. 'It's disrespectful.'

'*Disrespectful?*' Eddie repeated, laughing wildly. 'Fuck, man, have you actually *seen* what you're doing?'

'Just quit it,' Clive warned him.

Smirking, Eddie slotted the phone back into his pocket and prodded Joe in the gut with the gun. 'See that?' He nodded towards Clive. '*That*'s what you call loyalty. Now get over there,' he ordered, gesturing towards the chair. 'I said *MOVE!*' he roared, grabbing Joe by the front of his jacket when he didn't immediately obey and hurling him across the room.

'Aw, man, come on, there's no need for this,' Carl blurted out. 'He's done nowt wrong. What's up with you?'

Eddie lashed out, smashing Carl across the back of his head with the gun. 'Open your mouth again and I'll blow your fucking brains out!' he warned.

Turning back to Joe now, Eddie kicked him in the back of the knees to make him sit down. Then, snatching up the rope that Fred had placed on the second chair, he tossed it to Carl. 'Tie him up.'

'Why?' Carl moaned, rubbing at his head and giving him a confused look. 'What's he done?'

'He's a copper,' Eddie informed him, his gaze riveted to Joe to gauge his reaction.

'Don't talk shit,' Carl said with conviction. 'He's one of us, man. Through and through.'

'Yeah, that's what *I* used to think,' Eddie said, slamming the gun into Joe's temple and staring down at him. 'But that was before Daz recognised him.'

'Daz?' Carl pulled a face. 'What's that two-faced cunt got to do with anything? He don't even know Joe.'

'Oh, but he does,' Eddie hissed. 'You see, it seems he saw our *friend* here having a drink with some of his five-o mates over in Wigan earlier tonight. Isn't that right, *Joey* boy?'

Keeping his cool, Joe shook his head. 'I've got no idea why he'd be telling you something like that, considering I've never even met him. But I've heard enough about him to wonder why a smart man like you would take his word over mine when I've shown you nothing but loyalty.'

'That's right,' Carl agreed. 'Joe's one of the best. You can trust him with your life. *I* do.'

'If I want your opinion I'll ask for it,' Eddie spat. 'Now tie him up.'

'Aw, come on,' Carl said, resisting Eddie's orders. 'Don't do this. Daz is a fucking liar, you know that. He'll have made it up 'cos he's jealous of Joe taking his place on the crew.'

'Thirty seconds,' Eddie warned. 'And then you know what'll happen, don't you?' He flicked a pointed glance towards the dog.

Reminded of the night when Eddie had set the dog on Daz, Carl turned pale.

'Twenty-seven . . .' Eddie drawled.

'Just do as he says,' Joe told Carl, seeing the terror in his eyes.

'Oh, man, this is so wrong,' Carl groaned, his hands shaking so badly that he dropped the rope twice before he managed to loop it around Joe's wrists.

Circling the chair when his prey was bound, Eddie said, 'So, come on, Joe . . . let's have the truth. And we'll start with your real name, shall we?'

'You know my real name,' Joe replied, bracing himself in anticipation of the blows that he knew were about to come.

'Wrong answer,' Eddie said, lashing him across the face with the gun. 'Try again.'

'Aw, Jeezus, man, don't!' Carl yelped, crying now as he watched the blood spurt from Joe's broken nose.

'Real name?' Eddie repeated.

'Joe . . . Weeks,' Joe said, his eyes swimming with tears of pain.

'Wrong again,' Eddie snarled, slamming the butt of the gun down between Joe's legs now. Grinning with satisfaction when Joe screamed, Eddie circled the chair, giving his victim time to recover the power of speech. 'Ready to tell the truth yet?' he asked then.

'I *am* telling the truth,' Joe sobbed.

Eddie tut-tutted. 'I really thought you knew me better than this,' he drawled, shaking his head as if he was scolding a disobedient child. 'If there's one thing I hate more than a thief, it's a liar. At least you can hide your shit to stop a thief getting their hands on it, but you never know where you are with a liar. That's why you cunts have sniffer dogs, isn't it? 'Cos you know they can suss out a liar from miles off. They smell the fear, sniff their way right through the bullshit. Like my dog here . . .'

'Please don't, Eddie,' Carl moaned when he unlooped the dog's lead and walked the animal over to Joe.

'Last chance,' Eddie said, smirking down at Joe.

Joe's breath was coming in ragged gasps now. 'I'm telling the truth,' he insisted.

'Can't say I didn't give you a fair chance,' Eddie said as he released the dog.

It whimpered, and then lay down with its head on its paws.

'Get up, you pussy fuck!' Eddie commanded, booting the dog in its ribs. He let out a roar of rage when it yelped and tried to slither between Joe's feet to hide under the chair. Then he dragged it out by its back legs and started to kick it around the room.

'Pack it in!' Clive bellowed, leaving what he was doing and rushing at him. 'Look what you've fucking *done*, man!'

Breathing heavily, Eddie looked down at the bloody mess twitching at his feet. The dog's legs were clearly broken, and there was a deep indentation in its side where its ribs had punctured its lung.

'This is *her* fucking fault for softening it up with all that fucking stroking!' Eddie hissed. Then, his eyes glinting with pure madness, he turned on Joe. 'And yours, you cockeyed twat. Only she ain't here to pay for it so you'll have to pay double, won't you?' He aimed the gun at Joe's leg and fired it.

'Fucking hell, man!' Clive complained, holding his ears as the sound of the shot reverberated off the walls and clanged off the metal shutters. 'You could have give us some warning!'

But Eddie wasn't done yet, and he blasted a hole in Joe's other leg.

'*ENOUGH!*' Clive yelled. 'This is getting way out of hand.'

'No, it ain't – it's only just started,' Eddie told him.

'You shouldn't have done that,' Fred said quietly. 'You should've waited till you were finished here, then took him somewhere else. This wasn't part of the deal, so I'm out of here. You can finish it off by yourselves.'

'No one's going nowhere until the cunt tells me what

I want to hear,' Eddie said, his voice icy as he levelled the gun at Fred now.

'What you gonna do – shoot me as well?' Fred asked.

Staring him straight in the eye, Eddie said, 'Don't test me old man. Don't fucking test me.'

28

As he stood on the slip road, Daz felt as if his legs and his thumb had frozen solid. By the time he finally got a lift his teeth were chattering wildly. He climbed into the front passenger seat and nodded a thank-you at the driver.

'Where you headed?' the man asked, pulling off the hard shoulder and easing onto the motorway.

Daz's mouth was numb but he somehow managed to tell him that he was going to Wigan.

'Now there's a blast from the past,' the man said, smiling nostalgically. 'Used to go to the pier, back in the day. Wigan Casino, greatest place ever, that. That, and the Twisted Wheel. All-nighter, followed by a trip to Blackpool for the all-dayer. Man, they were the days.'

Glancing at the man out of the side of his eye as he prattled on about all the drugs him and his mates used to take to keep them up all night – which made Daz's own intake sound like kids' stuff – Daz sized him up. He was middle-aged and obviously some sort of travelling salesman, judging by the smart suit jacket hanging from the hook above the back door and the expensive shirt and tie he was wearing. Soft fuck, if ever Daz had seen one.

Forty minutes later, during which time he hadn't stopped talking, the man eased to a stop on the hard shoulder and sighed.

'This do you?'

'Yeah, it's great,' Daz said, able to speak now that he was warm. Unbuckling his seat belt, he made as if to open his door. Then, twisting around, he slammed his elbow into the man's overactive mouth before throwing an arm around his neck.

'Wallet,' he snarled.

Blood pouring from his split lip, the man tugged his wallet out of his pocket and handed it over without argument. But there was a comical mix of shock and betrayal in his eyes, a disbelief that Daz had turned on him after they'd had such a great conversation.

Daz emptied the wallet and tossed it onto the floor. Then, spotting the man's phone plugged into the cigarette-lighter socket, he wrenched out the charger lead and jumped out of the car before running up the grass verge and disappearing before the man had a chance to recover his wits and think about chasing him.

Slowing to a walk, he glanced back and saw the car tearing back onto the motorway. He smirked to himself. Served the cunt right for being so trusting.

Still fuming about the way he'd been so unceremoniously warned to leave town after having gone to so much trouble to help Eddie out, Daz slid the man's phone open and dialled 999.

He told the operator to connect him to the police and waited until an officer came on the line. Then he said, 'Just thought you might like to know that Eddie Quinn is about to kill one of your lot. That's *Eddie Quinn*,' he repeated slowly to make sure that the man had got it. 'And the copper's name is Joe. And they both live on the Grange estate in Ardwick. But I'd hurry if I was you 'cos it won't be the first time Eddie Quinn has offed someone.'

Disconnecting the call when the officer asked for his name, Daz tossed the phone into the grass and carried on walking. But he had a spring in his step now, and a smile of satisfaction on his lips.

No second chances for me, eh, Eddie? Well, none for you neither, you cunt!

29

Cheryl didn't usually set off until around nine, but she left the flat at seven this morning because her mum had askcd if she could take Frankie to his playgroup. Which was fine by Cheryl because she had a ton of washing to do and had promised to pop in to see Molly before lunch. And then she'd arranged to meet up with Vee for a spot of retail therapy – albeit only of the window-shopping variety because, as usual, she was flat broke.

She took the lift up to the fourth floor to get Molly's cat out of the way before she set off and frowned when she reached into the plant pot to find the key lying flat under a thin layer of soil. She always shoved it in point down and made sure that it was well covered. But if somebody had found it and used it to break in, would they really have bothered to put it back?

Telling herself that it was more likely that she'd been more careless about it than usual yesterday because she'd been in a rush, Cheryl unlocked the door and wheeled the pram into the hallway. But immediately she was in, the hairs on the back of her neck began to bristle. She'd been coming in here for weeks and had come to recognise the strange atmosphere that was unique to an empty home: the stillness of the undisturbed air, the lack of fresh body odour. But it felt different today, and there was a faint perfumy scent in the air.

She whispered at Frankie to stay quiet and crept down the hall to take a peek into the living room. At first glance everything appeared to be as she'd left it. But then Cheryl noticed that the curtains had been drawn almost all the way across, and she knew then that somebody had definitely been here because she only ever came during daylight hours and had never touched the curtains.

And where was the cat?

Cheryl went into the kitchen, her frown deepening as she looked around for the animal. By now it would usually be sitting by its bowl, giving her dirty looks as it waited for its food. But it was nowhere to be seen. And there was a cup that hadn't been there yesterday, standing upside down on the draining board.

Cheryl wondered if Molly had discharged herself from hospital and come home without telling her. It seemed like the most logical explanation but she wouldn't relax until she knew for sure. So, easing the cutlery drawer open, she slid out a knife. Gripping it firmly and holding it out in front of her, she went back out into the hall and peeked into the bathroom before going to the bedroom.

The door was slightly ajar, and when she neared it she heard the soft sound of breathing coming from inside.

'Molly?' she whispered, pushing the door open and approaching the bed on tiptoe. 'What are you doing coming home without . . .' Trailing off when she saw the dark hair on the pillow, she gasped. Then, anger replacing the shock, she yelled, 'Oi, what the hell are you doing in here?' Seizing the blanket, she yanked it off, her fury increasing when she saw who was lying beneath it. 'You cheeky bitch!'

Katya's eyes flew open and she gazed up at Cheryl in horror.

'How *dare* you break in here and make yourself comfortable like this!' Cheryl yelled. 'Get out!'

'Please, you've got it all wrong,' Katya spluttered, scrabbling to sit up without squashing the cat that was curled up beside her. 'I-I didn't break in. I used the key.'

'And that makes it all right, does it?' Cheryl snorted. 'Well, let's see if the police think it's all right, shall we?' She pulled her mobile out of her pocket.

'No, please, wait! You don't understand,' Katya cried. 'Joe . . .' Trailing off when she realised what she'd said, she clamped her mouth shut and gazed up at Cheryl wide-eyed.

Narrowing her own eyes, Cheryl said, 'What's Joe got to do with this?'

Katya shook her head. Then, dropping her feet down to the floor, she reached for her boots. 'I'm sorry, I shouldn't have come here. I'll go.'

'Oh no, you won't,' Cheryl said firmly, standing

341

between her and the door to stop her from leaving. 'Not until you've told me exactly what you're doing here, and what Joe's got to do with it. How do you even know him, anyway?'

Katya sighed and clasped her hands together, gripping them between her knees. 'I can't tell you,' she said quietly. 'Please, just accept that it is better that you don't know and let me go.'

'No chance.' Cheryl shook her head. 'You either tell me or you tell the police – your choice.'

'I can't,' Katya insisted, tears sliding down her cheeks now.

'Right, fine,' Cheryl snapped. 'I'll just go and ask Joe, then.'

'No!' Katya blurted out. 'Leave him out of this. Please, I'm begging you. You don't understand how dangerous this will be for him.'

Cheryl breathed in deeply and stared down at her. 'All right, I won't get Joe. But only 'cos he's my friend and I don't want you dragging him into whatever mess you've got yourself into. But I still want to know what's going on, or I *will* call the police.'

Katya squeezed her eyes shut and nodded. 'Okay, but will you let me go when I've told you?'

'I'll decide that when I've heard what you've got to say,' Cheryl said, folding her arms. 'So come on – let's have it.'

Taking a deep breath, Katya told her everything.

When she'd finished, Cheryl sat down on the bed beside her with a deep frown on her face.

'So, you're telling me that Joe's been coming to see you for weeks? And you're the one who phoned the ambulance for Chrissie last night?'

'Yes.' Katya nodded.

'But if you and your friends had just escaped, why would you come back?' Cheryl asked. 'I can't believe anyone would be that stupid. Not if it was as bad as you reckon.'

'I had to,' Katya insisted. 'She was hurt. And then I couldn't get away because the police were everywhere.'

Cheryl struggled to get it straight in her mind. It sounded like some kind of novel, and she wasn't sure whether she believed a word of it. She'd known Eddie for years and knew that he was a lot of things – but a vicious *pimp*? That just didn't sit right with her at all. He might be violent with other men, but she'd never seen him touch a woman in anger like that. And she couldn't believe that Chrissie would allow him to mess about with other women like that, either, never mind with *prostitutes*. And yet this girl was claiming that Chrissie had known all along, and had actively participated in their imprisonment.

'Do you see now why I need to leave?' Katya asked quietly.

'It's broad daylight,' Cheryl reminded her. Then, sighing softly, she stood up and said, 'Look, just stay put. I'm going to have a word with Joe.'

343

'No, please don't,' Katya implored.

'If he's helping you like you claim he is, then he needs to know I've found you,' Cheryl told her. 'It's all very well you being here but you obviously can't stay. And if you're telling the truth about Eddie, Joe needs to get you out of here before Eddie finds out. And he will, because he's got eyes and ears everywhere.'

'I don't want to cause Joe any more trouble,' Katya protested, crying softly again. 'He's been too kind already.'

'Too right he has,' Cheryl muttered, a little jealous that Joe had spent so much time with the girl, and that he obviously cared enough about her that he would put himself in danger with Eddie to protect her.

But she really needed to speak to him about it, find out what was going on from his point of view – and remind him what would happen if Eddie found out.

'I'll be back as soon as I can,' Cheryl said decisively, heading for the door.

Joe didn't answer when she knocked, so she started calling through the letter-box flap instead.

After a few minutes Kettler came out and informed her that Joe had gone out last night and hadn't returned yet.

'And I would appreciate if you didn't yell like a fish-wife in future,' he added tetchily. 'I've already had a disturbed night, thanks to him and that friend of his making an unholy racket in the early hours.' He cast a disapproving glance at Carl's door. 'When you see them, perhaps you could tell them that I've had just about enough of it and shall be calling the police if it happens again.'

'Get a life!' Cheryl snarled. Then, smiling tartly, she said, 'Oh, but I forgot, Joe *is* your life, isn't he? You know every move he makes, don't you, you freak?'

'I don't think there's any call for that,' Kettler retorted indignantly.

'Well, *I* don't think there's any call for sending stupid letters making up lies about your neighbours,' Cheryl spat back angrily. 'So just fuck off back to your fantasy world and keep your nose out of everybody else's business!'

Snorting with disgust when Kettler went back inside and slammed his door, Cheryl marched over to Carl's flat.

Mel's hair was all over the place when she finally answered the door, and her dressing gown was crooked so Cheryl could see almost everything.

'What do you want?' Mel demanded, peering out through bleary eyes.

'Where's Carl?'

'You tell me,' Mel said huffily. 'Probably still at his mum's, sulking.'

'No, he came back yesterday,' Cheryl told her. 'He didn't have his keys, so he was waiting for you to let him in. Haven't you seen him?'

'Nope.' Mel shook her head and yawned. 'That it? Can I get back to bed now?'

'Yeah, whatever,' Cheryl muttered, thinking that if it was *her* man she'd be a bit more concerned about where he'd spent the night. But then, Mel had probably guessed that he'd been with Joe, because the two of them had been pretty much joined at the hip since they'd been working together.

'Wanna see nana,' Frankie piped up just then, banging his feet on the pram wheels. 'Nana, nana.'

'All right, we're going,' Cheryl said, pushing him towards the lift. The girl in Molly's place would just have to wait until she got back.

She'd just entered the lift and pressed the button for the ground floor when the stairwell door opened and a man in a suit walked hurriedly across the landing, followed by two uniformed police officers. Stabbing the button to reopen the door when it began to slide across, Cheryl popped her head out in time to see them knocking on Joe's door. Almost immediately, Kettler rushed out of his flat.

'I'm the one who made the call,' he informed them with a pious look on his face. 'It's me you need to speak to. Phillip Kettler.'

Incensed now, Cheryl bundled Frankie's pram right back out of the lift.

'Whatever he's told you, it's a lie,' she blurted out. 'Joe's nowhere near as loud as he makes out. He's just got it in for him because Joe doesn't want to be his friend. No one does,' she added, flashing Kettler a spiteful glare. 'Look through your records – you'll see Joe's not the first neighbour he's harassed.'

'How dare you,' Kettler spluttered, his face reddening as his weird staring eyes almost popped out of their sockets. 'This is no concern of yours – it's a private matter between myself and the officers.'

The suited man held up his hands to shut them both up. Then, passing a key to one of the uniforms, he turned back to Kettler and said, 'Could you please go back inside, sir.'

'But I'm the one who called you,' Kettler protested, his gaze flitting towards the uniform, who had opened Joe's door with the key and was entering the flat.

'If you did, I'm not aware of it,' the man informed him. 'But I'm sure more officers will be dispatched to talk to you shortly, so if you wouldn't mind . . .' He waved an authoritative hand towards Kettler's door.

Kettler stiffened visibly but did as he'd been told.

Cheryl was nervous now. If the police weren't here because of Kettler, why *were* they here? And how come they had let themselves into Joe's flat like that? Was he in some kind of trouble? Was he being raided?

She backed away, hoping to slip back into the lift so that she could get away and ring Joe to warn him. But the lift door had closed, and by the time she'd pressed the button to reopen it the man had turned around.

'Just a moment, miss . . . I'd like a quick word.'

'About what?'

'You wouldn't happen to be Cheryl, would you?' Guessing that he was right when a cagey look leapt into her eyes, he gestured towards Joe's open door. 'Could you just step inside for a moment, please?'

Recovering from her shock, Cheryl shook her head and backed away.

'That's illegal. You're not allowed to just let yourself into people's houses while they're out. That's against the human rights act – or whatever they call it.'

'Inside,' the man repeated sternly, flashing his badge at her.

'All right,' Cheryl huffed. 'But I want your name, 'cos I'm reporting you as soon as I get out.'

When they were both inside Joe's flat the man closed the door. Keeping the pram between them, Cheryl folded her arms and glared at the uniform who had just come out of Joe's bedroom.

'Anything?' the man asked. Shaking his own head when the PC shook his, he said, 'Check the front room, then. And be thorough.' Turning to Cheryl now, he said, 'I'm Detective Inspector Moore, and I need to know when you last saw Joe.'

'And why would I tell *you*?' Cheryl replied snappily. 'People don't grass their mates up around here.'

'I have reason to believe that he may be in danger,' Moore informed her. 'And I happen to know that he trusts

348

you. So if you know anything about his whereabouts you need to tell me.'

'Why, what's going on?' Cheryl asked, frowning at Frankie when he started kicking at the pram again. 'And what do you mean about him being in danger?'

'I'm afraid I can't tell you that,' Moore said evasively. 'But it is urgent that we locate him. Do you know of a place called the arches?'

'No.' Cheryl shook her head, her frown deepening.

'But you do know Eddie Quinn?'

Wary again, Cheryl shrugged. 'So what if I do?'

'So, have you ever heard him mention this place?'

'No, I just told you – I've never heard of it.'

'And have you seen Eddie Quinn today?'

'*No*,' Cheryl said. 'But why are you asking about him? I thought you said you were looking for Joe.'

'We are,' Moore affirmed. 'But we think that he might be with Quinn.'

His stare was so intent that it raised the hairs on Cheryl's arms, and she started to read between the lines.

'Are you saying he's in trouble with Eddie?'

'I'm saying it's imperative that we find him,' Moore repeated, refusing to confirm or deny her suspicions. 'Do you know a woman called Patsy Mills?' he asked now.

Confused by the sudden shift of subject, Cheryl said, 'Yeah. But Joe doesn't, so what's she got to do with this?'

'Have you seen her lately?' Moore asked. 'Or her baby?'

'I didn't even know she had one,' Cheryl said truthfully. Then, 'Look, I don't know why you're asking me all these questions, but I haven't seen Joe since yesterday. Or Eddie. And I haven't seen Patsy in months. We all thought she'd moved till Carl saw her the other week . . .' Trailing off when she remembered something that the girl, Katya, had just said, she narrowed her eyes thoughtfully.

'What were you going to say?' Moore asked, pressing her.

'Nothing,' Cheryl murmured, an invisible curtain dropping over her eyes. 'I've just got to go, that's all. My mum's taking the baby to playgroup today and I'm going to be late if I don't go now.'

'Sir,' the uniform said, coming out of the living room just then.

Glancing towards him, Cheryl's eyes widened in horror when she saw the blood-covered pink rubber glove that he was holding.

Hearing her gasp, Moore said, 'What is it? What do you know?'

'Nothing,' she lied, her chin beginning to wobble.

'This is serious,' Moore said firmly. Then, aware that Cheryl was getting ready to bolt, and that he had no grounds to hold her, he said, 'Look, just come and sit down for a minute. Let me get you a glass of water.'

Waving for one of the PCs to keep an eye on Frankie, he led Cheryl through to the living room and sat her down on the couch. After pouring her a glass of water, he sat beside her.

'Look, I know you and Joe are friends,' he said, softening his tone. 'And I also know that you have history with Eddie Quinn, so I'm guessing that you're struggling with your loyalties right now. But would it make any difference if I told you that Quinn is the one that Joe's in danger from?'

A flicker of fear passed through Cheryl's eyes and then came the tears. Struggling to hold them at bay, she said, 'I don't know anything. If I did I'd tell you, but I don't.'

'Please, Cheryl, just *think*,' Moore implored. 'Joe left a message last night telling me that a woman called Patsy Mills might have been murdered. And we know that Quinn called Carl Finch and told him to bring Joe to a place called the arches, where, we believe, the body was being prepared for disposal. We also received a separate anonymous call telling us that Quinn was planning to kill Joe. That is why this is so urgent. So, whatever it is that you're hiding, I need to know.'

Cheryl was way out of her depth. The detective had been right about her struggling with her loyalties, because she'd known Eddie for a long time and he'd treated her really well since she'd moved here, making sure that everybody knew they would be answerable to him if they messed with her. But now that she was being forced to choose, she had to choose Joe. And not just because he was gorgeous, because she'd put that crush into perspective a long time ago, but because he was such a genuinely nice person. And a friend that you knew you could really rely on was worth a thousand Eddies.

'I don't know where that place is,' she told Moore. 'But someone said something about Eddie. She – she said her friend had heard him arguing with a woman about a baby he was supposed to have had with her. And then, last night, his girlfriend found out about it and went mad.'

'Chrissie Scott?' Moore asked.

'Didn't know that was her surname.' Cheryl sniffled, wiping her eyes on her sleeve. 'But, yeah, Chrissie.'

'And you say she and Quinn fought about this other woman?'

'No, her and the girl who told her about it,' Cheryl said. 'And now I'm wondering if that was *her* baby you found yesterday – Patsy's.'

'If it was, we'll know soon enough,' Moore assured her. 'There's a unit searching her flat now. Who is this girl who told you about the baby?'

'Just someone who used to live in Chrissie's flat,' Cheryl told him. 'She left last night, but she didn't say where she was going.'

It was a lie but, after everything she'd heard, Cheryl was beginning to believe that Katya had been telling the truth after all. Joe had obviously thought so to go to those lengths to protect her. And if she'd already suffered all that, Cheryl didn't want to add to her suffering by grassing her up and getting her deported. That wouldn't help anybody. Especially not Joe.

'You should speak to Chrissie,' she suggested. 'She'd be able to tell you more.'

Nodding, Moore said, 'I'll be calling up there after I've finished here.'

'She's in St Mary's,' Cheryl told him. 'She was supposed to have lost her baby after that fight last night, and she got rushed in.' Looking worriedly up at the detective now, she said, 'You don't really think Joe's in danger, do you? I mean, I know Eddie's got a temper, but he likes Joe. *Every*one does.'

'I don't doubt it,' Moore said. Then, sighing softly, he pushed himself to his feet. 'Thank you, you've been very helpful.'

Cheryl dipped her gaze and leaned forward to put her glass on the table. She felt guilty now, because she knew that she'd wasted a lot of time being obstructive. 'You will find him, won't you?' she asked, standing up.

'I sincerely hope so,' Moore said quietly, leading her back out into the hall.

'And you think he'll be all right?'

'Again, I can only hope so.'

Cheryl paused by the door and bit her lip. Then, asking the question that had been on the tip of her tongue since the moment when Moore had first said her name, she said, 'How come you knew who I was?

And all that other stuff – about me and Joe being friends, and that?'

'He told me all about you,' Moore said, smiling as he showed her out. 'And, for the record, he genuinely likes you. Just remember that when you find out what's been going on here. Okay?'

'Okay,' Cheryl murmured. Then, her frown deepening in line with her confusion, she pushed Frankie's pram into the lift. Pulling her mobile out of her pocket when it started to ring, she said, 'Sorry, mum, something came up. I'm on my way.'

30

After crying herself to sleep, Chrissie had soon been woken again and she hadn't managed to drop back off for the rest of the night. That was the cruel thing about maternity hospitals. They were designed for the delivery of healthy babies, and the specialised care of sickly ones. But they all got lumped in together, so even though Chrissie was in a single room she couldn't escape the sound of the babies in the ward on the other side of the door. The living breathing babies that had been crying throughout the night, while she had lain here crying for the dead one that had slipped all too easily from her body.

All night, and all morning so far, she had been blaming herself for that, telling herself that it must have known that it wasn't wanted; that it must have heard her at that clinic begging them to terminate it. And God must have heard her, too, and decided that she wasn't fit to be a mother after all. In fact, the whole sorry mess had probably been part of His grand plan, from her agreeing to move in with Eddie to him moving those girls into her flat, to that bitch pushing her into the table last night and finishing what Chrissie had left too late to finish for herself.

And now, just when she needed him most, Eddie had done what he always did and had let her down. He'd promised to come back but she should have known that he wouldn't. He was a liar and he always would be, and she'd lost absolutely everything because of him. Her flat, her independence, her self-respect. And now her mum, because there was no way Chrissie could ask her to come back after the way she'd upset her last night. She'd messed her about too many times, and it wasn't fair to expect her to come running when she called.

Lying in the bed now, Chrissie stared into space as the clock on the wall steadily ticked her life, her hopes and her dreams away. Too immersed in self-pity to bother looking around when the door opened, she closed her eyes when the man spoke her name. She was trying to make it clear that she wanted to be left alone.

'Miss Scott?' he repeated, a little louder this time. 'I know this is a bad time, and I'm sorry for your loss. But I really need to speak to you about Eddie.'

A tiny spark of fear flared in Chrissie's heart.

'What's happened?' she asked, snapping her eyes open and twisting her head to look up at the man.

'*That*,' Moore told her, 'is something I'm hoping you'll be able to help me find out. You see . . .'

Chrissie listened as he outlined what he already knew and her fear turned to bitterness, to anger, and then to pure, burning rage. It was true. The baby that bitch had told her about *had* been his. And now that she knew for sure, she also knew that he'd not only known about it but must have been seeing it regularly, whenever he went to the flat to pick up the gear or the money that he'd been stashing there.

But he wouldn't be seeing it again, or its mother, because they were both dead. And, according to this man, Eddie had not only killed the mother, he was now in the process of destroying the evidence. It wouldn't be the first time – or the last, by the sound of it, because right now he was holding a policeman hostage, too.

'I know where the arches are,' Chrissie told Moore when he'd finished. 'I was in the car with him once when his friend rang and asked him to drop some stuff off down there. He left me around the corner, but you'll easily find it. It's under the railway bridge, next to the canal off Warburton Street.' Pausing now, she breathed in deeply before continuing. 'There was another one. Last year. Tommy Jackson. And one a couple of months after that. I think his name was Jeff Price.'

'Are you sure?' Moore's eyes were calm as he peered down at her, but his heart was already pounding like a jackhammer in his chest.

'Positive,' Chrissie murmured, sighing, because she knew that there was no going back now.

31

It was fully light outside, and shafts of brightness were leaking in through the numerous cracks in the brickwork around the metal-shuttered door. No one wanted to be here, but since Eddie had completely flipped and threatened to shoot the whole lot of them if they dared to open their mouths again they had all resigned themselves to waiting until it was over.

Clive had taken the other chair over to the opposite side of the room. He was slouched in it now with his eyes closed, trying to convince himself that he was at home in his warm, comfy bed. Fred was sitting like a ghost in another corner, while Carl sat in a crumpled, traumatised heap beside the door.

Still tied to the chair in the middle of the room, Joe was alive – but only just. Eddie had mashed his face into an unrecognisable pulp, and Joe's entire body was one big bruise from the vicious kicking and punching that it had received. But it was the gaping holes in his thighs that were causing the blood loss that would kill him before too much longer.

Eddie was concerned about that, but only because he wanted to keep Joe alive until he'd admitted that he was a copper. That was all he wanted. For Joe to admit it, and tell him what he'd told his cunt mates about Eddie's business dealings. Then, and only then, would he be put out of his misery. And he *would* talk, Eddie was determined – even if he had to peel the cunt's skin off strip by painful strip.

He was pacing the floor in front of Joe now, with a kettle of near-boiling water in his hand – a few minutes ago he'd sent Fred through to the main unit to fill it up and plug it in.

'Ready to talk yet?' he hissed. Getting no answer, he held the kettle over Joe's leg and trickled a stream of scalding liquid down into one of the wounds.

Too weak to scream, Joe made a strangled whimpering sound.

'I'm waiting,' Eddie said, raising the kettle again.

'What was that?' Fred hissed just then. 'Did anyone else hear that? I think it came from outside.'

'You expecting anyone?' Eddie demanded.

'Not that I know of,' Fred told him. 'Could be a customer. I don't know.'

'Shit, man, it'd better not be,' Clive whispered worriedly. 'My fucking car's out there.'

'Shut up!' Eddie ordered, cocking his ear.

Before any of them could move, a booming sound ricocheted through from the other unit. Then another and another, followed by shouts of: 'Police! Stay where you are – we've got you surrounded!'

Clive was on his feet in a flash. Grabbing Fred, he shook him and hissed, 'Is there any other way out of here?'

'*IN HERE!*' Carl bellowed. '*WE'RE IN HERE, AND HE'S GOT A GUN!*'

He screamed when Eddie turned and took a wild shot at his head, then he rolled into the corner and scrabbled to squeeze himself in between the wall and the barrel. He heard the second shot a nanosecond before he felt the heat tear through his buttock. Then, mercifully, eveything went dark.

EPILOGUE

Joe had been in hospital for six weeks, and his small room was crammed full of get-well cards, balloons and teddies. And he had more fruit, chocolates and bottles of Lucozade than any human could be expected to consume in one lifetime. And yet, still, he felt as if something was missing. Because every last bit of it was from his old mates.

His *real* mates, he supposed he should call them. The friends and colleagues who had known him for years, and who knew him as Detective Constable Joe Mercer, not fictitious jack-the-lad Joe Weeks.

Now that he was back in the fold it was as if that other Joe had never existed, and everyone from his mates to his family had taken to changing the subject whenever he started to talk about his time on the Grange. It was almost as if they had decided that he needed to be debriefed somehow, the way that victims of crazy religious cults who had been indoctrinated with warped ideas were. But while he understood that they were doing it out of genuine concern, he didn't *want* to forget his time on the Grange. He had spent half a year of his life there, and had met some incredible people along the way; people he'd never have had a chance to get to know as he had if they'd known who he was from the start.

As the weeks had passed without so much as a card from any of *those* friends, he'd gradually come to accept that they had shunned him. And rightfully so, considering that they knew now that their friendships had been a lie from the start. So, when Joe heard a knock on his door today, the last person he expected to see was Carl.

'You not up yet, you lazy cunt?' Carl grinned as he popped his head around the door.

'Oi, language!' Cheryl scolded, pushing him into the room.

'Sorry. Keep forgetting.' Grimacing, Carl hobbled over to the chair beneath the window and sat down carefully. 'How's it hanging?'

'Not bad,' Joe said, sitting up straighter. 'All the better for seeing you two,' he added truthfully. 'I didn't know if I would until . . . well, you know – the court, and that.'

'Blame her.' Carl nodded towards Cheryl who was hovering at the end of the bed. 'I've wanted to come for a long time, but she didn't think you'd want to have anything to do with us.'

'Don't be daft.' Joe frowned.

'Yeah, well, I had an appointment in outpatients, so I thought, sack it, I'm going whether she likes it or not,' Carl said, reaching over for one of the chocolates that were sitting on the locker.

'Carl!' Cheryl hissed. 'You can't just help yourself, you've got to ask.'

'Me and Joe always help ourselves to each other's shit,' Carl reminded her.

'That was then,' Cheryl said quietly, averting her face to hide her blushes from Joe. 'Things are different now.'

'Oh, please don't act like I've grown two heads,' Joe groaned. 'Nothing's changed as far as I'm concerned.'

'No offence, but it has changed a *bit*,' Carl countered, agreeing with Cheryl now. 'Now we know you're a – *you* know.'

'Copper?' Joe supplied the dreaded word for him.

'Yeah, that,' Carl said. 'You're one, and we're not, so we can't just go back to the way things were, can we? You'd have to arrest us every two minutes.'

It was true, and they all knew it. But it didn't stop it from saddening them all, because they had grown close over the six months that Joe had lived among them.

'So, what's everyone been up to?' Joe asked after a while, hungry to hear about life back on the Grange.

Carl and Cheryl exchanged a hooded glance.

'Do you want to tell him, or me?' Carl asked.

'You,' Cheryl said, blushing again.

'We're together,' Carl blurted out.

'What, like as in couple?' Joe asked.

'Mmm.' Cheryl nodded. 'But we're not rushing things. We're just going to take it slow and see how it goes.'

'And it's going good so far, isn't it?' Carl said, winking at her.

'So far,' she agreed, giving him a shy smile.

'Wow!' Joe grinned. 'About time.'

'What do you mean?' they both asked in unison.

'Come on, are you trying to tell me neither of you knew you liked each other?' Joe said wryly. 'It was obvious.'

'Really?' Carl frowned. 'I mean, I knew *I* liked *her*, but I had no clue she liked me. And I never said nothing. Least, I didn't *think* I did. Mel would have had my bollocks for a keyring if she'd picked up on it.'

'Nice.' Joe chuckled. 'But while we're on the subject, what happened to you and her? And you and Shay?' he added, looking at Cheryl.

'Remember I told you I thought she was seeing someone else?' Carl said. 'Well, she was. *Him*.'

'You're joking?'

'Nah, man.' Carl shook his head. 'Discharged myself early from hospital, didn't I? Dropped in at my mum's to get my keys on my way home, thinking I'd surprise her. And I surprised her, all right. Caught them red-handed – in *my* fucking bed.'

'So what happened?'

'Well, I knew Chez would never believe me if I told her, so I rang her and told her to come up – made sure she saw it for herself. Then I kicked the fuck out of him.'

'And *I* rang Jayleen so *she* could see it for *her*self,'

added Cheryl. 'Carl was right – I wouldn't have believed it if I hadn't seen it. And neither would she, 'cos Shay had us both wrapped around his little finger.'

'And how do you feel about it?' Joe asked, guessing that she'd probably taken it hard.

'Gutted at the time,' Cheryl admitted. 'But I'm well over it now.'

'So you *should* be,' Carl snorted. 'You shed the pest and hooked the best. You should be buzzing.'

'Shut up, you idiot,' Cheryl said softly.

'Loves me really,' Carl said, winking at Joe.

'I'm pleased for you both,' Joe said, genuinely meaning it. 'And how's Frankie?' he asked then.

'Getting bigger by the day,' Cheryl told him, the love shining from her eyes as it always did when she spoke about her son. 'Hasn't even asked about Shay in weeks, has he, Carl?'

'No, 'cos he's too busy trying to tie me up in knots,' Carl laughed. 'I'll tell you what, he's going to know his way around a motor like a pro by the time I've finished with him. He already knows the names of all the engine parts.'

'Oh, you haven't told Joe about your thingy,' Cheryl reminded him.

'What's this?' Joe asked.

'He's got himself on a mechanic's course,' Cheryl announced, too proud to wait for Carl to say it himself. 'At college.'

'Good for you,' Joe said, reaching out to touch fists with Carl.

'Blame her again,' Carl said, rolling his eyes, although it was obvious that he was as chuffed about it as she was.

'So, how's everyone else?' Joe asked now. 'Any sign of Molly going home, or are you still feeding the monster cat?'

'Oh, she's been home for ages,' Cheryl told him, flicking a hooded glance at Carl. 'Soon as I told her about her squatter, she was up and out of the hospital like a flash of lightning.'

'Oh, God, I'm sorry,' Joe said concernedly. 'I didn't mean to cause trouble. I just didn't know where else to put her.'

'Oh, I wouldn't worry about it,' Cheryl laughed. 'They've been getting on like a house on fire. Subject of Molly,' she said now, heading to the door and leaning out to signal to somebody. 'You haven't met her grand-daughter Katherine, have you?'

Glancing up when a blonde girl walked in and looked at him shyly, Joe did a double take when he realised who it was.

'We told her to come in with us, but she didn't know if you'd want to see her,' Cheryl said, pushing the girl towards the bed. 'Like you wouldn't.'

'Wow,' Joe murmured, gazing up at Katya. 'You look so different with your hair like that.'

'I know,' she murmured, touching it self-consciously. 'But it's only temporary.'

'Good,' Joe said. Then, quickly amending it in case it had sounded like an insult, he said, 'I mean, it's nice, and all that. But I just thought your natural colour was gorgeous.'

'Thank you,' Katya said, her eyes glistening as she gazed at him.

Cheryl, watching from the other side of the bed, nudged Carl and gave him a soppy smile.

'So, how have you been feeling?' Katya asked Joe now. 'Are your legs very bad?'

'No, they're on the mend,' Joe said. 'They got both bullets out, and there wasn't too much muscle damage, so they reckon I should be able to go back to work soon.'

'Won't that be dangerous?' A cloud of concern shadowed Katya's dark eyes.

'Not much chance of danger when you're stuck behind a desk,' Joe assured her. 'But it won't be for ever.'

'Subject of for ever,' Carl interrupted. 'Is it true that Eddie's gonna get two life sentences?'

'At least,' Joe said, winking at Katya, who blushed immediately.

'As long as he doesn't get off with it,' Cheryl said disbelievingly. 'You know what he's like – he's probably already paying people to get at the witnesses.'

'Doubt anyone's going to put their necks on the line for him like that, now that his best mate's turned against him,' Joe said knowingly.

'What, *Clive*?'

'Yep. From what I've heard – and you haven't heard this from me – he's been spilling his guts in the hopes of getting a reduced sentence for himself. Whatever happens, Eddie's going down. And, with any luck, he'll be so old by the time he gets out that no one will ever take him seriously again.'

'Good,' Cheryl said approvingly. ''Cos the estate's been loads nicer since he's been gone. And Chrissie looks loads better now she's free of him, too.'

'Is she still there?' Joe was surprised. 'I thought she'd moved back in with her mum.'

'She has. I just saw her when she came back to get her stuff,' Cheryl told him. 'Anyway, never mind her. It's *this* one who needs her bum smacking.' She cast a mock-disapproving look at Katya. 'Molly loves having her there, and we reckon she should stay, but this silly cow's insisting on handing herself in. Talk some sense into her, will you?'

'What's this?' Joe frowned up at Katya. 'You don't have to do that. I haven't mentioned you to anyone, I swear.'

'I know, and I thank you,' Katya said regretfully. 'But it's time. My – my son needs me. He's nearly five now. He stays with my parents, and he is why I came here – so I could send money home for him.'

'She can send for him, though, can't she?' Cheryl said. 'Tell her, Joe. She'll be able to give him a much better life over here, won't she?'

'Don't,' Katya said quietly before Joe had a chance to open his mouth. 'I know it could never be. I am illegal, and he would be too. And he is happy with my parents. That is the only life he knows, so how could I take him away? I need to go home to him, not force him to come to me.'

Cheryl was still protesting, but Joe understood. Nodding, he said quietly, 'He's a lucky boy.'

'Thank you,' Katya murmured, biting her lip as her eyes filled with tears.

'Damien's here,' Carl said just then, glancing out of the window in time to see his friend's car pull up down below. Pushing himself to his feet, he extended his fist to Joe. 'See you in court, matey. And look after yourself till then, yeah?'

'You, too,' Joe said.

'Glad you're all right,' Cheryl said, rushing towards the bed and giving Joe a quick hug to hide the fact that she, too, was almost crying. 'You were a good mate.'

She rushed out then, and Joe saw Carl put his arms around her before the door closed.

'I have to go now, too,' Katya said sadly. 'But I won't see you again, so this is goodbye.'

'Are you sure?' Joe asked.

'Yes.' She nodded. 'I'm going to the police station from here. I'm ready.'

'Well, I wish you luck for the future,' Joe said softly. 'You deserve the best that life can offer.'

'So do you,' Katya murmured. Then, leaning over to kiss him, she whispered into his ear in her own language before rushing out.

Joe closed his eyes and leaned his head back against the pillows. Well, that was it . . . it was all over bar the court case.

Jumping when Mr T's voice suddenly boomed out from his locker ordering him to pick up his message, he reached over for it. The text had come from Cheryl's phone, and it read:

It meant I have dreamed of you since our eyes first met, and I will carry the memory of you in my heart for ever.

Dragging himself to the edge of the bed, Joe lifted his legs down and hauled himself onto the chair beneath the window. He pressed his face up against the glass and gazed down in time to see Katya passing Cheryl's phone back to her. She turned her head and looked up at him. Then, swiping at a tear, she climbed into the car.